MOTHERS

MOTHERS

TWENTY STORIES OF
CONTEMPORARY MOTHERHOOD

EDITED AND WITH AN INTRODUCTION BY

KATRINA KENISON AND
KATHLEEN HIRSCH

NORTH POINT PRESS

A DIVISION OF FARRAR, STRAUS AND GIROUX • NEW YORK

North Point Press
A division of Farrar, Straus and Giroux
19 Union Square West, New York 10003

Published in Canada by HarperCollins*CanadaLtd*
Printed in the United States of America
Designed by Debbie Glasserman
First published in 1996 by North Point Press
First paperback edition, 1997

The Library of Congress has catalogued the hardcover edition as follows:
Mothers : twenty stories of contemporary motherhood / edited and with
an introduction by Katrina Kenison and Kathleen Hirsch. — 1st ed.
   p.   cm.
  ISBN 0-374-21375-5
  1. Mother and child—Fiction.   2. Short stories, American—Women
authors. 3. Motherhood—Fiction. 4. Women—Fiction. I. Kenison,
Katrina. II. Hirsch, Kathleen.
PS648.M59M58 1996
813'.54080352042—dc20   95-52230

For our boys
Henry, Jack and William

Contents

INTRODUCTION 3

BEFORE *Mary Grimm* 19

ANOTHER MARVELOUS THING *Laurie Colwin* 33

FOR WOMEN EVERYWHERE *Perri Klass* 57

PAGAN NIGHT *Kate Braverman* 72

BABY PICTURES *Molly Giles* 87

SEPARATION *Mary Gordon* 99

THE TROUBLE WITH SOPHIE *Perri Klass* 112

YOU'LL BE CRYING IN A MINUTE *Ronni Sandroff* 126

KING OF THE SKY *Roxana Robinson* 132

QUALITY TIME *Barbara Kingsolver* 151

STARLIGHT *Marian Thurm* 165

CHANCES WITH JOHNSON *Paula K. Gover* 180

DEEDS OF LOVE AND RAGE *Marsha Lee Berkman* 203

THE INSTINCT FOR BLISS *Melissa Pritchard* 215

POLTERGEISTS *Jane Shapiro* 232

THE DAGUERREOTYPE *Julia Whitty* 254

IN THE GLOAMING *Alice Elliott Dark* 267

SWIMMING TO THE TOP OF THE RAIN
  J. California Cooper 290

LEAVING HOME *Sue Miller* 306

ZOO BUS *Eileen FitzGerald* 321

MOTHERS

INTRODUCTION

Mothers is, in our view, a belated first: a collection of short stories about motherhood in America today, written by mothers.

It grew out of our own experiences as professional women whose lives were transformed by children. When we first met, ten years ago, Katrina was an editor at a New York publishing house, specializing in fiction, and Kathleen was a journalist devoted to women's issues. We had careers, not children. In 1986, we came together as editor and writer on a book project, and a friendship was born. In the years that followed, we both became mothers and, as we grappled with the challenges of our new identities, we began to compare notes about our shifting priorities and the inner landscape of motherhood.

As anyone who has raised children will attest, motherhood is the world's most intensive course in love. We may experience it, by turns, as a state of grace or oblivion, entrapment or exaltation, profound joy or numbing fatigue. Sometimes we pass through all these emotions in the course of a single day. And yet, the next morning we are ready to resume. We bear our children, love them and struggle with them, learn to accept them as they are, and, ultimately, learn to let them go. In the process, we learn much about ourselves.

Some of these lessons have seemed to us, at times, too dark or painful to examine by the light of day; others we have shared easily. As Louise Erdrich wrote in her memoir *The Blue Jay's Dance: A Birth Year*, "Mothering is a subtle art whose rhythm we collect and learn, as much from one another as by instinct. Taking shape, we shape each other, with subtle pressures and sudden knocks. The challenges shape us, approvals refine, the wear and tear of small abrasions transform until we're slowly made up of one another and yet wholly ourselves."

Our Stories

Katrina: When I was pregnant with my first child, I spent hours visualizing various delivery scenes, trying in vain to imagine how it would feel to give birth. I worried about birth defects and premature labor, practiced breathing, and experimented with recommended delivery positions, and, like a good student, I read practical guidebooks about breast-feeding and newborn care. I thought I was preparing, as well as I could, to have a baby. But my daydreams rarely took me beyond the delivery room; birth itself was the main event, the one that seemed at once so frightening and so exciting. Once the baby arrived, well, it went without saying—we would all come home and begin our life together as a family.

How could I have spent so much time thinking about the birth process, and so little envisioning what might lie beyond it? Perhaps, deep down, I realized that there was no preparing for the experience of motherhood itself, or for the irrevocable transformation that would occur as my son was delivered out of my body and into my arms. A new person took his place on earth in that moment, and, in the same instant, I too became new. I was a mother. From that moment on, I have seen the world through different eyes.

As mothers, we are bound by depths of pain and waves of joy that those who have not raised children will never know. In each of our children we see a miracle of life—even as we realize, with sudden insight, that the world is full of just such miracles. I called my own mother at three a.m.—as the obstetrician sat on a stool between my legs, stitching my episiotomy with long black thread—and told her she was a grandmother. An hour and a half later, she slipped into my room, having driven alone in the dark, without directions, to a city hospital she had never been to before. She talked her way past the security guards and the night nurses, and she came to me. I was not altogether surprised to see her, though; it was just beginning to dawn on me what it means to be a mother.

Overnight, the world had changed. I felt like a traveler who sets foot on foreign soil only to realize that she has journeyed to the right place after all, that she has found home. Settling into this new home meant coming to know myself as a mother, discovering my child, and, with my husband, enlarging our marriage to include and embrace a third. Even as we began to create our own space and grow into these new roles, I found myself seeking stories of initiation, wisdom, experience. How do mothers love their children? How do they protect them, nourish them, celebrate them? How do they survive a child's betrayal, illness, or death? When I joined the tribe of mothers, the experiences of mothers everywhere became, in some measure, my own.

Kathleen: I didn't want to be pregnant. Or so I thought, through my vehement twenties and well into my still-strident thirties. I was a seventies feminist for whom a woman's creative freedom meant a room of one's own, and no one to answer to whenever I felt like taking in a late-night poetry reading or catching a train to some political event. I could not stop for the minutiae of motherhood, I told myself, when the world itself was like a sick child—hungry, homeless, crazed with material dreams—and in desperate need of advocacy. Mother love? No Pampers or strained peaches for me.

Rather, I would channel my nurturing energies into social causes, a writer with a sort of feminized earth-mother soul.

But the more I wrote, the less I believed in the power of words alone to heal. I came to see that just as all politics in the end are personal, so too is life's deepest poetry. Meaning began at home, and all the pain in the world wasn't deep enough to wipe out the impulse for personal renewal.

Thus, on the cusp of forty, I began trying to conceive a child. For five years I existed in a shadow land of yearning and disappointment. I learned what it was to want what I could not will. As I sat in clinic offices staring at photographs of alpine meadows and gorgeous mountain vistas intended to help me think positive thoughts, I grew more deeply engulfed in a grief that even loved ones could not know existed. The stories of mothers and their children were like enchantments to me, meditations from a state that I began to believe I would never attain.

And then one miraculous October day, a heart beat alongside mine. Hands reached toward the light through the amniotic ocean. The first time I saw my son's two-chambered heart, I wept. And the moment, eight and a half months later, when I heard his first yelp of assertion upon arriving in the world, I knew that creation had begun anew. As his ruddy head rooted at my breast, rapt with the newness of sense and hunger, I realized that to love this child through the arduous struggle into manhood would be the greatest creative act I would ever perform.

We both knew that there was no going back to those careers that had once seemed so all-consuming—at least not in the same way. And, in time, we began to wonder how we might broaden our dialogue to include mothers from other places and stages in life, and what we would have to say to one another. As women who had lived and worked with the stories born of contemporary American culture, it was only natural for us to turn to stories again. Through fiction, we felt, we could learn about the real lives of women in a way that is simply not possible with biography, history, or, often, even personal memoir. Reading stories about motherhood written just twenty or thirty years ago—by such authors as Grace Paley, Tillie Olsen, and Alice Walker—we realized that although, in many respects, the theme of mother love is timeless, many of the issues mothers confront have changed considerably. We decided to narrow our focus to stories that would portray the complexities of mothering in America today as we and other women of our generation are experiencing it—not as a footnote to career adventures, not as a subplot to romantic entanglements, but as a state of existence with an integrity all its own, rampant with grace, ambiguity, and bitter-sweet revelation.

We encountered a surprising phenomenon: despite the plethora of advice books on every aspect of parenting, there seemed to be a dearth of fiction. We found many stories *about* mothers, told from a child's point of view, but few that depicted a mother's view of herself in relation to her children. The stories we did find proved fascinating and irresistible. Some seemed to have been written in a rush of emotion; others were attempts to give shape and coherence to events or fears that had shaken their authors to the core—from the magnitude of birth to the death of a child. Invariably, we found ourselves asking, "Why aren't more women writing about moth-erhood?" Surely this is one of the most dramatic and complex roles we play in our lives.

Perhaps, we speculated, it is just too hard to sustain the tenuous world of the imagination while simultaneously being called upon to change a diaper and blow up a balloon. Storytelling requires a certain distance, a long view, and the relentless intimacy of motherhood rarely permits this kind of detachment. But women *were* writing about the equally intimate matters of sexuality and personal identity. The deeper we questioned and the more widely we read, we realized

that we could not avoid the issue of what has constituted "appropriate" literary topics in our society and the extent to which the
culture's values have determined what women choose to articulate
about their experiences. Perhaps—and this was the possibility we
found most disturbing of all—women have not regarded motherhood as a legitimate literary subject.

Notwithstanding the immense outpouring of women's literature
in the last twenty-five years, society's emphasis on women's advancement may have exerted a subtle form of censorship, causing a
generation of women to ransom a significant literature in the name
of progress. Looking back on our own formative years at women's
colleges in the 1970s, we well remember motherhood being regarded as a primary obstacle to artistic expression—literary or otherwise. In seeking to explain why so few women artists rose to
prominence before the feminist movement, young women agreed
(and our professors did little to dissuade us) that our predecessors
had been too saddled with the caretaking burdens of the home to
carve out the solitude needed to create. In seeking to explain why
so many early women writers had remained "minor" talents, we
found that the same wisdom applied.

During the 1970s and 1980s, motherhood became so unfashion-
able that maternity, rather than institutional sexism, was seen as the
chief hex on a woman's creative achievement. Is it any wonder,
then, that accomplished women writers would shy away from the
subject that, almost by definition, would relegate them to minor
status, or minimize their concerns as marginal for a generation of
women whose aims were far higher than the nursery? Women continued to have children, of course, yet children were rarely cele-
brated in our art.

When women writers proved silent on the topic of motherhood,
it was simply assumed that they didn't have children, or that they
had so successfully prevailed over motherhood's treacherous snares
that the existence of children in their private lives hardly warranted

mentioning. Given the times, the first of these assumptions had an element of truth to it. Between 1950 and 1976, America's birth rate dropped from 24.1 per thousand to a historic low of 14.6 per thousand. Women of all classes and educational backgrounds—including, certainly, writers—were having fewer babies. And the books that marked the era—works like Erica Jong's *Fear of Flying* and Marilyn French's *The Women's Room*—reflected vastly different concerns. Women wanted to break free from their mothers' physical and metaphorical constraints, to liberate their sexuality from the inevitabilities of motherhood, and to redirect their ambitions in order to compete equally in the marketplace of men.

In hindsight, this swing of the pendulum had significant literary repercussions. In an era marked by almost limitless candor, a let-it-all-hang-out openness, we have been virtually silent about the bearing and raising of our young. During what was inarguably one of the most turbulent periods in America's social history, we failed to produce a literature that positively embodied the relationship most essential to the continuity of society itself, that of parent and child.

To what extent this fact reflects women's own self-censorship, and to what extent it simply reflects the literary politics of the era, will perhaps always remain open to question. However, the marginalization of children and those who care for them persists today and is still reflected in gaps in the literature. Two recent anthologies of women's writings are illustrative. Not one of the forty contemporary short stories in *The Oxford Book of Modern Women's Stories* has motherhood as its theme. And yet most of these authors have raised children. Phyllis Rose's ambitious anthology *The Norton Book of Women's Lives* features autobiographical excerpts from the works of sixty-five nineteenth and twentieth century women, representing, according to Rose, "as broad a range of experience as possible." There is not a single piece about motherhood. In her introduction Rose suggests, "These women don't so much turn their backs on family life—many of them are married—as simply choose not to focus on it in telling

the story of their lives. In their books the deep satisfactions of marriage and maternity are often signaled only by dedications to spouses
and children.''

Mothers and children continue to be vulnerable to neglect and
exclusion in a society that elevates those who aspire to power and
productivity above those who aspire to nurturing relationships and
emotional well-being. Women who choose to stay at home with
their children are widely considered to have opted for a low-status
lifestyle. Those who work outside the home juggle feelings of guilt
toward their children with the need to prove that they can be as
valuable on the job as any man. Our nation's child-care providers
and teachers are underpaid and underappreciated. These cultural bi-
ases exert constant pressure on our maternal instincts, not to mention
our creative energies.

Thus, we may talk and joke about our children with other mothers at the day-care center or the playground; we may compare our
daunting workloads and complain about the second shift; but when
it comes to addressing our own deepest concerns—the primal force
of mother love, the deep-rooted need we feel to protect and nurture
our offspring; our often irrational fears for our children's safety or
our own sanity; the urge to hold a child too close, or the impulse
to escape those clinging hands—few mothers are willing to acknowledge these feelings among friends, much less expose them in print.

This collection breaks that silence. In fact, these stories may well
signal a shift in the value assigned to motherhood in America. Certainly they attest to the dramatic changes that mothering has under-
gone during the years that few were chronicling it.

Many of the authors represented here began their families during
the tumultuous seventies and eighties, and they write from out of
that experience. The subjects and situations they portray reflect the
diverse realities of motherhood today. Never have women had such
freedom in electing the circumstance in which we become mothers.
We are bearing the children of our husbands, married lovers, and

anonymous sperm donors. We are adopting and raising the children of other women. On the other hand, never have our struggles, once children are born, been so daunting. We no longer step into well-defined, circumscribed roles when we become mothers. On the contrary. Each and every one of us must reinvent the role for ourselves. These stories remind us just how far removed we are from the much simpler world in which our own mothers raised us, and how very isolated women may be by the new realities of motherhood. At the same time, they celebrate the underlying bond that continues to exist between mothers and their children, and which still connect one mother to another across the chasms of race, class, and time.

The stories in this book reflect a wide range of mothers' experiences, from pregnancy and birth, through the childhood years, adolescence, adulthood, and old age. But the themes that recur throughout the book—love, vulnerability, anger, and fear—cannot be so tidily arranged, for a mother's passionate involvement with her children does not end with childhood but, rather, extends to the very end of life.

The first three stories are about giving birth, but, even more, they are about the transformation that occurs in every woman as she integrates a new identity with the one she has known since childhood. Mary Grimm's young mother moves imperceptibly away from her lifelong friends as she prepares for her unplanned baby. "I'd known them all since grade school, and they should have been a comfort," she observes. "But I seemed to be looking at them from a long way off, across the great expanse of my stomach." Funny, irreverent, and brimming with confidence, Bonnie has no doubts about her ability to care for her baby, despite her youth. With her young husband's support she is able to bid farewell to "a whole fun world that was no longer open to me" and to embrace her new role, with a sense that she is ready to "settle into life"—albeit a bit earlier than she had imagined.

Unlike the impulsive Bonnie, Laurie Colwin's worldly heroine has planned and plotted for her baby's conception and arrival—and yet finds herself undone by the possibility that something could go wrong. Hospitalized for high blood pressure in her ninth month, the pragmatic Billie finds her very temperament undergoing a metamorphosis. "Billie had a horror of the sentimental," Colwin writes. And yet, "in secret, for she would rather have died than showed it, the thought of her own baby brought her to tears." Since it was first published in 1984, "Another Marvelous Thing" has become a classic short story in its own right, so universal is its depiction of the events and emotions surrounding the birth of a child. Based on Colwin's own experience of giving birth to her daughter, and her joy in creating a family in middle age, the story is even more poignant now, in the face of Colwin's untimely death in 1992 at the age of forty-eight.

Pediatrician, mother, and writer, Perri Klass has never shied away from writing about the deeper stuff of existence that mothers confront every day. In "For Women Everywhere," she breezily debunks the high seriousness of pregnancy and birth even as she offers a solemn reminder of every new mother's most urgent requirement —support, both moral and physical, from family and friends. Women may be biologically equipped to give birth to their babies, but no one can mother alone, for the triumph of birth quickly gives way to a day-to-day reality of overwhelming responsibility—a challenge that is, in the best of circumstances, all-consuming.

Dreams and fears, all the unbounded possibilities with which we greet the moment of birth, soon settle into the designs we come to know as our children's characters, the routine demands and limitations of daily life. In Molly Giles's "Baby Pictures," hope for a fleeting moment of creative time is dashed by a toddler's demand that his day begin. "What I won't believe, I think, as I lower the camera, is how little it takes to lose a good shot," says Giles's heroine. "I sigh at the sink of soiled dishes—ordinary plates in ordinary daylight—and set the camera down." And yet, as a self-congratu-latory friend with older children comes and goes from her kitchen, this mother achieves the maternal equipoise that honors, and makes an art of, the present.

Laughter does hair-trigger turns into tears in Ronni Sandroff's "You'll Be Crying in a Minute." Things seem to be going so well over an ordinary dinner that this mother of two is suddenly filled with the touchingly familiar certainty that it can't last. "We hear thumps and squeals from Kane's room—the hysterical laughter of a small boy being tickled by his older sister, tickled until his sides ache and he can't breathe and he wants to put his sneaker in her ribs," she notes, as she and her husband linger at the table. These are the moments strung out like common field stones to mark the paths of childhood, while mothers hover somewhere nearby, helping to shape their children's experiences into what will be viewed in hind-sight as rich hours, as true quality time.

Yet the quest for just this—quality time—is ephemeral and ser-endipitous, as Barbara Kingsolver's Miriam realizes. A single mother, Miriam juggles a part-time job, economic and logistical pressures, and the emotional needs of her five-year-old daughter, a resilient child who is doing her best to absorb life's realities. Never far from Miriam's mind are these harsh realities, and the intense vulnerability she and her daughter share in the midst of them. "When people remark to Miriam about how well-organized she is, she laughs and declares that organization is the religion of the single parent . . . But in her heart she knows what a thin veil of comfort it is that she's wrapped around herself and her child to cloak them from chaos."

As our file of stories grew thicker, a theme emerged that surprised us at first. We had expected to find stories celebrating the joys of motherhood, as well as those that acknowledge the tedium and frus-tration that are part of every mother's life. But we were less prepared for stories that would bring some of our deepest, most universal fears to the surface and then play them out to often shocking conclusions.

If the daily satisfactions of motherhood are woven into bonds of love and nurturance, fear and grief can just as quickly sever those connections, creating barren islands of isolation. In a number of these stories mothers find themselves cut off from the very sources of support and community they need most desperately. Kate Braverman's young drifter, blind to any possibility of choice in her precarious situation, prepares to abandon her unnamed infant in order to hang on to her alienated boyfriend. Brutal, disturbing, and all too convincing, Sunny's deliberations touch a raw maternal nerve—for most of us have had to contend, at one time or another, with a partner's jealousy toward a newborn, and with our own fantasies of somehow recapturing the freedom of a life unfettered by children.

Mary Gordon's chilling portrait of a mother–child relationship without boundaries is another extreme version of what can happen when a woman attempts to mother in isolation. JoAnn is as confused and lonely as Braverman's Sunny, and she makes an equally destructive choice, pulling her child back to her just when he most needs to enlarge his world and learn to trust others.

Homeless teenagers and emotionally unstable single women are not the only ones who lose their children, however. Roxana Robinson's Margaret is elegant, composed, and blessed with all the comforts of contemporary urban life. Yet she, too, feels trapped by her child. Her attempt to discipline her unruly little boy ends in tragedy, and the narrator's realization that, as mothers, "we are not in this together. The things that separate us are terrible and irreversible."

In "Chances with Johnson," Paula K. Gover also draws on the archetypal fear of losing a child—in this case, to a bitter ex-husband. With one son abducted and another left behind to wonder why his father hadn't chosen *him*, Elizabeth tentatively begins to reconstruct her life. And yet, she cannot fully love another man, or provide real security for her remaining son, as long as the fate of her child remains unknown. In the end, Elizabeth's shattered faith is restored when she realizes that her laconic lover wants to be more than a safe harbor for her—he also wants to be a true father.

These stories, painful though they are to read, serve a purpose, for they shed light on some of our own darkest imaginings, and they remind us that no one lives a charmed life for long—we are all vulnerable, in ways both large and small.

No defense, for instance, is strong enough to protect us from the day-care mishap, or the kindergarten teacher who informs us that our child is an unacceptable misfit. In Perri Klass's "The Trouble with Sophie," a mother does battle with the self-doubt aroused when her daughter's teacher makes therapy a condition of her continuing to come to school.

But this is just the beginning, for while we spend our children's early years arming ourselves against the heartless assaults of unimaginative teachers and neighborhood bullies, there comes a point when we must craft a different and far subtler form of protection. No one can hurt us as deeply as our own children can. And hurt us they do, sometimes even knowingly, as they struggle toward their own sense of who they are as people. Marian Thurm's Elaine, in "Starlight," must entertain her two young sons during a school vacation visit to Disney World, while trying to keep the anguish of her separation from them at bay. "She certainly wasn't about to ask them to come and live with her, to set herself up for being kicked in the teeth again. That was what it had felt like this winter—a swift, hard blow that left her so weak she could hardly move."

In Melissa Pritchard's "The Instinct for Bliss," Frances encounters the opposite problem. Her brooding preoccupation these days is that her adolescent daughter, Athena, "won't get fat or have sex or die." En route to a natural wool-dyeing workshop, where she hopes to be temporarily liberated from these maternal worries, she finds herself having to spring her daughter from jail and take her along. After a series of incidents both embarrassing and painful for Frances, her daughter provides her with a healing epiphany.

What brings Marsha Lee Berkman's mother and daughter together in "Deeds of Love and Rage" is the peace offering of a loaf of challah and, beneath it, the stabilizing force of a spiritual tradition laid over years of consistent practice and faith.

The struggles in these stories are particularly wrenching since the mothers they depict—like so many mothers of adolescents—are alone, divorced, or separated from the fathers of their children. These mothers are more vulnerable than we as a society want to see. With few of the structures in which children were traditionally raised intact any longer, women like those in J. California Cooper's "Swimming to the Top of the Rain" are compelled to shoulder ever-greater responsibility for society's young, and they often do so in a vacuum.

What is remarkable is that, even in such circumstances, women are able to forge heroic opportunities for renewal and human connection. In Julia Whitty's "The Daguerreotype," a single mother passes talismans from her own childhood on to her grown daughter, knowing that the unspoken history they represent will bind them together, even as her daughter takes her first steps toward independence in a distant land.

Jane Shapiro has the uncanny ability to make readers laugh and shudder at the same time—rather the way teenagers themselves do. Mothers of adolescents may simply nod their heads in rueful acknowledgment. And yet, despite the tensions that exist in this household of "hair-trigger adrenal glands," "Poltergeists" is, at bottom, a story of family connections maintained.

Shapiro's single mother and her children weather the violent storms of adolescence and emerge with their love and tolerance for one another tested but intact, for the lines of communication remain open—even when the messages are hard to swallow. The children's passage through adolescence marks a turning point for everyone, for the daily engagements and entanglements are about to come to an end forever. Watching her son graduate from high school, this battle-weary mother is buffeted by unexpected emotion: "At that moment, as I might have expected but hadn't, a wave of feeling broke over me; it was an unfamiliar combination—real, deep sadness and heart-stopping relief. I would miss them so much I'd never get over it—I couldn't live without them! At the same time, for my purposes they weren't leaving fast enough. I couldn't wait another minute to start not caring so much."

A child's departure demands perhaps a mother's greatest performance. We must learn to let go. And yet, much as we think we have rehearsed this act in the thousand small breaks we've experienced over the years, the leave-taking can feel like a death.

In Alice Elliott Dark's "In the Gloaming," the death is a real one. Janet realizes, as she watches her son die of AIDS, that he "had been the love of her life." Nothing will replace him, she admits, as she prepares to reenter the cold world of her marriage to a man who has never known her as deeply as her dying child does.

Sue Miller portrays the supreme test of grace and wisdom demanded of every mother in "Leaving Home": how to let go of our children when we carry in our hearts the painful foreknowledge of disappointment waiting for them just around the corner. Leah sees more clearly than her son the fault lines of his troubled marriage. "For a moment, as she walked silently across the kitchen, she worried about leaving the house, about what seemed like an abandonment of Greg, of them all. But she had no power anymore . . . to stave off ruin."

In being born, our children assert their first and essential freedom. Motherhood is that shifting relationship we maintain with this Other, and our biggest challenge over the years is to arrive at the point where we are able to embrace both the truth of who we are and of who our children have become.

Old age brings new dependencies, as Eileen FitzGerald's "Zoo Bus" beautifully depicts. "Gertrude will probably be there, but we'll just ignore her," the feisty Elise tells her young companion, as she guides them to the restaurant her sixty-year-old daughter frequents at lunchtime. "She could sit so close that Gertrude would hear her breathing and know she was alive." Elise reveals in unforgettable terms this last stage in a mother's life, when we are called to the most difficult letting go of all.

It takes courage to write about motherhood in a culture that sets women with children on the sidelines, and it takes even greater courage to give voice to the powerful emotions and fears that swirl deep beneath the surface of our daily lives, informing and shaping our relationships with our children and the world at large. *Mothers* begins the expanded dialogue we sought when we started this project. We hope that, as a group, these stories will also serve as a step toward a "mothers' literature," representing a broadened and matured perception of women and our creativity in late-twentieth-century America. Certainly they testify to the truth that to nurture a child is, in itself, a creative act worthy of celebration, and that to write about that experience is to acknowledge an aspect of our existence that has long been neglected. Whether we are new mothers or grandmothers many times over, we are anchored and succored by a special sustaining passion: mother love. And who among us does not thirst for stories?

Kathleen Hirsch
Katrina Kenison
September, 1995

BEFORE

◻

MARY GRIMM

I got pregnant on my honeymoon. We'd screwed everywhere we could for a year and three months, not using a blessed thing, so I had had this feeling that it was a matter of willpower—or not even willpower but just your body knowing that you were ready to settle into life. "Okay," the message would go from your brain down your backbone—*pow blip kazaam*—right to the ovaries: "It's time, *right now*," and things would release, open up. Your hands would fit themselves to—I don't know, knitting needles, diaper pins—your hair would start to grow itself into your mother's hairstyle, and you'd automatically stop wanting to go out and drink like a fool and dance all night. I figured this was going to happen when I was around twenty-six; I ought to have had nearly another six years. Oh, I planned to use birth control, I wasn't a total crazy. Just that once, though, just for that couple of days, we didn't want to waste time hanging out in a drugstore.

And, honestly, we were both embarrassed to go in and buy stuff. Now I slap those tubes of jelly on the counter along with the Hershey bars and ten-inch-fashion-doll clothes and corn plasters, and I don't give a damn. But then I didn't even like to see the little sign where the contraceptive stuff was kept that read FEMININE HYGIENE, as if potential babies were something to be scrubbed away. Some of the stuff said "Spermicide," too—something like an insect spray.

"You go," I'd say.

"No, you," Allen would say.

"I won't."

"You have to go," he'd say. "You promised, Bonnie."

"I did not."

And so on.

The upshot of this ignorance, this bashfulness, was a baby—or at first not the baby itself but its symptoms: a heavy burning ache behind my breastbone, an inability to stand toothpaste, the gradual swelling of my familiar body into a strange fruit—a gourd or a melon—from which my thin arms and legs stuck out like twigs.

This brought the relatives around to count backward from the due date and offer advice. Most Sundays Allen drove me to one house or another full of aunts, uncles, in-laws, cousins, family friends. I'd sit in big, soft chairs surrounded by people looking at my stomach, and I'd answer questions: "It's due in April" . . . "I'm going to work until the last month" . . . "As long as it's healthy."

Secretly, I wanted to have a girl. I already had Allen—it was hard enough learning to live with one male. Besides, I had it in my mind that I would be able to point out to this girl baby all the places I had gone wrong, and that would be at least one set of mistakes she wouldn't have to make. When I rode on the bus to work in downtown Cleveland and looked out the window at West Twenty-fifth Street, the way I'd been doing for years, when I washed the dishes staring at the yellow kitchen wall in front of me, when I waited in line at the bank or the supermarket, I'd be thinking of the things I'd have to tell her. About speaking up for yourself, about avoiding regret, how to tell if someone is lying, what to say when something is your fault.

And actually I was sure it would be a girl. I had only sisters, three of them, and I had the further evidence of other blood relatives:

nine aunts to three uncles. My mother's mother raised her children by herself after Grandpa left—years of hard work and no rest, and then at last about ten years of sitting back and having the fruits of her labor: respect, tiny grandchildren to pet and hand back, meals being cooked for her in her own kitchen by her daughters and daughters-in-law. We are a family of bossy women, talky women, women who intend to be taken seriously. So it was natural that from my body, so like my mother's and my grandmother's, I would pro-duce another woman. Allen had none of this sexual solidarity on his side. He had a brother and a sister, and no visible aunts or uncles. What could he say? He tried to get under my skin by bringing up rumors that twins ran in his family, but I took this for pure devil-ment.

We had an apartment then. What a trip it was, moving into that apartment. I remember how enamored I was of a green teapot—leaf green with gold trim. I put it up on a shelf over the sink and turned on the light nearby, to admire how it looked. That was the center of the apartment to me, that teapot on that shelf; it was the picture of what the rest of it would be when I fixed it up. It was night when we finished moving in and we all sat around and ate pizza—Annie from work, Allen's brother, John, and his buddy Ted; my best friend from school, Rose, and her sister Ellen; Jimmy Spicer and all that crew. All we had to drink was a six-pack of Champale that someone had brought and put in the refrigerator. No one would admit having brought it. We poured it into Dixie cups and drank it down, rank and beery-sweet.

Annie and Rose and I went to look at the bedrooms. Not Ellen —she wanted to stay with the guys: what a slut she was then. "This is going to be the baby's bedroom," I said to them. "It's going to be yellow and pink, two walls each color. Curtains with a yellow stripe." My old crib was in there already, scarred and scratched, wood-colored, pictures of lambs and rabbits at the head and foot. Probably we should have painted it, but I didn't want to cover up the lambs and rabbits—I'd looked at them, and so had my sisters, when we were too young to know what they were, and traced them with our fingers, and I wanted my girl to look at them with her unfocused eyes and pat them with her fat hands.

"Do you have a changing table?" Rose asked me. She didn't know a thing about changing tables and I knew it.

"No, and I don't want one," I said. "I'm going to use the top of the low dresser."

They looked at me, looked at my stomach, and looked away. They were horrified, I knew. I was horrified, too, in a way, by the swell of my stomach and by everything else, but also smug at having done it. Without even trying.

"Are you going to work after?" Annie asked me.

"When it's six months old, I'm going back." I was always very careful to say "it." I knew it was a girl but I felt it might jinx things if I said "she" right out. I was afraid something could shift in my body, a slow turn from one sex to the other.

"I don't think it's right to leave a little baby," Rose said. "Not until they go to school."

I sat down on a box and took my shoes off. "Give it a rest, Rose," I said. I knew she was saying what her mother said. They'd had no thought in their heads of babies, her and Annie. They weren't pregnant. They didn't know what to think of me at all. I leaned back against the wall and arched my spine, stretching, with the curve of my stomach pushed out. They looked at it, and their hands went to their own bodies. Annie put one hand on her stomach; Rose's fingers fluttered, touching her chest, her hips, twitching at her clothes.

"I'm going to breast-feed," I said.

"God, you're not," Annie said.

"I am, too," I said. "They get bigger if you do." All three of us looked at my chest.

This was bold talk on my part. Sometimes I felt quite different. Sometimes I wanted out of my body. I didn't feel bad, really—that wasn't it. I felt dreamy and sleepy. I sat for hours looking at baby books, reading about puréeing fruit and the order of immunization, sometimes sitting there looking out the window with my hand on the book, sometimes falling asleep with my cheek on the open pages. There was one book in particular that I liked, that said how to manage if you had one baby, then what to do if you had two, then three, then four. How to take four children for a trip on the bus was one of the things in this book. You were supposed to hold one by the hand who was holding another by the hand, one in a collapsible stroller, one in a sling against your chest. There was a picture of this woman wearing a dress and a hat, taking money out of her shoulder bag and giving it to the smiling bus driver, with all these round-faced children clustering around her like the angels that frame the margins of holy cards. I loved that book. I got it out of the library three times.

No, I felt fine, really. What worried me was this feeling of inevitability. I was going to have a baby and there was *nothing I could do about it*. I couldn't change my mind, couldn't say, "Wait, time out, I'd like to think about this for a minute." Somewhere in front of me were some solid hours of pain and a baby coming. I was going to grunt and bleed. My body was going to open. It was unbelievable, ridiculous, and yet I had to believe it.

I took the position of suspecting everything that was said to me. What did they know—"they" being the doctors and my female relatives? They were all so old. They'd been proved wrong already. I was proud I'd known I was pregnant before the doctor said so, even though the first two tests were negative. They'd said I'd have morning sickness, that I'd swell up with water, but I hadn't.

"What's the doctor doing for me?" I asked Allen. We were in bed and, against my protests, he was rubbing cocoa butter into my stomach, where the skin stretched over the baby. I wanted no special methods or precautions taken.

"What?" he said.

"Not a thing. Not a fucking thing."

He put his hand over my mouth. "Nice language for a mother."

I said I had to say it now, before I had to be a good example. I was feeling cross and cranky. I closed my eyes so as not to have to look at the greasy mound of my belly. I was seven-and-a-half months, and I finally needed to wear maternity clothes, instead of just unbuttoning the fly of my jeans and wearing a long shirt. My breasts were bigger already and Allen was showing signs of fascination with them, which I decided to find revolting and depraved.

"You have to go to the doctor," he said reasonably.

I hated him for saying this. "I go there and they make me give them a sample and the nurse weighs me and then I sit around in the waiting room with all these other swollen women and I read *Highlights* and then I go in and he gives me a hard time about gaining too much and asks if I've got any problems and I say no. That's it."

"Umhmm," Allen said. He moved his face against my shoulder, nuzzling from side to side, each side sweep carrying him a little farther onto my breast.

"Cut it out, Allen. Pay attention."

"Well, they can tell things from those tests, can't they?"

"You don't know anything about it. You don't know a thing." I threw the cocoa butter on the floor and rolled over.

It wasn't that I didn't want sex. Contrary to what the doctor had warned, I wanted it just as much as before. And I got a lot of attention, too, not only from Allen. I never would have credited it, but there are a lot of men who think it's sexy that you're pregnant. Even at nine months, when I was straining at the seams of these horrible maternity smocks, I got whistles when I was walking down the street. Guys would come up to me at parties and make jokes about buns in the oven, so as to have an excuse to pat my stomach. Partly it was curiosity, I'm sure. We'd never known anyone who got pregnant before—anyone our age, that is. I was the first in our crowd. Frankly, I looked great. My skin cleared up, for one thing.

So I wanted to do it. Allen wanted to do it. But when we did it, something was wrong. We seemed to be looking for each other, as if we were in a crowded room or a dark empty place; we knew the other person was there but we couldn't see each other. We kept trying, but it was no good. When we finished we'd hold each other, we'd turn on the radio and listen to late-night talk shows, and Allen would tell me jokes, and we'd fall asleep laughing. Some things were still okay.

But I worried about this full stop to the thrilling part of my sex life. Was this what had happened to all those sexless women my mother's age? You got pregnant and some switch in your body turned off all that teenage juice? You turned your cheek and pursed your lips instead of opening your mouth? You put your hands on his chest to push him away instead of to feel his hard little nipples? Watched TV together all evening, not talking, and then slept not touching?

By this time I'd cut my hours at the office to half, and all I had to do in the afternoons was sit around and think. How long does it take to do the dishes? I never made the bed. This is on principle: what's the point of making it look unused, unless it's to impress people? I could have baked but I was big as a house already. I could have watched the soaps. Actually, I did watch them sometimes, but half the actors and all the story lines were different from when I used to watch them in high school and I couldn't pay enough attention to catch up.

So I'd sit in the big armchair in the front room and look out the window and think. And I'd take long slow walks, thinking. Sometimes I thought about our honeymoon. It wasn't much, but it was fine. We went to Chicago, where we had friends we could stay with and save the cost of a motel, except one going and one coming back. With these friends, we went to some ball games and out dancing and hung out on the North Side the way we used to when we were all going to school there. At the time, I saw my adult life as a wonderful extension of my one year of college: lots of driving around, recreational drinking, and freedoms opening out one after another. The last day, we all went to the dunes on Lake Michigan with a picnic. We forgot the charcoal, but we were so hungry after swimming that we ate the hot dogs cold, with the warm wind blowing sand at us; grains of sand got between our teeth and made interesting gritty noises when we chewed. We grinned at each other, baring our sandy teeth, and we took pictures of our legs all lined up together, our pumped-up biceps, our arms buried from shoulder to wrist in sand, with only the hand sticking out, fingers wiggling. We all hugged each other after, and Allen and I drove off, still in our wet bathing suits, and immediately started looking for a motel, although it was only five-thirty. Even so, we didn't find one for a long time. Every NO VACANCY sign made us hotter. I sat as close to Allen as I could and tormented him while he drove, putting my hands inside his shirt and trying to undo his pants. A couple of times we pulled off the road and necked furiously, but we kept on. When we found a motel it was almost seven and we fell on each other, we melted for each other, we opened up all the way. That might have been the time, that one.

A month before my due date, supposedly spring, the weather was still gray, sleeting, dripping. I wasn't reading baby books anymore. All I had in front of me, between me and the baby coming, were a couple of "surprise" showers—one for my relatives, one for girlfriends. My mother had told me about them so I wouldn't turn up wearing something ratty. That was too bad. A surprise would have been distracting, at least—twenty dressed-up women hiding in closets and behind the living-room suite, jumping out. I sat around and felt sorry for myself for not having a surprise in my future.

  Annie, Ellen, and Rose came over sometimes. I'd known them

all since grade school, and they should have been a comfort. But I seemed to be looking at them from a long way off, across the great expanse of my stomach. I was so tired of it all, too tired to lift my hand or shake my head no when Annie brought me a cup of stinking herb tea. They sat and chattered about a whole fun world that was no longer open to me.

Shopping. I couldn't shop, couldn't bear to look at myself in a mirror. When I undressed at night I kept my eyes on a level so as not to see what was going on under my chin. Bad enough to see it with clothes over it. Going out for drinks after work. "Drinks," "work"—the words were no longer in my vocabulary. Sex, men, flirting: Ha. I wasn't a member of any sex anymore. I was a husk, a pod—a container, ready to split open.

I kept thinking and dreaming then of things coming open—of seams splitting, of cartons breaking and spilling their contents, of volcanoes, and, more horribly, of wounds, awful gashes that oozed unlikely substances: peanut butter, mud, ketchup. Sometimes it was melons slashed by a knife, all the seeds visible and gleaming wet. I could hardly stand to look at food just then, but I ate constantly, I just shoveled it in. Allen would watch me eat for another fifteen minutes after he'd finished—horrified, I think, to see all this stuff going in, maybe thinking I was going to explode, or give birth right there in front of him.

Allen was far away from me, too. Hugging was so ridiculous that I wouldn't let him do it. Kissing was out of the question, real kissing. To really kiss you have to wrap your arms around each other— neck, waist, wherever. You have to press up against each other, feel every part of his body pushing into or surrounding every part of yours. We lay in bed next to each other every night, holding hands, staring up at the ceiling until we fell asleep.

I stopped even thinking about the future. All there was, was now. There was my body with another body pushing around in it. I couldn't remember what my stomach, my breasts, had looked like before. I could hardly focus on the baby as any real thing. When Allen wanted to talk about names I really didn't care, but I made myself take a stand, on principle. There was no problem with a boy's name: Allen, for Allen; Joseph, for my father. We agreed about this, and, anyway, I still knew it would be a girl, and a girl had to be named this name I'd been carrying around since I was a kid, the name I'd wanted for myself instead of Bonnie: Rachel. It was not a silly name, not a name that could sprout a dopey nickname. It had a wonderful sound in your mouth. It was even biblical. But Allen wanted to name a girl after his sister. Debbie—I ask you. This is what we talked about those last weeks, constantly—at breakfast, at dinner, in bed. There was no compromise available, it seemed. We both hated all the other family names on both sides. We made lists. We read the *Best Baby Book of Names* to each other. It kept our minds off other things, like the fact that we were not allowed to screw anymore, even if we'd wanted to.

On a Saturday exactly two weeks before my due date, my mother-in-law drove over. Why? Who knows? Just to give us a hard time, is what I thought then. She came in and asked a lot of questions and poked around all over the apartment. Did I have my suitcase packed? Had I cooked up a lot of stuff and put it in the freezer for Allen to eat while I was in the hospital? Did I have a diaper service yet? The answer to all these questions was no. I could hardly bring myself to think about what was going to happen. I'd been telling myself there was plenty of time. It was just like when I was in school and there would be this big paper due that I had to do a lot of library research for, or I would have to make a clay relief model of South America with tiny products and resources glued to it. I would always start out with big plans, make lists, imagine the comprehensiveness of what it would be like when it was finished— the detail, the papier-mâché bananas, the small clay figures with miniature serapes. But I would put it off and put it off until there were only three days left, and then I'd panic for one day and rush around for another and stay up until two in the morning on the third, with my mother hovering anxiously over me as I grimly glued and pinned. So now the suitcase lay open and empty in our bedroom. The list of diaper services lay beside the telephone, unconsulted. I had no intention of freezing up big batches of lasagna or whatever.

"Allen wants to eat out while I'm gone," I said to my mother-in-law.

She was upset by this, I could see, but she had the good sense not to say anything.

To get out of the apartment, we went and got in the car and drove to the park near where we lived. It was real spring now, April, and actually warm. The sun was shining weakly. We parked and walked decorously down the path, the three of us. To our right there was a field with people playing catch and Frisbee, and some swings with children on them, swinging in great arcs, pointing their toes toward the sky. To our left there was the creek, and what Allen and I called the mountain. It was only a small hill, red clay and crumbling fast on its steep sides. But trees grew on it and there was a path on one side that you could scramble up to get to the top, which was a narrow ridge. Allen and I had often climbed it when we first lived in the apartment.

My mother-in-law was fussing with her purse as we walked. Allen had his hands in his pockets. He was scuffing up bits of leaves and gravel with the toes of his tennis shoes, walking his lively, good-natured walk. Even my mother-in-law, with her arthritic knees, was bouncing along. I felt like a sack of cement on stilts. What I wanted to do was climb the hill.

"Let's go up," I said to Allen.

"Don't be silly," my mother-in-law said.

"Come on, Allen," I said.

"You can't climb up there with that stomach," my mother-in-law said. She was showing alarm and I meanly enjoyed it.

"We can just go part way," I said to Allen, but I meant to go all the way once I got him up there.

He looked doubtful, but he followed me to the place where you have to step over the narrow arm of the creek that circles the hill. I stepped across, and stood waiting for him on the other side.

"Bonnie! Bonnie!" my mother-in-law called from the path. She was holding her purse in front of her with both hands.

"I'm going to do it!" I shouted to her.

We started up. The parts that were easy before were harder. The bits of the path where you had to plant your feet carefully because the ground sloped away were terrible. My balance was different. I felt like a tightrope walker, holding my arms out to keep upright. My stomach got in the way whenever I had to climb up and over the exposed roots of the trees, as if I were mounting a staircase. I had to scrabble up sideways and couldn't use my hands as much as I'd have liked. Finally we came to a part of the path that was like a chute, which you had to climb duckfooted, setting your feet at a careful angle, bending forward and rushing up, to use momentum. I did all that. Allen was just behind me. I made it up to the bend in the chute. I fell to my hands and knees.

"Bonnie! Bonnie!" my mother-in-law was yelling, and I could hear Allen gasping behind me.

"You dope, you jerk, you bitch," he said. He gripped me by my hips and shook them, put his arms around me, and pushed his face into the small of my back.

I let my arms relax until I was lying on my side, my face against the red crumbly clay, which was cool and slightly slick under my cheek. Looking up, I could see the top just above us, another ten feet—the hard ridge of the hill that I knew was bare of grass but carpeted with pine needles that slipped pleasantly under your feet. When you stood up at the top and looked down, the eroded sides, rawer and redder than the hard-packed soil of the ridge, sloped away from under your feet and you felt as if, with very little effort, you might slide down them into the water of the creek. Just one step, one small movement; no thought was necessary.

Allen was crying a little, which I thought was very sweet of him. "Oh, I'm all right," I said. I sat up so I could take his hand and kiss the palm. My mother-in-law was hesitating at the brink of the stepping-over place, holding her purse up almost over her head.

"I'm not going to do it!" I yelled to her.

"What?" she yelled back.

"I won't do it!" I yelled.

Allen and I started down. I slid down over the bad places on my butt, Allen going first to stop me if I fell. When we got to the bottom our clothes were dusty and smeared with red. My mother-in-law looked at us as if we were accident victims. "You'll be in the hospital before morning, after that," she said. I didn't care.

She was right, though. In the car on the way back I felt the first tightenings and loosenings, not yet pain. And after she'd gone home, I started to have mild contractions, and then a major one—the big pain rippling down, pushing my thoughts down, locating my center lower and lower. All the things I didn't know—when to start solid food, about Montessori, how to satisfy the sucking reflex—they didn't bother me a bit then, while I was going to the hospital with Allen in the car. It was like riding a comet or a roller coaster, this intense, purposeful movement after all those months of waiting. I didn't see anything ahead of me—not our lovely daughter; not the tired doctors who would talk to Allen afterward, my blood on their hands and their clothes; not my flattened, empty stomach; not my sallow face in the mirror the first time I could get up by myself and go to the bathroom; not Allen with a mask on his face bringing the baby through the door for me, with my lips saying "Rachel" for the first time. I didn't see any of that. But I could feel events rushing toward me as they wheeled me in. I could feel my life changing, the old familiar parts of it crumbling away and a new shape emerging that I would come to know, and, God, I was so excited I could hardly stand it.

"Before" began as a note in my ideas file, a bit of first-person narrative that came to me in a character's voice:

> *There's no use in sex education at all, take it from me. No matter how much you know, it's hard to take it personally. Sex and pregnancy are like death when you are young, things that you can see ahead like a train coming but it's a train you don't intend to get on. You change your mind about sex, I guess, but pregnancy, and death—they still hit you hard.*

I liked the sound and rhythm of the words, and also the woman I dimly saw who had spoken them, but I let them sit for a long time, more than a year. And then (when my daughters were nineteen and seventeen!), I finally was ready to write a story about the cataclysmic event that changed me from a girl into a woman and a mother. The year-old note was the first paragraph of the story (later cut) which I wrote in the voice of Bonnie, who was tougher and wittier than I have ever been, but still my sister.

M.G.

ANOTHER

MARVELOUS THING

□

LAURIE COLWIN

On a cold, rainy morning in February, Billy Delielle stood by the window of her hospital room looking over Central Park. She was a week and a half from the time her baby was due to be born, and she had been put in the hospital because her blood pressure had suddenly gone up and her doctor wanted her constantly monitored and on bed rest.

A solitary jogger in bright red foul-weather gear ran slowly down the glistening path. The trees were black and the branches were bare. There was not another soul out. Billy had been in the hospital for five days. The first morning she had woken to the sound of squawking. Since her room was next door to the nursery, she assumed this was a sound some newborns made. The next day she got out of bed at dawn and saw that the meadow was full of sea gulls who congregated each morning before the sun came up.

The nursery was an enormous room painted soft yellow. When Billy went to take the one short walk a day allowed her, she found herself averting her eyes from the neat rows of babies in their little plastic bins, but once in a while she found herself hungry for the sight of them. Taped to each crib was a blue (I'M A BOY) or pink

(I'M A GIRL) card telling mother's name, the time of birth, and birth weight.

At six in the morning the babies were taken to their mothers to be fed. Billy was impressed by the surprising range of noises they made: mewing, squawking, bleating, piping, and squealing. The fact that she was about to have one of these creatures herself filled her with a combination of bafflement, disbelief, and longing.

For the past two months her chief entertainment had been to lie in bed and observe her unborn child moving under her skin. It had knocked a paperback book off her stomach and caused the saucer of her coffee cup to jiggle and dance.

Billy's husband, Grey, was by temperament and inclination a naturalist. Having a baby was right up his street. Books on neonatology and infant development replaced the astronomy and bird books on his night table. He gave up reading mysteries for texts on childbirth. One of these books had informed him that babies can hear in the womb, so each night he sang "Roll Along Kentucky Moon" directly into Billy's stomach. Another suggested that the educational process could begin before birth. Grey thought he might try to teach the unborn to count.

"Why stop there?" Billy said. "Teach it fractions."

Billy had a horror of the sentimental. In secret, for she would rather have died than showed it, the thought of her own baby brought her to tears. Her dreams were full of infants. Babies appeared everywhere. The buses abounded with pregnant women. The whole process seemed to her one half miraculous and the other half preposterous. She looked around her on a crowded street and said to herself: "Every single one of these people was *born*."

Her oldest friend, Penny Stern, said to her: "We all hope that this pregnancy will force you to wear maternity clothes, because they will be so much nicer than what you usually wear." Billy went shopping for maternity clothes but came home empty-handed.

She said, "I don't wear puffed sleeves and frilly bibs and ribbons around my neck when I'm not pregnant, so I don't see why I should have to just because I am pregnant." In the end, she wore Grey's sweaters, and she bought two shapeless skirts with elastic waistbands. Penny forced her to buy one nice black dress, which she wore to teach her weekly class in economic history at the business school.

Grey set about renovating a small spare room that had been used for storage. He scraped and polished the floor, built shelves, and painted the walls pale apple-green with the ceiling and moldings glossy white. They had once called this room the lumber room. Now they referred to it as the nursery. On the top of one of the shelves Grey put his collection of glass-encased bird's nests. He already had in mind a child who would go on nature hikes with him.

As for Billy, she grimly and without expression submitted herself to the number of advances science had come up with in the field of obstetrics.

It was possible to have amniotic fluid withdrawn and analyzed to find out the genetic health of the unborn and, if you wanted to know, its sex. It was possible to lie on a table and with the aid of an ultrasonic scanner see your unborn child in the womb. It was also possible to have a photograph of this view. As for Grey, he wished Billy could have a sonogram every week, and he watched avidly while Billy's doctor, a handsome, rather melancholy South African named Jordan Bell, identified a series of blobs and clouds as head, shoulders, and back.

Every month in Jordan Bell's office Billy heard the sound of her own child's heart through ultrasound and what she heard sounded like galloping horses in the distance.

Billy went about her business outwardly unflapped. She continued to teach and she worked on her dissertation. In between, when she was not napping, she made lists of baby things: crib sheets, a stroller, baby T-shirts, diapers, blankets. Two months before the baby was due, she and Penny went out and bought what was needed. She was glad she had not saved this until the last minute, because in her ninth month, after an uneventful pregnancy, she was put in the hospital, where she was allowed to walk down the hall once a day. The sense of isolation she had cherished—just herself, Grey, and their unborn child—was gone. She was in the hands of nurses she had never seen before, and she found herself desperate for their companionship because she was exhausted, uncertain, and lonely in her hospital room.

Billy was admitted wearing the nice black dress Penny had made her buy and taken to a private room that overlooked the park. At the bottom of her bed were two towels and a hospital gown that tied up the back. Getting undressed to go to bed in the afternoon made her feel like a child forced to take a nap. She did not put on the hospital gown. Instead, she put on the plaid flannel nightshirt of Grey's that she had packed in her bag weeks ago in case she went into labor in the middle of the night.

"I hate it here already," Billy said.

"It's an awfully nice view," Grey said. "If it were a little further along in the season I could bring my field glasses and see what's nesting."

"I'll never get out of here," Billy said.

"Not only will you get out of here," said Grey, "you will be released a totally transformed woman. You heard Jordan—all babies get born one way or another."

If Grey was frightened, he never showed it. Billy knew that his way of dealing with anxiety was to fix his concentration, and it was now fixed on her and on being cheerful. He had never seen Billy so upset before. He held her hand.

"Don't worry," he said. "Jordan said this isn't serious. It's just a complication. The baby will be fine and you'll be fine. Besides, it won't know how to be a baby and we won't know how to be parents."

Grey had taken off his jacket and he felt a wet place where Billy had laid her cheek. He did not know how to comfort her.

"A mutual learning experience," Billy said into his arm. "I

thought nature was supposed to take over and do all this for us."

"It will," Grey said.

Seven o'clock began visiting hours. Even with the door closed Billy could hear shrieks and coos and laughter. With her door open she could hear champagne corks being popped.

Grey closed the door. "You didn't eat much dinner," he said. "Why don't I go downstairs to the delicatessen and get you something?"

"I'm not hungry," Billy said. She did not know what was in front of her, or how long she would be in this room, or how and when the baby would be born.

"I'll call Penny and have her bring something," Grey said.

"I already talked to her," Billy said. "She and David are taking you out to dinner." David was Penny's husband, David Hooks.

"You're trying to get rid of me," Grey said.

"I'm not," Billy said. "You've been here all day, practically. I just want the comfort of knowing that you're being fed and looked after. I think you should go soon."

"It's too early," said Grey. "Fathers don't have to leave when visiting hours are over."

"You're not a father yet," Billy said. "Go."

After he left she waited by the window to watch him cross the street and wait for the bus. It was dark and cold and it had begun to sleet. When she saw him she felt pierced with desolation. He was wearing his old camel's hair coat and the wind blew through his wavy hair. He stood back on his heels as he had as a boy. He turned around and scanned the building for her window. When he saw her, he waved and smiled. Billy waved back. A taxi, thinking it was being hailed, stopped. Grey got in and was driven off.

Every three hours a nurse appeared to take her temperature, blood pressure, and pulse. After Grey had gone, the night nurse appeared. She was a tall, middle-aged black woman named Mrs. Perch. In her hand she carried what looked like a suitcase full of dials and wires.

"Don't be alarmed," Mrs. Perch said. She had a soft West Indian accent. "It is only a portable fetal-heart monitor. You get to say good morning and good evening to your baby."

She squirted a blob of cold blue jelly on Billy's stomach and pushed a transducer around in it, listening for the beat. At once Billy heard the sound of galloping hooves. Mrs. Perch timed the beats against her watch.

"Nice and healthy," Mrs. Perch said.

"Which part of this baby is where?" Billy said.

"Well, his head is back here, and his back is there and here is the rump and his feet are near your ribs. Or hers, of course."

"I wondered if that was a foot kicking," Billy said.

"My second boy got his foot under my rib and kicked with all his might," Mrs. Perch said.

Billy sat up in bed. She grabbed Mrs. Perch's hand. "Is this baby going to be all right?" she said.

"Oh my, yes," Mrs. Perch said. "You're not a very interesting case. Many others much more complicated than you have done very well and you will, too."

At four in the morning, another nurse appeared, a florid English-woman. Billy had spent a restless night, her heart pounding, her throat dry.

"Your pressure's up, dear," said the nurse, whose tag read "M. Whitely." "Dr. Bell has written orders that if your pressure goes up you're to have a shot of hydralazine. It doesn't hurt baby— did he explain that to you?"

"Yes," said Billy groggily.

"It may give you a little headache."

"What else?"

"That's all," Miss Whitely said.

Billy fell asleep and woke with a pounding headache. When she rang the bell, the nurse who had admitted her appeared. Her name was Bonnie Near and she was Billy's day nurse. She gave Billy a pill and then taped a tongue depressor wrapped in gauze over her bed.

"What's that for?" Billy said.

"Don't ask," said Bonnie Near.

"I want to know."

Bonnie Near sat down at the end of the bed. She was a few years older than Billy, trim and wiry with short hair and tiny diamond earrings.

"It's hospital policy," she said. "The hydralazine gives you a head-ache, right? You ring to get something to make it go away and because you have high blood pressure everyone assumes that the blood pressure caused it, not the drug. So this thing gets taped above your bed in the one chance in about fifty-five million that you have a convulsion."

Billy turned her face away and stared out the window.

"Hey, hey," said Bonnie Near. "None of this. I noticed yesterday that you're quite a worrier. Are you like this when you're not in the hospital? Listen. I'm a straight shooter and I would tell you if I was worried about you. I'm not. You're just the common garden variety."

Every morning Grey appeared with two cups of coffee and the morning paper. He sat in a chair and he and Billy read the paper together as they did at home.

"Is the house still standing?" Billy asked after several days. "Are the banks open? Did you bring the mail? I feel I've been here ten months instead of a week."

"The mail was very boring," Grey said. "Except for this booklet from the Wisconsin Loon Society. You'll be happy to know that you can order a record called Loon Music. Would you like a copy?"

"If I moved over," Billy said, "would you take off your jacket and lie down next to me?"

Grey took off his jacket and shoes, and curled up next to Billy.

He pressed his nose into her face and looked as if he could drift off to sleep in a second.

"Childworld called about the crib," he said into her neck. "They want to know if we want white paint or natural pine. I said natural."

"That's what I think I ordered," Billy said. "They let the husbands stay over in this place. They call them 'dads.'"

"I'm not a dad yet, as you pointed out," Grey said. "Maybe they'll just let me take naps here."

There was a knock on the door. Grey sprang to his feet and Jordan Bell appeared.

"Don't look so nervous, Billy," he said. "I have good news. I think we want to get this baby born if your pressure isn't going to go down. I think we ought to induce you."

Billy and Grey were silent.

"The way it works is that we put you on a drip of Pitocin, which is a synthetic of the chemical your brain produces when you go into labor."

"We know," Billy said. "Katherine went over it in childbirth class." Katherine Walden was Jordan Bell's nurse. "When do you want to do this?"

"Tomorrow," Jordan Bell said. "Katherine will come over and give you your last Lamaze class right here."

"And if it doesn't work?"

"It usually does," said Jordan Bell. "And if it doesn't, we do a second-day induction."

"And if that doesn't work?"

"It generally does. If it doesn't, we do a cesarean, but you'll be awake and Grey can hold your hand."

"Oh what fun," said Billy.

When Jordan Bell left, Billy burst into tears.

"Why isn't anything normal?" she said. "Why do I have to lie here day after day listening to other people's babies crying? Why is my body betraying me like this?"

Grey kissed her and then took her hands. "There is no such thing as normal," he said. "Everyone we've talked to has some story or other—huge babies that won't budge, thirty-hour labors. A cesarean is a perfectly respectable way of being born."

"What about me? What about me getting all stuck up with tubes and cut up into little pieces?" Billy said, and she was instantly ashamed. "I hate being like this. I feel I've lost myself and some whimpering, whining person has taken me over."

"Think about how in two months we'll have a two-month-old baby to take to the park."

"Do you really think everything is going to be all right?" Billy said.

"Yes," said Grey. "I do. In six months we'll be in Maine."

Billy lay in bed with her door closed reading her brochure from the Loon Society. She thought about the cottage she and Grey rented every August in Jewell Neck, Maine, on a lagoon. There at night with blackness all around them and not a light to be seen, they heard hoot owls and loons calling their night cries to one another. Loon mothers carried their chicks on their backs, Billy knew. The last time she had heard those cries she had been just three months pregnant. The next time she heard them she would have a child.

She thought about the baby shower Penny had given her—a lunch party for ten women. At the end of it, Billy and Grey's unborn child had received cotton and wool blankets, little sweaters, tiny garments with feet, and two splendid teddy bears. The teddy bears had sat on the coffee table. Billy remembered the strange, light feeling in her chest as she looked at them. She had picked them both up and laughed with astonishment.

At a red light on the way home in a taxi, surrounded by boxes and bags of baby presents, she saw something that made her heart stop: Francis Clemens, who for two years had been Billy's illicit lover.

With the exception of her family, Billy was close only to Grey and Penny Stern. She had never been the subject of anyone's romantic passion. She and Grey, after all, had been fated to marry. She had loved him all her life.

Francis had pursued her: no one had ever pursued her before. The usual signs of romance were as unknown to Billy as the workings of a cyclotron. Crushes, she had felt, were for children. She did not really believe that adults had them.

Without her knowing it, she was incubating a number of curious romantic diseases. One day when Francis came to visit wearing his tweed coat and the ridiculously long paisley scarf he affected, she realized that she had fallen in love.

The fact of Francis was the most exotic thing that had ever happened in Billy's fairly stolid, uneventful life. He was as brilliant as a painted bunting. He was also, in marked contrast to Billy, beautifully dressed. He did not know one tree from another. He felt all birds were either robins or crows. He was avowedly urban and his pleasures were urban. He loved opera, cocktail parties, and lunches. They did not agree about economic theory, either.

Nevertheless, they spent what now seemed to Billy an enormous amount of time together. She had not sought anything like this. If her own case had been presented to her she would have dismissed it as messy, unnecessary, and somewhat sordid, but when she fell in love she fell as if backward into a swimming pool. For a while she felt dazed. Then Francis became a fact in her life. But in the end she felt her life was being ruined.

She had not seen Francis for a long time. In that brief glance at the red light she saw his paisley scarf, its long fringes flapping in the breeze. It was amazing that someone who had been so close to her did not know that she was having a baby. As the cab pulled away, she did not look back at him. She stared rigidly frontward, flanked on either side by presents for her unborn child.

The baby kicked. Mothers-to-be should not be lying in hospital beds thinking about illicit love affairs, Billy thought. Of course, if you were like the other mothers on the maternity floor and probably had never had an illicit love affair, you would not be punished by lying in the hospital in the first place. You would go into labor like everyone else, and come rushing into Maternity Admitting with your husband and your suitcase. By this time tomorrow she would have her baby in her arms, just like everyone else, but she drifted off to sleep thinking of Francis nonetheless.

At six in the morning, Bonnie Near woke her.

"You can brush your teeth," she said. "But don't drink any water. And your therapist is here to see you, but don't be long."

The door opened and Penny walked in.

"And how are we today?" she said. "Any strange dreams or odd thoughts?"

"How did you get in here?" Billy said.

"I said I was your psychiatrist and that you were being induced today and so forth," Penny said. "I just came to say good luck. Here's all the change we had in the house. Tell Grey to call constantly. I'll see you all tonight."

Billy was taken to the labor floor and hooked up to a fetal-heart monitor whose transducers were kept on her stomach by a large elastic cummerbund. A stylish-looking nurse wearing hospital greens, a string of pearls, and perfectly applied pink lipstick poked her head through the door.

"Hi!" she said in a bright voice. "I'm Joanne Kelly. You're my patient today." She had the kind of voice and smile Billy could not imagine anyone's using in private. "Now, how are we? Fine? All right. Here's what we're going to do. First of all, we're going to put this IV into your arm. It will only hurt a little and then we're going to hook you up to something called Pitocin. Has Dr. Bell explained any of this to you?" Joanne Kelly said.

"All," said Billy.

"Neat," Joanne Kelly said. "We *like* an informed patient. Put your arm out, please."

Billy stuck out her arm. Joanne Kelly wrapped a rubber thong under her elbow.

"Nice veins," she said. "You would have made a lovely junkie."

"Now we're going to start the Pitocin," Joanne Kelly said. "We start off slow to see how you do. Then we escalate." She looked Billy up and down. "Okay," she said. "We're off and running. Now, I've got a lady huffing and puffing in the next room so I have to go and coach her. I'll be back real soon."

Billy lay looking at the clock, or watching the Pitocin and glucose drip into her arm. She could not get a comfortable position and the noise of the fetal-heart monitor was loud and harsh. The machine itself spat out a continual line of data.

Jordan Bell appeared at the foot of her bed.

"An exciting day—yes, Billy?" he said. "What time is Grey coming?"

"I told him to sleep late," Billy said. "All the nurses told me that this can take a long time. How am I supposed to feel when it starts working?"

"If all goes well, you'll start to have contractions and then they'll get stronger and then you'll have your baby."

"Just like that?" said Billy.

"Pretty much just like that."

But by five o'clock in the afternoon nothing much had happened.

Grey sat in a chair next to the bed. From time to time he checked the data. He had been checking it all day.

"That contraction went right off the paper," he said. "What did it feel like?"

"Intense," Billy said. "It just doesn't hurt."

"You're still in the early stages," said Jordan Bell when he came to check her. "I'm willing to stay on if you want to continue, but the baby might not be born till tomorrow."

"I'm beat," said Billy.

"Here's what we can do," Jordan said. "We can keep going or we start again tomorrow."

"Tomorrow," said Billy.

She woke up exhausted with her head pounding. The sky was cloudy and the glare hurt her eyes. She was taken to a different labor room.

In the night her blood pressure had gone up. She had begged not to have a shot—she did not see how she could go into labor feeling so terrible, but the shot was given. It had been a long, sleepless night.

She lay alone with a towel covering one eye, trying to sleep, when a nurse appeared by her side. This one looked very young, had curly hair, and thick, slightly rose-tinted glasses. Her tag read "Eva Gottlieb." Underneath she wore a button inscribed EVA: WE DELIVER.

"Hi," said Eva Gottlieb. "I'm sorry I woke you, but I'm your nurse for the day and I have to get you started."

"I'm here for a lobotomy," Billy said. "What are you going to do to me?"

"I'm going to run a line in you," Eva Gottlieb said. "And then I don't know what. Because your blood pressure is high, I'm supposed to wait until Jordan gets here." She looked at Billy carefully. "I know it's scary," she said. "But the worst that can happen is that you have to be sectioned and that's not bad."

Billy's head throbbed.

"That's easy for you to say," she said. "I'm the section."

Eva Gottlieb smiled. "I'm a terrific nurse," she said. "I'll stay with you."

Tears sprang in Billy's eyes. "Why will you?"

"Well, first of all, it's my job," said Eva. "And second of all, you look like a reasonable person."

Billy looked at Eva carefully. She felt instant, total trust. Perhaps that was part of being in hospitals and having babies. Everyone you came in contact with came very close, very fast.

Billy's eyes hurt. Eva was hooking her up to the fetal-heart monitor. Her touch was strong and sure, and she seemed to know Billy did not want to be talked to. She flicked the machine on, and Billy heard the familiar sound of galloping hooves.

"Is there any way to turn it down?" Billy said.

"Sure," said Eva. "But some people find it consoling."

As the morning wore on, Billy's blood pressure continued to rise. Eva was with her constantly.

"What are they going to do to me?" Billy asked.

"I think they're probably going to give you magnesium sulfate to get your blood pressure down and then they're going to section you. Jordan does a gorgeous job, believe me. I won't let them do anything to you without explaining it first, and if you get out of bed first thing tomorrow and start moving around you'll be fine."

Twenty minutes later, a doctor Billy had never seen before administered a dose of magnesium sulfate.

"Can't you do this?" Billy asked Eva.

"It's heavy-duty stuff," Eva said. "It has to be done by a doctor."

"Can they wait until my husband gets here?"

"It's too dangerous," said Eva. "It has to be done. I'll stay with you."

The drug made her hot and flushed, and brought her blood pressure straight down. For the next hour, Billy tried to sleep. She had never been so tired. Eva brought her cracked ice to suck on and a cloth for her head. The baby wiggled and writhed, and the fetal-heart monitor gauged its every move. Finally, Grey and Jordan Bell were standing at the foot of her bed.

"Okay, Billy," said Jordan. "Today's the day. We must get the baby out. I explained to Grey about the mag sulfate. We both agree that you must have a cesarean."

"When?" Billy said.

"In the next hour," said Jordan. "I have to check two patients and then we're off to the races."

"What do you think?" Billy asked Grey.

"It's right," Grey said.

"And what about you?" Billy said to Eva.

"It has to be done," Eva said.

Jordan Bell was smiling a genuine smile and he looked dashing and happy.

"Why is he so uplifted?" Billy asked Eva after he had dashed down the hall.

"He loves the OR," she said. "He loves deliveries. Think of it this way: you're going to get your baby at last."

Billy lay on a gurney, waiting to be rolled down the hall. Grey, wearing hospital scrubs, stood beside her holding her hand. She had been prepped and given an epidural anesthetic, and she could no longer feel her legs.

"Look at me," she said to Grey. "I'm a mass of tubes. I'm a miracle of modern science." She put his hand over her eyes.

Grey squatted down to put his head near hers. He looked expectant, exhausted, and worried, but when he saw her scanning his face he smiled.

"It's going to be swell," Grey said. "We'll find out if it's little William or little Ella."

Billy's heart was pounding but she thought she ought to say something to keep her side up. She said, "I knew we never should have had sexual intercourse." Grey gripped her hand tight and smiled. Eva laughed. "Don't you guys leave me," Billy said.

Billy was wheeled down the hall by an orderly. Grey held one hand, Eva held the other. Then they left her to scrub.

She was taken to a large, pale green room. Paint was peeling on the ceiling in the corner. An enormous lamp hung over her head. The anesthetist appeared and tapped her feet.

"Can you feel this?" he said.

"It doesn't feel like feeling," Billy said. She was trying to keep her breathing steady.

"Excellent," he said.

Then Jordan appeared at her feet, and Grey stood by her head.

Eva bent down. "I know you'll hate this, but I have to tape your hands down, and I have to put this oxygen mask over your face. It comes off as soon as the baby's born, and it's good for you and the baby."

Billy took a deep breath. The room was very hot. A screen was placed over her chest.

"It's so you can't see," said Eva. "Here's the mask. I know it'll freak you out, but just breathe nice and easy. Believe me, this is going to be fast."

Billy's arms were taped, her legs were numb, and a clear plastic mask was placed over her nose and mouth. She was so frightened she wanted to cry out, but it was impossible. Instead she breathed as Katherine Walden had taught her to. Every time a wave of panic rose, she breathed it down. Grey held her hand. His face was blank and his glasses were fogged. His hair was covered by a green cap and his brow was wet. There was nothing she could do for him, except squeeze his hand.

"Now, Billy," said Jordan Bell, "you'll feel something cold on your stomach. I'm painting you with Betadine. All right, here we go."

Billy felt something like dull tugging. She heard the sound of foamy water. Then she felt the baby being slipped from her. She turned to Grey. His glasses had unfogged and his eyes were round as quarters. She heard a high, angry scream.

"Here's your baby," said Jordan Bell. "It's a beautiful, healthy boy."

Eva lifted the mask off Billy's face.

"He's perfectly healthy," Eva said. "Listen to those lungs." She took the baby to be weighed and tested. Then she came back to Billy. "He's perfect but he's little—just under five pounds. We have to take him upstairs to the preemie nursery. It's policy when they're not five pounds."

"Give him to me," Billy said. She tried to free her hands but they were securely taped.

"I'll bring him to you," Eva said. "But he can't stay down here. He's too small. It's for the baby's safety, I promise you. Look, here he is."

The baby was held against her forehead. The moment he came near her he stopped shrieking. He was mottled and wet.

"Please let me have him," Billy said.

"He'll be fine," Eva said. They then took him away.

The next morning Billy rang for the nurse and demanded that her IV be disconnected. Twenty minutes later she was out of bed slowly walking.

"I feel as if someone had crushed my pelvic bones," Billy said.

"Someone did," said the nurse.

Two hours later she was put into a wheelchair and pushed by a nurse into the elevator and taken to the Infant Intensive Care Unit. At the door the nurse said, "I'll wheel you in."

"I can walk," Billy said. "But thank you very much."

Inside, she was instructed to scrub with surgical soap and to put on a sterile gown. Then she walked very slowly and very stiffly down the hall. A Chinese nurse stopped her.

"I'm William Delielle's mother," she said. "Where is he?"

The nurse consulted a clipboard and pointed Billy down a hallway. Another nurse in a side room pointed to an Isolette—a large plastic case with porthole windows. There on a white cloth lay her child.

He was fast asleep, his little arm stretched in front of him, an exact replica of Grey's sleeping posture. On his back were two disks the size of nickels hooked up to wires that measured his temperature and his heart and respiration rates on a console above his Isolette. He was long and skinny and beautiful.

"He looks like a little chicken," said Billy. "May I hold him?"

"Oh, no," said the nurse. "Not for a while. He mustn't be stressed." She gave Billy a long look and said, "But you can open the windows and touch him."

Billy opened the porthole window and touched his leg. He shivered slightly. She wanted to disconnect his probes, scoop him up, and hold him next to her. She stood quietly, her hand resting lightly on his calf.

The room was bright, hot, and busy. Nurses came and went, washing their hands, checking charts, making notes, diapering, changing bottles of glucose solution. There were three other children in the room. One was very tiny and had a miniature IV attached to a vein in her head. A pink card was taped on her Isolette. Billy looked on the side of William's Isolette. There was a blue card and in Grey's tiny printing was written "William Delielle."

Later in the morning, when Grey appeared in her room he found Billy sitting next to a glass-encased pump.

"This is the well-known electric breast pump. Made in Switzerland," Billy said.

"It's like the medieval clock at Salisbury Cathedral," Grey said, peering into the glass case. "I just came from seeing William. He's much *longer* than I thought. I called all the grandparents. In fact, I was on the telephone all night after I left you." He gave her a list of messages. "They're feeding him in half an hour."

Billy looked at her watch. She had been instructed to use the pump for three minutes on each breast to begin with. Her milk, however, would not be given to William, who, the doctors said, was too little to nurse. He would be given carefully measured formula, and Billy would eventually have to wean him from the bottle and onto herself. The prospect of this seemed very remote.

As the days went by, Billy's room filled with flowers, but she spent most of her time in the Infant ICU. She could touch William but not hold him. The morning before she was to be discharged, Billy went to William's eight o'clock feeding. She thought how lovely it would be to feed him at home, how they might sit in the rocking chair and watch the birds in the garden below. In William's present home, there was no morning and no night. He had never been in a dark room, or heard bird sounds or traffic noise, or felt a cool draft.

William was asleep on his side wearing a diaper and a little T-shirt. The sight of him seized Billy with emotion.

"You can hold him today," the nurse said.

"Yes?"

"Yes, and you can feed him today, too."

Billy bowed her head. She took a steadying breath. "How can I hold him with all this hardware on him?" she said.

"I'll show you," said the nurse. She disconnected the console, reached into the Isolette, and gently untaped William's probes. Then she showed Billy how to change him, put on his T-shirt, and swaddle him in a cotton blanket. In an instant he was in Billy's arms.

He was still asleep, but he made little screeching noises and wrinkled his nose. He moved against her and nudged his head into her arm. The nurse led her to a rocking chair and for the first time she sat down with her baby.

All around her, lights blazed. The radio was on and a sweet male voice sang, "I want you to be mine, I want you to be mine, I want to take you home, I want you to be mine."

William opened his eyes and blinked. Then he yawned and began to cry.

"He's hungry," the nurse said, putting a small bottle into Billy's hand.

She fed him and burped him, and then she held him in her arms and rocked him to sleep. In the process she fell asleep, too, and was woken by the nurse and Grey, who had come from work.

"You must put him back now," said the nurse. "He's been out a long time and we don't want to stress him."

"It's awful to think that being with his mother creates stress," Billy said.

"Oh, no!" the nurse said. "That's not what I mean. I mean, in his Isolette it's temperature controlled."

Once Billy was discharged from the hospital she had to commute to see William. She went to the two morning feedings, came home for a nap, and met Grey for the five o'clock. They raced out for dinner and came back for the eight. Grey would not let Billy stay for the eleven.

Each morning she saw Dr. Edmunds, the head of neonatology. He was a tall, slow-talking, sandy-haired man with horn-rimmed glasses.

"I know you will never want to hear this under any other circumstances," he said to Billy, "but your baby is very boring."

"How boring?"

"Very boring. He's doing just what he ought to do." William had gone to the bottom of his growth curve and was beginning to gain. "As soon as he's a little fatter he's all yours."

Billy stood in front of his Isolette watching William sleep.

"This is like having an affair with a married man," Billy said to the nurse who was folding diapers next to her.

The nurse looked at her uncomprehendingly.

"I mean you love the person but can only see him at certain times," said Billy.

The nurse was young and plump. "I guess I see what you mean," she said.

At home William's room was waiting. The crib had been delivered and put together by Grey. While Billy was in the hospital, Grey had finished William's room. The teddy bears sat on the shelves. A mobile of ducks and geese hung over the crib. Grey had bought a secondhand rocking chair and had painted it red. Billy had thought she would be unable to face William's empty room. Instead she found she could scarcely stay out of it. She folded and refolded his clothes, reorganized his drawers, arranged his crib blankets. She decided what should be his homecoming clothes and set them out on the changing table along with a cotton receiving blanket and a wool shawl.

But even though he did not look at all fragile and he was beginning to gain weight, it often felt to Billy that she would never have him. She and Grey had been told ten days to two weeks from day of birth. One day when she felt she could not stand much more, Billy was told that she might try nursing him.

Touch him on his cheek. He will turn to you. Guide him toward the breast and the magical connection will be made.

Billy remembered this description from her childbirth books. She had imagined a softly lit room, a sense of peacefulness, some soft, sweet music in the background.

She was put behind a screen in William's room, near an Isolette containing an enormous baby who was having breathing difficulties.

She was told to keep on her sterile gown, and was given sterile water to wash her breasts with. At the sight of his mother's naked bosom, William began to howl. The sterile gown dropped onto his face. Billy began to sweat. All around her, the nurses chatted, clattered, and dropped diapers into metal bins and slammed the tops down.

"Come on, William," Billy said. "The books say that this is the blissful union of mother and child."

But William began to scream. The nurse appeared with the formula bottle and William instantly stopped screaming and began to drink happily.

"Don't worry," the nurse said. "He'll catch on."

At night at home she sat by the window. She could not sleep. She had never felt so separated from anything in her life. Grey, to distract himself, was stenciling the wall under the molding in William's room. He had found an early American design of wheat and cornflowers. He stood on a ladder in his blue jeans carefully applying the stencil in pale blue paint.

One night Billy went to the door of the baby's room to watch him, but Grey was not on the ladder. He was sitting in the rocking chair with his head in his hands. His shoulders were shaking slightly. He had the radio on, and he did not hear her.

He had been so brave and cheerful. He had held her hand while William was born. He had told her it was like watching a magician sawing his wife in half. He had taken photos of William in his Isolette and sent them to their parents and all their friends. He had read up on growth curves and had bought Billy a book on breastfeeding. He had also purloined his hospital greens to wear each year on William's birthday. Now *he* had broken down.

She made a noise coming into the room and then bent down and stroked his hair. He smelled of soap and paint thinner. She put her arms around him, and she did not let go for a long time.

Three times a day, Billy tried to nurse William behind a screen and each time she ended up giving him his formula.

Finally she asked a nurse, "Is there some room I could sit in alone with this child?"

"We're not set up for it," the nurse said. "But I could put you in the utility closet."

There amidst used Isolettes and cardboard boxes of sterile water, on the second try William nursed for the first time. She touched his cheek. He turned to her, just as it said in the book. Then her eyes crossed.

"Oh, my God!" she said.

A nurse walked in.

"Hurts, right?" she said. "Good for him. That means he's got it. It won't hurt for long."

At his evening feeding he howled again.

"The course of true love never did run smooth," said Grey. He and Billy walked slowly past the park on their way home. It was a cold, wet night.

"I am a childless mother," Billy said.

Two days later William was taken out of his Isolette and put into a plastic bin. He had no temperature or heart probes, and Billy could pick him up without having to disconnect anything. At his evening feeding when the unit was quiet, she took him out in the hallway and walked up and down with him.

The next day she was greeted by Dr. Edmunds.

"I've just had a chat with your pediatrician," he said. "How would you like to take your boring baby home with you?"

"When?" said Billy.

"Right now, if you have his clothes," Dr. Edmunds said. "Dr. Jacobson will be up in a few minutes and can officially release him."

She ran down the hall and called Grey.

"Go home and get William's things," she said. "They're springing him. Come and get us."

"You mean we can just walk out of there with him?" Grey said. "I mean, just take him under our arm? He barely knows us."

"Just get here. And don't forget the blankets."

A nurse helped Billy dress William. He was wrapped in a green-and-white receiving blanket and covered in a white wool shawl. On his head was a blue-and-green knitted cap. It slipped slightly sideways, giving him a raffish look.

They were accompanied in the elevator by a nurse. It was hospital policy that a nurse hold the baby, and hand it over at the door.

It made Billy feel light-headed to be standing out of doors with her child. She felt she had just robbed a bank and got away with it.

In the taxi, Grey gave the driver their address.

"Not door to door," Billy said. "Can we get out at the avenue and walk down the street just like everyone else?"

When the taxi stopped, they got out carefully. The sky was full of silver clouds and the air was blustery and cold. William squinted at the light and wrinkled his nose.

Then, with William tight in Billy's arms, the three of them walked down the street just like everyone else.

Although I am not an autobiographical writer, this story is a thinly disguised account of the birth of our daughter. As I lay on a gurney being whisked down the hall to have an emergency C-section, some voice said to me: If you survive this, it will doubtless be excellent material.

We all survived. Our daughter is now the tallest person in her class. As I watch her play, which often involves a small number of objects over which she is artistic director, voice, scriptwriter, and arranger, I realize that writers are grown-ups who never stopped playing in that way.

L.C.

FOR WOMEN
EVERYWHERE

□

PERRI KLASS

Alison, in her ninth month, finds she can no longer turn over in bed at night without waking up. The hydraulics of shifting her belly are just too complex, and to get from her left side to her right, she has to maneuver herself delicately, tucking her elbow under and using it as a lever, swinging her abdomen over the top. Turning over the other way, belly down, is not possible; if she could, she imagines, she would look like a circus seal balancing on a huge ball.

When her best friend from high school arrives to keep her company and wait for the birth, Alison hopes to be distracted; lately, she thinks of nothing but the advent of labor. When will this baby come out, when will the pains start that will be unmistakably something new, something she has never felt before? Her obstetrician suggested that they might feel like bad menstrual cramps, which Alison has never had. And she is now accustomed to the small tightenings inside her belly that occur every now and then; Braxton-Hicks, she tells her friend Doris, who thereafter asks her, if she should happen to clutch her belly, "Another Brixie-Hixie?"

It is very nice to have Doris around. For one thing, unpregnant, Doris is easily as big as Alison in her ninth month. Doris was big in high school and she's bigger now. She buys her clothes in special stores that sell silk and velvet and linen for the fat working woman, and all her lingerie is peach. She smells of a perfume named after a designer, which smells familiar to Alison because of little scented cardboard samples in a million magazines—open this flap to enjoy the magic—opposite honey-toned photos of naked bodies arranged like fruit in a basket. Doris's possessions fit surprisingly well into what she calls the tawdry jungle glamour of Alison's apartment. Among the overgrown plants with Christmas lights strung through them, and the life-size stuffed animals, and the bongo drum collection, Doris reclines in her jumpsuits, taking her ease as if waiting for her palanquin. When Doris and Alison walk down the street together on their way for hamburgers and onion rings, Alison feels like a phalanx. Finally she has the nerve to wear a big straw hat with fuchsia flowers out in public, stealing it off her stuffed giraffe. Hey, Big Mamas, she imagines someone shouting (not that anyone ever does). Together, she and Doris take up their share of the street and of the hamburger restaurant where the waitress now greets them by saying, "The usual, right?"

Alison is by now pretty well used to the rude and stupid and none-of-their-business things that people say to her. Good old Doris walked into her apartment, put down her two suitcases and her handbag and her camera case, and informed Alison, looking narrowly at her ballooned abdomen, "Alison, you are doing this For Women Everywhere." Then she gave a Bronx cheer.

"Right," said Alison, with relief, wondering how Doris knew. The world is full of well-meaning people who feel the need to tell Alison how brave she is, how they admire her. I always wanted a baby, but I don't know whether I would dare, they say; or, This is a really great thing you're doing. Alison's mother sends clippings from *People* magazine, keeping her up-to-date on Jessica Lange and Sam Shepard, Farrah Fawcett and Ryan O'Neal, Mick Jagger and Jerry Hall. Even Michael, when he calls up, shyly, to ask whether she really thinks this baby might be his, feels a politically correct need to tell her what a strong woman she is.

"Some people never grow up" is Doris's comment after Michael's next call, and at first Alison thinks she is referring to Michael, which is really unfair. Of the three of them, Michael could be considered the one who most notably has grown up; he has a house and a marriage and two children and all the correct car seats and coffee makers. "You," says Doris, "here you are at your age and the best you can manage is a friend you went to high school with and a boy you've been sleeping with since high school. Don't you ever think about moving on to a later stage?"

There is some justice there, Alison supposes, but if you are thirty-five and your favorite people are left over from when you were fifteen, then that's the way it is. Michael's marriage, acquired in adulthood, does not make Alison's mouth water. Neither does Doris's legendary liaison with a penthouse-dwelling real estate tycoon. Doris is mildly, or maybe avidly, curious to know who the other possible fathers are, and makes some pointed remarks about people who expect their friends to Tell All, and then hold back on their own juicy details, but Alison is not telling and not willing to be drawn into the same game of Twenty Questions that Michael keeps wanting her to play. Is it anyone I know? Is it anyone you care about? How many possibilities are there, anyway? "I am not," Alison says with pregnant dignity, "the kind to kiss and tell."

Alison is consuming something close to four rolls of Tums a day at this point. Automatically before and after every meal she reaches into her pocket for the cylinder, pops off three little chalky disks, and crunches them, feeling the burning go away. Doris tells her this is somewhat disgusting, and Alison informs her, loftily, "My obstetrician says I have progesterone-induced incompetence of the lower esophageal sphincter."

"Talk about disgusting," says Doris.

But it is a pleasure to have Doris there to go with her to the obstetrician, a pleasure not to go alone for the umpteenth time. She hands Doris the straw hat and steps on the scales unhesitatingly, watches the nurse move the weight from 150 to 200, then back to 150, then start messing around with the next smaller weight. One-eighty-two, very good. Smugly, Alison steps off the scale; how educational for Doris, she thinks, to realize that when you are pregnant you get on the scale proudly and hear a number like 182, and then a commendation. But Doris is studying a wall chart, a drawing of a full-term baby packed into a mother. Note the scrunched-up intestines, the way the baby's head presses on the bladder, and so on. "Yich," comments Doris, and follows Alison into the examining room, where she is notably unmoved by the amplified fetal heart.

Alison's obstetrician, Dr. Beane, is a good five or six years younger than Alison and Doris, and is such an immaculate and tailored little thing that it is rather hard to imagine her elbow-deep in the blood and gore that Alison imagines in a delivery room. Also, she has such tiny hands; can she really grab a baby and pull? Is that what an obstetrician does? Alison started out dutifully attending the classes, but she dropped out long before they got to the movie; she has never been one to read instruction booklets. Dr. Beane gives Doris the once-over, considerately doesn't ask any questions, and feels around on Alison's belly with those small, surprisingly strong hands. "You're engaged!" she says, as if offering congratulations.

Alison wonders briefly whether this is some terribly tactful way of acknowledging Doris's presence (better than, say, Is this your significant other?), but it turns out that engaged means that the baby's head has descended into her pelvis, and the baby is in place, all ready to be born.

"Have you thought about anesthesia?" asks the doctor, and launches into an educational lecture on spinals and epidurals, both of which involve having a needle inserted into Alison's back and pumping drugs into her spinal column.

"Yich," comments Doris.

"I think I'd rather die," says Alison.

"You won't die one way or the other. You'll just have pain. And if the pain is too bad, you can have Demerol, just to take the edge off for a while."

"In sorrow shall you bring forth children," says Doris, biblically enough.

"Pay no attention to that man behind the curtain," says Alison, not to be outdone.

"Any time now," says Dr. Beane, cheerful and unperturbed.

Twenty years ago in high school, Doris and Alison and Michael were the three smartest of their year, Doris and Alison were best friends and Michael and Alison eventually fumbled their way into bed. Michael and Doris, however, were the true co-conspirators of the high school, the ones who destroyed every sewing machine in the home economics classroom with a tube of Super Glue and a jar of Vaseline; the ones who reprogrammed the guidance computer so that every senior received a printout recommending Notre Dame as the single most appropriate college; the ones who slipped copies of *Oui* and *Penthouse* into the heavy plastic jackets reserved for *Life* and *The Smithsonian* in the library. Alison was more or less a chicken. Doris is now more or less the only person in the whole world who understands how Alison can go on sleeping with Michael every couple of weeks or so, year in and year out, and never want either to escalate or to de-escalate. And when Michael got married, and they didn't miss a beat, Doris was the only one to whom it was perfectly obvious that his relationship with Alison was covered by a grandfather clause. Alison knows that Michael called her up at the time, stricken with the kind of moral qualms with which he occasionally likes to agitate himself, and she knows that Doris told him to shut up and put out, and she is grateful. Michael's marriage is a brilliant success, as far as Alison can see, though she has not actually met his wife. They are both professors, Michael of math, of course, and his wife of something with ceramics in it, which is not art but high-tech semiconductors. Or something; Alison reserves the right not to be interested and wastes almost no time imagining the marriage, two total weirdo science drones trying to be domestic.

Alison and Doris parade themselves to the hamburger joint for the usual, once again. Alison has medium rare with cheddar and onions, Doris has rare with guacamole on top; both have onion rings. Alison's maternity wardrobe has dwindled; nothing fits and she cannot bring herself to buy anything since the whole process should be over in a week or two. She has one floral drop cloth, contributed by her mother, who also sent four pairs of support hose that are still intact in their cellophane. Over her one pair of cotton pants with a very stretched-out elastic waistband, she can put either a bright pink, extra-extra large T-shirt or else a breezy little yellow rayon number, bought at a yard sale, which was meant to be a pajama top for a very large lady. She has been working at home since her seventh month, easy enough since much of her work has always been done at home. She writes the in-house newsletter for a large company that manufactures communications equipment, and they have installed a modem in her living room. She is paid a ridic-ulous amount for this and has no intention of ever teaching freshman English again. The only problem, as of the last week or two, is that she cannot sit up at her desk anymore for long periods of time. The inhabitant of her abdomen starts to do calisthenics, and to have a full-size baby doing rhythmic jerks in her belly, it turns out, means she has to lie back on the couch and give it room.

She lies back, pulls up the pink T-shirt, pulls down the cotton pants, and she and Doris stare at her belly, at the road map of stretch marks. "God, it's like some kind of earthquake," says Doris, as the striated skin over Alison's belly button heaves upward. Today Doris, in honor of Alison's apartment, is wearing her leopard-print jumpsuit and blood-red earrings to match her fingernails.

"Are you quite comfortable?" Alison asks her abdomen. The acute angle of a little elbow juts out clearly, squirms around, then retreats into its crowded bath. Actually, Alison finds herself overwhelmed, reduced to awestruck mush, by the contemplation of her belly, by the thought that tightly curled up in there is a full-grown sardine of a baby. How can this possibly be? A fetus was one thing, for all its hormonal cyclone, the morning sickness and all the rest, but how can she be carrying something around that properly belongs in a baby carriage? And something with such a mind of its own; it seems now to want to put its feet just where Alison believes she keeps her own liver.

When Michael calls, Doris takes it upon herself to talk to him. She describes the action in Alison's belly, which she refers to as heavy weather in the Himalayan foothills. Alison, still lying on the couch, can hear the firm tones in which Doris discourages Michael's surreptitious questions. She's fine, we're fine, don't be ridiculous. You'll never know. You'll take care of your own children, Alison will take care of hers, and everyone will be just fine. Alison thinks of Doris in the tenth grade, when she wore only black and made frequent references to her dabbles in the occult sciences. Her room, in her parents' pleasant Tudor-style, two-car-garage house, had been converted into a sanctuary of Satan. Doris had removed the light bulb from the ceiling fixture and put two white, skull-shaped candles on either side of an altar on which the girls' high school gym teacher was regularly tortured in effigy before being sacrificed. Doris's mother had minded the writing on the walls more than anything else. But, after all, once the walls were written on they would have to be repainted anyway, so why not write on them some more? So Doris and Alison and Michael decorated them freely with song lyrics that seemed particularly meaningful at the time. Also, poems. The

Who, William Blake, Hermann Hesse, and Leonard Cohen figured prominently in the graffiti; Doris and Alison and Michael were all smart, but hardly exceptional. Anyway, lying on the couch, Alison remembers Doris in her high-priestess phase: massive in black, making oracular pronouncements, suggesting death or disfigurement for those she disliked, promising the favored that they would prosper.

"Lots of Brixie-Hixies, huh?" says Doris, finding Alison leaning against the wall in the kitchen, holding her belly.

"I don't know, this might be more than that."

"No false alarms now, you don't want to go getting me all excited for nothing."

"Let's time them," says Alison.

Twenty minutes apart. Fifteen minutes apart. Starting to hurt a little. Lasting thirty to forty seconds. Doris notes them down systematically in Magic Marker on Alison's one clean dish towel, contributed, needless to say, by her mother. She suggests to Alison that these numbers will make a humdrum dish towel a priceless precious memento. Alison tries to remember whether they said anything about breathing back in those first couple of childbirth classes.

"All right," says Doris, coming to the bottom hem of the dish towel. "Get that cunning little bag you have all packed and waiting and let's get moving."

"You really think it's time?"

"Do you want to wait for Sherman to take Atlanta? Get into the pony cart and let's go."

At the hospital, the nurse puts Alison into two little gowns, one with the opening in the front, the other in the back. Strangely enough, all the way over in the car, even as she experimented with panting, with taking big deep breaths, with moaning and groaning, Alison expected them to look at her blankly, to send her home, to wonder aloud why she was wasting their time. Instead, along comes this nurse, Madeline, a black woman even larger than Doris. The three of us, Alison thinks, would make quite a singing group. The nurse puts an IV into Alison's left hand and hooks belts around her waist to connect her to a fetal-heart monitor. Doris finds the monitor quite interesting and, when the nurse leaves the room, experiments with the volume control, turning up the gallop-a-trot of the baby's heart-beat as loud as it will go.

"Noisy baby you have there," she remarks. "I thought this was supposed to hurt. Does it hurt yet?"

"Are you looking forward to watching me writhe in pain?"

"Just remember, you will be writhing for women everywhere."

Alison is immeasurably glad to have Doris there. Does this mean, she finds two seconds to wonder in between contractions, that she is in fact going to want someone there from now on, that she is going to find herself alone with this baby and feel bereft? Well, maybe. But this is a fine time to start worrying about that.

"Don't worry," she tells Doris. "It's starting to hurt plenty. Don't be deceived by my stoicism and physical bravery."

"When you make a face like you're constipated and then pant like a dog, is that when it hurts?"

"I still can't understand why you didn't become a psychiatrist," says Alison, beginning to pant again.

"There's more money in stockbrokering," says Doris, who is in fact very rich.

"Well, thanks for coming," says Alison, suddenly not sure she has yet gotten around to saying that.

"I wouldn't miss this for the world." Doris looms over the bed, a great big woman with an auburn permanent and red nails, wearing green paisley lounging pajamas. What more could anyone want in a labor room? "Soon the fun will really begin—don't you get an enema?"

"I think that's out-of-date. Shit, Doris, this isn't a joke any-more."

"All you girls think you can just play around, and then when you get caught, you start whining."

The nurse, Madeline, comes bustling in, hears them shouting over the boom of the monitor. "Who turned this thing up so high?" she demands, turning it down.

"Why don't you take a little walk, see some of the scenery?" Madeline is unstrapping her from the monitor, rather to Alison's surprise; she hadn't expected them to grant her request.

"Is that okay?"

"Honey, you're moving pretty quick for a first baby, but you've got a ways to go. Just you go strolling with your friend, there's lots of corridors."

The people that Alison and Doris pass, as they promenade through the Labor and Delivery hallways, look meaningfully at Alison's belly. Most are doctors and nurses dressed in green surgical scrubs. There is one other woman in labor who is also up and walking, but her husband, who is six feet tall and bearded after the manner of John the Baptist, is practically carrying her. The walls are hung with non-descript Impressionist landscapes.

"Lovely on the Riviera this time of year," Doris says, each time they pass the French fishing village, and, "I hear the stained glass is simply stunning," when they pass the cathedral at sunset.

Eventually, walking begins to feel a little less probable, and Alison climbs back into bed. And along comes Dr. Beane to congratulate her on already being five centimeters dilated.

"God," says Alison, "this is becoming a real pain in the ass."

"Truer words were never spoken," says Doris.

Alison is no longer able to muster a sense of humor. Alison is in quite significant pain, and it is borne in upon her that she does not have the option of stopping these regular onslaughts. She would like an hour off, she wants to tell them, she would like to put this on hold and start again tomorrow. Instead, Madeline comes by every now and then and tells her to take deep breaths. They have her belted up again and keep telling her to listen to her baby's heart, how strong and regular it is. But this steady lub-a-dubbing seems to Alison to have very little indeed to do with that strong-willed little gymnast who has been kicking and wriggling so idiosyncratically. Alison wishes, truly and sincerely, to be back on her couch, watching her belly heave and swell. What a good working relationship that was, why go and spoil it now?

"I didn't know when I was well off," she tells Doris and Madeline. Dr. Beane is somewhere behind them, checking the strips that the monitor is printing out. An interesting geometrical dynamic, thinks Alison with perfect clarity, the three very large women and the tiny little doctor.

In fact, it goes very quickly for a first labor; everyone says so. Five hours after coming to the hospital, Alison is pronounced ready to push. Alison is no longer listening to anything that anyone has to say. This is, she has decided, the most ridiculous method for propagating the species that she can imagine. In those few precious seconds when the pain goes away, she thinks back to biology class, herself and Doris and Michael in the back row, acing every test. Think of all the alternative methods. Budding. Spore formation. Egg laying. Binary fission. And back comes the pain; howling, she has discovered, helps. Madeline does not seem to approve fully; there was something a little censorious about the way she closed the labor room door. "Mustn't let the other women in labor know that it hurts, huh," Doris was heard to say.

Sometimes she squeezes Doris's hand. Sometimes Doris squeezes hers. During one particularly unpleasant contraction, Alison gives out with a loud cry of, "Oh, fuckety fuck fuck the fucking fuck," and then her brain clears enough to hear Doris's response, "Do any more of that, darling, and you'll end up right back here."

What can she mean? Another contraction hits before Alison can actually think back to those familiar and surprisingly passionate nights with Michael, or to the nights with the other two men who will never know about this. Oddly enough, she can remember, as the pain ebbs, her decision to go ahead and get pregnant, that one particularly promising and active month when she got herself into this, but her mind cannot encompass the how. This is no moment to think about the more pleasant uses to which her lower body can be put. This is a moment to howl.

Dr. Beane, who has been off doing doctor things, reappears after Alison has been pushing for half an hour or so. Pushing is a little better than just contracting, but it is also hard work. "I have had enough of this," Alison tells her, loud and clear. "There is never going to be a baby. I want to go home."

"You're doing very, very well. You're going to have your baby soon."

"I don't want a baby. I changed my mind." She is dead serious, she is enjoying being a bad girl, she is kidding, she is contracting again, and Madeline is counting at her, ten nine eight seven six five four three two one, trying to get Alison to prolong the push.

"You heard the lady. She's changed her mind." Doris almost sounds dead serious herself.

Dr. Beane puts Doris on one side of Alison, Madeline on the other. Alison puts one arm around each of them, and each lifts up one of her legs, pulls it back. Dr. Beane is now a tiny pixie all dressed in surgical greens, rubber gloves on her hands. She looks at Alison severely. "You need to push this baby out," she says. "The monitor is showing poor beat-to-beat variability and you are ready to do it!"

"What is poor beat-to-beat variability?" asks Doris. Alison doesn't care.

"It means she has to push this baby out. Now, pull back on her legs, Madeline will count, and on the next push, I want to see progress."

It takes exactly sixteen more pushes for the baby to be born. Alison has suddenly remembered that she was promised Demerol for pain and is demanding it loudly. Dr. Beane tells her, somewhat brusquely, that she cannot have it so close to delivery, and Alison begins to make a speech about how unfair this is, how she has labored and labored and pushed and pushed. Then two things happen at once: another contraction begins and Doris leans in close to her ear and says loudly, "Stop whining and push! Something's going wrong with the baby!"

And, amazingly enough, Alison does care. Or at least responds. Or at least feels she has to respond. Or something. She stops making speeches, she grips the two pillars on either side and bears down for the full count. Dr. Beane encourages her. "I see the head!" she calls from her little steel stool between Alison's legs. Toward the end, Alison loses track of everything. She keeps her eyes fixed on Madeline's, since Madeline is the one who tells her this will be it, you'll do it next time. She bears down when Madeline counts, responding to the authoritative numbers like Pavlov's dog. And then, at the end, everything changes. Instead of pure pain and effort and her body straining and close to exploding, she actually feels it, she does, she feels something move down, something fall away from her, something slide out of her and the next moment everyone is laughing and cheering.

There is no separating anything out; Dr. Beane's triumphant announcement that she has a girl, the sudden shocking baby cries, slightly thin and then outraged, Madeline's assurances from across the room that the baby is perfect, ten fingers and ten toes. Before Alison can even contemplate that information, the baby, wrapped in a somewhat bloody blanket, is deposited on Alison's chest. Only then, lying back, does Alison realize the pain has actually stopped.

Dr. Beane and Madeline are still messing around at the bottom of the bed. Alison and Doris, however, are busy admiring the baby, who has stopped crying and is scrunched up in her mother's arms, occasionally opening her eyes to see if she can see who is responsible for this outrage. A little stretchy white cap on her head works its way off, and it turns out she has a great deal of dark hair. To Alison's relief, she looks like a newborn, like a monkey; there is no uncanny resemblance to Michael or any other adult.

"She's certainly beautiful," Doris says, as if surprised. Actually, she isn't particularly beautiful, Alison supposes, but on the other hand, she's the most miraculously divinely beautiful thing ever.

"I know what you mean."

"What happens now?" Doris asks, after a lull of admiring, during which Dr. Beane finishes up with the afterbirth and the stitches; a few twinges and a few ouches from Alison, but she is harder to impress than she used to be. The baby, eyes closed, nuzzles into her mother's neck, seeking warmth, or food, or contact, maybe missing the close confinement where up to now she has rocked and kicked and wriggled.

"Now Mother goes on up to the maternity floor and gets a little rest," says Madeline, "and Baby goes to the nursery and gets weighed and measured."

"Now I guess I take her home and educate her," says Alison, in wonderment.

"Well, good," says Doris. "As long as you have a plan."

"For Women Everywhere" was written when I was extremely pregnant. There was another piece of writing I was supposed to be doing, but the main character was not pregnant, and I found I couldn't imagine what her life was like. I wrote this story in part to distract myself from the daily discomforts of waiting out an overdue pregnancy (in August!), but the plot of the story turned out to be that same wait for a baby. I had imagined another woman, another life—but she was just as pregnant as I was. I couldn't lean across my stomach to reach my desk, so I put an ironing board across the arms of a big armchair and put the computer keyboard

on the ironing board. This is my daughter Josephine's story, then, the first one I ever wrote for her, written out of the excitement and disbelief that goes with expecting a baby—and the tedium and physical indignity which mark the final days of a pregnancy.

P.K.

PAGAN NIGHT

□

KATE BRAVERMAN

Sometimes they called him Forest or Sky. Sometimes they called him River or Wind. Once, during a week of storms when she could not leave the van at all, not for seven consecutive days, they called him Gray. The baby with the floating name and how she carries him and he keeps crying, has one rash after another, coughs, seems to shudder and choke. It is a baby of spasms, of a twisted face turning colors. You wouldn't want to put his picture on the baby-food jar. You wouldn't want to carry his picture in your wallet, even if you had his photograph, and she doesn't.

Of course, Dalton never wanted this baby. Neither did she. The baby was just something that happened and there didn't seem to be the time to make it not happen. They were on tour, two months of one-nighters between San Diego and Seattle, and when it was over the band broke up. When it was over, they got drunk and sold the keyboards and video cameras for heroin. Then they were in San Francisco and she still had the apartment. Later, they had Dalton's van.

Then they had to leave San Francisco. Something about the equipment, the amplifiers Dalton insisted were his, that they had accrued to him by a process of decision and sacrifice. Then they had to wind through California with her belly already showing, and all they had left were their black leather jackets and the silver-and-turquoise jewelry they had somehow acquired in Gallup or Flagstaff. Dalton kept talking about the drummer's kit, which he claimed was actually his, and they sold it in Reno and lived on the fortieth floor of an old hotel with a view of the mountains. They had room service for three weeks and by then she had stopped throwing up. After that there was more of Nevada and the van broke again on the other side of the state. There was the slow entry into Idaho, after mountains and desert and Utah, and the snow had melted and then the baby they had almost forgotten about was born.

Dalton can't stand the baby crying. That's why she leaves the van, walks three miles into town along the river. When she has a dollar-fifty, she buys an espresso in the café where the waitress has heard of her band.

Sunny stays away from the van as long as she can. Sometimes someone will offer her a ride to the park or the zoo or the shopping mall and she takes it. She's let her hair grow out, the purple and magenta streaks are nearly gone, seem an accident that could have happened to anyone, a mislabeled bottle, perhaps. Dalton says it's better to blend in. He's cut his hair, too, and wears a San Diego Padres baseball cap. He says it makes him feel closer to God.

Willow. Cottonwood. Creek. Eagle. She could call the baby Willow. But Dalton refuses to give it a name. He resists the gender, refers to the baby as it, not he. Just it, the creature that makes the noise. But it doesn't cost any money. She still feeds it from her body and the rashes come and go. It's because she doesn't have enough diapers. Sunny puts suntan lotion on the baby's sores, massage oil, whatever is left in her suitcase from the other life. Once she covered the baby's rash with layers of fluorescent-orange lipstick, the last of her stage makeup.

Sunny has begun to realize that if she can't keep the baby quiet, Dalton will leave her. It won't always be summer here. There will come a season when she can't just walk all day, or sit in the mall or the lobby of the granite city hall, pretending to read a newspaper. She won't be able to spend the entire winter in the basement of the museum where they have built a replica of the town as it was in the beginning, with its penny-candy store and nickel barbershop and baths for a quarter. She won't be able to spend five or six months attempting to transport herself through time telepathically. She could work in the saloon, find an Indian to watch the baby. Later she could marry the sheriff.

Today, walking by the river, it occurred to Sunny that this landscape was different from any other she had known. It wasn't the punched-awake, intoxicated glow of the tropics, seductive and inflamed. It didn't tease you and make you want to die for it. That's what she thought of Hawaii. And it wasn't the rancid gleam like spoiled lemons that coated everything in a sort of bad childhood waxy veneer flashback. That's what she thought of Los Angeles, where they had lived for two years. In Los Angeles, afternoon smelled of ash and some enormous August you could not placate or forget. Los Angeles air reminded her of what happened to children in foster homes at dusk when they took their clothes off, things that were done in stucco added-on garages with ropes and pieces of metal and the freeway rushing in the background like a cheap sound track. It was in sync, but it had no meaning.

This Idaho was an entirely separate area of the spectrum. There was something unstable about it, as if it had risen from a core of some vast, failed caution. It was the end of restlessness. It was what happened when you stopped looking over your shoulder. It was what happened when you dared to catch your breath, when you thought you were safe.

Sunny feels there is some mean streak to this still-raw, still-frontier place. This land knows it gets cold, winter stays too long, crops rot, you starve. This land knows about wind, how after storms the clouds continue to assemble every afternoon over the plain, gather and recombine and rain again, and this can go on for weeks. Her shoes are always damp. Her feet are encased in white blisters. Always, the thunderheads are congregating and mating and their spawn is a cold rain.

Some days the clouds are in remission, ringing the plain but staying low. On such afternoons, the three of them go down to the Snake River. They follow a dirt road to another dirt road and they've been instructed where to turn, near the hit-by-lightning willow. They park on a rise above the channel. Dalton leaves his guitar in the van and padlocks it, walks ahead of her and the baby with the fishing pole over his shoulder. They walk beneath black branches, find the path of smooth rocks down to the bank leading to a railroad bridge. It's a trestle over the Snake made from railroad ties with gaps between them and the tracks running down the center. This is how they cross the Snake, reach the other bank, where the fishing is supposed to be good. There are tiny grassy islands Dalton can roll up his black jeans and wade out to. Dalton traded somebody in town for a fly-fishing rod. He probably traded drugs for the rod, though she realizes she hasn't seen her black leather jacket for more than a week.

On Sundays yellow with orioles and tiger monarchs and a sun that turns the grasses soft, Dalton takes them fishing on the far bank of the river. One late afternoon he caught four trout. Sunny could see their rainbows when the sun struck their skin. They looked sewed with red sequins. They were supposed to be sixteen inches. That was the rule for the South Fork of the Snake. Their trout were smaller, seven and eight inches, but they kept them anyway, cooked them on a stick over a fire they made near the van. Dalton said the eyes were the best part and he gave her one and it was white as a pried-open moon and she ate it.

Now she is walking into a yellow that makes her feel both restless and invigorated. A yellow of simultaneity and symbols and some arcane celebration she can vaguely sense. When she ate the trout eyes, they were like crisp white stones. She thought of rituals, primitive people, the fundamental meaning of blood. If one mastered these elements, it might be possible to see better in the dark. She shakes her head as if to clear it, but nothing changes. Her entire life is a network of intuitions, the beginning of words, like neon and dome, pine, topaz, shadow, but then the baby starts crying.

Sunny knows it's all a matter of practice, even silence and erasure and absence. What it isn't is also a matter of practice. In the same way you can take piano or voice and train yourself to recognize and exploit your range, you can also teach yourself not to speak, not to remember. That's why when Dalton asks what she's thinking, she says, "Nothing." It's a kind of discipline. What she's really thinking about is what will happen when summer is over. What will happen if she can't make the baby stop crying?

Sometimes when she is frightened, it calms her to think about Marilyn Monroe. Sunny knows all about Marilyn's childhood, the foster homes, the uncles who fondled her breasts, kissed her seven-year-old nipples, and they got hard. Then Marilyn knew she was a bad girl. She would always be a bad girl. It was like being at a carnival, a private carnival, just for her. There were balloons and streamers, party hats and birthday cakes with chocolate frosting and her name written in a neon pink. And no one could tell her no. She had liked to think about Marilyn Monroe when they were driving in the van between gigs. The band was in its final incarnation then. Sunny was already pregnant and it was called Pagan Night.

When Dalton asks her what she's thinking and she says, "Nothing," she is really imagining winter and how she is certain there won't be enough to eat. Dalton says he'll shoot a cow. There are cows grazing outside of town, off half the dirt roads and along the banks of the river. Or he'll shoot a deer, an elk, he'll trap rabbits. He's been talking to people in town, at the Rio Bar. He's traded something for the fly-fishing rig, but he still has both guns and the rifle. He'll never trade the weapons, not even for heroin, even if they could find any here.

Today, on this cool morning, Sunny has walked from the river to the zoo. Admission is one dollar, but the woman in the booth knows her and has started to simply wave her in.

Sunny passes through a gate near a willow and she would like to name the baby Willow. It would be an omen and it would survive winter. Then she is entering the zoo, holding her baby without a name. She sits with her baby near the swan pond until someone gives her a quarter, a sandwich, a freshly purchased bag of popcorn. They simply hand it to her.

She has memorized each animal, bird, and fish in this miniature zoo. The birds stand by mossy waterfalls of the sort she imagines adorn the swimming pools of movie stars. She sits nursing her baby that she is pretending is named Willow. If anyone asks, and she knows no one will, she is prepared to say, His name is Willow.

Later, she stands in a patch of sun by an exhibit featuring a glassed-in bluish pool that should contain a penguin or a seal, but is empty. It smells derelict, harsh and sour with something like the residue of trapped wind and the final thoughts of small mammals as they chew off their feet and bleed to death. You can walk down a flight of stairs and look through the glass, but nothing is swimming. She knows. She has climbed down twice.

Sunny likes to look at what isn't there, in the caged water whipped by sun. This is actually the grotto that is most full, with its battered streams of light like hieroglyphics, a language in flux, lost in shifting ripples.

She pauses in front of the golden eagle. It will not look at her, even when she whistles. The information stenciled to the cage says the golden eagle can live thirty years, longer than many movie stars, longer than Hendrix and Janis and Jim Morrison and James Dean. This particular bird will probably outlive her.

Sunny is thinking about how hungry she is, when someone offers her half a peanut-butter-and-jelly sandwich. Actually, the woman has her child do this, reach out a baby arm to her, as if she is now some declawed beast you could let your kid near.

Her own baby is wrapped in a shawl, the same shawl she had once laid across the sofa in the living room of her apartment in San Francisco. She had gone there to study modern dancing, tap, and ballet. Her father had wanted her to go to nursing school. If she went to nursing school, her father could believe she had finally forgotten. He could conclude that she was well and whole, and he could sleep without pills. His ulcer would disappear. He could take Communion again.

Sunny took singing lessons and began to meet men with rock 'n' roll bands. Nursing school became white and distant. It became a sort of moon you could put between your teeth and swallow. She stopped envisioning herself in a starched cotton uniform with a stethoscope around her neck. What she wanted now was to smoke grass and hash and opium and stare out the window at Alcatraz. What she wanted to do was sniff powder drawn in lines across a wide square of mirror she kept on the side of the sofa, like a sort of magic screen where you could watch your face change forever.

Now, at the zoo, she stands on the wood slats surrounding the fish pond filled with keepers, twenty- and twenty-five- and thirty-inch rainbow trout. This is what keepers look like. On yellow Sundays, she and Dalton and the baby walk across the railroad trestle over the Snake River. But Dalton will never catch a fish this big.

She was afraid the first time they crossed the bridge. Dalton had to grab her hand. He hadn't touched her body since the baby was born. He had to pull her along. The bridge was higher than she had thought. The river was rushing underneath like a sequence of waves, but faster and sharper, without breath or cycles, and she was holding the baby. That day she was secretly calling the baby Sunday. And she was cradling Sunday with one arm and Dalton was holding her other hand, pulling her through the yellow. He was also holding the fishing rod he'd somehow procured at the Rio Bar, traded somebody something for, she is beginning to think it was her black leather jacket with the studs on the cuffs, the special studs sewed on by a woman who claimed she was a Gypsy in Portland.

Dalton must think she won't need her leather jacket in winter. He isn't considering what she'll need in winter. Maybe they won't still be in Idaho. Maybe they won't still be together. And the bridge was wider than she had at first imagined. It was like a pier with its set of two railroad tracks down the center, one thinner, the other fatter, one unused set covered with rust. The bridge was made from railroad ties and there were gaps between them where a foot could get caught, something small could fall through. Dalton said, "Make a pattern. Step every other one. Don't look down." That's what she did, stepped every other one, didn't look down, but still she could hear the river in a kind of anguish beneath her and she was shaking.

"It's an abandoned bridge, isn't it?" she asked Dalton.

The first few times he said yes, but when they had crossed the fourth time, he said no. She stopped, found herself staring into sun. "What do you mean?" she demanded.

"Look at the rails. The larger set are clean. Trains do this." He pointed at the tracks. "Or they'd be covered with rust."

"What if the train came now? As we were crossing?" she finally asked.

"There are beams every twenty feet," Dalton pointed to a kind of metal girder. "We'd hang on the side until it passed."

She tries to imagine herself standing on the girder, holding the baby which in her mind is named Sunday in one of her arms. She cannot conceive of this. Instead she remembers, suddenly, a story Dalton once told her years ago, before they had gone on the road, when they first recited their secret information to each other, their collection of shame, where they were truly from, what had happened, what was irrevocable.

Dalton told her about a night in high school when he had been drinking beer with his friends. Perhaps it was spring. They had been drinking since dawn and now it was after midnight. It was Ohio. That's where Dalton was from. His friends had wandered down to the train station. His best friend had tried to hop a train. Johnny Mohawk. That's what they called him, Mohawk, because he said he was part Indian. Johnny Mohawk tried to hop a train and fell. It ran over him, amputating both legs, his right arm, and half of his left.

"He was so drunk, that's what saved him," Dalton explained. It must have been later. They were riding in a tour bus. They had an album out and the company had given them a roadie, a driver, and a bus. Outside was neon and wind and houses you didn't want to live in. "He was so drunk, he didn't feel it," Dalton was saying. "If he'd been more awake, the shock would have killed him."

Dalton glanced out the window, at some in-between stretch of California where there were waist-high grasses and wild flowers and a sense of too much sun, even in the darkness. She asked him what happened. She tried to imagine Johnny Mohawk, but she could not. Her mind refused to accommodate the brutal lack of symmetry, would produce only words like tunnel and agony, suffocate and scream. Even if she had gone to nursing school, even if she went right now, enrolled in the morning, she could do nothing about Johnny Mohawk. It would always be too late.

"It was the best thing ever happened to him," Dalton said. "He was on his way to becoming a professional drunk. Like his father, like his uncles and inbred cousins. After the accident, he got a scholarship to State. They gave him a tutor and a special car. Now he's an engineer for an oil company."

Sunny thinks about Johnny Mohawk as she stands in the zoo, in front of a grotto with grassy sides and a sleeping male and female lion. Their cage seems too small to contain them if they wanted to do anything other than sleep in the damp green grass. She wonders what would happen if she fell in, over the low metal bar.

Near her, a pregnant woman with three blond daughters, each with a different colored ribbon in her long yellow hair, tells her two-year-old, "Don't you climb up on that bar now. You fall in, there'd be no way to get you out. That hungry old lion would eat you right up."

Sunny feels the baby in her arms, how heavy it is, how it could so easily slide from her, through the bar, into the grassy grotto. She could never retrieve it. No one would expect her to.

Then she is walking past the one zebra. When Dalton asks her if she wants to talk about anything, she shakes her head, no. She is considering how filled each no is, glittering and yellow. Each no is a miniature carnival, with curled smiles and balloons on strings and a profusion of names for babies. And in this no are syllables like willow and cottonwood and shadow and Johnny Mohawk. And in this no is the railroad trestle above one hundred thousand rainbow trout.

Sunny's favorite exhibit is the snow leopard. It is strange that a zoo in a tiny town should have such an animal. They are so rare. She reads what the snow leopard eats, mammals and birds. Its social life is solitary. How long does it live? Twenty-five years. Not quite long enough to see its first record go platinum. And it isn't really asleep on the green slope behind its grid of bars as much as it is simply turned away. Perhaps it is thinking about the past, and on its lip is something that isn't quite a smile. Or perhaps he is simply listening to birds.

There are always birds when they cross the railroad trestle on Sunday, the Snake below them, the bald eagles and blue herons and swallows and robins, orioles and magpies in the air near their shoulders. And there is no schedule for the train. She's called Union Pacific five times, waited for the man in charge to come back from vacation, to come back from the flu, to be at his desk, and there is no way to predict when the train runs over this particular trestle. It's a local. It gets put together at the last moment, no one knows when.

When they cross the bridge on Sunday, she is obsessively listening for trains. And there are so many birds, fat robins, unbelievably red, and orioles, the yellow of chalk from fourth grade when she got an A and her teacher let her write the entire spelling list for the week on the blackboard. And ducks and Canadian geese and loons, all of them stringing their syllables across the afternoon, hanging them near her face like a kind of party streamer. The baby is named Sunday or Sometimes and she feels how heavy it is, how it could just drop from her arms.

It's become obvious that these fishing Sundays are not about catching trout. It's a practice for something else entirely, for leaving, for erasure, silence, and absence. She understands now. It's the end of July. She won't be able to feed the baby from her body indefinitely or walk through town all day, looking for trash cans where she can deposit the diapers she has used over and over again.

Now it is time to rehearse. They are involved in a new show with an agenda they don't mention. It's a rehearsal for abandoning the baby. She practices leaving it on the bank, walking fifty steps away, smoking a cigarette. Then she rushes back to retrieve it, to press it against her. If she simply took a slightly longer path from the bank, permitted herself to smoke a joint, a third or fourth cigarette, she might not remember exactly where she placed the baby, not with all the foliage, the vines and brush, bushes and trees, the whole bank an ache of greenery. Something could have interceded, a sudden aberration in the river current or perhaps a hawk. She wouldn't be blamed.

In the children's petting zoo, a gray rabbit mounts a white one. Another white rabbit eats from a bowl. They eat and mate, eat and mate. In the winter, Dalton says he'll shoot a deer. He's made a deal with somebody at the Rio Bar, something about sharing and storing. There are always cattle, fish, rabbits, beavers, and otters that can be trapped.

During the day, Dalton says he's working on songs. He still has both guitars. He can only write music when the baby isn't crying or coughing. She wants to name the baby Music or Tears. Once she tells Dalton she wants to name the baby Bay. She remembers the apartment they had with the view of the bridge, the way at midnight the wind felt like a scalded blue. It was when everything seemed simultaneously anesthetized and hot. It was a moment she remembers as happy.

"It's not time to name it," Dalton said. He was strumming his twelve-string. He said many African tribes didn't name a baby until it had survived a year. Dalton looked at her and smiled. His lips reminded her of Marilyn Monroe.

That's when she realized each day would have to be distinct and etched. She licks the baby's face. She sits on a bench in the sun at the zoo by a pond with a mossy waterfall in the center. There are swans in this pond. She closes her eyes and smells the baby and decides to name him Swan. She kisses his cheek and whispers in his ear, "Your name is Swan. Your name is Moss. Your name is Bye-Bye."

"What are you thinking?" Dalton asks. It was during the storm two weeks ago. He was drinking tequila. Rain struck the van and she thought of rocks and bullets and time travel.

"Nothing," she replied.

Wind. Hidden networks. The agenda that sparks. You know how night feels without candles, without light bulbs, maps, schedules. This is what we do not speak of. Bye-bye-bye, baby. Bye-bye-bye.

Everyday, Dalton says he's going to write songs while she is gone. He has a joint in his mouth, curled on his side in the back of the van on a ridge above the Snake River where they now live. He has a bottle of vodka tucked into his belt. The vodka is gone when she comes back. Sunny has to knock again and again on the side of the van, has to kick it with her foot, has to shout his name, until he wakes up.

Each day must be separate, an entity, like a species, a snow leopard, a zebra, or a rainbow trout. Each one with a distinct evolution and morphology, niches, complex accidents. Last Sunday, she smoked a joint and drank tequila. Then they crossed the river on the railroad ties. She has a pattern, left foot, skip one with the right, left foot, skip one with the right, don't look down.

She knows it will happen on a Sunday, perhaps next Sunday. Dalton will say, "Come over, look at this."

"I can't. I'm feeding the baby," she will answer.

"Put it down a second," he'll say. "You've got to see this."

She'll place the baby in the center of soft weeds. She'll follow the sound of his voice, find Dalton on the bank with a great trout, twenty inches, thirty inches long. It will be their keeper and she will bend down, help him pull it in. Her feet will get wet. She will use her hat for a net, her red hat that says "Wyoming Centennial 1990."

The seconds will elongate, the minutes will spread into an afternoon, with no one counting or keeping track. When they've pulled the trout in, when they've finished the tequila, it will be dark. They will begin searching for the baby, but there will be only shadow. No one could say they were at fault. No one could say anything. No one knows about them or the baby, and the van has got at least five thousand miles left in it. They could be in New York or Florida in two days.

Perhaps it will be a Sunday when they are crossing the bridge. She'll be holding the baby named Sometimes or Swan or Willow, and they'll have to leap onto the steel girders as the train rushes by. The baby will drop from her arms into the Snake and it will be taken on the current like Moses.

They will never mention the falling. They will not speak of it, not once. It will just be something caught in the edge of their smile, like a private carnival that went through town and maybe you saw it once and too briefly and then it was gone.

She knows Dalton believes they are purer, more muscle and bone, closer to an archetypal winter beyond artifice. That was part of why they called the band Pagan Night. They are animals, barbarians, heathens. They are savage and recognize this, its possibilities and what it costs. In China and India, girl children are often drowned at birth. There are fashions of surviving famines engraved on the nerves.

Maybe this Sunday they will be crossing the bridge when the train erupts from a spoil of foliage and shadow, willows and herons and orioles. Dalton will have left his guitar in the van, padlocked with his paperback myths of primitive people. Perhaps it will be a Sunday after Dalton returns from the Rio Bar with heroin. They will have cooked it up and had it that night, all night, and the next day, all day, until it is finished and there is nothing left, not even in the cotton in the spoon.

When she stands on the Sunday railroad trestle, she will think about ineluctable trajectories. There is a destiny to the direction and journey of all objects, stars and birds, babies and stones and rivers. Who can explain how or why that snow leopard came from Asia to reside in an obsolete grotto in a marginal farming town among barley and potato fields in southern Idaho? What shaped such a voyage, what miscalculations, what shift of wind or currents, what failure of which deity?

Sunny knows exactly what she will be thinking when it happens. There are always acres of sun and their fading. It is all a sequence of erasures and absences. Who is to say flesh into water or flesh into rock is not a form of perfection? What of Moses on the river with an ineluctable destiny to be plucked from reeds by a princess? Perhaps on some fishing Sunday when the baby is named Swallow or Tiger and falls from her arms, someone on a distant bank will look up and say they saw the sudden ascension of a god.

We must set our mothers free. In truth, beneath and within the ghastly, suffocating ghetto of the sensibility this culture insists is the canon, our mothers are more varieties than the page has yet revealed. Some mothers are drug addicts and mad-women, angry, enraged, psychotic, exhilarated, on a trip. Some mothers scheme and gamble, find a frontier and explore it, naked, without a compass, in winter, if they must. Some mothers must. Some mothers are drawn to the periphery. They are in love with spikes, magenta in the hair, twenty-six gauge in the arm. They collect bad men and bad habits, get a tattoo, a taste for smack, for playing chicken with trains. They are entranced by tracks, superimposed on the earth or their flesh. Some moth-ers are compelled to fall from illusionary grace, and if they drop their child on the way, well, it happens. They are gathering stories to tell in middle age, if they chance to live that long. Some mothers don't just give birth. They also give death. And why not? They are, after all, only human.

In the sequel to this story, which I am not going to write, Sunny throws her baby over the rail and flees to Florida, where the van dies and she and Dalton break up. Sunny then becomes a med tech and marries an orthodontist she meets in the elevator of the office building. They have a boat, play bridge and tennis, go on Caribbean cruises, have a condo in Cancún. Sunny gets a good haircut and interior decorator. She gets a good tan. You've sat next to her at dinner. She belongs to your country club. She might be the girl next door. Good teeth and bones and she doesn't look back.

K.B.

BABY PICTURES

◻

MOLLY GILES

The light's right, bright as foil, a long silver sheet rolling in through the east kitchen window. I take one look and race back to the bedroom. "Mama?" Wynn calls as I pound past his door. "Mama? It's up time?"

"One second," I tell him. I find the camera where I left it, on top of the laundry. I snatch at it fast and race back to the kitchen. The light is still there, and everything blazes: the toaster, the step stool, the pears set to ripen on the sill. The dishes Robert left piled in the sink are the loveliest things I've ever seen in my life. I clamp the camera to my eye and hold my breath. The soiled plates, crushed napkins, and empty wineglasses burst into focus, each edge as sharp as if carved from a mirror. I lean forward, add Wynn's battered cup, subtract one gutted white candle, lean back, smile. It's going to be good. I steady the camera, touch the shutter—and just as I do, the back door flies open and Leslie Carney's shadow leaps over my shoulder to darken the drainboard. I turn with both hands raised. "Don't shoot me," Leslie giggles.

"Don't tempt me," I warn her. She's gleaming with sweat from her morning run, her face flushed, her hair stuck to her forehead.

"I knocked," she says. "You just didn't hear me. I had to come over. I've got the best news. You won't believe it."

What I won't believe, I think, as I lower the camera, is how little it takes to lose a good shot. I sigh at the sink of soiled dishes—ordinary plates in ordinary daylight—and set the camera down. Leslie pulls a yellow leaf from her sweatshirt pocket, hands it to me, and grins at my bathrobe. It's a long red Chinese robe with a torn hem and a grass stain on the knee; it was made in Paris and lined in silk, and despite Leslie's grin I can tell she admires it. Leslie is a jeweler; she too works at home, and she would give anything, I know, to have a robe of rich red silk to work in. I wear this robe for that—for making my pictures—and because I am pregnant again and need clothes that are loose.

"I'd like champagne," Leslie says, "but it's eight in the morning so I'll settle for tea. What kind do you have? Anything with rose hips is fine. I like rose hips when I've got cramps and oh man do I have cramps. I've got my period. My wonderful period. Two weeks late but I've got my period."

"That's your news?"

"That's part of my news."

"Leslie's here," Wynn sings from the bedroom. "Up time, Mama. Breakfast for Wynn time."

"I mean, I don't want to sound tactless," Leslie says, watching me put a pot of water on to boil for tea, "but if I were pregnant again right now I would kill myself. If I had to start over and do what you do all day, I'd never have time for myself." She follows me down the hall to Wynn's room, her voice a light hiss at my heels.

Wynn has taken the pillowcase off his pillow and put it over his head. Since he is wearing nothing else, the effect is predictable, and Leslie, whose own children are ten and twelve and girls besides, stares at him sorrowfully and says, "See. I just couldn't take it." I scoop Wynn's damp pajamas and diapers from under the mattress where he has stuffed them, toss them toward the hamper, grab jeans

and shirt from half-opened drawers, and carry him, kicking and singing, masked and naked, back into the kitchen.

"No bath?" he asks from beneath the pillowcase. "No bath
today?"

"Later," I tell him. "He hates to have his hair washed," I explain
to Leslie.

"They all do," Leslie says. I let it pass. Leslie is my age but acts
like she's older. She's been married longer and had children earlier
and seems to have always known what she wanted to do with her
life. I feel as if I'm just beginning to find out. I started taking pictures
five years ago—about the same time I met Robert—and I had my
first, and last, exhibit the month before Wynn was born. It's hard,
Leslie has told me, to handle marriage and children and career—
hard, but not impossible. Leslie herself has lived in the same house
with the same man for fourteen years, and she has worked on her
jewelry steadily through pregnancies, breast-feedings, childhood ill-
nesses, Scout troops, and orthodontists' appointments. If she can do
it, I tell myself, so can I. I lift the pillowcase off Wynn's head and
contemplate his rosy face.

"He threw up last night," I explain to Leslie. "In his crib. I didn't
give him a full bath then because it was late and the tub was full of
my trays and equipment."

"You need your own darkroom," Leslie says, shaking her head.
"I've told you and told you . . ."

"He hasn't thrown up since," I interrupt. "I hope it's not flu."

"Lara used to throw up all the time when she was two," Leslie
says. "It's their digestive systems. They aren't developed yet."

"Digestive systems," I repeat, impressed. Wynn, bouncing, singing, lets me dress him, then slips off my knees, runs into the living
room, turns on the TV, and plumps down to a babble of cartoons.
I am aware of Leslie's disapproval (she does not own a TV) and I
feel that disapproval deepen as she watches me wander around the
kitchen fixing Wynn's breakfast. The dry cereal, I realize, has too

much sugar, the milk is not nonfat, the juice is not fresh-squeezed. Leslie contents herself with a brief sigh and starts to touch her toes. I carry Wynn's breakfast in to him, set it down, and kiss him softly on top of his head. His hair smells foul and as soon as Leslie leaves I'll start his bath. I dread it already. He'll fight. He'll hit me and scream. I'll scream and hit back. We'll both be drenched with bath water, struggling, slipping, cursing, he on his knees in the water, me on my knees on the tiles, both of us shouting "Stop it!", both of us in tears, neighbors phoning police, an ax splitting the door, sirens, trained dogs, a reporter calling Robert at the office.

Leslie is doing leg lunges when I come back in, her short solid body posed like an archer's in the doorway. "She's not like your other friends," Robert said when he met her. "She isn't crazy and she isn't pretty." I was surprised that Robert, usually so astute, could not see Leslie's beauty. Perhaps he's never noticed her eyes. They are small and half-hidden under the thick blond bangs she forgets to clip back, but they are beautiful eyes, shy, quick, and as luminous as the moonstones she works with. She works with ebony, ivory, and opals too. She designs bracelets and breastplates—big, heavy pieces—Amazon armor. She told me once, without smiling, that she was developing a personal mythology, based on her study of the goddess Artemis. I answered, unsmiling, that I knew what she meant. My goddess has neither name nor mythology, but I wait on her too, and watch for her blazing. Leslie straightens now and pats her flat stomach.

"You know what I'd be doing today if I hadn't gotten my period?" she asks. "I'd be at the clinic, waiting in line for an abortion. Carney would be in line behind me, with a gun at my back. You know how he is. The last thing he wants is a baby right now." Leslie assumes I know her husband better than I do, but in fact I've only met him once. Carney is a contractor who came to our house, alone, to talk about building a darkroom for me. I remember a slight, soft-spoken man in a baseball cap. There was nothing distinctive about him, and if I were to pass him on the street without his cap I would not be sure enough to say hello. Sometimes Leslie wears his cap when she rides her bike, but I always know Leslie, in all her disguises. I recognize her in her blue jeans, in her sweat suit, in the long lace dress she wears to the art fairs. I recognize her at the market, in the schoolyard, in front of the post office. We meet, I sometimes think, like spies; we hide behind our grocery bags the way spies hide behind newspapers. We stand in broad daylight and exchange secrets. We know all the passwords. Our password is "He."

"He," Leslie says now, "already made me have one abortion. Best thing he ever made me do, too." She takes the cup of tea I pour her and sits down at the table. "So," she says. "You've traveled all over. What's a good place to stay in New York?"

"New York? Who's going to New York?"

She grins. "Remember that craft show I applied for? Well, they took me. I got the letter yesterday. They liked the slides I sent—especially the series of winged headbands. They said my work was just what they were looking for. Man! Can you believe it?"

"Yes!"

We are shrieking and laughing across the table. "I'm so excited," Leslie cries. She claps her hands over her eyes. "But what do you think I should do?"

"Do? What do you mean? You should go."

"What if Carney won't let me?"

"Won't *let* you?"

"What if he tries to stop me?"

I laugh again. Leslie does not. Pouring my own tea, I say, "How can he stop you?"

"He broke my arm once."

I look up, shocked. Leslie shrugs. "I don't think he meant to. Some guy was coming on to me, once, at an opening; Carney thought I was flirting or something. He's kind of insecure lately. So he's not going to like the idea of me flying off for a week in New York."

"You mean you haven't told him yet?"

"I've been thinking I may never tell him. Until the night before I leave." She drops her eyes, stirs her tea. Wynn hollers, "More toast," and as I get up to make it I say, "You could take Carney with you."

"I can't afford his ticket. As it is, I'm going to have to use money he doesn't even know about. This friend of mine—this lawyer I met at the tennis courts—he helped me set up a special account. In my maiden name. Carney can't touch it."

I'm thinking what I'd give for a week with Robert in New York, but I don't say that. One of the best years of my life was spent with Robert in New York; we were starting out and everything was free and easy between us. We were determined to be different from other couples we knew—we were going to be kinder and smarter and more successful. We were never going to fight and we were going to share everything—dreams and responsibilities—equally. I block the breadboard so Leslie can't see me putting marmalade on Wynn's toast, and then I carry it in to him. When I come back to the kitchen I see that Leslie is leafing through a book of Imogen Cunningham's photographs on the table.

"What's your favorite?" she asks me.

"Favorite? That's hard. Maybe this one . . ." I open the book and point to a picture of an unmade bed, all soft folds and shadows. "I love this one. When Cunningham's children were little she did what I'm trying to do now—that is, she took pictures of things around the house and garden. Some of her best work was done when she was a housewife." I smooth my bathrobe over my belly, feeling the baby move, as I stare down at the picture. "It can be done," I say. I follow Leslie's speculative look toward the dishes in the sink, and laugh. "Those," I dismiss them, "those are Robert's. It was

Robert's night last night. He was supposed to wash up but he forgot."

"Men don't do a damn thing," Leslie says.

I take a deep breath. "He," I say, "was supposed to watch Wynn and do the dishes last night so I could go to a lecture at the college. When I came home I found Wynn asleep in his crib with vomit on his blanket. Robert hadn't even undressed him. His shoes were still on."

Leslie shakes her head. We have finished our tea, but I don't make more. Thinking of Robert's laziness has made me lazy. Thinking of Robert's selfishness has made me want to withhold. I'm remembering how Robert tricked me into making love to him last night when I came home; that's what I cannot forgive—that he fooled me into all the old exhilaration, then let me pad by myself into our child's room, stretching, smiling in wifely content, to discover there the sort of man I'd married. I was angry last night and I'm angry today. Anger feels almost natural now, to me and to Robert too; we take it for granted, accept it as an everyday mood. We no longer think of ourselves as a couple set apart. "His accounts . . ." I explain. "He said he had to work on his accounts and since I had 'so much free time' today . . ."

"Free time," Leslie repeats. She laughs. "The only time I feel free," she says, "is when I'm alone." Her words seem to surprise her, for she bends to tie her shoelace. I notice her left hand is bare. She told me once she had never liked her wedding ring; Carney had picked it out for her. "And you know Carney's taste." She straightens, drums her fingers on her knees, and says, "Men are such babies."

Wynn, at the sound of the word *babies*, comes running in and climbs on my lap. He sticks his tongue between his teeth and gets an absorbed, stupid look on his face as he starts to pull the front of my bathrobe open. "Don't do that," I warn him.

"Want to," Wynn says.

"No."

"*Want* to."

"It's hard when they're little," Leslie says. "You'll have more freedom next year." She turns to Wynn. "You be nice to your mother."

Wynn says, "No! *You* be nice!" He is about to say more when he hears the music of a favorite commercial. He gives me a brilliant smile, slips off my lap, and runs back to the television.

"Of course next year," Leslie continues, "you'll have the new one." She stands. "I've got to get going. Finish my run. I do twenty-five miles a week now. It's really amazing how strong I've grown." For a second I'm afraid she is going to make me feel one of her muscles, but her eyes are on the floor and her face looks sad. "I feel better than I ever have in my life," she says, "and the better I feel and the stronger I feel, the more restless I get. I can't explain it. I just feel . . . restless."

I know she is talking about sex. I am silent.

She sits down again, jiggles her knees up and down, and says, "The other night Carney and I were fooling around on the couch and I wrestled him down to the floor. You should have seen his face. Nothing like that had ever happened to him before in his life. He was so surprised. But he liked it too. Men like strong women. Just so long as they know they're still stronger." She throws me a knowing woman-to-woman smile that fades very fast. "When Carney and I were first married I couldn't drive a car. I couldn't balance a checkbook. I had to ask him for every cent before I went to the store. Now I do it all. I pay the bills and fix the car and put in the garden and he's just, you know, the same old Carney. Losing his hair. Getting a paunch. I feel sorry for him in a way. But I can't stop growing. I can't go backwards. I have to go forward. What else is there?"

She is looking at me, expecting an answer. "Well . . ." I begin.

I don't know how to finish. There is the second in between back-wards and forward that sometimes blazes and can sometimes be cap-tured. But I can't explain that.

"It's not fair," she says flatly. "Someone's always losing. You can't gain something without someone else losing." She picks the yellow leaf off the table, pulls it apart. "The other day," she says, "I was talking to this guy, this lawyer, and he was telling me about a trail ride you can take, up into the Sierras, you rent your own horse, and I thought, Oh man, wouldn't I love to get away. Just get up and go, all by myself."

We are both silent. We are both imagining the Sierras, the high, dry sunlit air, the buzzing of bees, the flight of an eagle, the scent of sugar pine and smoke. I will take my camera, I think, and a knapsack of film. I will spend one day on clouds, one day on re-flections, one day on . . . "Mama," Wynn sighs. He stands before me, aims, throws a toy car at my foot. It strikes and burns my ankle. "Thanks a lot," I tell him. He ducks his chin down. I can tell he is sorry. He doesn't like having Leslie here so early. He likes me to himself in the mornings. I like me to myself in the mornings too. "I want to get away," I say. There's a twitch to my voice—the anger that's become so familiar. "I want to get away and finish my portfolio. Do you know what's in my portfolio?"

Leslie shakes her head.

"Baby pictures," I say.

We both laugh. I think of my pictures: Wynn an hour old, a day old, a month old, a year . . . Wynn with Robert in the garden, at the beach, his arms around Robert's neck as Robert studies his ac-counts at the table . . . Wynn in a basket, a backpack, a walker, on foot . . . baby pictures. And although the baby changes in each one, turns into someone new who turns into someone else again, al-though the stately infant in lace becomes the radiant, skinny-legged shouter on the trike, although nothing has been lost or gained that I haven't caught, or tried to catch, at the instant of passing, although

I have done my best, baby pictures they are, and remain. Leslie is right to treat me as someone younger, someone who still has a great deal to learn.

"Your time will come," Leslie promises. "Just hang on in. And oh, by the way, I have those earrings you wanted me to make for your mother-in-law. They're good. She'll like them."

"How much will you let me have them for?" I know Leslie's work is expensive, but she's already said she will give me a break.

"Money?" she says. "Let's see. I hadn't thought about money. You took those slides for me . . . let's say eighty."

"Dollars?"

"They'd sell for twice that at any gallery."

Too much, I think. Leslie and her husband both ask too much. Carney wanted a fortune to build the darkroom. Robert shook his head when I gave him the price. "You'll have to wait a little longer," Robert told me. But can I wait a little longer? I haven't sold a photo in over six months. At night I wake up wide-eyed, frightened. I listen to Robert breathing beside me; I get up and check on Wynn in his crib. I walk back and forth through the house in my bathrobe. I should take pictures then, in the dark; I should start a new series on insomniac housewives. Ghostly refrigerators, moonlight on mirrors, a bag of onions beginning to sprout. Leslie has told me she used to wake up too; she used the time to research Artemis.

She is explaining that gemstones are expensive as she clears off the teapot, rinses it, and sets it on the counter to dry. She tells me she uses only the finest materials. She tells me she has high standards and always manages to meet them. I know this. I approve. The little rabbit tails on her tennis socks flick as she paces around my kitchen. If I'm not interested in quality . . . if I want cheap stuff . . . "Leslie," I sigh. She subsides.

"I just don't want you to think I'm ripping you off," she mutters. "If you don't want to take them, someone else will."

"Let me think about it," I say. But I'm thinking that eighty dollars will make a good start toward building a darkroom. I walk Leslie to the door and watch her drop into her leg lunge again. The sun is strong as bleach now, stripping her hair, making her face, as she lifts it, shiny and tired. "I shouldn't have had that tea," she says. "It's going to slow me down. But thanks anyway." She turns, pauses, grins over her shoulder. "Where did you find that bathrobe again?"

"Paris," I tell her. "My first gift from Robert."

She groans and waves and I wave too as she jogs from sight. Then I close the door and look around the kitchen. I have to clean. I have to cook. I have to shop. I have to dress. I have to make one beautiful picture and then another and then a portfolio of beautiful pictures. But all I do is stand by the kitchen sink, eating crusts of toast off Wynn's breakfast plate, staring at the leaves falling onto the patio. I am remembering the last time I went to Leslie's house. We sat on the floor of her studio, surrounded by tools neatly nested in marked boxes, sunshine pouring in on everything, alchemizing even the smell of burnt metals into an essence airy, pure; we drank wine with our sandwiches and laughed because we were so lucky, because we had it all, home and husbands and children and good health and our own good work to do too. I turn from the sink. Wynn has been watching from the doorway. A shaft of mid-morning sun falls on his hair.

"Is it later yet?" he asks, and I know at once he means bath, is it time for the bath, time for our struggle.

"Not yet, my love."

"I don't like later."

"I don't like it either. I like now."

"What's now?"

"This."

I reach up, lift the camera off the top of the refrigerator where I left it, uncap the lens, and focus on Wynn. I catch him as he turns, hair filthy and on fire in the sunlight, already shouting, half gone, in flight.

This morning I received a tearful phone call from my oldest daughter, who writes full time for a newspaper. She went to her son's third-grade open house last night, and when she asked if there would be any after-school program, the teacher made a face and said, "Day care? The mothers in this district don't work and we don't need day care; that's why the children here are so good." My daughter spent a restless night, worried that her son won't be considered "good" because she is pursuing a career she loves. I in turn have spent a restless morning wishing she did not have to fight the same fights I did raising her and her sisters.

"Baby Pictures" was conceived and written in panic. The original narrator was a poet. Redbook rejected it, saying they did not feel poets were "careaboutable" and would I consider resubmitting the story making the narrator a book reviewer. After I finished roaring—which took a while—I settled down and remembered a TV documentary I had seen about the wonderful photographer Imogen Cunningham. She had been asked how she had managed to raise her sons and manage her career, and she shrugged and told the interviewer it was no problem for her, she didn't understand the difficulty women were always complaining about. And then she paused, and with wonder and a hushed apology in her voice, said one word: "Dinner." It turned out she had had a German girl living with her when her children were small, and this girl had cooked dinner every night, freeing Cunningham to work in her darkroom. I loved this admission, and I loved her for making it. I looked at her—a mischievous elf of an old lady—and decided she was "careaboutable" in a way I could care about, and then I looked at her photographs—those luminous unmade beds—and decided I could serve both Redbook and my own conscience by making my narrator a photographer.

In this respect, I suppose, I did manage to get the best of both worlds, and just remembering this makes me want to call my daughter back and suggest she write a newspaper series about working mothers in her school district and get a grassroots movement started to organize a day-care center there. For I still believe, as do my characters in "Baby Talk," that it is possible and, in fact, necessary to have everything—our kids, our careers, our cakes with extra frosting.

M.G.

SEPARATION

◻

MARY GORDON

The social worker said: "I think he needs a group experience."

Not looking at JoAnn, handing a piece of paper with a black design JoAnn saw later was the steeple of a church. Ascension Play School.

"It's no trip for you," the social worker said to JoAnn. "See that building there, behind the Episcopal church. They wrote to us, saying they're offering a scholarship to any child of ours who might benefit from a group experience."

Child of *ours*?
   Of *yours*?
   No one's but mine.

She put her hand over her mouth, to keep back something. Sickness? Bad words that would cause trouble later on? Words that would be put down in the file. She knew their ways. This Mrs. Pratt was not the first of them, she'd had a lot of them in towns over the years.

The game was shut your mouth.

The game was shut your mouth and keep it shut.

The game was shut your mouth and give them what they wanted.

Town after town. Arriving. Making your way to the county seat, the hall, the metal desks, the forms to be filled out, the bad lights with their buzzing noises, and the questions.

Name?

Her husband's. Not an out-of-wedlock child. Her son. Hers, but everything all right before the law. The husband, not abandoning, but driven off. Pushed out. No room for him, he knew it, and was sorry, but he knew. One day: "Well, I'll be shoving off."

"All right."

A night she stayed up, when the baby had the croup. Her husband saw her happiness. He saw how happy she was, after the steaming shower and the rush outside to the cold air, after all this, the easy, even breathing. And her humming. Song after song.

"Well, I'll be shoving off."

"All right."

Rubbing the boy's wet head with a dry towel. Wet from the steam she'd set up in the bathroom. His hair that smelled like bread. She put her lips to it, and breathed it in. His easy breath, the wet smell of his hair. And looked up at the father, at the husband, sorry for him, but it was nothing, he was right to leave, there wasn't any place for him.

Humming, his damp head and his easy breathing. Happy, happy. All I want.

He needs a group experience.

All I have ever wanted.

■

Her childhood: blocks of muteness. Of silence because what was there to say. Neglect, they called it. She was kept alive. Fed. Clothed. She saw now that could not have been so easy. The flow of meals, sweaters, jackets, in the summer short-sleeved shirts and shorts, a bathing suit, washed hair, injections that were law. She felt sorry for her mother, whom she could barely remember now. She had trouble calling up the faces of the past.

Her memory: the outline of a head, a black line surrounding nothing. The faces blank. Unharmful ghosts, but nothing, nothing to her. And of course no help.

It was why she didn't like the television. All the filled-in faces. She wanted, sometimes, to ask people about their memories. Do you remember people when you are away from them? The faces? At what point do they come alive?

Even her husband's face grown ghostly.

But she never said these things. She kept to herself. Smiling, quiet, clean. She and her son.

Never causing trouble.

Keeping things up.

Arriving on time for the social worker.

The clinic.

The dentist, who said it was all right if she sat on the chair and he sat on her lap to be examined. Otherwise he'll scream.

Fine, then, Mrs. Verbeck. Just keep it up. Keep him away from sugar snacks. Fresh fruit. Apples or carrot sticks. Water rather than soda or other sweetened drinks.

Yes, thank you. Yes.

You've done a good job. Not one cavity. You floss his teeth?

I will.

We'll show you how. Miss Havenick, the hygienist, will show you.

"Let's open our mouth, Billy."

Not yours. His.
And mine.

She wanted to phone the call-in radio and ask one of the doctors.
   Are the faces of people empty to other people as they are to me?

Except his face. The one face I have always known.

At night while he slept she sat on a stool beside him just to learn his face. So that she never would forget.

An angry baby. Happy only in her arms.
   He doesn't take to strangers. Thanks, no, I can manage. Thanks.

Did anyone look at her face? In the shadowy childhood, family of shadow, furniture the part of it that she remembered most. The green couch. The red chair.
   Did anyone look at my face?

He needs a group experience.

But we are happiest alone.
   But never say it. She knew what people thought. Children need other children. They believe that, everyone believes it.
   Only I do not believe it.
   Only he and I.

■

Happy, happy in the studio apartment, in the trailer, in the basement rented in the rotting house. Happy in the supermarket, laundromat, bank where we stand on line to cash the check from welfare. Singing, eating meals we love, the walks we take, bringing back leaves, pinecones. Puzzles we do in silence, cartoon shows we watch.

She wanted to say to them: "We're very happy."

She never said these things. She moved.

Five towns. Five different states.

He needs a group experience.

This time she thinks they may be right. Now he is four years old. Next year, no hope.

No hope. No hope.

All I have ever wanted.

On the first day of school, she dresses him. She didn't dare to buy new clothes for school. She puts on him the clothes that he has worn all summer. Black jeans with an elastic waist. An orange short-sleeved shirt with a design of a bear on the left breast pocket. White socks, his old red sneakers he is proud of. Velcro. He can do them himself.

The teacher says: "He's never had a group experience?"

"No, just with me."

"Maybe, then, for the first few days you can stay with him. For a little while. Until he adjusts to the group situation."

She sees the other mothers bought their boys and girls new clothes. And for themselves. She parks the car behind the church and waits till they have all gone in the little building, like a hut, built for the children. All the other mothers know each other. Like each other. And the children.

There is no one that we know.

The teacher is standing at the door. "Good morning Jessica, Kate, Michael, Daniel, Jason, Alison."
    "And here comes Billy."

Children are playing on the swings and slides.
    Children are playing in the sandbox.
    Girls are pretending to cook at the toy stove, using toy pots and spoons and dishes.
    Boys are in the corner making a house of large blocks, then shoving it down, building it, knocking it down, fighting, building.

Billy hides his face in her shoulder.
    "I won't leave you."
    "Maybe tomorrow," says the teacher. "After he gets more used to the group, you'll feel that you can leave after a while."

■

The teacher's pants are elastic-waisted, like the children's pants. She wears blue eye shadow, her fingernails are pink as shells. She is wearing sandals with thin straps. She is wearing stockings underneath the sandals. JoAnn wonders: Maybe they are socks that only look like stockings. Maybe they stop.

At night he says: "Don't take me back there."

"All right," she says. Later she says: "I made a mistake. We have to go."

The second day of school he will not look at anybody. When the teacher puts her hand on his shoulder to ask if he sees anything he might like to play with, he pushes her hand away and looks at her with rage. "No one said you could touch me." He hides his eyes. He grinds his eyes into his mother's shoulder blade.

She's proud that he can speak up for himself. But she is frightened. Now what will they do?

In the playground, he lets her push him on a swing. She lights a cigarette. The other mothers don't approve, although they try to smile. They tell her about their children, who had problems getting used to school.

"My oldest was like that. Till Christmas."

No one is like us. No one is like he is.

One morning he says he's tired. She tells him he doesn't have to go to school. She keeps him home for three days. Both of them are happy.

But the next day it's worse in school. Only one of the mothers smiles at her. She says: "You know, maybe Billy's finding the group too large. Maybe he could just come over to our house. Daniel's used to the group. If they made friends, maybe that would help Billy in the group."

"Thank you," JoAnn says. "But we're so busy."

The social worker says: "You're not working on this separation."

Everything has been reported. The social worker takes it as a bad sign that JoAnn refused the other mother's invitation. Which she knows about.

"If I were you," she says, ". . . or maybe some counseling. For both your sakes."

JoAnn is terrified. She tells the other mother she would like to come. The other mother writes her name and address down on a piece of paper torn from a pad in the shape of an apple with a bite out of it. It says "Debi—35 Ranch Road." And in parentheses "Dan's mom."

For this, she buys her son new clothes.

He never cries anymore. Nobody can make him do anything he doesn't want to. His eyes are bright green stones. No one can make him do anything. This makes her feel she has done right.

The morning that they are going to the house they take a bath together. They laugh, they soap each other's backs. Lately she sees him looking at her sex a second longer than he ought to, and his eyes get hard and angry when he sees she sees. She knows they will not bathe together much longer after this year. But this year. Yes.

■

Debi, the mother, has to look several places for an ashtray. JoAnn hasn't realized there are no ashtrays until she has already lit up. They are both embarrassed. Debi says, "Somehow most of the people I know quit." She goes through her cabinets and then finds one from a hotel in Canada. "We stole it on our honeymoon," she says, and laughs.

Billy knows his mother doesn't want him to play with Danny. She knows he knows. But she can feel his bones grow lively on her lap; she feels his body straining toward the other children. Danny and his sisters, Gillian and Lisa. And the toys. The house is full of toys. Trucks, cars, blocks, toy dinosaurs are scattered all over the wooden floors. But the house is so big it still looks neat with all the toys all over. The house is too big, too light. The house frightens JoAnn. She holds Billy tighter on her lap. He doesn't move, although she knows he wants to. And she knows he must.

"Look at the truck," she says. "Should we go over and look at that truck?"

Debi jumps out of her chair, runs over to the children.

"Let's show Billy the truck. See Danny's truck, Billy?" She gets down on her knees. "Look how the back goes down like this."

JoAnn doesn't know whether or not to go down on her knees with Debi and the other children. She stands back. Billy looks up at her. His fingers itch to touch the truck. She sees it. She gives him a little push on the shoulders. "Go play," she says. She lights another cigarette and puts the match in the heart-shaped ashtray she has carried with her.

Billy isn't playing with the other children. He is playing alongside them. Danny and his sisters are pretending to make dinner out of clay. They don't talk to Billy; they don't invite him to play with them; they leave him alone, and he seems happy with the truck. She sees he has forgotten her. For him she is nowhere in the room.

■

Debi says, "Let's go into the kitchen and relax. They're fine without us."

JoAnn feels the house will spread out and the floor disappear. She will be standing alone in air. The house has no edges; the walls are not real walls. Who could be safe here?

In the kitchen in a row below the ceiling there are darker-painted leaves. She tells Debi she likes them.

"I did them myself. I'm kind of a crafts freak. Are you into crafts?"

JoAnn says she always wanted to do ceramics.

"I do ceramics Thursday nights," says Debi. She brings a cookie jar shaped like a bear to the table. "I made this last month," she says. "And while you're at it, have one." She offers JoAnn the open jar. "I made them for the kids, but if you won't tell I won't."

The cookies frighten JoAnn. The raisins, and the walnuts and the oatmeal that will not dissolve against her tongue.

"If you want, there's room in our ceramics class on Thursdays. I think it's important to have your own interests, at least for me. Get away, do something that's not connected to the kids. Get away from them and let them get away from you."

JoAnn begins to cough. She feels she cannot breathe. The walls of the big room are thinning. She is alone in freezing air. Her ribs press against her thin lungs. Debi says: "You okay, JoAnn?"

"I smoke too much. This year, I'm really going to quit. I've said it before, but now, this year I'm really going to do it."

They hear a child scream. They run into the living room. Danny is crying.

"He hit me with the truck."

"Did you hit him with the truck?" JoAnn says. "Tell Danny you're sorry."

Billy looks at them all with his bright eyes. Except at her. He does not look at his mother. He knows she doesn't want him to apologize. He knows that she is glad he did it. He did it for her. She knows this.

"We've got to be going," says JoAnn, picking Billy up. He presses the truck to him. "Put the truck down," she says.

He doesn't look at anyone.

"Don't go," says Debi. "Really, they were doing great. All kids get into things like that. They were doing great for a long time."

"We've got to go," JoAnn says, looking in the pocket of her plaid wool jacket for the keys. "Billy, give Danny back his truck."

"Danny, can Billy borrow the truck till school tomorrow?" Debi asks.

JoAnn pulls the truck from her son's grip.

"Thanks, but he doesn't need it," she says, smiling, handing back the truck. "It isn't his."

The truck falls from her hand. It makes a hard sound on the wooden floor. Hearing the sound, Danny begins to cry again.

"Let's try it again," says Debi. "They were really doing great there for a while."

JoAnn smiles, holding Billy more tightly. "Sure thing," she says.

At night, while he sleeps and she sits on the stool beside his bed to watch, she thinks of him in the room with the other children. Him forgetting. She thinks of him pushing the truck back and forth on the floor beside the other children, thinks of the walls thinning out, and her thin lungs that cannot enclose the breath she needs to live.

Alone. Alone.

All I have ever wanted.

■

In the morning he says: "You should have let me take that truck."

She says: "Do you want to go back to that house?"

"I want the truck."

"Danny's a nice boy, isn't he?"

He says: "Are you going to leave me alone today?"

"I don't know," she says. "I'll see."

When they arrive, the teacher says: "I think Billy's ready for a regular day today. I think the time's come definitely."

She doesn't look at JoAnn when she says this. She takes Billy's jacket off and hangs it on his hook below his name. She does not let go of his hand. "Billy, I heard you played with Danny yesterday. That's so terrific. He brought in the truck today, for you to play with while you're here."

The teacher leads him into the class, closing the door behind her so JoAnn can't see them. So that he cannot look back.

She stands in the hall. Her hands are freezing. She pulls the fake fleece collar of her plaid coat around her ears. Her heart is solid and will not pump blood. She walks into the parking lot. She gets into her car and starts it. She does not know where she will get her air, how she will breathe. The engine stalls. She pumps the gas pedal and starts the car again.

And then she hears him. He is calling. He is running toward the car. She sees that he has put his coat on by himself. She sees him standing at the car door, opening it, getting in beside her.

She can breathe, the air is warm and helpful for her breathing. They are driving, singing. They are happy.

She says to him: "Let's pack up all our things. Let's find another place, a better place to live in."

Happy, singing.

He will leave me soon enough.

The genesis for this story was watching mothers leave their children each morning in my son's nursery school class. One particularly extreme case suggested an even more extreme situation to me. But it was clear to me that the extremity was only another part of the story of all mothers and all sons.

M.G.

THE TROUBLE
WITH SOPHIE

PERRI KLASS

Mrs. Peterson's kindergarten class is holding a strawberry breakfast for the mommies and daddies, and attendance is very close to one hundred percent. Of course, many of the mommies and daddies will be late to work, but Dabney is the kind of school where most of the parents, hardworking and driven though they may be, can come late to work if they want. In their workday suits, their silk scarves, their tasteful ties, they can demonstrate their parental affection by wedging themselves into teeny plastic chairs and allowing their offspring to bring them paper plates of not very good late summer strawberries. And, thinks Hannah, who with her nondescript sweater and khaki skirt is the least-dressed-up mother in the room, they can congratulate themselves: What a perfect room, what a perfect school.

Across the table are two daddies with video cameras: instead of eating their strawberries, they are making movies of them.

"I just love your rain forest," says a very well-groomed mommy to Mrs. Peterson, who is moving gracefully around the kindergarten room, her kingdom. She is a small woman, full of disciplined energy, like an Olympic gymnast.

"Did Elias tell you that he helped make the trailing vines?" Mrs.

Peterson says. "He did a really wonderful job!" And Elias's mother smiles proudly at her son, who leads her back to the rain forest corner to admire, once again, the trailing vines.

Hannah is not comfortable in her seat and, to tell the truth, is not really comfortable in this kindergarten room. She loves her daughter, Sophie, and is proud and happy that Sophie comes every morning to this warm, lovely room with the marionette theater and the rain forest corner and the shelves of gorgeously illustrated children's books. Yes, this is the right place for Sophie, but the wrong place for her mother. Hannah is keenly aware of what it means for her to be late to work today: a seminar of ten students delayed half an hour. She should be in that small drab room with other people who are interested in fruit flies and their chromosomes. She is not generally at ease with small children, not in fact generally much at ease with people, period. A research scientist down to her toes, she doesn't like conversation unless it conveys information. As a matter of fact, Sophie's conversation usually does exactly that; one-on-one with her daughter, Hannah is fine. But here in this bubbling crowd of strawberry-eating parents, Hannah feels awkward and very distinctly, and guiltily, bored.

One of the videotaping daddies puts down his camera and smiles a cheerful shark's smile at Hannah. "You have to hand it to them here at Dabney," he says. "We looked at a lot of schools, but there wasn't any real attempt to nurture the child's creativity, not the way there is here."

With great relief, Hannah sees her husband approaching. Howard is a smiler and a glad-hander, a deal maker. Let him talk to Mister Nurture-the-Child's-Creativity. They probably work at adjoining law firms, probably play squash on the same courts at noon.

Howard smiles at her and hands her a paper cup full of black coffee, and then he does indeed glad-hand the father across the table. Then, as Hannah takes a grateful scalding gulp of coffee and thinks regretfully about her own stiff inability to mingle, along comes Sophie, pushing up next to her mother at the table, butting another parent out of the way.

"Say excuse me," Hannah and Howard admonish in unison, but fondly. These two adults, who are so very different in their public selves, so very different even in their most private obsessions, have in common a bewildered appreciation of their daughter, of her determination, her resolute inability to notice obstacles, her oddly lovely turns of phrase. She pushes us around like nobody's business, Hannah has heard Howard boast to friends, as if his daughter were the sharpest litigator of them all.

"I am the only kid that is holding the gerbil," Sophie announces, thrusting the animal into her mother's plate of strawberries. Sophie, the child of two tall, brown-haired people, is a tiny blonde, a child with a triangular elflike face and masses of twisting blond tendrils.

Mrs. Peterson materializes, a gentle hand on Sophie's shoulder. "I think it's a little too scary for the gerbil out here with all these people," she says, perfectly pleasantly. "Why don't you take your mommy and daddy over to the zoo corner and let them see how you put her back in her cage?"

Sophie's face freezes in an expression Hannah knows very well; thwarted, unable to believe that anyone is trying to make her do something other than what she had planned, poised on the edge of screams, sobs, refusals. Hannah feels a sudden fierce triumph at seeing Mrs. Peterson's expert modulations meet with this response, but mostly she feels terrified that, amidst all the other well-behaved parents and children, Sophie is going to make a scene.

"Does the gerbil live in a *cage*?" Hannah asks in wonder. "And do you know how to open it up all by *yourself*?"

Sophie lets go of her grievance. "I'll show you," she says importantly to her mother. And they march off together. A horrible scene averted.

But then, as Hannah and Howard are leaving, Mrs. Peterson stops them at the door and asks if they would please schedule a meeting

with her; she would like to talk to them about how Sophie is doing.
When they have agreed and thanked her and escaped, and are standing out in the school parking lot, Hannah and Howard look at each
other, and though he tries for a wry shrug and she for a mock-
helpless grimace, both of them know that this is no joke, and this is
no good news.

They have, it seems to others, a somewhat odd and unexpected
marriage. People are sometimes surprised to hear in those late-in-
the-dinner-party, wine-tinged conversations that Hannah and Howard have been together since college, when she was a biology major
and he was prelaw; even then, their worlds did not overlap. Perhaps
to those who know them now, they seem more like two peculiarly
assorted people who might have met in their thirties, desperate to
couple off. A personals ad, a hired matchmaking service, even a
friend-of-a-friend connection: Hey, I know someone else who's
very smart, very interested in settling down.

But it wasn't like that at all. Oh, they've had their summers apart
and their doubts, but basically they are one of those peculiar and
somewhat irritating couples who knew right from the beginning that
this was it. And what they have in common, what no one can
necessarily see, looking at the straight-ahead trajectories of their careers, their relationship, their lives, is they both believe the world is
a strange and hostile place, and the only hope for safety is in your
home, your fortress, your secret sanctuary.

They take different approaches to this knowledge. Howard believes in getting out there and walking the walk and talking the talk
and mixing it up with all comers. The law, for Howard, is a handy
institutionalization of what he knows to be the truth of the world:
me against all of you, winners and losers, attack or be attacked.
Hannah, on the other hand, believes in staking out a tiny territory,
preferably a territory whose charms are invisible to most people, and

staying low to the ground. As a fruit-fly geneticist, she is legendary for her compulsive care and caution; she will bring forward no results until they have been verified and reverified beyond all doubt. She will not whisper, not even dare to dream, what she has not protected and defended well in advance. And because she is careful, talented, and even lucky, she has done well.

And so now they live together with Sophie in one of those sunny big apartments that people live in right before they give up on the city and move to the suburbs for the sake of good public schools. But they will not move to the suburbs; they have promised each other that, and so they took Sophie through the private school dance and ended up at Dabney.

The night after their conference with Mrs. Peterson, Howard cannot sleep. He is pacing, fuming. Hannah at first does drift off to sleep, but she wakes up after an hour or so, disturbed by the crackling in the air, the tension in the room.

"Honey?" she says, shifting on her pillow. Then remembers: the classroom with Mrs. Peterson and the headmaster.

"That worthless lump of left-out Play-Doh," Howard says.

The headmaster's initial function at the meeting was to tell Howard and Hannah how proud Dabney was of Mrs. Peterson, the teaching awards she has won. Hannah nodded solemnly; Howard folded his arms and looked dubious.

Then Mrs. Peterson launched into her prepared speech: why Sophie is having emotional problems adjusting to kindergarten.

Soon, inevitably, Howard was fighting with her. And then with the headmaster, with both of them.

"Isn't that why you call it choice time?" Howard asked, with the exquisite, aggressive courtesy of a lawyer eager to trap a witness in the silken knot of her own words. "Because the child makes a choice?"

"Yes," Mrs. Peterson told him, "choice time is a chance for the children to exercise their own decision-making abilities in a safe and developmentally appropriate choice environment."

"So in that case," Howard said, "what's wrong with my daughter exercising her decision-making abilities?"

Patiently, as one who is well accustomed to helping distraught parents understand that their children have serious emotional problems, Mrs. Peterson explained yet again. "Sophie makes the same choice every day. She refuses to take advantage of any of the diverse learning opportunities that the classroom offers, and instead focuses in an unhealthy way on one small area of fantasy play."

"But if it's *choice* time," Howard roared, losing that exquisite courtesy, "then she's entitled to make any choice she damn well wants!"

Then the headmaster came to the rescue, explaining kindly and gently that this was not intended as criticism, it was just Mrs. Peterson, with her award-winning skills, picking up on some emotional-adjustment difficulties that little Sophie seemed to be undergoing; the choice-time issue was emblematic of those stresses, which in turn might represent more serious home-based issues, which deserved attention before they got any worse.

Hannah preempted Howard, who was obviously not at his best; she loved him for galloping to Sophie's defense, but her own instinct to conciliate and smooth over might actually be in Sophie's best interest.

"Tell us more," Hannah said, and Mrs. Peterson, of course, obliged.

And that night, after they made Sophie's favorite supper, macaroni with lemon sauce, and hugged and kissed her into bed, Hannah and Howard polished off a six-pack of beer, and both became hysterical with laughter over the image of Sophie performing civil disobedience in the kindergarten rain forest.

Because that was what Mrs. Peterson described; Sophie spent each and every choice time curled up among the green construction paper lianas, the photographs of poison arrow frogs and venomous snakes. When the time came to dismantle the rain forest, to make way for the igloo for the Eskimo project, Sophie took up a position lying across the squares of green carpet remnants, hugging the trunk of a tree, and wept for hours.

Mrs. Peterson, placed in the position of the despoiler of the Amazon, gave way. She refused to play the role of the soulless multinational corporation, agreeing, finally, to Sophie's terms: the rain forest would be left intact. And so Sophie continued to choose rain forest at choice time, alone of all the children, since the others had long ago lost interest. You have to admit, Hannah and Howard told each other, it's pretty funny.

So they drank the beer, a very unaccustomed weeknight indulgence for them both, and cleaned up the kitchen and made Sophie's lunch for the next day, and went up to bed themselves. But Howard could not sleep, and at two in the morning they ended up turning on their light and hashing it out again.

"She's a fascist with a degree in early-childhood education," Howard said. "She's mad because Sophie is smarter than she is and has a stronger will. She wants to punish all of us."

"I think you're reading some of this in," Hannah says, sitting up in bed.

"I am *not* reading it in. This is thought control," Howard says. "This is a teacher who likes having her own way and comes up against a little girl who just won't take it from her." There is nothing in his voice but admiration and love.

"But honey, she does have to get along in school," Hannah says, and sees from his face that she has made herself into a traitor.

"What are you talking about?" Howard demands. "You think we should put a perfectly sane, intelligent child into *therapy* because her jargon-stuffed imbecile of a kindergarten teacher loses a few tugs-of-war with her?"

Because that is what they want, Mrs. Peterson and the headmaster.

They even offered a list of approved therapists, "who have worked well with Dabney before." Sophie is troubled and disturbed; she refuses to have anything to do with marionettes, she would not wear pajamas on pajama day. "Pajama day?" Hannah had asked, trying to keep her end up. "I didn't know you had a pajama day." Mrs. Peterson and the headmaster exchanged satisfied glances. Sophie had concealed pajama day from her parents. She needed therapy immediately.

"Come to bed," Hannah says. She'll be exhausted tomorrow. She opens her arms, and Howard comes and lies beside her; she switches off the light and fits her body up against his. He holds her, even kisses her neck. But tension is still the strongest emotion in the bed.

It's always a little bit of a lottery, waking up Sophie, who, if left alone, would sleep well on toward noon. Hannah goes into her bedroom never knowing whether Sophie will come to life sweet and cuddly, or as savage as a bear disturbed in hibernation. And then there are the mornings she seems to awaken with a well-established identity: "I'm Barbie!" she will announce, and the prudent thing to do is to say, "Why Barbie, good morning!" and wait patiently while she roots around on her shelves for the five Barbie dolls that need to be carried to breakfast.

This particular morning Sophie opens her arms to her mother, who kisses the top of her head. Sophie's curls are pulled into a ponytail while she sleeps; this prevents some of the worst tangles and therefore the most violent hair-brushing arguments. The weight of her daughter on her lap is at once so exotic and so familiar that Hannah could cry with it, especially on this particular morning, when she has to accompany Sophie to the therapist's office. All of Howard's bluster about suing the school, and is this what we pay them all that money for, has come to nothing. There have been two more conferences and several notes home. If they want Sophie to stay at Dabney, this kindergarten, which she says she loves, where her best friends Dennis and Cara go, then Sophie needs therapy.

Howard, Hannah realizes, feels ashamed, as well as angry. He will not even consider accompanying Sophie to the therapist; Hannah has now gone three times, waiting out in the beige waiting room while Sophie has her session. But today it will be mother and child.

Sophie looks up into her mother's face. Dreamily, she smiles and says, "I know a way for you to love someone but be angry at them. You just tell them, 'I like you but I don't like what you did.' "

"Yes," Hannah says. "That's very true. I like that."

"I knew you would," Sophie says smugly. "That is why I saved it to tell you as your special treat."

Hannah wears the flowered dress and the blazer she sometimes wears on the first day of classes. She dresses Sophie in a flowered dress as well, and gives in to her with no argument when she announces that she is going to wear her party shoes. Let her think that going to the therapist is a treat.

Hannah is terrified, the therapist will surely confirm the judgment of the teacher and the headmaster: This is a troubled child. Emotional problems, adjustment difficulties. Perhaps the therapist will look at Hannah, stiff in her flowered dress, and say, Well, what could you expect with such a mother. Hannah, who has kept herself so carefully defended all her life, realizes once again the most essential lesson of parenthood, the terrible vulnerability of the parent. If she put into words what she is feeling as she carefully pulls the car out into traffic, what she would probably say is, I don't want anyone or anything to change the way I think about my daughter.

Back before that strawberry breakfast, it seems to Hannah, she lived in a happy fairyland, thinking the world saw Sophie as she and Howard did, charmed by a child's assertive originality. If you had told us of a child who refused all the other kindergarten choices and spent all day in the rain forest, Hannah thinks, we would have been charmed by the individuality, the strength of character. But that was not how her world saw Sophie, and now, most insidious of all, Hannah and Howard see her a little as that world does.

Hannah drives more slowly than usual; she has become in every way more cautious, she thinks. There was a time when motherhood seemed likely to make her into someone she had never been, someone spontaneous and uninhibited and always ready for an unexpected giggle, but she knows now that she is the same old Hannah.

Howard has withdrawn completely. He is working harder than ever, out most evenings. When Hannah told him, "We have an appointment tomorrow at the therapist's, he wants to see the whole family," Howard looked briefly pained. "I probably won't be able to make it," he said, and she nodded.

"Look!" Sophie yells from the backseat. "Look at my favorite store in the whole world going by outside my window!"

Her favorite store in the whole world is a five-and-dime. Well, what the hell. They are early, of course; Hannah always leaves extra time. She parks the car and spends seventeen dollars on whatever Sophie wants. A magenta plastic egg stuffed with chocolates. Two necklaces and six bangles. A white patent-leather purse with a mirror inside. Gold clip-on earrings. And a small pot of Swedish ivy. In front of them in line is an old lady not too much taller than Sophie, or so it seems from Hannah's height. The lady wears, like Hannah and Sophie, a flowered dress. But hers trails on the ground in back and the hem is coming down. She is buying two bags of licorice and a night-light, digging in a well-worn change purse. Her fingers, which are twisted, put the coins on the counter: a quarter, a nickel, a pair of pennies. The girl at the cash register waits patiently, and Sophie is absorbed in the contemplation of her earrings, but Hannah is impatient: Just dump the money on the counter, for heaven's sake, and get it over with. A dime. Another penny. A nickel and a quarter.

Then suddenly the old woman's shaking fingers tear right through the thin leather of her change purse, tear the leather right off its metal rim. A cascade of coins falls to the floor, bouncing and ringing against the metal candy stand. Hannah stares, not immediately seeing what to do with the plant, the necklaces and bangles, the plastic egg in her hands. But Sophie thrusts the earrings into the hand of the old woman, who is staring at the devastation. "I will pick up your moneys all by myself," Sophie announces. "Watch!" And she is down on the floor scooping up coins. Hannah, putting down her purchases, bends to help her daughter, but Sophie waves her away, saying triumphantly, "I am the only one who knows where is the money that I didn't already get!"

And truly, Hannah thinks dizzily, there is something blessed about this moment. Sophie puts the money into her new white patent-leather purse and presents it to the old lady. When the checkout girl has efficiently bagged the licorice and the night-light, she rings up their purchases, Sophie and Hannah's, without charging them for the purse.

"That's a good little girl you have there," she says earnestly to Hannah, handing over their bag. She is maybe eighteen, her name-plate, Tanya, displayed on a full bosom, her fingernails the long red talons that Hannah has never had and Sophie would kill for.

Waiting outside the store as Hannah hurries them out to the car, since they are now a little bit late, is the old lady, who puts one twisted hand on Sophie's head and looks intently into the little girl's eyes.

"There is a mirror inside the pocketbook so you can look at yourself," Sophie says, from around one of the chocolates; she has already opened the egg and started in.

"I will, thank you very much," says the old woman, in an un-expectedly firm and rich voice.

They are not really late, five minutes at most, but the door to the inner sanctum is open, denoting that the therapist has already come out and looked for them. Feeling flustered, noting that Sophie's face is smeared with chocolate, Hannah leads her into the room, pulls a tissue from her pocket, and starts to wipe around Sophie's mouth—all before noticing that the therapist is not alone. Howard is sitting in one of the armchairs, rocking slightly on its uneven legs.

The therapist is a man about Hannah and Howard's age, but where Howard is neat and groomed, the therapist has a bushy mustache and hair going in all directions and a paunch that strains against his shirt.

"Hi, Sophie," he says. "You look like you've been eating something."

Although she knows it's silly, Hannah cannot help wondering whether he will record this as some small tick against her as a mother: feeds her daughter candy right after breakfast. But at least he looks like a man who knows how to enjoy a chocolate pig-out.

Sophie smiles at him, bewitchingly, enchantingly, then wheels around and goes to a cabinet. With confidence she opens it and removes a family of flexible dolls. Carries them to another cabinet and removes a red bin filled with plastic jungle animals. Then sits down on the floor, her back to her parents and the therapist, and begins to move the dolls and the animals in a game, murmuring their conversation, too low to be heard by the adults.

"Is that what she's done the other times she's come here?" Hannah asks.

"Pretty much," the therapist says. "We went through all the toys I've got, and she settled on that combination of dolls and animals."

"And is that supposed to prove something?" Howard asks angrily, and Hannah, whose heart has lifted with joy at finding him here, at once is worried.

"Well, I would say it proves that your daughter is a child who knows what she wants," says the therapist, smiling. And Sophie, perhaps hearing him, turns around briefly and favors the three adults with one of her charming, delicious flashes of teeth.

Howard waits until she turns back to the toys, then says softly, "So what happens now?"

The therapist considers the question, which has not been asked with any hostility, which has in fact, Hannah realizes with love and relief, been asked only with desperate sincerity. "Well," says the therapist, "I would say that what happens now is we watch your daughter, who is without question a smart and determined little girl, and make sure her world is the place she needs it to be."

"She's fine, then," Hannah says, definitively, to her husband and the therapist both.

Howard takes a deep breath; Hannah can actually see his shoulders rise and fall. Hannah suddenly feels safe, warm—not the feeling that she is in a safe place, but the feeling that perhaps it *is* possible to create safety, to bring it forth out of love.

Sophie speaks: "Look what I can do!" Her parents and the therapist turn and look, and she holds out the magenta plastic egg. Dramatically, making extravagant gestures, she opens it into its two halves. "See, there is no candy inside anymore," she says, and Hannah nods, sees the other two nodding as well. Sophie puts her nose to one empty magenta egg half and takes a long happy breath. Lifts her face up, radiant with joy and surprise, and cries out, "Oh! As I sniff the chocolate air!"

"Can we do it?" Hannah says. "Can it be done?"

"She'll do it herself," the therapist says firmly, and takes a long, happy breath himself, as if he too could smell something sweet and promising in the air.

"The Trouble with Sophie"—I think this story grows in part out of the discovery of parental vulnerability; any criticism of your child, any suggestion that there may be "a problem" goes so directly to your heart. You send your children out into the world, that is, into school, knowing that they are the most wonderful things that ever happened—and then, of course, you find out how others see them. This is a story about a child who is reinterpreted to her parents by a jargon-laden teacher, and

also, I think, about the damage that these reinterpretations do. I wrote it thinking of parents whose pleasure in their children has been dampened or overshadowed by specialists who make every variation into a pathology. It is meant to be a story about enjoying your child and trusting your instincts; it is also, of course, a mean-spirited and vindictive reaction to politically correct educational gibberish and the perfectly well-meaning efforts of those who visit their ideas on children but cannot express themselves clearly in normal English.

P.K.

You'll Be Crying
in a Minute

■

RONNI SANDROFF

With other people suffering so much anguish, it doesn't seem fair that the wings of trouble keep passing my family by. The four of us sit at dinner, evening after summer evening, without so much as a cold among us. Our house is not in a flood area, on an earth-quake ledge, or near a combat zone: none of us is on methadone, taking fertility pills, or under indictment for a crime. I don't work at a dead-end job. I have nothing to worry about.

And yet I'm as busy with worry as a woman trying to knit a sweater before her child can outgrow it. Worry knots my fingers: it rubs them raw. I tally all neighborhood suicides and accidents as if I were a bookmaker keeping odds on survival.

I wasn't always this way. I was so busy tugging at the perimeters of our lives to make them take a shape that pleased me, so busy amending, revising, and adjusting our routines, that I had no idea I'd be filled with dread as soon as everything was right. I was raised to be heroic in times of crisis—to get the children to the hospital emergency room first and faint afterward. I was never taught to handle satisfaction, admiration, praise.

Cara sat next to me in the company cafeteria today, and after a comment about hard pears and soggy bread she asked the usual question: "How do you manage both children and a job?"

The next time I give a serious answer to that question, I thought, I'll have to be paid for it. "Badly—I do it all badly," I said, and tried to turn the talk to the one current film my husband, Gary, and I have managed to see.

"You don't do it badly," Cara said. "You just got a promotion —after only three months—and your son and daughter are beautiful."

I put my sandwich down on its paper plate. Pastrami is hard to chew anyway, but it's inedible when my mouth is full of motherhood. I tried to be patient with Cara. I admire her long, limp skirts and eyelet blouses, her permanent wave, her salad lunches.

"I can't imagine having kids," Cara said, her fork darting for an olive. "And I'm almost thirty-three. Neil and I haven't much time to decide."

I batted her a few reasons for *not* having children. I exaggerated Sarah's aggressiveness ("Almost every day I get a call from the mother of some child she's bloodied") and Kane's prying ("I think he listens at the door when we make love"). I told her of the spring of the great chicken-pox epidemic; about going home from our quiet office to find that no one's put the potatoes in to bake; that Kane needs help with math and, horror of horrors, Sarah has an art project due the next day and there's not a shoe box in the house.

Cara kept the same bemused expression on her face no matter what I said. "Does it hurt a lot, having a baby?"

"Yes. It hurts a lot and it keeps on hurting," I said meanly. Damn her narrow hips and graceful arms, I thought. Damn her questions. I don't want to be forced to make up explanations for what I do with passion, by instinct, blindly. If I'd thought about it as much as she thinks about it, I might have talked myself out of having children too.

The lunch with Cara leaves me shaken. It's bad luck to hear someone say out loud, as Cara did, that I've had more than my share of goodies from life. Something could go wrong at any minute. After I began to work, whole afternoons would go by when I'd forget to worry about the children. I'd try to make it up to them when I got home.

As I drive down our street I see a white truck with a revolving red light parked near our house. I know it isn't an ambulance. I know it is not parked in front of our house. But what if it were? During the one-block drive I picture both children laid out on stretchers with burns covering ninety per cent of their bodies: There is no place I can touch them without causing pain. Their lungs are scorched; they cry in silence; their eyeballs melt.

The white truck belongs to the electric company. Men are digging in the asphalt in the middle of the street. But even the sight of my family sprawled in front of the huge TV set can't stop me from completing imagined funeral arrangements for them all. There are rows of sobbing school friends; a grandmother faints at the grave.

The baked potatoes are in the oven. The table is set. The children make a salad while I broil the chops, and although we keep bumping against each other in the small kitchen and green cucumber peels slap the floor, dinner is on the table in twenty minutes.

I sit down in my chair, put my face in my hands, and wait until the anxiety I have felt since lunch can ebb. When I look up, my family is staring at me.

"Hard day?" Gary asks.

"No, not particularly."

"You look tired," Sarah says.

Kane wiggles his eyebrows at me, his blue eyes popping in his latest imitation of a TV commercial.

I put sour cream on my baked potato and pour juice for Kane and Sarah. I pass Gary the chops. I tell Sarah not to sit on her feet. I ask Kane to stop wiggling his eyebrows.

The children eat quickly and leave the table before I've finished my salad. They go into Kane's small room, right off the dining alcove, and close the door.

"Remember Kalligan, the man who owned the liquor store on Ocean Avenue?" Gary asks.

I brace myself for a tale of trouble. "What happened to him? Was he hit by a truck? Did he leap from a burning building? Was he arrested for bribing a state liquor inspector?"

"I don't make these things up."

"You always bring home terrible news. What happened?"

"I'm not going to tell you if you're going to take it personally." But he cannot hold out. "The poor man had a heart attack. He dropped dead in his store. A customer found him."

"That's too bad. I liked him." When will other people say such things about us? Too bad about Sarah and Kane. Too bad about Gary's accident. Too bad about Sheila's nervous breakdown—did you hear? They're giving her shock treatments. She sobs all day, mourning the future victims of a nuclear war.

I start to laugh and Gary gives me one of his looks—jaw rigid, eyes cold as aluminum—warning me back to sanity.

"It strikes me as funny sometimes," I say. I drop a tomato from my fork as I try to explain. "All the world's problems loom over us like monsters in a nightmare, but we just keep chasing after our personal happiness. The human race is so dumb, and funny, and cute."

Gary smiles tentatively. "Cute, huh?"

"Yes, cute. Especially you."

We hear thumps and squeals from Kane's room—the hysterical laughter of a small boy being tickled by his older sister, tickled until his sides ache and he can't breathe and he wants to put his sneaker in her ribs.

"They'll be crying in a minute," I say to Gary. He nods. I rise to rap on the closed door. "Keep the noise down."

"Okay," they say, still giggling. I can hear the thumps of pillows being thrown across the room. My mother's words are struggling to be said: You'll be crying in a minute. At the most ecstatic moments of my childhood I heard that.

The laughter turns to shrieks. I try to open Kane's door, but it is blocked by their bodies piled in a jumble of limbs. I squeeze through a small opening.

"We're having fun," Sarah calls.

Kane peers out from beneath her chest and wiggles his eyebrows.

I know someone will get hurt. It's dangerous to feel so good. Too much happiness attracts the evil eye of disaster. Or is it dwelling on disaster that brings it on? It's hard to know which superstition to believe. The children, frozen in mid-tickle, stare at me. I hold myself tight, refusing to contaminate them with my fears.

"I didn't have the heart to stop them," I tell Gary, falling back into my chair. "Their idea of fun is to tickle and scream until they turn blue."

Gary touches my hand. "They're both at a good age. Not babies anymore but too young to have a driver's license. Did you hear what happened to the oldest Kenmore boy?"

I smile at him. He's looking awfully good with his face tanned. I stop wondering why some slim-hipped secretary doesn't walk off with him; I've fed the snapping jaws of worry enough today.

And I resist asking what happened to the Kenmore boy. Our children are at a good age, if you can stand the noise, and we're at a good age too. We'll all be over the edge soon, but meanwhile, in the sliver of time before the sobbing starts, I let the dangerous feelings of contentment fall like a light shawl on my shoulders and slip off my watch so I won't be able to count the minutes until the eleven o'clock news.

"You'll Be Crying in a Minute" remains one of my favorite pieces. The story was written at a time when motherhood was out of fashion amid all the excitement over women entering and succeeding in the workplace. Those of us who were pioneering working moms got plenty of encouragement for our career advancement, but no acknowledgment for the incredible emotional labor involved in parenting. Although I had a demanding magazine editing job, I always knew that I went to work to rest.

R.S.

KING OF THE SKY

□

ROXANA ROBINSON

I stood, that day, before the deep closet in the front hall, taking off my coat. The small domestic view gave me modest satisfaction: an orderly row of neat shoulders, our various selves. There was Gilbert's sleek and dressy herringbone tweed, his grimy tan trenchcoat, my velvet-collared chesterfield. No bright colors, nothing exciting, but everything was well made, clean, looked after. Among the others I hung my everyday self, the dull green loden coat that I wear all winter—to the supermarket, to the small local museum where I volunteer three days a week, and on the twice-daily trips I make from Gramercy Park, where we live, to Jock's school, four blocks south.

"Come on, Jocko, take off your things," I said, turning back to the hall.

Jock, who is nine, didn't answer. He was in the middle of something private. His red boots still on, his jacket flung open down the front, he was kneeling next to a needlepoint-covered chair and aiming his gun-shaped hand at something in the distance. His eyes were focused, not on our meekly flowered wallpaper but on a muddy battleground somewhere. He was talking urgently under his breath, and between the bursts of hissed and whispered words were periodic explosion noises.

In third grade, boys' fantasies are almost entirely violent. Mayhem and death lie at their cores, and all require the powerful and satisfying sound of an explosion. This noise is something all boys—and few girls—can do properly. It begins at the moment of detonation: the cheeks balloon slightly, and a deep gargle at the back of the throat produces a muted rumble. The lips part slightly to allow the sound loose into the world, and the vibrating root of the tongue and the arched roof of the palate produce a series of slow reverberations. The echoes continue deep in the throat, distant and sinister. Their majestic pace, their diminishing volume, their final lapsing into an elegiac silence, all suggest the end of everything. Nine-year-old boys need to suggest—particularly to their mothers—their dangerous capacity to end everything.

I knelt on the rug next to Jock's small, supple body. Ignoring me, he leaned on the chair seat and sighted along his extended finger, one eye closed for accuracy. I faced the pale clear skin of his cheek, the faint purple delta of veins at his temple, the fragile translucent whorl of his ear. Jock has Gilbert's high forehead and pointed chin, and his own silky gold-brown hair that lies flat and fine against his skull.

I began easing his boots off. Jock allowed this, stretching out each leg in turn for me to grasp, but he continued to ignore me and what I was doing. It is as though the least hint of connection or cooperation with this large domestic female would destroy the secret, other, *real* life that Jock has so carefully created. I don't insist on recognition, I don't care. As long as Jock allows our worlds to function peaceably side by side, and occasionally to interlock, I don't complain. I have other parts to my life besides the part that contains him—why shouldn't Jock? And for him, it is a desperate matter, his independence.

When our things were off we got back on the elevator. We were going to the ninth floor to visit Willie, who is one of Jock's best friends, and Willie's mother, Margaret, who is one of mine. We all live in an old building on the north side of Gramercy Park. It's a quiet neighborhood; the avenue stops there, and there's not much through traffic. The park itself is small and elegant, and merely the sight of it—always a pastoral surprise among all that urban geometry—seems to slow the tempo. It's a peaceful, old-fashioned place, and our building is peaceful and old-fashioned as well. Our doormen are hushed and attentive, the lobby and halls are clean and well ordered. It's safe, and we don't lock in the day-time. On nine I pushed open our friends' heavy front door and called out hello.

"Come in," Margaret called back. "We're in the kitchen."

Jock set off at a run. Margaret's apartment is bigger than ours, a duplex, with a terrace over the park outside the living room. Margaret has a great eye and has wonderful things; I ambled slowly down the long book-lined hall, through the big square dining room with its modern mahogany table. I was admiring, as I always do, her style: the enigmatic nineteenth-century paintings, the complicated Oriental patterns underfoot. Margaret thinks of things that would never occur to me: she'd found a sculptor who worked in iron and commissioned him to make wonderful ornamental bars for the windows. The new ones were just being installed, and I could see fanciful baroque designs across every view.

In the big white kitchen Margaret was sitting on the tiled floor with Willie, wrestling with one of his boots. Margaret is tallish, long-boned, long-waisted, precise in her movements. Her hair is glossy blond and perfectly straight. She wears it blunt-cut, just below her jawline, and parted exactly in the middle. A small tortoiseshell bar-rette on either side holds it neatly in place. Margaret works nearly full-time as a lobbyist for an environmental group, and she was still dressed for the office. She was in a dark green long-sleeved buttoned-up blouse and black pants: very elegant. Margaret always looks elegant, in a quiet way. It's all in the details: black suede shoes, a high silk collar, a dull gold chain. Margaret likes details, and she's good at them. I'm told she's brilliant at work; lobbying means taking charge, planning strategy, changing people's minds. She's assertive and effective: I admire her for that; they're things I'm not.

Willie is Margaret's only child; she always said she couldn't manage with any more. He looks just like her, with the same pale skin, the narrow, brilliant blue eyes, and the sleek cap of blond hair. Temperamentally, however, they are fiercely opposed: Margaret demands order, Willie chaos.

Willie was lying on his side, propped up on one elbow. He was using his hand as a fighter plane and making jet-engine noises. Jock ran over to him with a nine-year-old's eccentric gait, haphazard and lurching. As he reached Willie, Jock knelt and skidded to a stop on his knees, his hands on his thighs. Willie gave him a sidelong glance and went on with the air war. Neither spoke.

"Hi, Margaret," I said. "Hi, Willie."

Willie ignored me, his puffed-out cheeks full of sound.

I would have ignored his ignoring, but at once Margaret said, "Willie, say hello to Mrs. Jamieson."

Willie did not look at her. He made more powerful jet-engine noises and set his plane on a dangerous course past his shoulder.

"Willie," Margaret said again. Willie ignored her. His eyes were fixed on his hand: this was aerodynamically flattened, and his fingers were split into wings. His engines revved, reaching a higher and higher whine.

"Willie," Margaret said ominously.

"Don't worry about it," I said, wishing I hadn't said hello to Willie in the first place. But now Margaret ignored me.

"Willie!" Margaret said again, her voice peremptory. Willie heard in it the end of the negotiating period. He looked up at me for a split second.

"Hi," he said, not quite insolent, his eyes flicking off my face at once. His voice returned to combustion engines.

"Hello, *Mrs. Jamieson*," Margaret said.

"Mrs. Jamieson," Willie added airily to his flying hand.

Margaret shook her head, her lips tight. She looked at me grimly. "We've been having a wonderful time today. We're in such a good mood," she said.

Margaret's views about boys are different from mine. Willie's resistance drives her crazy. Of course, Willie's resistance might drive me crazy, too. There's something manic about Willie, something locked and frantic and driven. He lunges toward crazy, and then so does Margaret. They goad each other on. The more one insists, the more resistant the other turns, and though their goals are different, their methods are the same. They seem sometimes like two halves of the same fierce and indomitable personality, trapped in the same skin, battling for control.

I always thought it was just a phase. I think people are better parents at some ages than at others. I'm probably at my best right now, with a nine-year-old. Though I adore him, though I know he adores me, with Jock I can sleepwalk through my days, each of us in our own worlds. When Jock is a teenager, and I have to pay attention and get into the real issues, I'll probably be terrible. But I always thought that when Willie became an adolescent, Margaret would come into her own. Once she was freer to work, once she could return to her own world, she'd encourage Willie to inhabit his. She'd admire his independence, she'd support his originality. She'd pull back and he'd relax. That's what I thought. All this conflict seemed temporary; they would just have to live through it.

Now Margaret yanked at Willie's second boot. Willie, loose-limbed, uninvolved, came along with his foot, and was pulled smoothly toward her on his back. Strands of his sleek pale hair lifted magically from his head, as though he were free-falling through space. Jock had joined him on the floor, and at Willie's involuntary slither they both began to laugh, the low, irresistible belly laugh of the supine. It made me laugh too, that loose, jellyish gurgle, but Margaret didn't even smile. She ignored them, sliding her hand inside the boot and finally worming out the foot. Her face was dark and her mouth set, as though the resistance of the boot, the tactile cling between rubber and leather, was Willie's fault, part of his stubbornness.

She pulled the boot off at last and shook her head. "God!" she said, and put the boots side by side next to the wall. She stood up, wiped her hands on her black pants, and smiled at me. "Okay," she said briskly, and moved over to the big gas range.

"It's all airplanes here this week, we're all pilots. Willie's king of the sky," Margaret said, turning on the flame beneath the kettle. "I don't know why. Before that we had police shoot-outs and drug runners, but suddenly it's all airplanes. Do you have airplanes, or is it only us?"

"We're a mix," I said. "We have some comic-book heroes, airplanes, and a lot of spaceships."

"I'm glad we're not Exterminators anymore, anyway," said Margaret.

"*Terminator,*" Willie said loudly, from flat on his back, still not looking at her. "Terminator."

"Terminator," said Margaret. She looked at me and quoted wryly from an imaginary report. "Mrs. Welch can't seem to keep track of her son's interests. She belittles him by forgetting the names of his favorite toys."

"What a name, anyway. 'Terminator,'" I said. "Why don't they just come right out and name them Death, or Hatred?"

"The kids would love it," said Margaret. "They'd all want one."

She fixed tea for us, and soup and crackers for the boys, and we all sat at the butcher-block table. The boys were on stools across from each other. They were involved in something, staring intently and mirthfully into each other's eyes as they ate. Pasita, Margaret's Colombian housekeeper, was doing the laundry. We could hear the steady lunging drone of the washing machine, and the faster, ringing sound of the dryer. Pasita sat behind us at the ironing board, her arm moving smoothly back and forth over the clean cotton. Next to her was a pile of ironed clothes, white and crisp. Outside it was cold and windy, and the bare-limbed park trees showed light dustings of snow, but inside the air was steamy and warm. It felt entirely safe.

I grew up in New York, on East Seventieth Street. When I was little, in the afternoons it seemed that all of Park Avenue was full of children walking home from school. The girls walked with their mothers, their fine hair in messy braids, their socks drooping around their ankles. The little boys, noisy, daring, walked without parents, dressed in blue blazers, carrying knapsacks. The doormen kept a watchful eye on them. The doormen had authority and would call out sternly to a group of rowdy boys, "That's enough, now! Settle down," as they passed noisily by on the sidewalk. And the boys eyed the doormen and did not answer. They did, for the moment, settle down. They knew that they were part of a neighborhood, that their parents had friends in their building, that they were part of a watchful, strict, benevolent network that commanded and protected its children.

But things have changed, though doormen still call out to rowdy boys on upper Park Avenue and here in Gramercy Park. The world outside that network is more threatening now, and our children are at risk in a way I was not.

When I was little, accidents were the gravest danger to children. There was, at that time, a tacit agreement among grown-ups that children were to be cherished. Strangers risked their lives to save other people's children, pulling them heroically from burning houses, out of rivers and wells. That has changed. Now a stranger approaching a child is an enemy; children are targets. Now there are grown-ups and teenagers who harm children, deliberately. That fact is always, always, at the back of my mind, of all parents' minds.

When Jock was five, he and I had a fight. He stood in the hall outside his room and yelled up at me, a small fiery figure in brown corduroy pants and a striped cotton jersey, his slipping-off socks dragging beyond his toes. He shouted that he hated me, and I shouted back that I didn't care: these were loud, angry, pulse-pounding moments. I was outraged that he should challenge me, and I towered angrily over him. Compared with him I was immense, giantesque. My huge hands on my wide and powerful hips mimicked and ridiculed his own, his small hands set bravely on his narrow hips.

"I don't care that you don't care," he finished shrilly, and whirled away from me. He stalked angrily into his room and slammed the door. He stamped his feet with each step, but in socks, on the carpet, his small feet made only faint thuds.

I went into the kitchen to calm down, and a few minutes later Jock appeared in the doorway. He was wearing shoes, and his yellow slicker. The peaked hood was pulled up over his head, casting a deep glowing shadow over his face.

"I'm running away," he announced.

I was no longer angry; I was ready to make up. I looked at him, this small defiant golden figure, and I was struck by how powerless he was. Children have control over nothing in their lives; everything is determined by us, who claim to have their best interests at heart. But who's to say we do? We have our own best interests at heart, as always: self-esteem, authority, convenience. It seems so unfair to these tiny people, who stand up to us so bravely, who struggle so hard to be real, to make us know that they are real.

I said, "All right."

Jock stood still, uncertain.

"Forever," he warned.

He had thought I would argue. He watched me carefully, for a trick, for a second thought.

"If you want to run away, you can. I can't stop you," I said docilely. "But don't forget, you aren't allowed to cross the street."

"I know that," he said crossly. He still watched me, and I smiled at him.

"I love you," I added, and at that he regained his dignity, and turned proudly away. He walked to the hall door. I stood in the doorway and waved as he got into the elevator, his arms crossed on his chest, his elbows cradled in his palms, the peaked hood shading his small brave face.

What I should have done was follow him, I know that now. I should have gone down right after him in the next elevator. I should have shadowed him around the block, stepping quickly into doorways like Sherlock Holmes when Jock turned around. But I had some notion of playing fair, and I thought I should not invade his adventure.

Instead, I went to the front window and leaned recklessly out, the sidewalk below drawing me dizzyingly toward it. It was early spring, and the trees in the park were just beginning to unfold the fresh green of their leaves. There weren't many people on the block. No one else was in a slicker: it wasn't raining. I could easily see the small yellow figure, the pointed hood—which he had always refused to wear before—addressed upward, to me. He was walking slowly, for someone with such a fierce purpose, and I wondered if the world now seemed larger, noisier, more arbitrary than he had remembered it upstairs in our kitchen. I watched him until he reached the corner, and I saw him turn dutifully down the next side of the block. Then I waited, watching the clock, leaning out the window over and over, until finally I saw him again, coming from the other direction. He was at the far end of our block, making his steady way up the sidewalk toward the canopy over our door.

I was standing on our landing when the elevator door opened to reveal him. His face, in the golden shadow, was meditative and proud.

"I'm back," he announced.

He was back, unharmed, and proud. That was what I had intended. But at what risk! I still wake up in the night with the nightmare vision of someone stepping toward him on the sidewalk, taking Jock's trusting hand and leading him away. A stranger taking possession of this child that occupies my heart. Oh, God, I think at two o'clock in the morning, my limbs locked with tension and fear, how could I have let him go?

It is a puzzle to me, this memory, a riddle about freedom and safety, independence and responsibility. I don't know the answer to it. When I zipped up Jock's pale yellow slicker and sent him into the world, I meant him to know he could turn from me, that he was free. But I shouldn't have done it, I shouldn't have taken that terrible risk. When I think of it now, it seems as though his survival was a miracle, an extraordinary and undeserved piece of luck. It seems dangerous, that luck, something I may have to pay for later.

Now Margaret asked, "Are you going to the parents' meeting on Tuesday?"

"I think so," I said. "But we have tickets for the opera that night. So if we go to the parents' meeting, Gilbert will have to give the tickets to his secretary."

"Who likes Wagner, I'm sure. So what will you do?"

"Negotiate," I said.

"Who will win?" asked Margaret.

"It depends," I said. "I always say we should go to those meetings, but I don't even know how important they are. You know you should go, but why? At the last parents' meeting we listened to Tommy Grimshaw's mother tell us how sorry she felt for herself, and how difficult her ex-husband is."

Margaret smiled. "I know what you mean," she said. "But I think you do it for solidarity. We're all in this together. Anyway, I go because I want to know everything the teachers know. I want to know everything they think about my kid. I want to know what their theories are and what they suggest. I may not do what they suggest, but I want to know what it is."

Actually, Margaret did need to know what the teachers thought about Willie: he was a discipline problem, and in constant trouble at school. But she was right, too, about solidarity: that's what mothers owe each other—support, complicity, humor. I felt ashamed that I was willing to offer so little, that I was so lazy and insular. I was chastened by Margaret's response, the fact that she was determined to do things properly, to take part, to be involved.

"You're much more responsible than I am," I said. "I still have the feeling that kids grow themselves up, that it just happens."

"But you're probably right," said Margaret cheerfully. "They probably do. I'm wildly overresponsible: what can I say?"

"What does Frank think?"

"Who knows what Frank thinks? I'm so crazed about taking charge of everything that he backs off. Who knows what he'd be like as a single parent?"

"Wouldn't it be awful if our husbands brought up our children?" And we laughed at the thought, full of shared horror.

"Nan Wallace was on a flight home from the Caribbean last winter. It was just after she and Steve had gotten married, and her kids were with their father. The plane started bumping, which Nan hates. It got worse and worse and finally Nan grabbed the stewardess and said, 'Could you please tell the pilot to quiet this plane down? If it crashes, there are two wonderful children in New York who will have to grow up with their father.' "

We both laughed again, and I said, "It's a chilling thought, isn't it? But why? It's not that the fathers don't love them."

"Oh, no. Of course they love them. It's just that they don't know anything. They don't know *anything*," said Margaret firmly. "They have no clue. They'd get everything wrong."

"But wouldn't they learn?" I pictured Gilbert widowed, bravely quelling his grief, earnestly attending school meetings, soberly walking Jock to school.

"Please," said Margaret. "Frank knows every corporate law precedent going back to 1900, but he can barely remember what Willie's name is. The two of them living alone together would be a disaster."

Willie and Jock were in the middle of some sort of contest. Their heads were lowered over their bowls, and they were staring intently at each other, slurping from their soup spoons, and laughing raucously. Still staring fixedly at Jock, Willie said, "Daddy knows my name."

Margaret looked at him, irritated. "Of course Daddy knows your name. That was a figure of speech."

"Daddy knows my name," Willie repeated, "and I *want* to live with him. I'd *like* to live alone with Daddy." He put a huge spoonful of soup in his mouth. At once he lapsed into a high cackle. The soup, deliberately or accidentally, it was hard to tell, came spraying out in a wild fan, all over the table and over Jock. This was a declaration of mutiny, and Jock, of course, began laughing as well, rocking dangerously on his high stool and kicking his feet.

"Oh, *Willie!*" said Margaret. "*Look* what you've done." She was really cross. She stalked to the sink and got the sponge. "Get down off your stool," she snapped. "Willie, get *down*. Now."

Willie still did not look at her. He got down off the stool and then put his hands on the table. He began little springing jumps, kicking himself off against the floor, as though he were going to heave himself up and sit in the middle of the soup-sprayed surface. He was flopping his head from side to side and laughing wildly. Jock was doing the same: hysteria had set in, the last refuge of the child-about-to-be-punished.

"Willie, *look at me,*" Margaret said, kneeling in front of him, the sponge in her hand, trying to mop the soup off his shirt. But Willie would not look at her. He kept flopping his head from side to side and laughing.

"Jock," I said, "stop laughing and come over here." Jock shook his own head wildly, closing his eyes. "Jock," I repeated, and without looking at me, still with his eyes shut, he slid off his stool. He began making his way over to me, holding out his hands like a blind man. He wobbled and staggered, deliberately missing my stool, while Willie screamed with laughter.

I grabbed Jock by the arm and pulled him over next to me. "Jock, stop," I said sternly, but I wasn't really cross.

Willie was still flopping his head back and forth, and he had closed his eyes too. Like Jock, he feigned blindness, groping with his hands in front of him. He touched Margaret's face, roughly bumping her nose, and he screamed joyfully.

"Eeeyeww! What is it?" He went into high-pitched giggles. "What weird, squishy thing is this?" He bumped Margaret's face again, rudely.

"Willie," Margaret said angrily. She grabbed him by the shirt and shook him. "Stop it. I mean it."

Willie's hand strayed away from her face, but he did not open his eyes, and he did not stop his laughter, shrill and false.

Margaret now took hold of his shoulders, and her voice rose. "Willie, stop it. Stop it right now."

Willie's eyes were still pinched shut. He shrugged his shoulders violently, away from his mother's hands, and began jumping wildly up and down, his voice in a high whine. "Eeeyeww," he said, over and over, "eeeyeww, what is it? Is it human?"

By now Willie and Margaret were deep inside the thicket that they had created and shared: thorny, isolate, barbaric. Within it, each of them struggled fiercely to destroy the authority, the reality, of the other.

Margaret grabbed Willie's shoulders again and shook him, hard. He went limp, wobbling bonelessly. I felt sorry for both of them, both so angry, now so committed to their struggle. But Willie was being so awful, so wild, so arrogant, so contemptuous, that part of me felt just like Margaret. There was a part of me that felt mean, tyrannical, swollen. Part of me wanted that child subdued, wanted him shaken until his teeth chattered, until his will was broken and he stopped his derisive whine. I knew the feeling, all parents do, of the rage that threatens sanity. I knew why there was child abuse; we've all come close.

"Willie, listen to me," Margaret said violently, talking through her teeth. "*Listen to me.* If you don't stop this, right now, this minute, you are spending the rest of the afternoon in your room. Alone. Jock will have to go home. Now *stop it!*"

There it was, the big threat. I try not to use it, because Jock always rises to the challenge. And following through on it is always inconvenient. Now we all waited, suspensefully: everyone's afternoon hung in the balance, Jock's and mine and Margaret's, to say nothing of Willie's. But Willie never hesitated.

He yanked himself away from Margaret again and began springing up and down into the air, crouching, and then shooting up into the air. His eyes were still screwed shut, and over and over he made violent explosion noises. He was a rocket, a cannonball, a spaceship, a bullet, anything but a submissive child.

"All right," said Margaret, furious, "all right. Is this what you want?" But she didn't move. "Is this what you're trying to do? Stop it, Willie, I mean it," she said.

He bounced up, landed, crouched, and launched himself again, unimpeded.

Margaret stood up now and shook her head. It was as though nothing had happened, no wildness, no threat, no feeble retreat. She cleaned the soup off the table and sat down again at the table, ignoring the boys.

"Honestly," she said to me, "it's like having lunch in the lion house."

Jock watched, interested: this is not what would have happened at our house. And I watched, unhappy: Margaret's strategy baffles me. It seems that if you don't follow through, there's no point in making threats at all. It seems to me you're just teaching a child that there's no risk to rebelling. But I said nothing to Margaret. No matter what she says about all of us being in this together, I know that you never tell another mother what to do. And besides, how do I know I'm right? Why is my instinct better than hers? What about letting Jock go off on his own, at five years old, in New York City? What kind of sage and responsible act was that? No, we all make our own mistakes; we all act crazily, indefensibly. We are saved by time passing and by miracles, not by the interference of our friends.

But Willie was not to be denied a climax. Behind Margaret, in a dazzling throwaway gesture, he upset his bowl, sending heavy split-pea soup in a great floating wave onto Margaret's back, soaking her elegant silk blouse.

"All right!" she shouted. "All right, Willie! That is enough! You come here with me." This time she took Willie's arm and yanked him along behind her, out of the kitchen. Again, Willie relaxed all his limbs and let himself be dragged, limp, letting gravity declare his reluctance.

When they were gone, Jock and I looked solemnly at each other.

"Poor Willie," I said. "He doesn't seem very happy."

Jock shook his head, but he would not speak to me, he would not take my side against his friend. He sat silent and mournful, taking small spoonfuls of his soup, his head down. I drank my tea. When Margaret came back, she was brisk and glowing, her cheeks pink with fury. She had changed her shirt and put on a thin cashmere sweater. I wondered if you could ever get split-pea soup out of silk.

"Sorry," she said, sitting down again. "I'm sorry, Jock, but Willie forgot his manners and he forgot the rules. He's going to stay by himself for a while and think about them."

"When can Willie come out?" Jock asked. He seemed very small and quiet. It was now hard to imagine him laughing raucously, kicking his legs under the table.

"Willie has to stay in his room until his father comes home," Margaret said brutally. She picked up her mug of tea in both hands and brought it to her mouth. It concealed her face except for her eyes, which were blazing. She looked wild, distraught, and I thought she was close to tears.

Jock's face fell. His afternoon was emptied of color, and he played dejectedly with the cracker on his plate. He crumbled it messily, rubbing at its soft pale crispness until it collapsed in bits. I wanted to comfort both of them, but I could think of nothing to say to Margaret.

Finally I said, "Well, Jocko, you and I will go to the park, if you like, or we can go home and I'll play a game with you. Whatever game you like." He glanced up at me, weighing this offer soberly, though we both knew it didn't make up for his afternoon with Willie.

I waited before I moved, but Margaret didn't look at me, or answer, so I thought she was letting me know that she didn't want to talk about whatever she was feeling.

"I think we'll get going," I said to her. "Sorry this happened, but don't worry about it. I'm sure we played a part in it; it wasn't all Willie." I wanted to make her feel less isolated, less frantic, but she shook her head.

"Oh, don't *you* worry about it," she said, walking us to the front door. "It wasn't Jock's fault. Willie has to learn what the rules are, that's all." Her face was stiff now, her head was up, and she had her hands deep in the pockets of her trim black pants. She looked very cool, very much in charge.

"Well, don't let it get you down. God knows, it happens all the time," I said, shaking my head slightly, as though Jock spent all his daytime hours shut in his room. But Margaret looked politely uncomprehending, as though she didn't know exactly what I was talking about. I couldn't think of any other way to reach her, and it seemed clear that she didn't want to be reached. So we left her alone, in her apartment, with Willie on the other side of a grimly closed door.

I should have stayed with her, I see that now. She had said, We're all in this together. What support was I giving her by leaving her alone, by letting her pretend that everything was all right?

What happened was that Willie decided to escape. The new window bars were being installed that week, and in Willie's room the old ones had been taken out and the new ones set in place. They were only set there, they hadn't yet been bolted into the window frames, but only the sculptor knew this. The bars looked solid, but, as it turned out, a bold nine-year-old could dislodge them.

Willie opened his window wide. It was cold outside—it was December—and when he opened the window he must have paused at the damp winter wind that swept into his room. Like Jock, he bundled up dutifully before he set out, as his mother would have asked. He got a sweater from his bureau and put it on by himself, backwards, the label under his chin. His room overlooked the terrace, and when he climbed out onto his windowsill, the terrace must have looked inviting. It was diagonally beneath him, not directly below, but on the way there were windowsills, ledges, cornices, safe things to grip. The climb would have looked dangerous but feasible to Willie, and it was both. There were places he could cling and balance as he clambered down and sideways, through the singing air, the wind holding him against the building, until he had sidled far enough over to drop the last few feet onto the terrace.

This is the part that is hard to think about. The French doors to the living room were locked. Willie stayed on the terrace, maybe shivering, maybe hoping and not hoping to see his mother. She passed the living room several times that afternoon, but she heard nothing, she saw nothing. She tries to remember now if she might have heard something. If he had called, if he had knocked, would she have heard? But she heard nothing. Perhaps, when she passed, he was there. Perhaps when he saw her he hid, sobered by his climb, fearful at last of her rage. Perhaps he had been sobered by what he had done: going out into the real world, he had felt himself flattened against the cold brick side of the building, he had felt the terrible singing call of the drop, the rush of the sidewalk, nine stories down. Perhaps, after this, he had lost his nerve; perhaps the thought of facing her rage as well was too much for him. But he was there on the terrace for a while. He left a plastic superhero there, balanced on the sill outside the French door, waiting for it to open. He didn't knock on the door, he didn't shout out for his mother to let him in. He made no demands. For some period of time he stayed alone out there, in the wind, his sweater on backwards. Maybe he played for a while with the superhero, under the lowering December sky. But it's hard to imagine him playing, it's hard to imagine him, by then, as anything but subdued.

At some point Willie decided to climb back up. He was trying to undo his mistake, to be good. He was trying to put himself back where Margaret wanted to find him; he had thought better of his escape. When Margaret finally knocked at his door, calm, her heart no longer closed against him, her rage no longer in charge, Willie wanted to be sitting in his room, the window shut, the sweater off.

He clambered first up onto the broad parapet. There he stood, his sneakered feet tiptoed and teetering as he stretched for the first window ledge. But climbing up is very different from climbing down, and this time the ledge was slightly too high, slightly too far, for his grip to hold his weight.

We are not in this together. The things that separate us are terrible and irreversible. What lies now between me and Margaret will lie there forever, a chasm nine stories deep.

These things should not happen. With luck, any luck at all, things would have gone differently. Margaret would have seen him, the terrace doors would have been unlocked, the window ledge would have been closer. And neither Margaret nor Willie ever wanted to be in that thicket of hostility. They love each other, mothers, children, no matter what they say, what they do. That should count. And repentance is meant to save.

Most often there are miracles; most children are saved. When a miracle doesn't happen, when you hear that a child is lost, the terrible sound of it echoes within your mind, a series of slow reverberations. They continue, deep inside you, distant and sinister. You feel terror, the vertiginous pull downward, the drop that you escaped for no reason. And you hold your own child close to you, close, no matter how he struggles.

I write about things that trouble me. Several years ago there was a cluster of incidents in New York involving children who fell from high windows. It seemed so terrible to me, the image of a child falling through the air: a child's body is much heavier than an adult's, because it carries so much more emotion, so much more unlived life. And that long passage through the air: endless, irreversible, informed by such pure and passionate regret. This image of the falling child haunted me, and to lay it to rest I made up these characters, and this story.

R.R.

QUALITY TIME

□

BARBARA KINGSOLVER

Miriam's one and only daughter, Rennie, wants to go to Ice Cream Heaven. This is not some vision of the afterlife but a retail establishment here on earth, right in Barrimore Plaza, where they have to drive past it every day on the way to Rennie's day-care center. In Miriam's opinion, this opportunistic placement is an example of the free-enterprise system at its worst.

"Rennie, honey, we can't today. There just isn't time," Miriam says. She is long past trying to come up with fresh angles on this argument. This is the bland, simple truth; the issue is time, not cavities or nutrition. Rennie doesn't want ice cream. She wants an angel sticker for the Pearly Gates Game, for which one only has to walk through the door, no purchase necessary. When you've collected enough stickers you get a free banana split. Miriam has told Rennie over and over again that she will buy her a banana split, some Saturday when they have time to make an outing of it, but Rennie acts as if this has nothing to do with the matter at hand, as though she has asked for a Cabbage Patch doll and Miriam is offering to buy her shoes.

"I could just run in and run out," Rennie says after a while. "You

151

could wait for me in the car." But she knows she has lost; the proposition is half-hearted.

"We don't even have time for that, Rennie. We're on a schedule today."

Rennie is quiet. The windshield wipers beat a deliberate, ingratiating rhythm, sounding as if they feel put-upon to be doing this job. All of southern California seems dysfunctional in the rain: cars stall, drivers go vaguely brain-dead. Miriam watches Rennie look out at the drab scenery, and wonders if for her sake they ought to live someplace with ordinary seasons—piles of raked leaves in autumn, winters with frozen streams and carrot-nosed snowmen. Someday Rennie will read about those things in books, and think they're exotic.

They pass by a brand-new auto mall, still under construction, though some of the lots are already open and ready to get down to brass tacks with anyone who'll brave all that yellow machinery and mud. The front of the mall sports a long row of tall palm trees, newly transplanted, looking frankly mortified by their surroundings. The trees depress Miriam. They were probably yanked out of some beautiful South Sea island and set down here in front of all these Plymouths and Subarus. Life is full of bum deals.

Miriam can see that Rennie is not pouting, just thoughtful. She is an extremely obliging child, considering that she's just barely five. She understands what it means when Miriam says they are "on a schedule." Today they really don't have two minutes to spare. Their dance card, so to speak, is filled. When people remark to Miriam about how well organized she is, she laughs and declares that organization is the religion of the single parent.

It sounds like a joke, but it isn't. Miriam is faithful about the business of getting each thing done in its turn, and could no more abandon her orderly plan than a priest could swig down the transubstantiated wine and toss out wafers like Frisbees over the heads those waiting to be blessed. Miriam's motto is that life is way too complicated to leave to chance.

But in her heart she knows what a thin veil of comfort it is that she's wrapped around herself and her child to cloak them from chaos. It all hangs on the presumption that everything has been accounted for. Most days, Miriam is a believer. The road ahead will present no serious potholes, no detour signs looming sudden and orange in the headlights, no burning barricades thrown together as reminders that the world's anguish doesn't remain mute—like the tree falling in the forest—just because no one is standing around waiting to hear it.

Miriam is preoccupied along this line of thought as she kisses Rennie goodbye and turns the steering wheel, arm over elbow, guiding her middle-aged Chevy out of the TenderCare parking lot and back onto the slick street. Her faith has been shaken by coincidence.

On Saturday, her sister Janice called to ask if she would be the guardian of Janice and Paul's three children, if the two of them should die. "We're redoing the wills," Janice reported cheerfully over the din, while in the background Miriam could hear plainly the words "Give me that Rainbow Brite right now, dumb face."

"Just give it some thought," Janice had said calmly, but Miriam hadn't needed to think. "Will you help out with my memoirs if I'm someday the President?" her sister might as well have asked, or "What are your plans in the event of a nuclear war?" The question seemed to Miriam more mythical than practical. Janice was a careful person, not given to adventure, and in any case tended to stick to those kids like some kind of maternal adhesive. Any act of God that could pick off Janice without taking the lot would be a work of outstanding marksmanship.

Late on Sunday night, while Miriam was hemming a dress of Rennie's that had fallen into favor, she'd had a phone call from her ex-husband, Lute. His first cousin and her boyfriend had just been killed on a San Diego freeway by a Purolator van. Over the phone, Lute seemed obsessed with getting the logistics of the accident right, as though the way the cars all obeyed the laws of physics could make this thing reasonable. The car that had the blowout was a Chrysler; the cousin and boyfriend were in her Saab; the van slammed into them from behind. "They never had a chance," Lute said, and the words chilled Miriam. Long after she went to bed she kept hearing him say "never had a chance," and imagining the pair as children. As if even in infancy their lives were already earmarked: these two will perish together in their thirties, in a Saab, wearing evening clothes, on their way to hear a friend play in the symphony orchestra. All that careful mothering and liberal-arts education gone to waste.

Lute's cousin had been a freelance cellist, often going on the road with the likes of Barry Manilow and Tony Bennett and, once, Madonna. It was probably all much tamer than it sounded. Miriam is surprised to find she has opinions about this woman, and a clear memory of her face. She only met her once, at her own wedding, when all of Lute's family had come crowding around like fog. But now this particular cousin has gained special prominence, her vague features crystallized in death, like a face on a postage stamp. Important. Someone you just can't picture doing the humdrum, silly things that life is made of—clipping her toenails or lying on the bed with her boyfriend watching *Dallas*—if you hold it clearly in your mind that she is gone.

Lute is probably crushed; he idolized her. His goal in life is to be his own boss. Freelance husbanding is just one of the things that hasn't worked out for Lute. Freelance fathering he can manage.

Miriam is thinking of Rennie while she waits through a yellow light she normally might have run. Rennie last week insisting on wearing only dresses to nursery school, and her pale, straight hair just so, with a ribbon; they'd seen *Snow White*. Rennie as a toddler standing in her crib, holding the rails, her mouth open wide with the simplest expectation you could imagine: a cookie, a game, or nothing at all, just that they would both go on being there together. Lute was already out of the picture by that time; he wouldn't have been part of Rennie's hopes. It is only lately, since she's learned to count, that Lute's absence matters to Rennie. On the Disney Channel parents come in even numbers.

The light changes and there is a honking of horns; someone has done something wrong, or too slowly, or in the wrong lane. Miriam missed it altogether, whatever it was. She remembers suddenly a conversation she had with her sister years ago when she was unexpectedly pregnant with Rennie, and Janice was already a wise old mother of two. Miriam was frantic—she'd wanted a baby but didn't feel ready yet. "I haven't really worked out what it is I want to pass on to a child," she'd said to Janice, who laughed. According to Janice, parenting was three percent conscious effort and ninety-seven percent automatic pilot. "It doesn't matter what you think you're going to tell them. What matters is they're right there watching you every minute, while you let the lady with just two items go ahead of you in line, or when you lay on the horn and swear at the guy that cuts you off in traffic. There's no sense kidding yourself, what you see is what you get."

Miriam had argued that people could consciously change themselves if they tried, though in truth she'd been thinking more of Lute than herself. She remembers saying a great many things about choices and value systems and so forth, a lot of first-pregnancy high-mindedness it seems to her now. Now she understands. Parenting is something that happens mostly while you're thinking of something else.

Miriam's job claims her time for very irregular hours at the downtown branch of the public library. She is grateful that the people at Rennie's day care don't seem to have opinions about what kind of mother would work mornings one day, evenings the next. When she was first promoted to this position Miriam had a spate of irrational fears: she imagined Miss Joyce at TenderCare giving her a lecture on homemade soup and the importance of routine in the formative years. But Miss Joyce, it seems, understands modern arrangements. "The important thing is quality time," she said once to Miriam, in a way that suggested bedtime stories read with a yogic purity of concentration, a mind temporarily wiped clean of things like brake shoes and MasterCard bills.

Miriam does try especially hard to schedule time for the two of them around Rennie's bedtime, but it often seems pointless. Rennie is likely to be absorbed in her own games, organizing animated campaigns on her bed with her stuffed animals, and finally dropping off in the middle of them, limbs askew, as though felled by a sniper.

Today is one of Miriam's afternoon-shift days. After leaving Rennie she has forty minutes in which she must do several errands before going to work. One of them is eat lunch. This is an item Miriam would actually put on a list: water African violets; dry cleaner's; eat lunch. She turns in at the Burger Boy and looks at her watch, surprised to see that she has just enough time to go in and sit down. Sometimes she takes the drive-through option and wolfs down a fish sandwich in the parking lot, taking large bites, rattling the ice in her Coke, unmindful of appearances. It's efficient, although it puts Miriam in mind of eating disorders.

Once she is settled inside with her lunch, her ears stray for company to other tables, picking up scraps of other people's private talk. "More than four hundred years old," she hears, and "It was a little bit tight over the instep," and "They had to call the police to get him out of there." She thinks of her friend Bob, who is a relentless eavesdropper, though because he's a playwright he calls it having an ear for dialogue.

Gradually she realizes that at the table behind her a woman is explaining to her daughter that she and Daddy are getting a divorce. It comes to Miriam as a slow shock, building up in her nerve endings until her skin hurts. This conversation will only happen once in that little girl's life, and I have to overhear it, Miriam is thinking. It has to be *here*. The surroundings seem banal, so cheery and hygienic, so many wiped-clean plastic surfaces. But then Miriam doesn't know what setting would be better. Certainly not some unclean place, and not an expensive restaurant either—that would be worse. To be expecting a treat, only to be socked with this news.

Miriam wants badly to turn around and look at the little girl. In her mind's eye she sees Rennie in her place: small and pale, sunk back into the puffy pink of her goosedown jacket like a loaf of risen dough that's been punched down.

The little girl keeps saying, "Okay," no matter what her mother tells her.

"Daddy will live in an apartment, and you can visit him. There's a swimming pool."

"Okay."

"Everything else will stay the same. We'll still keep Peppy with us. And you'll still go to your same school."

"Okay."

"Daddy does still love you, you know."

"Okay."

Miriam is thinking that ordinarily this word would work; it has finality. When you say it, it closes the subject.

It's already dark by the time Miriam picks up Rennie at TenderCare after work. The headlights blaze accusingly against the glass doors as if it were very late, midnight even. But it's only six-thirty, and Miriam tries to cheer herself by thinking that if this were summer it would still be light. It's a trick of the seasons, not entirely her fault, that Rennie has been abandoned for the daylight hours.

She always feels more surely on course when her daughter comes back to her. Rennie bounces into the car with a sheaf of papers clutched in one fist. The paper they use at TenderCare is fibrous and slightly brown, and seems wholesome to Miriam. Like turbinado sugar, rather than refined.

"Hi, sweetie. I missed you today." Miriam leans over to kiss Rennie and buckle her in before pulling out of the parking lot. All day she has been shaky about driving, and now she dreads the trip home. All that steel and momentum. It doesn't seem possible that soft human flesh could travel through it and come out intact. Throughout the day Miriam's mind has filled spontaneously with images of vulnerable things—baby mice, sunburned eyelids, sea creatures without their shells.

"What did you draw?" she asks Rennie, trying to anchor herself.

"This one is you and me and Lute," Rennie explains. Miriam is frowning into the river of moving headlights, waiting for a break in the traffic, and feels overcome by sadness. There are so many things to pay attention to at once, and all of them so important.

"You and me and Lute," Miriam repeats.

"Uh-huh. And a dog, Pickles, and Leslie Copley and his mom. We're all going out for a walk."

A sports car slows down, letting Miriam into the street. She waves her thanks. "Would you like to go for a walk with Leslie Copley and his mom sometime?"

"No. It's just a picture."

"What would you like for supper?"

"Potpies!" Rennie shouts. Frozen dinners are her favorite thing. Miriam rather likes them too, although this isn't something she'd admit to many people. Certainly not her mother, for instance, or to Bob, who associates processed foods with intellectual decline. She wonders, though, if her privacy is an illusion. Rennie may well be revealing all the details of their home life to her nursery-school class, opening new chapters daily. What I had for dinner last night. What Mom does when we run out of socks. They probably play games along these lines at TenderCare, with entirely innocent intentions. And others, too, games with a social-worker bent: What things make you happy, or sad? What things make you feel scared?

Miriam smiles. Rennie is fearless. She does not know how it feels to be hurt, physically or otherwise, by someone she loves. The people at TenderCare probably hear a lot worse than potpies.

"Mom," Rennie asks, "does God put things on the TV?"

"What do you mean?"

Rennie considers. "The cartoons, and the movies and things. Does God put them there?"

"No. People do that. You know how Grandpa takes movies of you with his movie camera, and then we show them on the screen? Well, it's like that. People at the TV station make the programs, and then they send them out onto your TV screen."

"I thought so," Rennie says. "Do you make them sometimes, at the library?"

Miriam hears a siren, but can't tell where it's coming from. "Well, I organize programs for the library, you're right, but not TV programs. Things like storybook programs. You remember, you've come to some of those." Miriam hopes she doesn't sound irritated. She is trying to slow down and move into the right lane, because of the ambulance, but people keep passing her on both sides, paying no attention. It makes Miriam angry. Sure enough, the ambulance is coming their way. It has to jerk to a full stop in the intersection ahead of them because of all the people who refuse to yield to greater urgency.

"Mom, what happens when you die?"

Miriam is startled because she was thinking of Lute's poor cousin. Thinking of the condition of the body, to be exact. But Rennie doesn't even know about this relative, won't hear her sad story for years to come.

"I'm not sure, Rennie. I think maybe what happens is that you think back over your life, about all the nice things you've done and the people who've been your friends, and then you close your eyes and . . . it's quiet." She was going to say, ". . . and go to sleep," but she's read that sleep and death shouldn't be equated, that it can cause children to fear bedtime. "What do you think?"

"I think you put on your nicest dress, and then you get in this glass box and everybody cries and then the prince comes and kisses you. On the lips."

"That's what happened to Snow White, isn't it?"

"Uh-huh. I didn't like when he kissed her on the lips. Why didn't he kiss her on the cheek?"

"Well, grown-ups kiss on the lips. When they like each other."

"But Snow White wasn't a grown-up. She was a little girl."

This is a new one on Miriam. This whole conversation is like a toboggan ride, threatening at every moment to fly out of control in any direction. She's enjoying it, though, and regrets that they will have to stop soon for some errands. They are low on produce, canned goods, aluminum foil, and paper towels, completely out of vacuum-cleaner bags and milk.

"What I think," says Miriam, after giving it some consideration, "is that Snow White was a little girl at first, but then she grew up. Taking care of the seven dwarfs helped her learn responsibility." Responsibility is something she and Rennie have talks about from time to time. She hears another siren, but this one is definitely behind them, probably going to the same scene as the first. She imagines her sister Janice's three children bundling into her life in a whirlwind of wants and possessions. Miriam doesn't even have time for another house plant. But she realizes that having time is somehow beside the point.

"So when the prince kissed her, did she grow up?" Rennie asks.

"No, before that. She was already grown up when the prince

came. And they liked each other, and they kissed, and afterward they went out for a date."

"Like you and Mr. Bob?"

"Like Bob and I do sometimes, right. You don't have to call him Mr. Bob, honey. He's your friend, you can call him just Bob, if you want to."

Instead of making the tricky left turn into the shopping center, Miriam's car has gone right, flowing with the tide of traffic. It happened almost before she knew it, but it wasn't an accident. She just isn't ready to get to the grocery store, where this conversation will be lost among the bright distractions of bubble gum and soda. Looping back around the block will give them another four or five minutes. They could sit and talk in the parking lot, out of the traffic, but Miriam is starting to get her driving nerves back. And besides, Rennie would think that peculiar. Her questions would run onto another track.

"And then what happened to the seven dwarfs?" Rennie wants to know.

"I think Snow White still took care of them, until they were all grown up and could do everything by themselves."

"And did the prince help too?"

"I think he did."

"But what if Snow White died. If she stayed dead, I mean, after the prince kissed her."

Miriam now understands that this is the angle on death that has concerned Rennie all along. She is relieved. For Miriam, practical questions are always the more easily answered.

"I'm sure the dwarfs would be taken care of," she says. "The point is that Snow White really loved them, so she'd make sure somebody was going to look after them, no matter what, don't you think?"

"Uh-huh. Maybe the prince."

"Maybe." A motorcyclist dodges in front of them, too close, weaving from lane to lane just to get a few yards ahead. At the next red light they will all be stopped together, the fast drivers and the slow, shooting looks at one another as if someone had planned it all this way.

"Rennie, if something happened to me, you'd still have somebody to take care of you. You know that, don't you?"

"Uh-huh. Lute."

"Is that what you'd like? To go and live with Lute?"

"Would I have to?"

"No, you wouldn't have to. You could live with Aunt Janice if you wanted to."

Rennie brightens. "Aunt Janice and Uncle Paul and Michael-and-Donna-and-Perry?" The way she says it makes Miriam think of their Christmas card.

"Right. Is that what you'd want?"

Rennie stares at the windshield wipers. The light through the windshield is spotty, falling with an underwater strangeness on Rennie's serious face. "I'm not sure," she says. "I'll have to think it over."

Miriam feels betrayed. It depresses her that Rennie is even willing to take the question seriously. She wants her to deny the possibility, to give her a tearful hug and say she couldn't live with anyone but Mommy.

"It's not like I'm sending you away, Rennie. I'm not going to die while you're a little girl. We're just talking about what-if. You understand that, right?"

"Right," Rennie says. "It's a game. We play what-if at school." After another minute she says, "I think Aunt Janice."

They are repeating their route now, passing again by the Burger Boy where Miriam had lunch. The tables and chairs inside look neater than it's possible to keep things in real life, and miniature somehow, like doll furniture. It looks bright and safe, not the sort of place that could hold ghosts.

On an impulse Miriam decides to put off the errands until tomorrow. She feels reckless, knowing that tomorrow will already be busy enough without a backlog. But they can easily live another day without vacuum-cleaner bags, and she'll work out something about the milk.

"We could stop here and have a hamburger for dinner," Miriam says. "Or a fish sandwich. And afterward we could stop for a minute at Ice Cream Heaven. Would you like that?"

"No. Potpies!"

"And no Ice Cream Heaven?"

"I don't need any more angel stickers. Leslie Copley gave me twelve."

"Well, that was nice of him."

"Yep. He hates bananas."

"Okay, we'll go straight home. But do you remember that potpies take half an hour to cook in the oven? Will you be too hungry to wait, once we get home?"

"No, I'll be able to wait," Rennie says, sounding as if she really will. In the overtones of her voice and the way she pushes her blond hair over her shoulder there is a startling maturity, and Miriam is frozen for a moment with a vision of a much older Rennie. All the different Rennies—the teenager, the adult—are already contained in her hands and her voice, her confidence. From moments like these, parents can find the courage to believe in the resilience of their children's lives. They will barrel forward like engines, armored by their own momentum, more indestructible than love.

"Okay then, potpies it is," Miriam says. "Okay."

I am frequently asked if my fiction is autobiographical, and the answer is no. I don't write about myself, or my family, or my friends. But I do write about the experience of self, and family, and friends, and I could never do that if I didn't know the territory. I can hardly count the ways that being a mother has broadened my writing, deepened my connection to all other women, and galvanized my commitment to the Earth and its fate. As difficult as it is, sometimes, to find a way to be a writer while taking care of children, I think it would be harder to be a writer who has never known what it means to care for a child.

B.K.

STARLIGHT

◻

MARIAN THURM

Elaine and her mother had spent the day shopping, going from one department store to the next—from Lord & Taylor to Saks to Jordan Marsh to Burdines. It was Elaine's third day in Florida, and they had been looking for gifts for her two boys: Jesse, who was nine, and Matthew, who was eleven. Elaine hadn't seen either of them in months, and she hoped the shirts and sweaters she had bought were the right sizes. The last time she saw them was in early December, when she left their house in New Jersey with three large suitcases crammed with her winter clothes. At first she had felt an overwhelming grief when the boys told her they preferred to live with their father; the humiliation had come later, along with a sudden, cold anger. She got over her anger soon enough—how could you be angry at children who were too young to know they had hurt you? The grief stayed with her much longer, but she was finally over that, too. It was the humiliation that lingered. As her mother and father had said more than once since Elaine's arrival, "Who ever heard of young children like that just coming right out and picking their father over their mother, no two ways about it?"

Even Peter, Elaine's husband, had been amazed at the boys' decision. He hadn't been all that pleased about it, either. Keeping Jesse and Matthew meant keeping the house and finding someone to take care of things until he got home from work. It wasn't anything like what he had envisioned for himself. He didn't go into details, but Elaine knew that whatever it was he wanted was going to be harder to get now that there were two children to be looked after. When he first told her why he wanted out, she stared at him in disbelief. She was boring, he said. Nothing she did or said or wanted was interesting anymore. They were on their way back from the city, where they had had dinner with a friend of Peter's from college— a criminal lawyer who specialized in defending celebrities who'd been arrested on drug charges. He had asked them to a big party he was giving, where there was sure to be plenty of really good dope, and Elaine wanted to know why Peter had said they'd love to come, why he'd said it sounded like a great way to spend an evening. We're not college kids anymore, she yelled at him in the car as they crossed the George Washington Bridge. You really are a drag, he said quietly, and he didn't let up until they pulled into the driveway of their house. They sat in the car for what seemed to be hours, Elaine shivering as they talked. What did he want her to do? she asked him. Take up skydiving? Get a job as a trapeze artist? Put a ring through her nose? That's when he told her he wanted out and gave his reasons. Her own reasons, at least, made sense; it was impossible to love someone who criticized her at every opportunity, who belittled her in front of her children, her friends, strangers, the whole world. After thirteen years, she had had enough. Even so, Peter had the last word. Whenever Elaine heard a book or a movie or a TV program described as boring, her skin prickled with goosebumps, as if she were in danger.

"You had a phone call," her father said. He had just unlocked the apartment's four locks to let Elaine and her mother inside.

"Who was it?" her mother said.

"Sweetie, did I say I was talking to you?" her father said.

"Who was it, Daddy?" Elaine said.

"It was Peter. He said the airport in Newark was snowed in, and the kids wouldn't be down until tomorrow. Or maybe the day after. It all depends on the weather."

"Was he civil to you, at least?" Elaine's mother said. She and Elaine put their shopping bags down in the foyer. The apartment was the perfect size for two people, with an L-shaped living room and a kitchen that could only take a small, round table. Elaine had been sleeping in the second bedroom her parents used as a den, but once the boys arrived she'd have to camp out in the living room. The three of them went out onto the screened-in terrace. The terrace overlooked the Intracoastal Waterway; just as they sat down, a motorboat went by, buzzing so loudly neither of them caught her father's answer. "Well, was he or wasn't he?" her mother said.

"Bastards," her father said. "I wish those creeps would stay out of my backyard."

"What else did he say?" Elaine asked her father.

"Peter? He was very polite. He asked how all of us were. He said the boys were very disappointed about the trip's being postponed. They can't wait to see all of us. Especially you, Lainie Bug, needless to say."

"Needless to say." Elaine knew her father was lying—his voice sounded unnaturally hearty, as if he were speaking to someone too old or too young to be told anything close to the truth.

"Well," her mother said, "disappointed though we all may be, you can't do anything about the weather, and that's that."

"Thank you, Mother, for your wit and wisdom in these trying times," Elaine's father said.

"Please don't talk to her like that," Elaine said.

"Your mother knows I like to kid around. That's the way I am."

"I don't mind. Or most of the time I don't. After forty years—"

"Well, you should mind," Elaine said. She stood up and looked out over the water at the condominiums that seemed to take up every last square foot of land. Just across the way, a hundred yards in the distance, she could see men and women lounging around a long rectangular swimming pool, and a diver poised on the board, ready to take off. She watched as he flew into the water and disappeared. It was a mistake to have come to Florida, she realized. But the boys had never been here before, and she had wanted to meet them on neutral ground, to vacation with them far enough from home so that she wouldn't have to worry about their calling for their father to come and get them in the middle of the night. And she had wanted to be among allies, people she could count on for comfort if things went disastrously with her children. What she hadn't counted on was her parents' making her feel worse than she'd felt all winter long. Her father was especially hard to take. Since his retirement, he'd mellowed, but she never knew what to expect. It was easy enough to be fond of him from a distance; living with him in such close quarters these past few days, she'd begun to wonder if she'd last the week or end up running out to find herself a motel.

The telephone rang.

Her mother said, "Arthur?"

"Don't look at me," her father said. "I'm just sitting here enjoying the view from my terrace."

"If it's for you, I may just hang up."

"Suit yourself."

Her mother picked up a phone that was on the terrace floor, next to a seven-foot-tall cactus. "Brenda," she said after a moment. "It's not bad news, is it?" She carried the phone past the sliding glass door into the living room, rolling her eyes as she went.

"Who's Brenda?" Elaine said, running her hand along the spines of the cactus.

"One of your mother's friends from O.A."

"I give up," Elaine said. Her fingertips were bleeding; she put them in her mouth.

"Overeaters Anonymous. Your mother can be on the phone day and night with those people. If any of them feel like they're about to go stuff their faces with a nice Sara Lee cake, for example, they call someone in this network they've got set up and talk their heads off instead of finishing the cake. Mommy lost fifteen pounds, by the way. Looks great, doesn't she?"

"Terrific." Elaine turned around in her chair so she could see her mother. "Wonderful," she said.

"You, on the other hand—"

"I'm fine."

"Feel like talking your head off to your old father?"

"About what?"

"Whatever. How about what you're going to do to get the boys back."

"This is the last time I'm going to repeat this," Elaine said, "so pay attention: they're perfectly happy where they are. Perfectly."

"They can't be. Children belong with their mother. That's the way it works in this world."

"It seems to me I've heard that before—twice yesterday and once the day before that."

"Does it sound any better today?"

"Worse," Elaine said.

Her mother came back out onto the terrace, eating the largest carrot Elaine had ever seen, and she was reminded of Jesse and Matthew, aged three and five, dressed in their Popeye pajamas, holding carrots in their hands as they sat on their knees in front of the television set watching some dopey program—*Gilligan's Island*, she thought it was. They were young enough then that their heads smelled sweet when she bent to kiss them. She hadn't noticed when the sweetness disappeared; one day, it was simply gone.

She couldn't explain why her children had done what they had. The morning after she and Peter had driven home from the city, they had just finished breakfast and Jesse and Matthew were about to leave the table when Peter said, "Sit still a minute." They listened to him talk, staying silent until Peter said it was all up to them, whatever they wanted to do was fine. "Think carefully. Take your time," Elaine started to warn them, but already Matthew was saying he would stay with his father and Jesse was nodding his head up and down, saying that was what he wanted, too. They shrugged their shoulders when she questioned them, and she didn't have the heart to press the issue. If they had been daughters, it might have been different; she just didn't know. After she left, she settled herself into an apartment in Fort Lee and found a job as a secretary in a private school in Manhattan—the first job she'd ever had. She stayed away from the house in Fair Lawn and talked to Peter briefly now and then. She spoke to Matthew and Jesse only once; she was near tears throughout the conversation, and couldn't wait to hang up. They talked about school—book reports, and new gym uniforms, and the science teacher who made Matthew come in at the end of the day and stare at the clock on the wall for half an hour as punishment for talking in class. The boys talked easily, as if it had been hours rather than months that had passed since they heard her voice. At the end, she told them she missed them, then hung up before she could hear their response.

It was spring vacation and she was ready to see them, finally; to see what would happen. She wouldn't expect too much of them— if they were stiff as strangers at first, she was prepared to draw back and let them approach her at their own pace. Maybe, after their week together in Florida was up, they would decide to see each other every weekend, or every other weekend. Beyond that, she couldn't speculate. She certainly wasn't about to ask them to come and live with her, to set herself up for being kicked in the teeth again. That was what it had felt like this winter—a swift, hard blow that left her so weak she could hardly move.

Her parents kept wanting to know what she had done. It's easy enough to be a lousy mother, her mother told her. You think you're doing everything right and then one day it turns out you were all wrong.

Elaine knew what her mother had done wrong. She had been a mother who couldn't wait for her children to grow up. Elaine and Philip, her younger brother, were always treated like adults; whenever there was trouble, they were expected to act calmly and reason things out. Once, at the train station, when they were on their way to the city to see *My Fair Lady*, Philip, who was terrified of escalators, couldn't bring himself to put one foot in front of the other and step onto the moving stair. "Just get a grip on yourself," their mother had shouted, while Elaine, who was twelve, ran down the other escalator to Philip and took his hand. It was the middle of the winter, but Philip's hand was moist and warm. Elaine promised him that it didn't matter whether they ever got to the city to see *My Fair Lady* that day, she only wanted him to stop crying. After the train left without them, their mother came down from the platform. "Get away from him," she said to Elaine. "I don't want you feeling sorry for him. The whole world knows how to deal with escalators. What's so special about him?" Elaine watched her brother lick tears from the corners of his mouth, and she wanted to lift him off the ground and fly him high above the escalator all the way to the city, leaving her mother behind with a look of absolute astonishment on her face. But Philip finally made it up the escalator and was forgiven. It was her mother who was never forgiven—not by Elaine, anyway.

"Do I care that Brenda has to put her mother into a nursing home?" her father was saying. "Does Elaine care?"

"What?" Elaine said.

"Tell your mother you couldn't care less."

"All right, I get the picture," her mother said.

"Can't we talk about something pleasant for a change?"

"What should we talk about? The weather? Even that kind of talk gets me in trouble."

"Talk to your daughter. Find out what's on her mind."

"I'm going to take a nap," Elaine said. "That's what's on my mind."

"Are you tired?" her mother said. "I'm not surprised. A long day of shopping can be very exhausting."

"I'm a people watcher," Elaine's mother announced in the airport coffee shop the following afternoon. During breakfast, they'd got a call from Peter saying the boys would be arriving at three-fifty-five. After the call, Elaine had gone alone to the beach in Fort Lauderdale, taken a quick swim, then slept in the sun for an hour, and returned to the apartment feeling fairly self-possessed. (It was the one time she'd been away from both her parents—the one time she'd successfully avoided them.) Now it was almost three-thirty, and she was close to panic.

"People fascinate me. I could look at them for hours," her mother went on. "Look at the couple over there." She motioned toward a man wearing a cowboy hat and a big red mustache, and the black woman who sat opposite him. Their baby was asleep in a plastic infant seat they had placed on the table. "Now, what do you think motivates people like that?"

"What do you think motivates your mother?" Elaine's father asked. He smiled at her. "Plain old-fashioned nosiness?"

Elaine smiled back, but her hand shook as she reached for her water glass.

"Go ahead and laugh," her mother said. "I guarantee you ninety-nine percent of the people in this world would understand my point."

"I think," her father said, "the time has come for me to make my speech."

"If it's the one about mothers and children and who belongs with whom, you can cancel it," Elaine said.

"Give me a chance," her father said. "I just want to give you a little piece of advice, that's all. You listen to what I'm going to say to you and you'll have those children eating out of the palm of your hand one-two-three."

"Excuse me," Elaine said, and pushed back her chair.

"You can't afford to make any more mistakes, Lainie Bug," her father called after her as she headed for the rest rooms at the back of the coffee shop.

Inside, she rushed past a teenage girl who was tweezing her eyebrows in front of a large mirror over a row of sinks. She locked herself into a stall, dropped the seat cover, and sat down on the very edge. She closed her eyes. The stall reeked of strawberry-scented deodorizer; still, it was easier to breathe now that she was alone.

In the dark, she told herself who she was: a grown woman scared to death of two little boys. Her own children. She had always wanted to be a mother, had always wanted babies. You couldn't go wrong with babies; there was no possibility of disappointment. You could hold them as close as you needed to, tell them all day long how much you loved them, and never feel foolish.

One night last summer, already suspecting her marriage was lost, Elaine had led the boys into her darkened bedroom, and in their pajamas Jesse and Matthew stretched themselves out on the floor and stared in amazement at the hundred glow-in-the-dark stars and planets she had stuck on her ceiling that afternoon—a whole galaxy that shimmered endlessly above them. Peter was away in Japan on a business trip, on the other side of the world; there was no one to question what she had done with her day. After the boys were settled, Elaine got down on the floor, concentrating on nothing except the perfect faces of her children. When she awoke two hours later, her neck was stiff and the boys were gone. There was a light summer blanket covering her; someone, Jesse or Matthew, or maybe both of them, had bent over her while she slept.

"We thought you fell in and drowned," her father said when Elaine made her way back to the table. "Like that time at the

World's Fair when you and your friend What's-Her-Name disappeared into the bathroom for a nice relaxing smoke. I couldn't imagine what you two were doing in there for so long. Of course, as soon as I got a whiff of you I knew what it was all about."

"You all right?" her mother said. She touched her lips to Elaine's forehead. "Nice and cool."

"Do you want a Coke or something?" her father said.

"Not me," Elaine said. "We really should get a move on. I don't even know why I sat down again."

They got to the gate just as the first passengers from Newark appeared. Matthew and Jesse were right up front, dressed identically in tweed jackets, tan pants with cuffs, and Weejuns. Jesse was wearing glasses and had a flesh-colored patch over his right eye. Elaine ran to him. "What's the matter with your eye? When did you start wearing glasses?" she said. She kissed him and then she kissed Matthew. Neither of them kissed her back, though Jesse hugged her and Matthew shook her hand.

"Can't you give your mother a kiss?" her mother said.

"I'm in seventh grade," Matthew said. "I shake hands."

"And what about your brother?"

"Me?" Jesse said. "I hug, but I don't kiss."

Elaine said, "What's the patch for? Tell me what's wrong." She sat down in a padded chair opposite the check-in counter. Everyone else stood around her.

"It's just a lazy eye," Jesse said cheerfully. "It won't do any work unless I force it to. With a patch over the other eye, the lazy eye has to do all the work. You understand what I'm saying?"

"Why didn't your father tell me?" Elaine said. "Why didn't you tell me?"

"He says hi," Matthew said. "I forgot all about it."

"You know what? His girlfriend bought us Star Wars costumes, even though it wasn't Halloween," Jesse said.

"God, what a jerk." Matthew put his hand over his brother's mouth.

"It's all right." Leaning forward, Elaine took Matthew's hand away from Jesse and held it. "Your father can have as many girl-friends as he wants. It makes no difference to me whatsoever."

"Well, he doesn't have one anymore. She dumped him."

Jesse said, "She used to make breakfast for us a lot on Saturdays and Sundays. She'd be there real early in the morning, like seven o'clock. She was a real early bird, Dad said."

"This kid is unbelievable," Matthew said.

Quickly Elaine's mother said, "Who would like to go for a mid-night swim tonight? The water will be nice and warm, and we'll have the whole pool to ourselves."

"If it's really summertime here, can we have a barbecue?" Jesse asked.

"Sorry, guys," her father said. "No barbecuing allowed. Those are the rules of the condominium."

Jesse tried again. "Instead of a barbecue, can we go to Disney World?"

"You don't want to go to Disney World," her father said. "It's a four-hour drive each way. And you've already been to Disneyland, haven't you?"

"Are we going to have fun on this trip, or what?" Matthew said. "What did we come down here for?"

"What do you mean? You came down here to be with your mother," Elaine's mother said. "That's the main thing."

Elaine studied her shoes, yellow espadrilles that she had bought just for the trip. The little toe on each foot had already worn holes through the canvas, she noticed. When she looked up, Jesse was dancing, shifting his weight back and forth from one foot to the other, his arms in the air, his elbows and wrists bent at right angles. Some sort of Egyptian dance, Elaine thought.

"Look at me. I'm Steve Martin," Jesse yelled. " 'Born in Arizona, moved to Babylonia. King Tut.' "

"Terrific," Elaine said, and clapped her hands.

"Oh Jesus," Matthew said.

Ignoring her mother's warning and her father's dire predictions, Elaine took the boys everywhere they wanted to go: Monkey Jungle, Parrot Jungle, and the Seaquarium. The boys seemed excited and happy, though often they would run ahead of her, too impatient to stay by her side. Once, from a distance, Elaine saw Jesse casually rest his arm on his brother's shoulder as the two of them stood watching a pair of orangutans groom each other; she kept waiting for Matthew to shake Jesse off, but it never happened. Two nights in a row, they went to see the movie *Airplane!* A couple of nights, they played miniature golf. At the end of each day, Jesse and Matthew told Elaine they had had "the best time." She supposed that this meant the trip was a success, that they would have nothing to complain about to their father when they went back home. She had kept them entertained, which was all they seemed to have wanted from her. She might have been anyone—a camp counselor, a teacher leading them on class trips, a friend of the family put in charge while their parents were on vacation. There was plenty of time to talk, and they told her a lot—long, involved stories about the fight Jesse had recently had with his best friend, the rock concert Matthew had gone to with two thirteen-year-olds, the pair of Siamese fighting fish with beautiful flowing fins they'd bought for the new fish tank in their bedroom—all about the things that had happened to them in the four months they had been out of touch. But she still didn't know if they were really all right, if they loved their father, loved her. You couldn't ask questions like that. When, several years ago, her brother had started seeing a shrink, he'd complained that his parents were always asking him if he was happy. It's none of their business, the shrink told him—if you don't feel you want to give them an answer, don't. As simple as that.

It was nearly midnight; the boys had just gone to bed. Elaine went into her parents' room, where her mother and father were sitting up in their king-size bed watching *Columbo* on a small color TV. Dick Van Dyke was tying his wife to a chair. He took two Polaroid pictures of her and then he picked up a gun. His wife insisted he was never going to get away with it; he aimed the gun at her and pulled the trigger.

"Wait a minute," Elaine's mother said. "Is this the one where Columbo tricks him into identifying his camera at the—"

"Thanks a lot," her father said. "You know how I love Peter Falk."

"Who knows, maybe I'm wrong."

"You're not," Elaine said. "I saw this one, too."

"Well, it's nice to be right about something."

Elaine lay down on her stomach at the foot of the bed, facing the TV set. She yawned and said, "Excuse me."

"All that running around," her mother said. "Who wouldn't be tired?"

"It's not necessary to run like that all day long," her father said. "Didn't those two kids ever hear of sleeping around the pool, or picking up a book or a newspaper? Maybe they're hyperactive or something."

"They're kids on vacation. What do they want to read the newspaper for?" her mother said.

Elaine sat up and swung her legs over the side of the bed. "It's my fault," she said. "I couldn't bring myself to say no to them about anything."

"Did you accomplish anything all those hours you were running?" her mother asked. "Do you feel like you made any headway?"

Elaine was watching an overweight woman on TV dance the cha-cha with her cat along a shining kitchen floor. "What?" she said.

"Of course, if they really are just fine there with Peter and his sleep-over girlfriends, that's another story," her father said.

"Quiet," her mother said. "Look who's here."

Jesse stood in the doorway, blinking his eyes. "There's a funny noise in my ears that keeps waking me up," he said. He sat down on the floor next to the bed and put his head in Elaine's lap. "You know," he said, "like someone's whistling in there."

Elaine hesitated, then kissed each ear. "Better?"

"A little."

"More kisses?"

Jesse shook his head.

"Let me take you back to bed." Elaine walked him to the little den at the other end of the apartment, where Matthew was asleep on his side of the convertible couch. Jesse got onto the bed. On his knees, he sat up and looked out the window. "I can't go to sleep right now," he said quietly. Beneath them the water was black; above, the palest of moons appeared to drift by. There were clouds everywhere, and just a few dim stars.

"Did you want to tell me something?" Elaine waited; she focused on the sign lit up on top of the Holiday Inn across the waterway.

"We're getting a new car. A silver BMW," Jesse said dreamily. "We saw it in the showroom." He moved away from the window and slipped down on the bed. "We might drive it over to Fort Lee and come and see you. And when Matthew has his license, the two of us will pick you up every day and take you anywhere you want to go."

Elaine still faced the window; she did not turn around. "To the moon," she said. "Will you do that for me?"

Jesse didn't answer for a long time. "We can do that," he said finally, and when she turned to look at him he was asleep.

It was my father who offered me a few sketchy details of a woman he knew whose children had chosen to live with their father after a divorce. "How could this happen to her?" my father asked me, as if I knew the answer. "Starlight" was my response to his question. My own child was just a year old at the time, and Elaine's situation was, for me, almost too painful to contemplate.

M.T.

CHANCES WITH JOHNSON

PAULA K. GOVER

There's all kinds of madness in the world, that's what I tell Johnson. Some of it gets you locked up. Some of it puts you on pills so you don't have to think, just remember to breathe and eat. Most of it leaves you in the here and now, not quite broken, not quite whole.

Johnson and I talk late at night, falling off holding hands, sometimes in the middle of a thought. Before I met him, I always went to bed with the television going. I'd call for Herman and he'd pad up the stairs, slow and sleep-heavy, footsteps sounding almost human, then he'd stretch out on the rug at the foot of the bed. Sometimes the hurting washed over me so strong I'd call out his name just to hear the answering thump of his tail as it dropped against the floor.

Now I've got Johnson to talk to. I tell him, "I've been crazy, you know, really crazy." He smiles when I say this, not because it's funny, but because he knows what I've been through and he knows what I mean. Nights are the worst time for thinking, he tells me. He met me a year after my ex-husband Jim took off with our oldest son, Eddie, and Johnson says that's enough to drive anyone out of their mind. There are times I feel the edge looming up when I think

180

about Eddie off God-knows-where with his father. It's like standing at the roar of Niagara Falls, staring down and hearing your heart say to jump. But there's my younger son, Joey, to think of, forcing me to keep one foot in the world, and Johnson helps bring me around.

We live in an old red-brick house with white shutters on the bluff looking west over Lake Michigan. Sometimes after Joey's in bed, Johnson and I walk down the narrow sandy path to the beach. In the summer you can see the lights of the tankers moving heavy and slow toward Wisconsin. On nights when the wind tapers off and the surf rolls in gently, the moon reflects in a pale yellow plate on the water. When it's calm like that, Johnson takes my hand and we wade in up to our knees. I tie my skirt in a knot at my hips and we walk where the bottom is smooth between the breakwaters. He says he loves this place. That makes me happy, because he hasn't been living up here that long, and I want him to stay.

Johnson kept on teaching high school biology in Saginaw after his wife left, putting himself into his work so hard he won a state-wide award. He's got a gold plaque from the governor, and it's hanging over our dresser. There's no question in my mind that he makes a good teacher. He likes people in general, all kinds. And he might have stayed in Saginaw forever, unhappy about the divorce, but working just to keep himself sane, except two students pulled a gun on him and stole his wallet, then hit him over the head. They charged two thousand dollars on his American Express card before they were caught. He says the part that hurts most is the boys had been students of his at one time, and he liked them. He knows all about crazy firsthand.

We both like to swim before bed when the water is warm enough, stripping down naked on our dark end of the beach, tossing bits of driftwood out into the lake for Herman to fetch. He comes pawing across the surf, prancing and growling and shaking water. Then he drops the wood at our knees in the water and we throw it back out again.

I got the dog when I moved up here with the boys, because we were all afraid in the house at night until we couldn't sleep. All those years and noise of the city behind us, and not even a thought back then as to what existed beyond the front door once the deadbolt was slid into place. There we were, all afraid in the silence of our house on the bluff, a house that grew larger in the dark, looking down on the gently lit lap of the town we'd made home. I lay awake sorting out the noises in the dark, sometimes with the boys pressed against me, and we'd whisper explanations to one another. A limb against my window. A night bird fanning down to the harbor. The buckle of a car door along the hill. The house itself, settling and creaking into sleep. We'd lived so long in the city that a big house in a small town made us jumpy, and that's what I mean about madness.

The summer nights are what Johnson likes best about living up here. We sit on the porch after supper, watching the sun as it slides into the lake, then naming stars as they appear one by one east to west. We go up to bed and pull back the covers and lie there with the breeze coming in through the windows that line one whole wall of the bedroom. The young petty officer at the Coast Guard station said the house used to belong to a ship's captain. I say that maybe our bedroom was his, the captain's, because from the windows you can see out on the lake and down the shoreline for miles. A captain would like that. Johnson says I should think about going back to school because I have a good imagination, and people with good imaginations know how to think, and that I would do really well in all my classes. Johnson says then I could get a degree and a job. I say I like how things are, and I bring in enough money renting out rooms. Besides, I tell him, I could get a job if I wanted. I've had jobs before.

We lie there talking late, sometimes with the news playing low on the television, and we tell each other how it was before we met. There are nights this goes on a long time, because we've only been together five months. He talks about his kids and how the divorce broke him up. He tells me that he couldn't believe for the longest time his wife really left him, and how she wasn't coming back. He says that he used to be happy-go-lucky, that he could bounce back from anything. Then his ex took their kids to Tampa with her new husband, and Johnson hasn't seen them for a year and a half, which is exactly how long Eddie's been gone. And he says that his spirit's been broken. I say, "Yeah, mine too."

Sometimes he gets me to talk just a little about Eddie. I try to imagine what he's doing, and if he's still totally crazy about baseball. Johnson says boys don't outgrow things like that, especially baseball. We talk about Joey too, and Johnson says Joey doesn't like having him around. I tell him I wouldn't be too sure about that, but he says Joey feels awful because first his dad took Eddie off, and now his mother has a new boyfriend. Johnson says Joey might think I don't need him as much, and I say it's all such a mess I don't want to talk about it.

Every so often Johnson presses me too hard, asking questions about Jim and Eddie's disappearance when there aren't any answers, and I start feeling like there's a storm stuck inside of my skull. One night we were lying in bed, talking about Eddie, and he kept repeating himself, asking, "How could a father do that to a kid? How could he do that? How could he do that?" He'd go quiet for a moment, talk about something else, then he'd start up again. He kept asking, "How could he do that? How could he do that?"

"How am I supposed to know?" I finally screamed, sitting straight up in our bed. "How the hell am I supposed to know? Do I look like I know? Do I? Do I?" I hadn't known I'd start screaming like that, and I'd been surprised by the sound of my voice. The room seemed oddly silent once I'd finished, so quiet I could hear my own heartbeat drumming in my ears. Then Johnson sat up beside me when I started to cry.

"Hey," he said as he pulled me close, his jaw moving against my

cheek. "I'm not the enemy." I lay there against him, crying for a
while, then drifting at the edge of dreaming as he stroked my hair.
We were still sitting side by side when he reached across me, switch-
ing off the bedside lamp and pulling the quilt up around our shoulders. "It's okay to get mad," he whispered at my ear, and after that
I was sleeping.

Johnson and I met at a dance in the V.F.W. Hall downtown. I
didn't want to go to the dance at first, but Yubi, my friend, insisted
what I needed was to get myself out of the house. She said that
winter was turning me into someone she didn't know or like. Most
days I spent the afternoon writing letters to Eddie with no place to
send them, or calling Friend of the Court, trying to think what to
do to bring Eddie back. So Yubi said, "Come on, girl, you're going," just like that. She got all dressed up in a green satin dress and
matching heels, saying, "If there's only going to be one black woman
at this thing, then she sure as hell is going to be one beautiful black
woman," and I laughed, because Yubi's never had to worry about
how she looks. Even in the morning she comes downstairs looking
great, no makeup, just those big shining eyes and a smile.

She sat at my dressing table that night, twisting her head as she
tried on earrings, smiling at my reflection in the mirror where I lay
belly-down at the end of the bed. Watching her humming and fussing, I decided, what the hell, why sit home, and I put on black
slacks and a red turtleneck sweater. "It'll be fun, just you wait,"
Yubi told me as we rode down the hill into town.

It was right at the end of January and snowing just a little, and
we parked in a lot two blocks from the hall. Everything glowed soft
and misty under the streetlights and we walked like we weren't in
any kind of hurry, and Yubi went, "There's something in the air."
I smiled, because there is almost always something in the air for
Yubi, and she looked like some kind of beautiful angel with snow
feathering all across her green coat.

We had to pay three dollars each to get inside, but Yubi said,

"It's all the beer you can drink, don't complain," as the doorman tattooed a black ink FIRST CLASS on our hands with a rubber stamp. Inside the hall, white crepe-paper streamers hung in loops from the ceiling, and a mirrored light reflected tiny rainbows on the planks of the dance floor. Yubi knew a few women from work, and they waved and smiled at her as we walked the edge of the hall, calling out to her by name, holding up cups of beer and winking. I didn't know anyone except the chubby, redheaded teller from the bank who gave us our beer and said, "Well, isn't it nice to see some new faces coming around."

We sat at the end of a long table that was covered with white paper and sprinkled with pastel confetti. The music was loud and we couldn't talk without having to shout, so we just sat at the side of the room and drank from our styrofoam cups, but even just watching was fun. Yubi moved her head from side to side in time with the music the deejay was playing, and I tapped my feet. Since nobody asked us to dance, we danced together a couple of times. Yubi said that's how you do it, that's how you let men know you like to dance. And she was right, because pretty soon men were asking her to dance. Every once in a while, she'd check back to make sure I was okay, sweat beading up at her temples, and she'd blot at her face with a paper napkin, then go back out on the floor. And I was pretty happy just watching everybody have fun, especially Yubi, because she really loves to dance fast and knows how to move her hips so it looks just right.

I drank my beer and Yubi's beer, and I got a little drunk. Then I got more when our cups were empty. After I sat back down, a guy in jeans and a sweatshirt came up and asked me to dance. I said, "No, not to this, not fast. I'm too old for this kind of dancing," and he asked me how old I was. He looked about thirty, so I said, "Ten years too old for you," and right then a polka came on and he smiled and took my wrist, leading me out on the dance floor. We danced in two big circles on the floor, and every time Yubi's circle passed

mine she'd squeal out "Elizabeth," as if she was on a roller-coaster
ride. Then when the polka was over, a slow song came on, and we
danced to that. After that, I said I had to sit down and he said thanks
for the dance, and that was that. Or it would have been that, except
for the fact that Yubi got the car stuck when we left at midnight,
and we were walking up the hill to the house when Johnson came
by in his pickup and drove us home.

So that's how we met, and Johnson likes to talk about it sometimes, because he says he was miserable back then. And I guess I
like to talk about it too, because I was lonely when I met him, even
if I didn't realize it, even if I hadn't believed I could fall in love
again, ever.

I have a sink of strawberries from Lander's farm, and I'm paring out
the stems to make freezer jam. It's June and the kitchen is hot.
Outside the sun is white, and the sky is white, and the lake stretches
out like sheet metal all the way to the horizon. From the window
I watch as a steamer breasts the breakwater. I burned my back and
arms picking berries yesterday, and Joey burned too, from his neck
to the top of his shorts, and both of us are wearing white T-shirts
today and have Nivea greased across our shoulders. I can see him
from the window, his little rump sagging in the red hammock that
hangs between the oak and the pole to the clothesline, and he's
reading a book about volcanoes while Johnson mows the lawn. I'm
worried about the grass stirring up Joey's asthma, but Johnson says
ninety-nine percent of all asthma is psychological and that maybe I
shouldn't worry so much. Johnson knows a lot about everything but
not in a know-it-all way.

I'm standing there at the sink with a box fan on the table going
full blast at my back. I've got the radio turned up loud to the Devonsport station when Johnson pulls up on the mower he borrowed
from our neighbor and comes in the back door mad. He walks to

the refrigerator and opens the door, stands there a minute, then pulls out the water bottle.

"Get a glass," I tell him. If I don't say that he'll drink right out of the jug. He doesn't move, he just looks at me with sweat slipping down his face and grass plastered to his calves where it flies up from the John Deere. So I pull a blue plastic tumbler from the side drainer and hand it to him. He's breathing fast and he's biting his lip, so I know something's eating at him, I just don't know what. So I say, "Johnson, what's wrong?" He just stands there, shaking his head as he drinks the cold water from the tumbler in a steady series of swallows. So I say, "Johnson, is something wrong? Did you get a letter from your kids or something?" I don't usually prod him this way. He's a talker. I don't have to prod. "Johnson?" I say.

"Jesus, Joseph, and Mary," he sighs. He's a great one for sighs. On bad days, like ex-anniversaries, he wakes up with heavy breaths and sighs all through breakfast. On bad days he goes on with his sad sighing until I grab him and rub my hands through his curly dark hair and tell him he's going to hyperventilate if he doesn't stop breathing that way. "Life's too short to go around making yourself faint-headed," I warn him.

He's standing there sighing and wiping his neck with two squares of pink-flowered paper towel. Then he says, "God damn your ex-husband, Elizabeth," and I look at him over my shoulder as I pull the drain in the sink. "This thing with Eddie is doing Joey in, you know that," and I nod my head. "He's out in the hammock, and I've been trying to talk to him. I even tried to get him to ride the mower with me, said I'd teach him to work the gears. But he says that he's worried about Eddie, and he's sitting out there watching cars go by because he thinks his dad might come back and get him too. And it stinks that he has to go through this. It really stinks."

"Johnson," I say, "I've looked for Eddie. I've gone to the police, I hired an investigator, you know that. And the court doesn't know where he is any more than we do," I say, and he frowns. Then he slams his fist against the refrigerator so Joey's magnetic letters rattle and some drop to the floor. "And I've called Jim's family and gone every place I can think of where they might be," I add softly as the last bit of sand and water sucks out of the sink. The berries spread thick over the white enamel, and I say, "It's awful, I know, but we just have to live with it for now. And I'm doing the best I can."

"I can't imagine you married to a man like that," he says, and I wince, fighting tears as I start scooping berries into the colander.

"That was a long time ago," I say, breathing deeply. "But you know what's the worst?" I add. "It's that he took Eddie and not Joey, or didn't take them both, because Joey is not as clever or slick as his brother, that's what. And he gets sick right and left. And he looks just like me, pink and blond and fuzzy, and Eddie looks just like a real Italian, just like Jim," and now I am crying in earnest. "Parents aren't supposed to pick favorites."

I bought the house in Devonsport after Jim and I called it quits. Yubi called me in the city and told me to move on up. We'd been friends since high school, even back when black girls and white girls didn't hang around much. We'd been friends since we both lied about our ages to get jobs at the Dairy Queen on Division Street, saying we were sixteen when really we weren't. One night at closing the place got robbed by a guy with panty hose over his head who tied me and Yubi together with an extension cord in the restroom. When you're fifteen, even the bad things turn out good. Like Yubi and me. There's nothing that can come between us after spending eleven hours back to back in a dark smelly bathroom, afraid that guy would come back and kill us like he said he might.

After Jim and I broke up, Yubi said to come up and see her, to get out of the city, to clean out my heart. She'd gone up to Traverse for summer work, cherry picking, canning factories, work she said let her mind go off while she did it. Work so easy she could sing to the radio while doing it and not make any mistakes. It was Yubi's idea to settle up here like this, to buy one of the old houses in Devonsport and rent out the rooms, even if I was only thinking about temporary things at the time. I'd lived my whole life in Grand Rapids. I'd lived my whole life in other people's houses, with my mom till she died, then with Jim in one rental house after the other, moving sideways and never really up.

I bought my own place, a three-story brick house, and it sits at the top of the town looking down over the bluffs and dunes that run along the lake. Jim and I had split up our savings and it took every penny to make the down payment, but it was worth it. The winters are cold because the place doesn't have much insulation, which is the reason we got it so cheap, but Yubi and Johnson are planning to fix that in August. And the place feels good when I walk in the door, like home should, with high ceilings, and I've stripped all the woodwork, and I've got four boarders and Johnson.

I'd been in the house almost a year, from January to November, when Jim took Eddie and never brought him back. Yubi says Jim's a cold-hearted bastard, that he's trying to break my spirit, that he's trying to drive me crazy. I say if anyone knows how to break me, it's Jim, even if he once said he loved me more than life itself and wrote me a poem to prove it.

Sometimes at night I sit on the bed and stare at myself in the mirror. I try to see what's different, what's changed, what's there now that wasn't there with Jim. He said I was the one who changed, after all, not him, but I only see who I am. Me. Elizabeth. I don't really think Jim's trying to hold on to the past, at least not how it was when we were married. I think he's trying to teach me a lesson, and he thinks he can do that with Eddie, and it's rotten how he's hurt Joey in doing it.

He blamed me for the divorce, saying if I'd never taken that job at the V.A. hospital that our life wouldn't have gotten so messed up. Something happened to me when I took that job, and that's what I can't see when I look in the mirror, trying to figure it out. The closest I can come to explaining it, is that the world inside that place was more real than the world outside. I was an attendant, so I really got to work with the men there, and I realized how you can't predict what life will give you, even if you plan. I'd be with those guys all day, spooning in food to someone who didn't know me from Adam, changing diapers, or shuffling cards for the ones without hands. There were old guys there, guys from World War II, and ones from Korea, Nam, stroke victims, guys with plates in their heads, quadriplegics, guys with kids, guys that used to have the world by the balls. Eight hours a day I'd love those men who'd been dumped off there to die. I'd go home to Jim and the kids after work and get scared, start thinking how nothing lasts forever, everything is just for now, how there is no promise of life ever being what you expected. Jim said I should quit because he was tired of coming home to a woman all tied up in knots over nothing. He said, "Over nothing." That killed me. But I couldn't quit. I needed what I got from those guys, needed it like a fix, because it made me so full, and Jim couldn't do that.

Maybe that is a little thing to break up a marriage over. I don't know. I just know I needed Jim to wake up and see that life is something new each day, to look at his kids and say, "Jesus, I made these kids with Elizabeth," to say, "The sun came up this morning and isn't that pretty great?" But Jim was going to be the best production manager at Keebler, ever. He was going to whip his crew into shape and change their attitudes. He went off to work at six every morning and came home at seven or eight in the evening. His clothes smelled like cinnamon and nutmeg and almonds. The scent never washed off his skin.

One night he came home and I was crying because Don D'Ambrosio died on my shift. The boys were watching television, and I was trying to fix goulash, but every other second I was crying and trying not to. I was trying to believe that Don really was better off dead, because he'd been so unhappy lying in bed and not really living like he did before half his belly got blown away. Jim came in and took one look at me and said, "What the hell's going on here?" and I told him about Don, how I was holding his hand when he died. Then he told me to get hold of myself, because the boys shouldn't see me so upset.

"I am upset," I told him. "And maybe the boys should see me like this. Maybe they should realize that life is not all one big party. Maybe they should see that things get a little rough sometimes."

"They're going to think something is wrong here," Jim said.

"Well," I said. "You know what? Something is."

Johnson comes over to the kitchen sink and stands behind me. He places his wide hands on my shoulders and spreads his fingers, pressing gently against my T-shirt and sunburn. "Elizabeth," he says softly, and I turn, leaning into him hard and quick. "God, I wish I could help you," he says. "I go around here fixing things up, but the one thing you need most, I can't give you. Do you want to get another lawyer?" he asks as I cry against the sweaty, damp warmth of his chest. "Yubi says we could hire a different investigator."

I twist then and look through the window to the yard. Joey is standing near the edge of the road, kicking in the dust so it rises in a cloud at his ankles. I've paid three different agencies to track Jim down, but they've all trailed just a step behind him. They can tell me where he's been, not where he is at this minute.

Johnson feels me looking out the window, and he turns just enough to see Joey lift his hand to his eyes and rub. "I wish I could help him," he adds, and I start to cry harder, choking against Johnson's chest.

We're standing there when Yubi comes up from the basement. She's humming some church song under her breath, and we don't move apart when she walks into the kitchen. She goes, "Oops," teasing, like maybe she's caught us kissing, then she sees I'm upset. "What's going on here?" she says, and puts her hands at the flare of her hips. She stands there looking at us with the wicker laundry basket overflowing at her feet, and she says, "What's the problem, Baby Bets?" I'm her Baby Bets, white, tightest friend.

Johnson shakes his head. "Elizabeth is just having a hard time. We were talking about Eddie and how Jim took him off."

"Girl," she says, and whistles through her teeth, "that is enough to make anybody cry. Cry a river, if you ask me, Baby Bets. Lord," she says as she turns, carrying the laundry down the hall to the den, and we hear her going on. "That Jim is nothing but a cold, ugly, nasty S.O.B., I'm telling you, God ain't done with him yet, no sir, he's going to have to do some kind of praying to save his white ass when they catch him." Then the television comes on loud with soap opera music, and she closes the door, and it's quiet again.

Johnson and I just stand there awhile, and after a bit I quit my crying, shuddering down inside his arms. I pull away from him then, from the lawn-mower scent of his chest, and I smile. I look at his face and rub a smudge of motor oil from his chin. He's been crying too. "You miss your kids, don't you?" I say, and he nods. "Aren't we a pair?" I laugh gently, and he closes one eye, then he opens both of them wide, green eyes with thick, black lashes.

"That we are," he says, and he pulls me against him, so close I can hear his heart.

Jim and I fought about sex. He said what I needed was to go see a shrink, because after Joey came along, I didn't enjoy things so much. It hadn't always been like that. Once upon a time, I couldn't wait for him to get home from baking cookies to jump into bed with me. Once upon a time, in another world, I'd stick Eddie down for a nap at lunch, and Jim would race in for a quickie. It was just that after Joey arrived, things changed. There was laundry and diapers and feedings and flu shots and earaches to deal with. And Joey's delivery itself was a nightmare.

I went home from the hospital with my belly all flabby and a sunken, sore half-moon where they'd finally had to reach in and save Joey. I couldn't nurse him like I did with Eddie, because I was sick the second time after losing so much blood. Then the incision got infected, and my bladder prolapsed. So there I was, carrying around a baby who was all gassed up on formula and crying, my bladder leaking into my panties, and Jim grouching out loud that I was just about as fun as a corpse. Life isn't always fun, I told him.

A few months of living in the middle of all that, and I decided on my own to get help. As I dialed through the list of family counselors in the phone book, the hardest part was explaining the exact kind of help I thought I needed. Even once I figured out what I had was marital problems, I hadn't been prepared for being placed on a waiting list. I left my name with half a dozen clinics and got referred to several others, and not one with any opening sooner than two months away. Then just when I'd given up believing that I'd ever find help, Dr. Lois Harper left a message at work for me to call her.

In the middle of my afternoon break, Dr. Harper took my call as I stood there at the pay phone in the hospital lobby. "Elizabeth," she greeted me. Her voice was throaty and warm, and not what I'd expected. "I got your name through Family Central, and I have an opening tomorrow evening if you'd like to come in." It was as simple as driving downtown after work. It was as simple as saying I'd be there.

From our very first session in her third-floor office, I knew Dr. Harper was exactly what I needed. She was a large, round woman, fleshy all over, and with a great shelf of breasts that rested on her belly. While she appeared over forty, that might have meant fifty or sixty, but I couldn't quite guess, as her face was pale and plumply softened. She filled the door to her office side to side, and had a big head of bouncing red curls and blue eyes. I'd expected to meet someone in a gray skirt and jacket, perhaps topped with a white cotton lab coat, and I got Dr. Harper in a lavender jumpsuit tied off with a paisley sash. I'd expected a woman wearing horn-rimmed glasses and sensible shoes, and I got purple velvet slippers and burgundy nails. I'd expected something else, but I found what I needed. I found someone who laughed as much as she listened.

Dr. Harper's laughter surprised me at first, as I'd been hurting inside for so long. The first week we sat there face-to-face in matching blue recliners, rocking forward and back until I'd gone through the list of my problems at home. "And?" she smiled brightly when I seemed to finish up.

"And?" I echoed back, then I paused. "And I think I'm going crazy, that's what," I cried, and she lay back in her chair and started laughing out loud.

"I'd feel crazy, too," she announced. "I'd feel absolutely mad," she smiled. "It's okay to feel crazy." Then she rocked forward and handed me a box of blue tissues, staring straight into my eyes as I blew my nose. "And there are ways to make things better," she promised in a whisper.

Dr. Harper's laughter let me learn I could turn crazy into something else. Between listening and laughing, I started to believe there were all kinds of chances for things to work out, and that life could be a balance of both pain and hope. I learned that I could take responsibility for enjoying sex, if I wanted to, but that was the part Jim didn't get. The part about wanting to. I went alone to my appointments at first, then Jim started going with me when we kept having problems in bed. That was Dr. Harper's suggestion, but mostly Jim just liked to tell her what was wrong with me, and how nothing was wrong with him. She suggested ways to help me to learn to relax and explained how he could ease up a bit. But Jim never'd been easy before that, and he kept on hovering over me, rubbing me so hard that I felt like I was being erased. I was tired, and my heart turned away. So I faked it, moaned out some version of ecstasy, and of course I felt guilty and horrible. And sad.

I talked to Yubi about it. I had to tell someone. She said she'd probably fake it too, if she were me. "Absolutely, Baby Bets." Then she added, "And if I was afraid of losing my man." And she said, "Are you?"

"Am I what?" I said.

"Afraid of losing him?" She smiled.

"No," I sighed, and I meant it. "You know what I want, Yubi? I want a little tenderness, a little patience, just a little. That's all," I said.

"Girl, don't we all," she said. "Don't we all."

Johnson's thirty-three and I'm forty-one, and I tell him I like the difference. He says my age makes me more stable, more compassionate. More grounded, he tells me.

"Than young girls with smooth skin?" I ask him, and he blushes.

"That's not what I mean," he says. I tell him there are a lot of us around. "No," he says. "Not like you. See," he explains, "you weren't looking for somebody."

He likes to throw off the covers at night and look at me naked, run his fingertips over my nipples and trace my scar with his lips. I get embarrassed, tell him not to look so close or he'll get scared, but a part of me likes it. His ex is an aerobic dance instructor with black hair cut close to her head. Sometimes I think about that when we're in bed, think that I might not measure up. But Johnson's so patient, those thoughts don't stay around for long.

Johnson's got wide shoulders, but he's a little flabby. Not much, but not perfect either. And when we're in bed I don't forget how I look, but it just doesn't matter so much anymore, because I am just me and Johnson is just Johnson, and it's all that we got. And sometimes when we're done, I lie there and smile and he goes, "A penny for your thoughts," or something silly like that.

So I tell him, I go, "You know what's so great is that this is so ordinary. So lovely and ordinary," and he smiles. It's the closest I get to talking about love.

In August I tell Johnson I will give him the money if he wants to fly his kids up for a visit. "No," he says. "But thank you for offering. Maybe at Christmas."

We're on the third floor, putting in a shower and a stool so there'll be a john up there for the boarders. It was Johnson's idea to fix up a bathroom for them. He says it'll be more private that way, that the two floors we live on will be our own then. So I go, "Hey, if it's the money that's keeping you from saying yes, please take it. I have enough from the rent."

"No," he says. "Besides, I think Joey is getting used to having me to himself." Then he says, "I got a job in September."

"You're kidding," I say. "No one gets work up here out of season."

"I did," he smiles. "I'm going to fill in at the high school for a woman who is out on maternity leave. I'll teach biology and earth science."

"You said you didn't want to teach if you didn't have to," I say. "You said Saginaw ruined you on that, especially high school."

"I said that?"

"Yes. You said that last spring."

"Well," he says. "A lot has happened since then. Right?" he says. "Right?" He frowns for a moment as he tightens the shower head, then shouts, "Watch out," and turns on the water. "It works!" he cries in genuine surprise, which surprises me back. I think he's a genius. He pulls me inside of the fiberglass stall, then he kisses me under the water. When I close my eyes, it feels just like rain.

Joey is ten, and he's always had asthma in the fall, every year, no fail. But this year it isn't so bad, and the doctor says being on the lake helps. And Johnson has allergies, so the two of them come home from school and take their medication and hang out together. Sometimes they work in the yard, or they watch television together on the couch. Joey tells Johnson things he never tells me, and I'm surprised at the things I hear secondhand. Johnson's right about Joey thinking his father doesn't love him, but he doesn't push him to talk about it. And I don't think he's trying to replace Jim. Not really. I think he's trying to be a friend.

In September, when everyone is gone during the day, I get a little itchy thinking about Eddie. Now that cherry-canning season is over, Yubi got hired on at the lumber store as a cashier. I don't have her to talk to, and the boarders all work daytime jobs. So it's just me in the house thinking about things and painting the front hallway and freezing vegetables in Ziploc bags and labeling them.

And then late one Friday afternoon the phone rings, and it's Eddie. I can hardly believe it, because I'm always thinking about him, but when I hear his voice on the phone I can't figure out what to do. He goes, "Mom, I want to come home. I miss you and Joey."

So I get my voice real level, because I am about in tears, and I say, "You can come home any time you want. Just tell me where you are."

"I'm in Grand Rapids with Dad. We've been here six months, but he said you knew I was here," he sniffles. "Dad said you wanted me here because I needed to spend time with him, and that with Joey getting sick all the time, that two boys were too much trouble for you," and then he is crying and trying to catch his breath.

I'm mad as hell at his father, but I try to sound calm. "Listen, honey, your father didn't tell you the truth. I've always wanted you here, and I've never stopped wanting you here, ever, and I mean that. Just tell me where you're living, and I'll come and get you."

"Dad'll kill me," he says.

"Eddie," I cry out then, "your dad broke the law when he took you away." My voice is shaking. "I can't come and get you unless you tell me where you are," I explain.

"3149 Westphalia," he answers. "But I think we're moving."

"Why?" I say. "Why?"

"Dad is packing all our things again," he says, then he starts crying again. "Mom," he says in a quiet little voice, "come get me."

"Don't worry," I tell him, trying to reassure him, even though my heart is breaking up in my chest. "You just hold on, because I'll be there."

By the time Johnson's car is coming up the hill, I'm wild and running out the door. I'm still telling him about the phone call as we drive out of town. Joey is sitting in back, and he's asking a million questions and I tell him to just take it easy, that nobody knows what will happen. But we're too late, because by the time we get to the address on Westphalia, the sun is setting, and Eddie and Jim are gone. We go to the houses in the neighborhood and ask people if they know Eddie or Jim, but they don't. And I can't believe Jim's been with Eddie in Grand Rapids all this time, almost on the street we once lived on as a family, and I can't believe they are gone, and nothing Johnson can say will stop me from crying. Nothing.

The next couple of months I'm really low, and I tell Johnson I feel like I've gone past the bottom and I'm hanging in space. I spend my days calling long-distance directory assistance in Michigan cities and asking for listings under Jim's name, but without any luck. He's vanished again, and I can't pass a minute without thinking about Eddie. Half the time I can't eat, and when I do I throw up. Johnson's good with Joey, taking him roller skating and to play putt-putt golf in town. I go from feeling helpless about Eddie, then to feeling bad about how Joey's stuck in the middle of this mess. More than anything at this point, even with Johnson to take up the slack, Joey's my son, and he needs to believe that I won't let him down, but I'm in a slump and I can't get out.

One day we go into town to eat at the inn and there's a family there with six kids, and the mother, a skinny redhead, keeps saying their names, and they all start with *K*. She goes, "Kerry, stop that. Kim, let go of Kyle. Kelly, wipe your face. Krissy, Kevin, sit up and eat." I sit there and watch them and my food gets cold, and I can't stop watching them. Johnson takes me home and puts me to bed and sticks a thermometer under my tongue and a heating pad at my feet. He says I need to see a doctor. I say I will. But most of all I need to see Eddie, and I feel like I could kill his father. I could. If only I had the chance.

So I go to the doctor and find out I'm pregnant. I guess I knew all along. But I can't make up my mind to tell Johnson. I can't decide if I really want to be a mother again at my age, and with things like they are. And just when I decide I could love a new baby if I had one, that maybe it would be the best thing, I find a note from Johnson on the edge of my dresser. He tells me he'll be gone for a while, and to please, please not worry. And it's signed, "Love, Johnson."

Yubi says Johnson really has gone to see his kids because the school says that too. In the note he said he'd be back, all that kind of stuff, but I don't believe it and I don't care. The doctor says I'm almost three months along, but it's not really a baby to me, not in my head. Not like it was with the boys when I wanted a family so bad, even if Jim and I fought. So at three full months, I'll make up my mind, decide if I'll have it. I tell Yubi I got a bun in the oven, and she says it's a sign, and I say she's crazy. I don't believe in mystical junk like that. All I know is, there is this little knot growing inside me, and I should have told Johnson I loved him.

It's the middle of November, and it still hasn't snowed, and Johnson's been gone three weeks. I tell Yubi I think he cut out. She says she doesn't think so, Johnson's not that kind of guy. I say what does she know, maybe he got back with his ex-wife aerobic dance instructor with the sleek body. Yubi says not to think like that. I tell her I can if I want. She says go ahead, nobody's stopping me.

So I wake up on a Thursday, the day I told Yubi I'd decide about the baby. If Johnson had come back. Yubi says to make up my mind for myself, because the one thing that should be important is what I think.

Around noon, I put on my coat and red rubber boots and walk down the beach to the breakwater. All the kids are in school, and the summer people have left, and the dunes are empty. The wind's blowing sideways, flattening the tufts of grass that cling to the sand. Both foghorns are sounding, first one then the other, echoing back and forth between the lighthouse at the end of the pier and the Coast Guard tower on shore. The water is rolling in so hard I can barely make out the wailing of the seagulls hovering over me, and each time a wave hits the breakwater it bursts into spray. I stand at the end of the pier for a while and think about what I should do, listening to the call and response of the foghorns.

Mostly I'm thinking about chances with Johnson, about chances for happiness, the chance for this baby, the chance that I'll end up alone again. I stand there at the end of the pier and I make up my mind. I'm going to have this baby. I will have this baby because I miss Eddie, and Joey needs a family, and because I think Johnson is long gone. And in the end I know I've made the right decision, even if it was a hard one, even if I had to make it alone.

The next morning I take the old bread and rolls from the kitchen and climb down the hill to the lake. It rained all night long, and the day is thick with mist. The gulls hover and cling in a swooping circle as I toss up crusts and crumbs. I'm walking back up the hill to the house, thinking about how I'll tell Yubi I'm keeping the baby, when I see Joey coming around back by the porch. His yellow rain slicker is sailing behind him, and I start to run toward him, holding my arms out. And then I have to stop for a minute. My breath is short from climbing, and I can already feel the baby pressing against my bladder.

I'm standing there holding my side and thinking about making French toast for breakfast, when another boy rounds the house, taller than Joey, dark, and yelling, and I know in a flash that it's Eddie.

There's no stopping me then. I'm racing over the wet grass, slipping in the mud by the garden as Eddie rushes against me. I'm holding him then, so tight and hard that he squeals, lifting him up until his legs wrap around my waist.

I've got Eddie at my shoulder by the garden when Yubi comes around the corner of the house, shouting and picking her way barefoot across the backyard. Her hair's still up on her head in red plastic rollers, and she's shouting and laughing. She's laughing and hollering out, "Baby Bets, hold on." She's hollering my name, and right behind her is Johnson, with Eddie's suitcase in his hand.

My son was eight when my father died, and as I attempted to come to terms with my own sense of loss over the next few years, I wasn't always aware of the exact nature of the grieving I'd left him to do on his own. Throughout the first six years following my divorce, my father had joyfully taken over the role my son's father had abandoned. However, it wasn't until I dove back into the work of transforming an earlier draft of "Chances with Johnson" that I realized that my son's loss of his grandfather had struck a double blow: simply put, losing the second male figure in his life underscored the absence of the first. As I worked through the process of leading Elizabeth and Johnson into their dance of tentative steps, I realized the ways in which Joey embodied the many sadnesses I'd come to recognize in my own child. And with each movement I crafted between Joey and his mother, I returned to the world of my son with a greater sense of what would allow him to feel grounded and secure and protected. Now, as my son races toward adulthood, I realize that I've provided him with far more than I'd thought possible a few years back. I allowed him the opportunity to watch me learn the feeling of hope, and I have taught him that there are all kinds of chances for happiness in this world.

P.K.G.

Deeds of Love
and Rage

◻

MARSHA LEE BERKMAN

We are a troubled family. Ephraim left three months ago and
Cecilia and I have had to confront each other like enemies who
suddenly find themselves at the same party. Yesterday we quarreled
and today, dressed in a pair of faded blue denim shorts and a yellow
T-shirt that says "Foxy" in flowery iridescent letters, she moves
through the house sulking. She is the only thing in motion on this
hot sultry day.

My only child . . . Her dark uncombed hair straggles around a
thin face and sad thirteen-year-old eyes swollen from lack of sleep.
Last night through the flimsy walls of our apartment, I heard her
weeping, and this morning her whole face slumps in sorrow and
rage. It is all my fault. I can see it in the frown that bridges her
forehead. If only I would make concessions, try harder, her father
would come back. And so we are doomed to this summer that
continues to stretch endlessly before us, a time that hardly seems to
be real at all but just a series of minutes, hours, days to be gotten
through and endured together. How we have begun to dislike each
other. By the end of summer Ephraim and I shall come to a decision
for the sake of the child, but now we are still wavering back and

forth. Yes, I can tell from the way her black eyes glow with a fierce fury: she is as tired of me as I am of her.

At the beginning of June Ephraim packed up his bags and took an apartment and a job on the other side of the city. He does not have enough space, he says. How foreign that word sounds on his tongue. We had begun to chip each other into little bits and pieces. Ephraim will not admit it, but sometimes I think it was the strain of the child.

As a baby she was perpetually restless and moody. She came into the world too soon, bounding feet first from the womb. I had nothing prepared. No, not even her name. I had to snatch that also without thought. She cried day and night, refusing any of the usual things, and Ephraim and I would take turns rising from our sleep, moaning with fatigue, too tired to comfort each other for this strange being who had taken over our lives.

Thirteen years and still she remains a puzzle to me, her moods flashing back and forth, a mood for every moment of the day. A look, a remark, or some dark demon within can change her in an instant. I was too old to have her. Yes, I am certain it must be that. But Ephraim is a religious man. He used to say that suffering cleanses the soul, that burdens are to be borne.

"It is a sign," he said then, clasping his heavy hands together, closing and unfolding them nervously, considering it. To Ephraim there is a purpose in the world that escapes me. There are things that we are not supposed to understand. He prefers the difficult to the simple, certain that God is testing him. He was not an easy man to live with.

This morning when Cecilia asks if her father is coming for the Sabbath, which begins at sundown, I tell her that it is hopeless. "Your father is impossible," I blurt out in a weak moment, saying it passionately, throwing up my hands in a gesture of despair. I can hear my voice rising unpleasantly, and as soon as the words are out of my mouth, I am sorry. But it is already too late.

She turns on me. "Bitch," she says without a sound, mouthing the letters with her lips. At first I ignore her. It is far too hot to respond, to become embroiled in another one of these arguments. Anyhow, what would be the use? Let her vent her wrath on me. Let her get it out of her system, think that her father's absence is my fault. What harm can it do? But then she says it again, and this time she whispers it, but loudly enough for me to hear the ugly sound reverberate in the room.

"Bitch," she says a third time, growing bolder. The word explodes from her mouth, chilling me to the bone although the sun is seeping resolutely through the drapes and the room is sweltering with the heat.

"Bitch," she says again and again, unable to stop, her face contorted with rage. I feel my heart beating faster within the cage of my body, fluttering against the armor of my bones, and, rising, I slap her face, so hard that it stings my hand and leaves an ugly red mark on her skin.

She runs to her room and the door slams shut. I can hear the click of her lock snapping closed, then loud sobs as she gasps for breath. I imagine her flung sideways across her bed, her hair falling wildly over the edge, beating the pillow with her tight closed fists, and suddenly I am filled with pity for her and shame for myself.

Through the long hours of the morning she remains in retreat and will not come out. Finally I pound on the door and order her to open it, but the only sound is the steady whirring of a fan. Frightened that she has done something rash, racked with guilt that I have lost control, I take a hanger and, bending it, work diligently at the keyhole until at last I swing open the door.

She has stopped crying but her face is splotched with red and there is still an angry imprint where my hand crossed her cheek. She is pouting on the bed, her eyes puffy, her lower lip thrust forward. She will not even look at me. The curtains are drawn against the heat and in the dim shadowed light of the room I see that she has strewn candy wrappers over the floor. An empty Coke bottle sprawls on its side against the dresser. A lonely sock protrudes beneath the bed. A trail of dirty clothes trace a path through the room and end in a corner next to stacks of *True Confessions* magazines littering the rug.

"Come out," I say as calmly as I am able, swallowing hard for what we have done to each other, what we continue to do. "We'll make up. Everything will be all right." I try to appear more confident than I really am. "You're only hurting yourself, you know." The words sound as hollow and meaningless as when my own mother uttered them, and I am aware that this sort of logic will never reach her.

"Look," I say, trying to keep my voice steady. "It has nothing to do with you." I keep my eyes fixed firmly on her face although she continues to stare stubbornly at the floor. "It's between your father and me."

At last she lifts heavy lids to look up defiantly. A difficult age, I think, and she is more difficult than most. Beneath that yellow T-shirt with the ludicrous letters, her breasts rise as supple as ripe fruit. Under her arms I see black prickly hair sprouting like desert scrub. She will not let me see her naked anymore. Once I came into the room, catching her by surprise, and saw with a shock that triangle of womanly hair on her body. Now we stare at each other without speaking. Suddenly overcome with remorse, I long to tell her that I am sorry but the moment passes and instead I say nothing. I retreat and she rises mournfully to take a shower.

When I hear the water running full force, I decide to call Ephraim. He is an engineer, capable of correcting the errors of vast machinery.

Perhaps it is still possible for him to correct the errors of our lives. I dial his number at work and he answers the phone himself, startling me, as though he has been standing there all along, arms crossed over his chest in a familiar posture, waiting for me to call.

"Ephraim," I begin, without bothering to ask how he is, "come home tonight. We are eating each other alive."

"On Sunday," he says wearily, for we have been through this before. Ephraim refuses to come on Friday for Shabbes. It is too far he says. He is afraid that something will happen before he gets here and he will have to travel after sundown when it is forbidden. A thousand and one disasters pass through his mind. The car will stall and leave him stranded. A train could have an accident, God forbid. A bus could be hijacked on the highway (he has read of it happening), and he will be caught as night falls and the Sabbath descends without a prayer to stand on.

"Too late," I say. "By Sunday we'll both be dead."

"Don't worry," he answers solemnly as though he hasn't even heard me. "I will pray for us." Suddenly I can see him standing in the fading light, his prayer shawl draped over his shoulders, a skullcap on his balding dome—at dawn, at dusk, in heat or cold, swaying and rocking on the balls of his feet, summoning the God of Israel, communing with his Maker. He is in the wrong century, I think, the wrong life. He should have been Abraham journeying beneath a starry sky, Moses adrift in the wilderness, Jeremiah making his lonely vigil through the desolate city of Jerusalem.

"Ephraim, Ephraim," I plead, desperation overtaking my voice. "Live a little! Take a chance. What harm can it do?" But he is older, more set in his ways. I can hear him sighing and struggling with himself.

"Yes, I'll pray," he repeats again, but he sounds exhausted, as though what is happening to us is all too much for him.

"What good will your prayers do? What good is your God?" I cry, aware that I am beginning to descend over the edge. Then I decide on another tactic and this time my voice is softer, cajoling. "Come home, Ephraim," I say. "I need you. I want you."

I can almost hear the catch in his voice, the hesitation as he thinks it through.

"For the child, Ephraim," I persist.

"It is too difficult," he murmurs at last.

"Ah, Ephraim," I say, "*life* is difficult," but he has made up his mind. He is firm, refusing to commit himself. "For shame," I cry, and slam down the phone.

Tonight, tomorrow he will not even answer it. Once I let the phone ring a hundred times just to test him, knowing that he was there, swaying silently in the dark. Cecilia calls him late at night when she thinks I am asleep. I can hear her whispering about me, telling him how hard it is for us to get along, how she wishes he would come back. Now, hearing footsteps, I wonder if she has been standing there all along. I turn on the tap and quickly splash my burning face with cold water. But even so I can feel myself flushing as though she has caught me in a disreputable act. Her eyes are red and rimmed with fatigue but she has changed her clothes, and clipped her wet hair back from her forehead. Yet the place where I struck her continues to stain her cheek, forming a barrier between us. She says nothing, her face an impassive mask. Perhaps she has not heard anything after all and it is only my imagination which tortures me.

"Come," I say, trying to make the best of a bad day. "It's time to get ready for Shabbes." Before the sun sets we must clean the house, polish the silver, cook the dinner, and bake the bread. In these matters Ephraim has trained her well. She obeys me silently, without a word of complaint. I uncover the dough that we prepared earlier, and we take out the bread tray and the silver candlesticks that need polishing. On the shelf next to them a sad solitary imprint marks the spot where Ephraim's wine cup stood.

She places a board on the kitchen table and her fingers move deftly over the dough, pounding and kneading it into shape, her face coloring with the heat, her eyes intent on her task. At last she twists it into thick braids to slip into the oven, pinching off a piece which she burns in an ancient ritual, closing her eyes and moving her lips in silent supplication as she has seen me do. What does she yearn for behind those sorrowful eyes? What thoughts does she think? For the past year she has suffered with nightmares that wake her up screaming in the middle of the night, as though striving to be released from some dread torment that will not leave her alone. In the morning when I come into her room I see her sheets twisted into knots, as though demons have tied them during the night.

"A stage," the doctor says, but I know better. She has always been this way. Now just more so. Sometimes I think that when I am old and defenseless, unable to take care of myself, I will have to live with her and then she will vent her stored-up rage upon my helpless body like that dough beneath her hands.

I want to say, "Tell me what you're thinking, Cecilia," but she is far away, her gaze focusing on something else, caught in a web of her own thoughts.

Yesterday to calm us both I prepared a picnic supper to take to the park. Other families were there, too, and we spread a blanket on the grass and had cold slices of roast beef and potato salad. When the ice cream man came around we bought cherry Popsicles and sat at the edge of the playground to eat them. Children were swinging, and, watching them, Cecilia decided to pump her own skinny legs high over the sandboxes, soaring higher and higher until her face was filled with a strange, gentle joy. Afterward, she sat very close to me and laid her head upon my shoulder, her eyes tranquil, her expression subdued. But by evening it was obvious that she was brooding. We quarreled, and later I heard her crying until I finally turned over and fell asleep.

She is still working soundlessly as the heat builds to a peak of intensity and I pause to step outside on our small balcony, where we have some hanging plants that are rapidly wilting, and two old porch chairs that Ephraim keeps meaning to paint. We are on a quiet street at the very end of a cul-de-sac, and an occasional car, coming down here by mistake, will turn around beneath our porch. But now there is not a sign of life. Across the street windows are sleepy lids, blinds and drapes closed against the broiling sun. The heat is suffocating. From next door I hear the blast of a TV, then a muffled sound as it is quickly turned down. But it is not only the heat which suffocates me. It is the knowledge of what has become of the three of us, of what we are doing to each other.

When I go back into the house Cecilia is still intent on her tasks. She raises her head and looks at me suspiciously without saying anything. The kitchen has become unbearably hot, the sun pouring through the curtains onto the linoleum floor, the futile beating of a fan on top of the refrigerator the only noise that breaks the silence. I join her and we work side by side without uttering a word. Beads of perspiration gather on her forehead and above her upper lip, and I wonder again what she is thinking behind those inscrutable eyes.

"Cecilia," I long to say, "let's make up, let's not fight," but something holds me back. Her mouth is pursed tightly together, her jaw clenched, and I decide not to say anything.

Instead, I open the oven and take out the bread, setting it on the counter to cool. It is dark brown, the top of the braids blackened slightly at the tips, and she glances approvingly at it. For a moment she seems about to speak, but then stops as though pride still prevents her. I season the chicken and put it in to roast. The sun continues to splash across the kitchen in waves of heat. I stop to take a bath and nap before dinner, and still we have not spoken since morning.

When I appear an hour later I see that she has spread a white cloth upon the table and set out the best dishes and silver, placing the candlesticks in the center. Over the mound of fragrant bread is a green-and-gold embroidered cover Cecilia made one summer at camp with the word Sabbath in Hebrew. She has changed again, this time into a clean white blouse and white shorts, and her hair is tied back with a light blue ribbon. I am wearing a long print skirt and a colorful top I bought one year in Mexico, and my hair, which is beginning to thread with gray at the sides, is pinned on top of my head with a large tortoiseshell clip.

I turn off the fan and open the windows, drawing back the curtains. For the first time in days the heat has begun to break. A cool breeze stirs the material and they flutter lightly against the screens. Before the sun is ready to disappear behind the tops of the houses like an angry red eye, I light the candles and stand before them, arms upraised to say the blessing that ushers in the day of rest. Cecilia takes her place next to me and even though my eyes are closed I can feel her hands circling the air next to mine, drawing the Sabbath closer.

"A good Shabbes," I say, forcing myself to reach out and put my arms around her shoulders, but her spine stiffens at my touch. Her body remains rigid and she averts her somber pupils from mine, her front teeth biting down hard on the middle of her lower lip.

I set the dinner on the table and then we both sit down, neither of us wanting to acknowledge Ephraim's empty place at the head of the table. Memory recalls his strong blunt hands above Cecilia's bowed head, intoning the patriarchal blessing that always brings such a strange quiet joy to her face.

In his absence I say a prayer of thanksgiving over the bread, breaking it apart with my hands, and then we eat it in thick chunks, greedily, suddenly ravenous.

"It's good," I say. "*Very* good," and she blushes with the praise, her tan cheeks turning rosy beneath the surface.

"Do you really think so?" she asks, and her expression changes as she speaks to me for the first time since morning. "You're not just saying that?"

"No. Really. It's good," I say again and I can see that she is pleased. A slight smile passes over her lips and like soldiers on a battlefield it is clear that we have decided to call a truce for the holiday.

But then, in spite of myself, I remark bitterly, "It's a pity your father couldn't be here to taste it."

For the second time that day I am sorry as soon as the words are out of my mouth. A look of pain crosses her face and her eyes linger longingly on the candles. "But he's coming Sunday, isn't he?" she asks intensely.

"Yes," I say. "Of course. On Sunday." I say it calmly this time to reassure her and perhaps myself as well. It seems to sustain the two of us, and we relax and begin to eat with relish. Gradually a strong breeze gathers outside and blows through the room, releasing us, and it appears that the weight of thirteen years does not rest as heavily on her shoulders. The muted light of the candles catches her features in an unexpected expression, and I am startled to see that it is Ephraim's face before me.

As we eat, lengthening shadows fall over the walls in ghostly shapes. Darkness enfolds us, broken only by the bright headlights flooding the living room when they come to the dead end of our apartment.

Cecilia's brow is furrowed in concentration above the slender bridge of her nose. We make desultory talk and I think how far away we are from each other. At last I set out two melons for dessert and crushed grape ices that we spoon into the hollowed centers of the fruit.

We linger for a while longer, still not speaking, and then I clear off the table while she rises to help, thrusting her arms into the soapy dishwater.

She hands me the dishes and I dry them, placing them one by one on the white counter as we work silently, the light of the candles finally sputtering to a close. The smell of burnt wax fills the air. A full moon illuminates Cecilia's slight figure and I see that the red mark on her cheek is nearly gone.

When we finish I hang up the towel to dry and our glances meet as she turns to go. How fragile she looks, how young, I think, so that I yearn to cry out to her as she disappears into the hushed darkness of the hallway. I am filled with a rush of love for her. Flesh of my flesh. Bone of my bones. Then, as though she has read my mind, suddenly she returns and standing on her tiptoes, kisses me goodnight. "Mother, I'm sorry," she says, and then just as quickly she is gone.

On Sunday Ephraim will come and perhaps things will work out after all. Who knows? But for a while at least in the stillness of this moment there is peace. At last there is peace. And tomorrow or the next day anything seems possible now, anything at all.

Although "Deeds of Love and Rage" is not autobiographical, the events of my own life at the time were somehow transmuted by that mysterious process known as artistic creation into the mother and child of the story. It was written in a burst of passion one hot and difficult summer when I was torn by duty to a trying adolescent, the expectations of a traditional marriage, and my own needs. The story is certainly the most painful I have ever written, and in my effort to write as honestly as I could about the complex emotions of a mother toward her child, it represented a pivotal point in my own development as a writer. For the first time I realized that my experiences, as a woman and as a mother, were as valid as any of the more familiar themes of the male writers I knew. Eventually, it taught me an important lesson: to listen to the pulse of my own heart and to trust my own instincts. However, at the time I was unaware of all that the story would mean—to myself—and to others. Writers with whom I shared the story, particularly men, were so disturbed by the character of the mother that I put it away for two years. One day I came upon it by chance, reread it, and felt again the initial impetus that had generated its birth. I made some minor corrections and decided to send it on its way. More than any other piece I have written, it has somehow touched the deepest nerve and elicited the most moving response. I am grateful to have written it and more grateful still that it has spoken so profoundly to so many.

M.L.B.

THE INSTINCT

FOR BLISS

□

MELISSA PRITCHARD

Frances Waythorn, her face ghastly as a mime's from a souring paste of yogurt, scrubs walls and wainscoting, praying for bleach, polish, order, something, to check her daughter's latest slide from innocence. Pockets the Bic lighter, so Athena can't smoke. Weasels under the bed, dredging out a feculent nest of candy wrappers, cigarette butts, lewd notes, blood-soiled underwear, so Athena won't get fat or have sex or die. Frances's motions are selfless and efficient, her behavior a worship extending into grief. She refuses to acknowledge the poster of Jim Morrison. If she follows her own heart, stripping his deviant's baby face off the wall over her daughter's bed, who knows what might happen. Mothers like Frances are no longer immune from the retaliation of their daughters. Her face beginning to itch under the dried yogurt, Frances swivels a plush bunny into the center of the eyelet-edged pillow. Her child's room is pulled back, once again, into an immaculate relief of white, except for the poster, unexpungeable as a stain.

Athena, legally halved, is batted lightly between her parents. On alternate weeks she is not at her father's, she resides with Frances, her white room declining into a dank, fetid emporium of sloth. Those Sunday afternoons when Athena arrives, a canny refugee, on

215

her mother's doorstep, a soiled, lumpy pillowcase of belongings over one shoulder, declaring she is an atheist who has drunk the blood of stray cats, Frances's labor, much like that of Sisyphus, begins anew, no hope for reprieve, only the diligent untanglement of familiar, defiant knots.

Frances is, in fact, uncrumpling and reading, rereading Athena's smutty notes before packing for her drive to a Navajo wool work-shop when the doorbell rings. Hollering, "Wait," then "Sorry," unlocking the door, her face dripping water and patchy, as if with plaster, she sees he has a lovely, surprisingly tender face, this Officer Ruíz, telling her Athena is at the police station with another girl, arrested for shoplifting. He has been busy, attempting to notify the girls' parents. (Guiltily, Frances remembers three distinct times the phone rang as she scavenged under Athena's bed.)

"Where in God's name is her father? She's staying with him this week."

"Ma'am, from what your daughter claims, Mr. Waythorn is in Albuquerque until tomorrow."

He then informs Frances she can come get Athena, or agree to her being held overnight in juvenile detention.

"Of course I'll get her, though I am about to leave for Arizona. What about the other girl?" Frances asks, not really caring, angry that once again, and predictably, Athena's father has left her in the dark, told her nothing of his plans, neglected his daughter, and spoiled her own small hope for independence.

"Her parents have requested she be held overnight."

"In the Taos jail? Good lord. At their age I was in a convent. Reciting Shakespeare. Doing as I was told. Though Athena's father was a delinquent, a truant, he's boasted that often enough."

Frances's tone is bitter, as if she had known him even then, as if she had been harmed, even then, by her husband's errant boyhood.

■

So far, Frances decides, this driving across the hammered-flat desert is largely a matter of virulent silence.

Athena catches at a shifting avalanche of cassettes falling from her lap.

"May I play the Red Hot Chili Peppers? Their lyrics are banned." With Frances, almost any "Mother may I?" worked.

"Banned?" Frances attends carefully, thinks she identifies the phrase *donkey juice* shouted over and over.

"I can't clearly make them out, honey. The words."

Pleased, Athena spritzes her face and arms with water from the plastic spray bottle she's brought, fogging herself like some fragile, costly plant.

"Want some?"

Tepid mist hits Frances, wetting her face. She has a pale rash from the yogurt.

Right now she would rather feed than punish Athena, pad her with double cheeseburgers, damp fries, chocolate shakes. If she's fat, no boy will want to have sex with her. If she's fat, she might not steal. Possibly no one but her mother will want her. She casts a look at Athena, the combat boots, unpolished and heavy-looking as bricks, shredded jeans, black tank top, the front of her hair in two taffetalike maroon flaps, the back of her head a shaved greenish stubble. The starlike design inked onto her upper arm—Frances is afraid to ask if it is a satanic emblem or simply the declaration of an atheist. What if Athena belongs to a cult, a gang? Frances remembers the heavyset woman in a purple tunic on Oprah Winfrey, sobbing, saying you never, ever, know what your children do once they leave the house, you think you do, but you don't. Her son had been machine-gunned outside the front door. Actually, it is Frances whose stomach is bloating, whose thighs have widened.

"Ma-maah." Athena says it like a doll. "Where are you heisting me?"

"To a workshop on dyeing wool. I signed up for it at an arts fair last month, a freak impulse because I've never woven or dyed a thing in my life. But, Athena, at my age, let me tell you, inventing a new life is no zip-i-dee-doo-dah flick of the wrist."

"May I drive?"

"No."

"Pleeze, Ma-mah? Dad lets me drive his truck sometimes."

"Absolutely not. You're supposed to be in jail. And your father's decisions, as you well know, are never mine. Look how he's abandoned you."

"He lets me do what I want, that's different. It is grotesque out here, Ma-maaah."

"Really? I think it has its own beauty. Deserts are spiritual places. Points of transcendence."

This observation rebounds, stilted. And why is Athena talking to her like a rubber doll?

"A couple of things we're to remember when we get there. Can you lower that a bit?"

Athena blunts, reluctantly, her music.

"When you're introduced, you're not to look any of the Navajos directly in the eye."

"Why not?"

"They consider it overly intimate."

"Cool."

Frances glances over. She never knows what will be cool or why.

"A simple enough thing for you."

"What?"

"You never look me in the eye, Athena. Not anymore."

"Not." She pins her mother with a look startlingly lethal.

"Is that genuine? That's frightening."

Athena shrugs. "What was the other thing? You said there were two."

"Fish. You can't eat fish around them. Navajos believe fish are embryonic, unformed humans, something like that. I can't remem-

ber. It's in here." Frances pats the guidebook on Navajo culture she
has brought, largely unread.

"Fish sticks make me puke anyways."

"Anyway."

"Any-waaaays . . ."

With the toe of her boot, Athena turns up the banned, incoherent
lyrics.

What finally wakes her, after the others are up, is a sullen drone of
flies along the heat-warped window ledge. In a white plastic bucket,
blacking the surface of their drinking water, is a cobbled rug of
drowned flies. A single fly still walks, if walking, she wonders, is
how to describe it, along the battered lip of a tin cup. Frances rolls
her sleeping bag next to Athena's, against one of the eight cinder-
block walls of the hogan. She hasn't the least idea how to function
in a Native American environment, but neatness is never an error.
Manners are the same the world over, to quote her mother, and
politeness, not sex, the true mortar of civilization. Frances's resolve,
now that she is divorced against her will, is to "follow her bliss," a
phrase she'd recently heard at a Wild Women of the West seminar,
where one of the most astonishing things she had participated in was
humping the earth to release pent-up male energy. This is why she
has driven all the way out here, to a Navajo reservation. On instinct
for bliss. She hasn't the least experience with dyeing wool or weaving anything. She can't even sew. What attracted her was being told
this would be a place where, temporarily, no men were allowed.

Scraping open the wood door, Frances sees her red car parked
under the mercury yard light, haughtily disassociated from the three
trucks, two of which have I ♥ SHEEP stickers on their bumpers while
her car has a blue sticker, stuck there by Athena, an upside down
cow on it saying MEAT IS DEAD. Athena had left the window on
her side down, and with the car so close to the hogan, Frances sees

a ratty-tailed saffron rooster patrolling the front seat, back and forth, back and forth, its flat eye proprietary, arrogant.

"Hey, Ma-mah, coffee."

Athena holds out a green chipped mug, wearing yesterday's clothes, her mouth smeared a pinkish mahogany, a beauty dot penciled above the bow of her top lip. Over Athena's bare shoulder, if she squinches up her eyes, Frances can make out a half circle of Navajo women bent over an animal of some sort, trussed and quivering on its back.

"Ma-mah, poke on your glasses. You need to see this. They're going to kill a sheep."

Before leaving the hogan, neatly dressed in ironed jeans and a white-fringed turquoise sweatshirt, Frances, her eyeglasses on, hesitates before a Navajo loom, its cotton warp a pale and tranquil lyre rising up from the muted, traditional design. Cocoons of wrapped yarn hang neatly along the rug's perfect edge, where the weaver stopped. Reluctant to go outside and face any sort of butchery, Frances traces the design's black fretwork with one slowed finger, out to its edge.

She drinks her coffee, sitting on the ground beside a small cedar fire that burns with tallowy, weak effect in the morning sunlight. The grandmother squats behind the animal's throat, in a wide, pink-fanning skirt, red argyle socks, and tennis shoes, her skirt the same medicinal pink as the outhouse, angled downhill as if it might tumble any time, exposing whoever sits, unfortunate, inside. Athena stands near the workshop instructor, a young Navajo woman named Valencia, who brushes a cedar branch, in blessing, over the animal. The grandmother, a white kerchief splashed with red roses concealing most of her face, pulls hard on its head, twists it, breaking the neck, then saws her long knife like a resined bow so blood sprays then spills with a green rushing of spring into a low white bowl, and the animal's bowels loose a sheen of knobbled dung onto the flat, colorless ground.

The fleece is split into a kind of jacket, its creamy lining veined with rich coral. The carcass still cinched within its parchment membrane, legs splayed in four airy directions, suggests to Frances, except for the knob of breast, an upside-down table, fit to work on. The head, facing Frances, is set down in the fire. One eye swells, a black, glazed plum, the other sears and spits shut, then both eyes close, though unevenly, so it cannot look back upon its old form. The tongue doubles, prizing open the charring jaw. The yellow wool blackens, crisps, stinks. Now the spirit of the animal is released from all boundary, is everywhere.

This placid slaughter consoles Frances. A useful dismemberment, ritualized and strangely clean. The carcass squarely hung by hind feet from a cedar pole near the outdoor kitchen, the parchment membrane flensed back, the pursey insides unlocked, emptied out. The wine-brown brooch of liver, for Frances goes to touch it, like warm sea glass. The taupe-gray skeins of intestine are pulled and stretched, the Navajo women pour hot water through the lengthened guts from an old tin coffeepot, squeezing and dribbling out the dung-colored stuff. A ripe jeweling of ruby and pewter, pearled matter, a supple kingdom falling over the plain hard canvas of dirt, the dull, droughted, troubled-seeming earth spotted with blood like vital specklings of rain. The stomach with its sallow chenille lining, the drying gloss of lungs, liver, kidneys draped over a narrow pole. And rising under the callus of blood in the milky flat-faced dish, like a mineral pool, strings of bubbles, a languorous spitting of bubbles, as if something deep under its weight still breathed.

Frances studies these women, the practical details of their butchering, their reverent pulling apart of a life and making it into other, smaller, useful things.

■

Two emergency-room nurses from Lubbock are the only other participants in this workshop, and Frances has made no effort to talk to either one of them. A Married Rule, that pretense of sociability. The nurses, both skinny, both earnest and, for some reason, wan-looking, stick close to the Navajo women, speak in enthusiastic twangings. Frances prays she doesn't resemble them, though she has signed up and paid for this experience, is conscious of being that evil necessity, a tourist with money to purchase a 3-D postcard, "Navajo women at work on the reservation." She wants to tell these Indian women she understands, but what is it she understands, and does she?

"Maa, Maaah . . ."

Bleating, Athena shuffles outside the tilting outhouse, her nose pinched, her voice nasal.

"You realize there are no males here. None. Except the sheep, and we've just killed him."

"Oh, there are men." Frances's voice is muffled, weary. "Always and eternally there are men." She steps out of the terrible-smelling pink box. "My intent, Athena, was to go someplace where, for once, there weren't any. And where the Navajo men who usually live here have gone, I can't imagine. I'm sure it's rude to ask."

They walk back down the slope, Frances whacking at her dusty pants. White pants. What had she been thinking?

"I need some smokes. I have to go into town."

"Town. For heaven's sake, Athena. Look where we are."

"Well, a trading post then. Plus I gotta wash my hair, it's getting completely gross. There's a bathroom in their house, I went in and found it, but no water. You turn the faucets and air spits out. There's not even water in the toilet."

"There's a bad drought. I heard Valencia say it's got something to do with the strip-mining, with the slurry water the mines use. All month they've been hauling water from town."

"These people should move to where there's more trees, more

water. God." Athena narrows her eyes over the arid, hopeless, scrabbly landscape, blowing mournful smoke from her last cigarette. "Look. That dumb chicken's still on your front seat."

Athena runs, arms flapping, cigarette dangling, to swat the rooster out of the car. The Navajo women stop what they're doing to look, and Frances cannot interpret their faces. She jogs to catch up. She had looked forward to this trip by herself. She had hoped to learn something, or at least stop thinking about what exhausts and obsesses her. Now, looking into Athena's bright, provocative face, Frances sees how precisely, like a scissor cut, it matched her own at that age.

"Athena. You have to behave yourself. When you're the guest of another culture, you blend in, you ask intelligent questions."

"I am. I'm going to ask where the nearest store is and where the men are stashed."

"Athena."

"What."

"Please."

"What."

"You could be in prison right now. I could have left you there until your father decided to come and get you."

"Yada yada yada."

"What were you stealing?"

"Undies."

"Underwear? I just bought you plenty of . . ."

"Sexy underwear, Ma. You've never bought me that."

"May I ask you a simple question? What makes you so sure you are Jim Morrison's wife reincarnated?"

"You're the one who told me about reincarnation."

"Yes, but you can't just make up who you wish you had been. Oh, wouldn't I love to think I was once Thomas Jefferson or Sarah Bernhardt or even Luther Burbank."

"Thomas Jefferson?"

"I've always wanted to be Thomas Jefferson. Do you know who I was in love with at your age?"

"Dad?"

Frances pauses dramatically. "Carl Sandburg."

"Who's that?"

"He's dead now, but he was a famous poet. I wrote Carl Sandburg several passionate letters. He was in his seventies."

"Cool. Mom in love with an old dude."

"I never mailed them. I knew he had a wife and a goat farm in North Carolina, and probably he was happy."

"What about Dad? Oh, never mind. You'll just say something nasty. You're in that stage now."

"Stage?"

"Of divorce. Denial, rage, stuff like that."

"Where'd you pick up that idea?"

"Dad. He has books on divorce. Just like you."

"The same books?"

"Yup. Exactly. You guys are exactly alike."

Right, Frances thinks. Except he's chosen someone else. He's betrayed me.

Doing as she is asked, Athena drags the charred head from the fire by one gristled ear, sets it on a wood block, scrapes off filings of ash with a stick so the head can be wrapped and baked. And when she is certain her mother sees, for isn't her mother always watching, spying, jealous, easy to fool, a cinch to scare, to give her something really to be scared about, Athena swoops one finger across the bowl of dulling blood and drives it deep into her own mouth. Not long after that, Frances will stand in the parrot-yellow kitchen, stuffing gray, salted mutton into her mouth until the women, laughing, caution her to stop, until they stop laughing and take the plate away, saying this will make her sick. Mutton hunger is what they will say she has.

After lunch, they ride in the nurses' truck to the base of a sort of mountain. Everybody gets a plastic grocery sack. They are to follow the grandmother, collect twigs, leaves, roots, and mosses, plants Valencia names for them, mullein, lichen, sumac, mountain mahogany, chamisa.

Athena lags behind with the most tired-looking nurse, while Frances tracks the grandmother, what she can of her, two red argyled ankles flashing up a rigorous incline. Frances slows from the midday heat, the altitude, the enervating whiteness of the sun. In every direction, sealike troughs of land push up clumps of piñon and cedar, like rich, bronze-green kelp. A hawk skates the air above her in fluid, mahogany curls.

Frances nearly trips over the grandmother, crouched by a blunt formation of black rock, on her knees with a table knife, chipping chrome-yellow powder from the rock and dusting it off her hands into a plastic bag.

Valencia looks up kindly. "We use this to get our black, mixing it with piñon pitch and cedar ash. It's pretty hard to find, but grandmother is amazing, she goes right to where it is."

The taller nurse stands like a sentinel, a lank poplar, behind Frances.

"That stuff looks like uranium. Exactly."

Frances takes her turn scraping, grazing her knuckles; the uranium idea has unnerved her.

"You could hike up here once a year, get a gigantic load of this stuff to last you."

Frances thinks no one has heard, though the nurse's voice is tactless enough. The grandmother is resting in the compressed, thick

shade of a piñon tree, while Valencia, wiping sweat from her forehead, answers, a perceptible teacher's edge to her voice.

"We take only what is needed each time. And Grandmother has
taught us to leave an offering, a gift, before separating anything from
where it is found."

"Halllooooo!" Athena, her arms making rapid pinwheeling motions, appears to be urging them up to the next highest ledge.
Frances is busy, spit-washing a smudge of uranium off her turquoise
shirt.

When the three white women attain the highest ledge, they hold
their plastic bags of roots and twigs, panting, confounded by what
they see. Inches deep across the ground lay thousands of pottery
shards. The women, winded, hot-faced, are told they are standing
on a trash dump, where Anasazi Indians, centuries ago, had thrown
their broken pots and garbage.

The Navajo women sit and rest, observe the three white women
stooping and bobbing, pecking about for bits of clay, their arms
blooming with what they cannot seem to gather up fast enough. At
first, the women call back and forth excitedly, then lapse into an
almost funereal quiet, the weight of anthropology, the burden of
choosing among priceless relics falling almost gloomily upon them.
Like children, their greed eventually tires them, and they become
aware of the Navajo women, quietly watching. They stop, arms and
pockets and bags loaded down, their small congress embarrassed, bits
of pottery dropping off them like leaves.

"Perhaps just two or three," says one nurse.

"Those that mean the most," suggests the other.

As Frances sets down her cumbersome pile, Athena, who had
wandered off, returns. Between her hands rests a large, perfect potsherd, a black lightning streak down its reddish, curved flank. Ex-
claiming over its size and near-perfect condition, Frances begins to
thank Athena, grateful for the largeness of gesture, the love implied.

"It's for Dad," Athena says softly. "I wanted to bring him something."

"Oh." Frances drops to her knees, shuffling through her little clay bits, as if to choose.

"Did you leave an offering?"

"Yuppers. My last cigarette, one I copped from the nurse."

On the ride back, they stop beside a faded sprawl of prickly pear to pick its mushy red fruits for pink dye. The driving nurse, feeling unwell, decides to drive to the trading post for stomach medicine. Both nurses drop the women back at the hogan except for Athena, who's begged a ride.

Frances labors alongside her instructor, hefting enamelware kettles and a halved oil drum filled with hauled water onto different fires. She sorts through gathered plant materials, carries bags and baskets of handspun wool skeins out from the hogan, admires Valencia's long, black hair, twisted in a shining bundle at the nape of her neck, noting its resemblance to the skeins of wool, to the little bundles of yarn dangling from the edge of the rug inside the hogan. She wonders how Valencia would raise a daughter, how do the women raise teenagers out here, how, in her own case, could things get much worse.

Swirling the stained waters with an ashy stick, made sleepy by the steam of plants, bitter- or sweet-smelling, or dense as soured earth, Frances begins to hope Athena might not return until much, much later.

At once she hears the truck, observes it dipping and rising over the rutted gullies, with Athena, cross-legged in the bed of the truck, in a somber corona of dust, brandishing a cigarette. As her daughter trips unsteadily past her, blowing smoke out both nostrils, her maroon hair tangled and shreddy-looking, Frances studies the shaven back of her head, so disturbingly infantlike, watches her wobble around a cast-iron pot of chamisa dye, right herself, then pitch behind one side of the hogan and begin, audibly, to vomit.

One of the nurses comes up to Frances.

"I found this in the truck bed."

Frances stares at the half-empty bottle.

The bottle lodged under her arm, Frances uses a peeled stick to raise out of the water one of the skeins of yarn. It hangs from the end of the willow stick, a twist, an eight, of deep, ardent gold.

Worse than finding Athena on the ground is seeing the rooster, pecking with cold disregard, at her daughter's vomit. Frances is about to kick the rooster, when suddenly, admitting nature's genius, she leaves it to clean the mess Athena has once again made of things.

"G'way." Athena's tattooed arm takes a sodden, backward sweep at the air. "G'way, stupid."

Her profile, smooshed into the ground, is a mask of vomit and dirt.

"All right. I will go away. I will go get something to wash your filthy face with. You disappoint me, Athena."

Athena's visible eye stays blearily fixed on the rooster.

Inside the dim, stifling hogan, Frances finds the one available cloth, her pink western bandanna. The only water she knows of is in the white plastic bucket. Biting her bottom lip, plunging her arm deep to wet the bandanna, she has to shake off a burred sleeve of flies. She stands quiet before the loom, an object of great dignity, a pursuit, elusive to Frances, of stillness and purpose. Hadn't she tried to make their marriage like that, into fine cloth, an enduring design?

Balling up the tepid pink bandanna, wringing it hard, she squats behind Athena, turning her head and wiping her soiled face. As she scrubs under her daughter's chin, a muddy backwash of rage hits.

"There." She throws down the stained rag. "You find something to do with that. I'm taking our things to the car. We're going home, not that either of us has much of a home anymore."

As she finishes stuffing the trunk with their few things, Frances hears the nurse, the one who had shown her the half-empty whiskey bottle, behind her.

"Mrs. Waythorn, your daughter took off running that way. If you take the car, you'll catch up to her. It won't be dark for another fifteen minutes."

The woman's voice is so nursely, so merciful, so professionally equipped for trauma, Frances wants to collapse against her ordinary sweatshirt, her calm and practical shoulder. She wants to say, Oh you take care of this, somebody else manage this, I only want to rest.

Even in the drought-smeared violet light, Frances easily makes out the skinny speck of her daughter shambling along the gravel-and-dirt road. In the middle of nowhere. Going nowhere.

As her car creeps closer, Frances, seeing Athena's set, miserable profile, does a most unexpected thing. She pumps hard on the accelerator and shoots past her daughter, steering with great angry lurches and radical swerves, up over the crest of a small hill and down.

She stops, exhilarated, considering what she has done. Abandoned her daughter. Gone beyond her. Swooped by. Yes.

Her arch has a dark wetted gash across it. Athena's potsherd, the gift for her father, has rolled off the seat and smashed into pieces around her foot. Frances rests her forehead on the steering wheel. After a long while, she becomes aware of darkness. My God. She switches on the light overhead, lifts up to see the top third of her face in the little mirror. Smeared with dirt, tears, old mascara. Her pants, too, ruined. Her shirt, poisoned with uranium.

Wildly, she feels for the ignition, in a panic, shoves into reverse, backs up the car, coasts down the little hill she's concealed herself behind.

Frances gets out of the car, sees blurrily, a mile or so away, the mercury yard light she had aimed for the night before. Hears, as if it isn't hers anymore, the sound of weeping.

The car light switched on, Frances is on her knees, searching under the seats, trying to gather back pieces of the clay pot. On the day she had been scrubbing down her child's room, on the day of her daughter's arrest, she had found, while on her belly under Athena's bed, a green cardboard shoe box. Inside the shoe box were the souvenirs Frances had kept hidden from everyone. The dry, yellowish triangle of Athena's umbilical cord, a wavy, black shank of her ex-husband's hair, the auburn braid of her mother's hair, cut six months before she'd died, and, like twin, eerie rattles, two tiny boxes of Frances's own ivoried baby teeth. Athena, searching through her mother's secret things, had taken, out of instinct or curiosity, all she needed.

"Ma-mah? What is it? What are you doing?"

"My foot's cut."

"Poorest Mommy. You can't drive, bleeding and crying like that. Shh, shh, okay, shh. I'll help you. Shh."

Stripping off, wrapping the black tank top around her mother's foot, Athena, not bothering to ask, gets her old wish to drive. And as the reservation night covers, uncovers her white, scarcely touched breasts, as her mother guards, unyielding, the broken potsherds, bits of hair, and dried cord, Athena will piece together a stubborn, defiantly remembered, child's way home.

"The Instinct for Bliss" is a grafting of circumstance onto wholesale invention, of exaggeration onto the sort of wild fretfulness and self-doubt that chronically accompanies living with an adolescent. My oldest daughter was, at the time I began the story, in full-scale and somewhat justified rebellion against the life she found herself in—she refused its society. Out of relief as well as some leftover capacity for ad-

venture, I seized on a friend's invitation to visit with a Navajo family she knew well in Arizona. The story is a magnetization between what did happen, what almost happened, and what never happened. Writing it became the urgent hear-task of shaping what I'd been given as a mother into what I most desired—reconnection with my firstborn child.

M.P.

POLTERGEISTS

□

JANE SHAPIRO

The other evening, after talking on the phone with my daughter, Nora, who lives in Rome, I walked over to the Mexican place, the nearest restaurant to my apartment, where I had a narrow escape— I almost stepped into a deeply strange, forgotten, familiar world. I stopped on the threshold, looking in at the stucco room hung with striped rugs and dusty sequin-trimmed sombreros; it was early, but the place was packed, unnaturally so, and the mood was wrong— not loud but still too keyed up. Then I saw why the restaurant seemed to have shrunk: all the patrons were high school kids. They looked gigantic; even the girls appeared to need a place with higher ceilings and more commodious chairs. They weren't braying or throwing food or dropping their pants or anything; in the intense attitudes that were normal for them, they were eating burritos. I backed out. Moments later, when I came to, I was strolling toward the Thai place, remembering a lost time, my children's high school days.

In 1985, I was still living in New Jersey in the house Willie and I had bought when the kids were small, and when Zack and Nora got into their senior and junior years the three of us were suddenly agitated and constantly struggling to appear serene. I was alone.

That's what it felt like: I'm living alone, with only my adolescent children and our hair-trigger adrenal glands. The epinephrine was cycling through our nervous systems with no outlet. Since Nora and Zack had started high school, there had been a few occasions when I went over the top and screamed. It came on only once or twice a year, and afterward I was ground down by ordinary guilt. Still, I understood perfectly the state of mind of the parents who shrieked and frothed daily, tried to rip the earrings out of their children's ears, and rolled around with the kids in mortal combat on the rug. With even the most hysterical of the parents of teenagers I knew, I felt a sort of tender affiliation: they had been blindfolded and poked until maddened; they were flying, on an adrenaline high that couldn't be contained.

Mornings were okay. In the mornings, things were normal, with the indefinable heightened quality we were getting used to: supra-normal, metanormal. Zack and Nora were glossily beautiful, standing in the kitchen in pure ringing silence, conserving their deep reserves of energy. Zack's breakfast was four pieces of toast and a quart of milk; Nora's was a Diet Coke. Every few days I squeezed oranges and carried the glasses of juice to their bedrooms, where they were blow-drying their marvelous hair. *Oh, thanks,* they'd call patiently, through the dryers' roar. While I watched, they'd take a sip.

That year, I was really busy. I spent a fair number of evenings going out with my women friends, all of us wearing our earrings, and suits with big shoulders, and being glamorous, irrepressible modern American divorcées together, then straggling home. And I was still working full-time at a training school for bad boys (breaking and entering, assault with intent, car thefts), a place where I had a role to play that was simple and made sense: I was trying to teach kids to read. On my way to work I'd drop my own kids at the high school and I'd watch as they crossed the lawn; they looked dynamic but pacific—they were washed to a shine, arrayed in calculated, shabby, sexy black. I had a persistent, weird feeling: I couldn't prove it, but I thought that those were not my children. The crossing guard looked like the same guy he had always been. But the kids had been replaced by Martians.

Daytime was the Martian time, when all the normal stuff happened. Graciously, they did the usual things: Nora did gymnastics, and Zack played his guitar; they were both lacrosse players, student council representatives, actors, and members of the Black Literature Club. After school, Zack worked at a health food restaurant, making sandwiches invented during the sixties; Nora helped run a theater program for tiny children, walking the kids to the bathroom, tying their masks onto their little faces, restraining the biter. If I got home late from work, the house would already be thumping, a giant heartbeat in the walls—Nora's Jane Fonda video. This was still daytime. Nora and Zack were doing the well-known, complicated adolescent impersonation of people fully engaged with the daytime things. In fact, everything happened at night.

They were going to concerts. Some Saturdays, they set out in the morning and rode long distances, to faraway venues. Hours before the show, there'd be a city of cars in the parking lot, and packs of young people in the late sun and then in the gathering darkness, lurching around and handling each other, and buying and selling and consuming loose joints, pills, the standard seductive killer drugs, and a fluid called Liquid Lady. Nora and Zack told me about these events. Of course I asked, Did their friends drink and take drugs? Zack had long been a master of the noncommittal amiable remark. He said, "The bottles to beware of are the ones that look like cologne."

Other Saturdays, they stayed home. After dinner they walked around their rooms for three hours, dressing and phoning. At ten, scrubbed as if for surgery and artfully got up, they rushed out. At two, hoarse and depleted, they staggered home.

At parties, muscular, stoic boys would kneel and take a piece of tubing deep into their mouths and tip their heads back like sword swallowers, and their friends would pour whole beers through a motor-oil funnel, straight down their throats. Girls did it, too—Nora reported that when this happened she sometimes left the room. This was dangerous, I said; drinking like that, those boys could get very sick. "Get sick?" Zack said. "Actually, Mom, that's pretty euphemistic. They could die." I planned to call the parents of the beer swallowers, to inform them. Which parents would you single out, the kids said. It happens all the time. Please, Mom. It's the least of it.

"Mom," Zack said. "Here's a typical incident, but you can't do any phoning."

"What is it?" I said.

"We can't tell you these things if you start talking about calling people."

"What is it?"

"Is it about Benjy?" Nora asked, starting to laugh. "Oh, it's ridiculous! It's nothing, Mom."

"What?"

They were laughing so happily, so healthily. They pounded each other, stamped their feet, wiped their eyes. They both cried, *"Benjy drank three beers through his nose!"*

Zack's girlfriend, Bibi, looked as much like Nora as somebody else could—a sexier, ruder Nora, in muddy cowboy boots. In the daytime, Bibi smelled like a puppy—she was working after school for a veterinarian, planning to become one. She liked to tell long, bloody, oddly arousing stories about veterinarian life. Bibi was very beautiful and sloppy. I was jealous of her. The first time she came to our house, she immediately picked up our cat, pressed him to her, and licked his fur; Zack sat down suddenly, as if to avoid swooning. Now, whenever she had a chance, Bibi would come over and stay for many hours, with her jeans straining to cover her strong, elegant legs. She would slip off the boots and lie down with her feet in Zack's lap. Then she would fondle the cat in several remarkably inventive ways, and Zack would watch her. She drove me nuts.

Nora suddenly got a boyfriend—a deep-voiced guy named Mark. He was less annoying than Bibi—shallower, less clever, and not around much. I kind of liked him, and he may have kind of liked me. A sophomore, he was already planning to be a surgeon. On our first meeting, I asked how he knew that for sure, and he said sonorously, "I have a special aptitude," and wiggled his fingers. He grinned. Nora blushed horribly. We all stared at Mark's jiggling, dexterous hands.

I had a boyfriend myself; that is to say, there was someone I'd been seeing since a few months after Willie and I divorced. Steven and I weren't by any means in love, but we were certainly old enough to be placid together, reasonably happy in the way recommended by best-selling books: we didn't expect too much. The only thing I had ever tried to change about him was early on, when I made him cut back on the after-shave.

Steven stayed over on the Saturdays he didn't have his son with him. Every other Sunday morning he drove out and bought eight bagels, and he and I ate two of them in the wonderful silence, and by the time the kids stumbled from their beds he had usually gone home. "Where's Dome?" they said. (His only unusual physical characteristic was a slightly overrounded forehead, and you really had to be paying attention to notice it.) Once a month or so, he'd still be there when they woke, and they'd say things like "Hi, Steve. Thanks for the bagels—these six bagels as well as the last nine hundred bagels."

On a back road late on Halloween night, driving home from a party at about ninety miles an hour, two kids rolled a car. They climbed out, stood up, vomited on their ghost costumes, and walked away in the moonlight. After that, some parents of party-givers started making all the guests sleep at their houses so they wouldn't drive home drunk; when you arrived at the party you had to surrender your car keys before you could repair to the keg or upend the bottle through your nose. Zack didn't have his driver's license yet; Bibi did. Zack and Bibi and Nora got in the habit of pretending that they'd been driven by someone else, and in the middle of the night, after everybody had fallen down on the mattresses, they'd slip out and meet on the lawn and run for Bibi's car and make their getaway. The three of them would drive out to the diner, comb their smoky hair, eat platters of scrambled eggs, and when they felt coherent enough, drive on home.

"Do any of these parents happen to refuse to serve alcohol?" I asked once, kind of wearily.

Zack said that the parents didn't serve marijuana and cocaine, but that inhospitality had virtually no impact on events.

"*Cocaine?* Is that a *common* thing?"

He looked at me absently. He said it was a pain, because cocaine traditionally happens in the bathroom, so anytime you wanted to go to the bathroom you had to go out in the yard.

Nora laughed. "It's really true!" she said. "Julie comes to be lookout."

"So what would happen if no alcohol was served? Would anybody go to the party?"

"Sure," they said. "It happens. Everybody goes."

"And then nobody drinks?"

Zack said, "People bring vodka and drink it in cups of tea."

"I don't want you to drink and drive!"

"We never do," they said. "Are you crazy?"

"Do you smoke joints?"

"Mom," they said kindly, holding my gaze.

"I don't want you to drink or smoke at all."

"We know that, Mom. We know you don't."

My pal Annie came over to have tea and talk about our lives—what we used to do, what we would do later, when all this was over. Annie's daughter was a Saturday gymnast, like Nora; her son worked alongside Zack at Tempting Treats, squeezing the carrots, massing the sprouts in the pitas, melting the Monterey Jack—killing a little of their enormous surplus of time. Annie and I had been banking on these pursuits to keep the kids safe. In fact, Annie had gone further—had got her former husband to ante up a lot of support money to keep their kids in the private day school instead of the public school. So we considered her children marginally safer than mine: they were receiving *individual attention*. Now Annie and I sat in the dining room with the teapot in its ineffectual little cozy, giving each other keen looks. Zack was in his room. His door was closed, and through the door came, instead of sound, the usual waves of sexual energy pouring into the house and agitating the air. I imagined him in there finishing his college essays, desperately pulling on his hair. "Probably not his hair," Annie said glumly. She said she used to worry that when they reached high school they'd start having lots of sex—dangerous, fifties sex—and that would be traumatic, and now there was AIDS, which was unimaginably worse. Still, if they wore their condoms and chose their partners carefully, she had decided, the safest illicit activity currently available to the kids was making love. "At least while they're having sex they can't be driving the car a hundred miles an hour," she said.

Passing the dining room, Nora called pleasantly, "Why can't they?"

■

After an eventful New Year's Eve, when Zack got his butt squeezed by a mystery girl, and also underwent a conversion and rededication to academic excellence, he devoted eighteen consecutive nights to studying for his third round of S.A.T.s, like somebody possessed. Then he and Nora stayed over with friends and came home on Saturday morning gray and staring. Here's what they said:

We watched *Love Connection*. Then *The People's Court*—a case about a beagle and some rat poison. Then the five-o'clock news—Lou Gossett was on. Then *World News Tonight*—we love it. Reagan was real happy down in Mexico, shaking hands with the Mexican president. Then we got souvlaki and took it to the party. We left early and went back to Holly's mom's and watched *The Shining*. Then *Repo Man* came on. Then Robbie said "I'm Robertson Parson Shattuck III" about forty times and tiptoed out and tried to walk on the edge of the upper terrace with his eyes closed and fell onto the bluestone lower terrace and broke his arm. Then we took him to the emergency room and waited for his dad, and his dad rode over in his Jaguar with his Haitian driver. Then two guys from the high school came in; they had been beaten up and their faces were meat. Then *Tom and Jerry*. Then morning came.

"Then what happened?" I asked.

Zack: "Sun came up."

As the year progressed, the parties seemed to grow more drastic, more extreme. Shooting the Boot was introduced—each guest gulped a sneakerful, out of the host's high-top. Vomiting, of course, was perennially big: the Technicolor yawn, riding the porcelain bus, talking to Ralph on the big white phone. Urination was big: a kid named Soup liked to go into the bathroom immediately and piss into the shampoo. One couple or another always had to have a fight, and one or both of the lovers had to run out of the house, and maybe the girl would key-scratch the guy's car. There was always the abused guy. There was always the depressed girl who pulled guys seriatim into a bedroom or closet. Something valuable always had to get broken. If, as could happen, the parents were fools enough to leave town, everybody showed up, and then there'd be the trashed house and weird things going around in the dryer, and maybe the whole population of the high school outside on the deck, some of them in mid-urination when the deck fell down.

Nora didn't drink. She reported that a boy had asked, When did you stop? I never drank, she said. Never? Unsteadily, he held out his big, strong feverish hand for a crunching handshake. He nodded sagely. He said, *I'm very impressed.*

Some narcs came to school. Nora said that the narcs—a man and a woman—were wearing amazing disguises: bell-bottoms, fringed vests, *hair.* They looked about thirty-five. Nora claimed the narcs had sidled up and asked where to buy "stuff," and she'd said, "Officers, I have no idea."

In fact, you could buy your drugs in the auditorium. Or outside the gym, against the wall, where the regular daytime dope-smokers stood dreaming. Every Friday, a blue van pulled up behind the gym, and the dealers, three seniors—Jason, George, and Robbie—ran out, got in, and in two turns around the block bought the school's supplies for the week. From Nora, their pal, I got a clear impression of the dealers: Robbie was a neglected, handsome, depressed rich boy; George was a gentle, skinny, cocaine-dependent poor boy; and Jason was a hardened criminal.

I made an appointment with the principal. He was a tall fellow, always as precisely turned out as one of his students, as clean-shaven as a person can be. The skin of his cheeks shone like a baby's, and he had a baby's clear, guiltless eyes. When I arrived, he turned this face toward me and looked pleasant. "What are you doing about the drug problem?" I said, and he held his pleasing expression.

"Please sit down," he said. As for the narcotics, the administration was aware, they were paying steadily close attention, there'd been marked improvement, hopes were high. "A van comes every week to sell dope," I said. He said he wasn't at liberty to say publicly what was being done about that possibility. "Have you considered stopping it?" I said. "That seems pretty straightforward."

It wasn't that simple, he said amicably.

"It *is* that simple. You pick up the phone, you dial, you tell the cops. They drive out and they arrest the drug dealers."

This was a community of very concerned parents, he said. It was a community full of resources.

"I don't get it."

We gazed at each other with hatred.

He said that no parent in this community—perhaps, and he certainly thought so, myself included—would want to see the future of any local student jeopardized by what many might argue could be a very unnecessary police presence.

I said, "You mean Robbie Shattuck is too rich to bust."

He told me that the concern of parents like me was a source of support and nourishment for the high school administration, and he could only impress upon me that they were continuously at work on addressing the pressing problems facing us, not just narcotics-related, not just alcohol-related, not just violence-related, not just prejudice-related, but across the board. While saying this, he stood, and all the wrinkles fell out of his suit. He said some more. Meanwhile, I imagined him studious in cruel bathroom light, scraping the razor time and again over his cowardly face. I lunged across the desk and we shook hands—our hands were wet. He promised to keep me and people like me apprised. At last we gave up and said a brief, loud, disgusted goodbye, like lovers who were sickened to recall they had ever shared a moment.

■

Steven turned forty-five and started bringing in a lot more money. He began to mutter about changing his already extremely rewarding life. His son was ten, so he had energy for this remaking—I was bitter about that and laughed a lot. The result of his deliberations was, for somebody in his situation, an ordinary one: he upgraded from a Honda to a metallic Porsche. Whenever he came over, the kids looked for new ways to compliment him on the phallic nature of his choice: *"Commanding,"* they'd say. *"Potent. Really smooth and rounded."* Steven and I shared friendly sex, a desire to be with another person, and a talent for not causing trouble—was there more? This year I had been surprised to develop, by imperceptible increments, an awareness that Steven and I might actually part; I couldn't face it. Meanwhile, every other Saturday night the new Porsche stood all night in the driveway, gleaming, solid, dependable, a still point in a shifting universe.

Zack, to Nora, when he thought I was out: "It's stifling. It's stifling here. It's so *stifling* living in this house! There's not enough air in this house to support life!"

Nora wanted to go to Florida with her boyfriend. "You've got to be kidding," I said. She said, "That is *not* a nice tone." I was drawing some flash cards for school, using basketball terms and the names of Knicks. I printed HOOK SHOT.

Her boyfriend had two plane tickets to Fort Myers and an uncle's empty condo on Captiva Island. I said that was economical but cut no ice with me.

She said, "Well, I want to go."

"Ask your father," I said. Saying this gave me a tiny, standard sort of thrill: Let *him* deal with it. Wreck *his* week. Nora snorted—she and Willie were getting along badly. She was secretly not talking to him; that is, technically she spoke with him, but meanwhile she knew she was only pretending to speak.

While I printed FOUL LINE, FAST BREAK, TOUCH PASS, and RORY SPARROW, Nora explained my philosophy to me: that I took the position that they had to make their own decisions, always balancing their decisions against my concerns and feelings, that that's how we'd arrived at their curfews, that's how we'd arranged things for years—I trusted them. This was no different. I said, "Well, my feelings are very strong. I don't want you to go."

"Excuse me, Mom, but I think that's kind of hypocritical."

"And why is that?"

"Because Mark is already my boyfriend, and we're not going to do"—ominously—"anything in Florida that we *can't do here.*"

That didn't matter, I said, even if true, which I doubted: what mattered was the intensity of the honeymoonlike situation, the five days alone, my sense that although I didn't need to intervene in their inevitable sexual life, I did need to make my own statement about precisely what my hopes and, yes, I said bravely, my expectations were for her, and what my own values continued to be, and so on. I warmed to my topic and, hoping to gain the advantage, lavishly gesturing with my Magic Marker, jawed on.

"Well, I'm sorry, Mommy!" she said finally, and she began to cry.

"Why are you crying?"

"You're a wonderful mother," Nora squeaked. "And I really feel bad about this."

"There's no harm done," I said.

"I can see that you and me are going to have to have different views."

"We certainly do."

"I feel so bad. I hate to not do what you want!"

"I'm sure you'll do the right thing," I said.

"That's why I'm upset!"

"Why?"

She said miserably, "Because I'm going!" Then she dried her face and went to phone her friends to borrow their many infinitesimal iridescent G-string-based bathing suits.

I yelled after her, into the next room, "Don't you kids ever have any *real* problems?"

Nora, a week later, at dinner, apropos of nothing: "Mom, I hate to say it. But I don't know what's wrong with you. It's like you're turning into a different person."

I now had, of course, a psychiatrist. My psychiatrist was cautious, stubborn, wily, deft, like somebody whose survival in a hostile world depended on extreme cunning and vigilance. It made sense: he was a Freudian—his type was supposed to have already vanished, like the theater and Yiddish. His office contained a prominent couch, which I wouldn't consider lying on; a couple of kilims, like Freud's; a small card thanking the patients for not smoking; a tissue box decorated with kitty cats entangled in their yarn balls. Early on, he had accidentally revealed that he loved Cheech and Chong, and then nothing for months. I had been talking to him all year: he appeared sometimes drowsy or faintly addled, sometimes alert; behind him the light falling through the window brightened, dimmed, brightened; the newest rug seemed to fade slightly; a humidifier joined us and the air grew moist. The most comforting thing my psychiatrist ever said to me, and it was extremely comforting, wasn't even a full sentence. He murmured, "The inevitable disquietude of spirit in a house where adolescents live."

Zack was in *Three Sisters*: a shortened version, cut by the drama teacher—three acts, fewer military men, and only half the pronouncements about life. The kids called it *Two and a Half Sisters*.

After the play's run, eight of the cast members came for dinner and sat at our round dining table wearing idiosyncratic and sexy clothes, flushed and attentive like a ring of children at a birthday party. I served a turkey, although it was February, and one bottle of California champagne for all of them—for a toast to Chekhov and themselves. When I brought in the platter, their dilated pupils shone and they all cried, "Turkey! My favorite food!" They pantomimed abject disbelief—all their lives, they'd had turkey only once a year. Vivaciously, they toasted the turkey, as if he were a pal. They all had to go to the bathroom constantly; each time, whoever left said goodbye to the turkey carcass. After dinner they drank many cups of tea. Then everybody strolled to the front door, and they all stood there and looked at Zack overintently while he said to me, "Oh, where is it, where has it all gone, my past, when I was young, gay, clever, when I dreamed and thought with grace, when my present and my future were lighted up with hope?" Then the others took turns thanking me with lines from *Two and a Half Sisters*, tossed their hairdos, and rushed into the night. Zack went with them. This was a good moment. I stood on the step a long time, staring out into total darkness.

Steven was away for the weekend—no Porsche, no bagels. At midnight, after a video outing, Nora got home, looking sensible. Her planned mock honeymoon was still three weeks away; we weren't talking about it. She had been lying low, leading a remarkably staid life. She seemed to be playing a character in an imaginary young person's novel: *Nora Green, Good High School Girl*. Now she pulled on her boxers, yanked back her hair, washed her face for half an hour, kissed me twice, and went to bed.

At two, Zack's expected arrival time, he wasn't home. I decided to read. At two-thirty, he wasn't home. At three, he wasn't home. At three-fifteen, the phone rang once, then stopped. At three-thirty, I heard Bibi's car slowly approaching, coasting in—she was driving with admirable care, and they were almost home. But they weren't.

The car paused, then moved on. When I went to look out, it was gone. Empty street, in quiet darkness.

I thought I could call Willie and wake him, to say—what? I could call the parents of Zack's fellow actors. Half an hour more, and I'd be willing to go that far.

I waited. I could wake Nora and ask her where Zack had planned to go. Of all the alternatives, that seemed preferable—waking a young person instead of some parents who, troubled, compromised, were still somehow managing in the middle of a Saturday night to catch a few pathetic winks. At four, I tapped at Nora's door, then tiptoed in. Her lamp was on, casting soft light on her tangled bed. Nora was gone.

I dialed Willie, let it ring. He was out. I enjoyed one moment of resentment, very brief and rich.

I phoned the parents.

Three of the actors were in their beds. Nora's boyfriend, Mark, wasn't in his bed. Bibi wasn't. Tim, the senior class president, wasn't; Katya, the eager environmentalist, wasn't; Jessica, the mathematician, wasn't. Beebop, the boy with four earrings, wasn't. Holly, the girl with the shredded jeans and visible underpants, wasn't. Alan, the tall weight-lifting boy with the velvet hat, who was going into the army, wasn't. It was four in the morning. Almost all the parents answered on the first ring; struggling to awaken, they were remarkably gracious, as if genuinely welcoming my call. None of them were curt with me, and none sounded at all resentful. They didn't sound as though they bore any resemblance to the parents I'd imagined encouraging crowds of future Ivy Leaguers to ingest beer through gas station funnels and vomit onto their shoes. One couple, whom I'd never met, and whose son was home and sleeping, offered to come over and sit with me because I was a single parent. Two of the fathers offered to drive out and look, but we couldn't think where they should go. One of the fathers offered to go out, find them, and run them over with the car, and his wife and I laughed hysterically for a long time. Bibi's mother called the police, who had no information. Let's get off the phones, we said. Maybe they'll call.

At six, in birdsong and rising light, they arrived. Nora slipped her key in the lock like a safecracker, slid the door open, and stepped in. Her lips were rosy and puffy, prominent in her ravaged face. "Oh Mom!" she said groggily. "Oh no! You're up!"

And I was also *really disappointed* and I was also *really mad*, I cried. How could they do this? Hadn't it occurred to them I'd be worried? What was in their minds? Half the parents in this town had been awake half the night! *"And I cannot believe not one of you had the consideration to call! It's absolutely incredible that—"*

"One of who?" she said.

"All of you!" I cried, and I stamped my foot in its fuzzy slipper. *"I have had it! I can't believe you guys would betray my trust like this! You go out there right now and tell Zack to send Bibi home and get in here!"*

She looked horribly confused. "What do you mean?" she said.

"What do *you* mean?"

"Isn't Zack here?" she said.

"Zack wasn't with you?" I said.

Pause. Tiny voice. "I was with Mark."

"What a surprise," I said. "But where is Zack?"

"Well, Mom, I'm sorry," she said. Then she added mildly, the way she had said the same thing to the hippie narcs, "I have no idea."

I recalled something funny the psychiatrist had said. The Kleenex box was over near the couch. Occasionally, sitting across the room, I threatened to sniffle, and then we both half rose and he shoved the box toward me through the empty air. Once, he murmured in consolation, while shoving the box, that a poltergeist was like a sort of ectoplasmic manifestation of adolescent libido.

"What?" I said.

"Poltergeist," he said.

I snuffled.

"The ghost that makes noises and throws plates off the shelves," he said.

I said damply, "Please. It's really not helping. I could use some *advice*."

He said, "Fine. Here it is: Put the babies up for adoption."

I was standing on the driveway in my bathrobe and coat, looking at the frosted lawn and the ascending sun, when Bibi's car, one fender crumpled, pulled in. Zack and Bibi got out and walked toward me slowly. They'd both been crying. One of Zack's shirtsleeves was torn off and wrapped around his arm as a bandage. He dropped Bibi's hand and put his arms around me, and for a moment I laid my head on his shoulder and hugged him back. "Oh, I hope you weren't worrying," he said softly. And he said that the line had been busy when they'd called last night—four tries and then they had thought it was too late.

I said that was ridiculous, I was furious at all of them, and where the hell had they been?

"Oh no. I hope you weren't up worrying," he said again.

Of course I had been, I said, and so had Bibi's mother. What had happened?

"Gee, I'm sorry." He looked exhausted, and so disheartened that it made me feel quiet. "Your sister has just taken all the flak for you," I said, but my heart wasn't in it. "What *happened*?"

He said to Bibi, "Will you come in with me?" When he reached to take her hand, she pulled it away—her palms were covered with little cuts. Inside, the cat threw himself against her legs, and she looked at him absently but didn't pick him up. We sat down, and they started telling their story moment by moment.

A long tangled night. Implausible, undoubtedly real events. It had taken on a life of its own—it *unfolded*. First they'd started to drive to Washington to see the Vietnam Memorial—to show it to Alan, who'd been threatening for months to join the army. They were going to call me from the road. Holly's father, a doctor, lived in Philadelphia, and she wanted to stop at his apartment to show Alan a photograph of him, taken twenty-five years earlier: her handsome young dad in green beret and full regalia, in Panama, in front of a grocery store, giving the camera his typical look of confidence. In two cars they drove down to Philadelphia. On South Street, Bibi's car got a flat. It seemed a little menacing—many guys in shadowy doorways. Bibi drove Holly's car to a phone and called me, but my line was busy.

Still in my coat, sitting at the kitchen table, I was listening hard. They were across from me, leaning slightly against each other. Zack's good hand was in Bibi's jacket pocket. Their story was oddly persuasive, told in those intense soft voices.

Zack and Tim and Alan changed the flat; they all drove to the divorced father's apartment, he was gone for the week, they couldn't find the photograph, they ate some English muffins out of his freezer, thought of calling me but got distracted, then it was too late to call, they got exhausted, lay down.

"Eight of you lay down?"

Well, yes, they said.

They slept awhile. Some people were smoking recreational amounts of dope in quiet darkness on the living room rug; the others were in the father's room, on the bed and in the chair, under their jackets, sleeping. Later, the living room people slept, and the bedroom people woke up. The apartment smelled like dusty smoke. Holly was gone. There was confusion. Much later it turned out she'd been outside, wearing her father's navy blue overcoat, walking around the block—Spruce, Fifth, Pine, Fourth, over and over again. It was cold out, with a high, white moon. When Bibi and Zack got organized and went out to look for Holly, they stepped out into the dark street and there she was!

They reorganized themselves as a group, turned on some lamps, brushed their teeth with the absent father's toothbrush, opened, then closed, the windows, patted at the cushions. Alan was upset—maybe he was planning to make the wrong move. Holly was upset—this short night in her father's apartment, surrounded by his furniture, was in some strange, powerful way the most intimate time she'd ever had there. Some of the group wanted to debate with Alan; others talked quietly with Holly. After a long time standing in the foyer, they went out.

They found their cars. ("Why did you have to *find* your cars?" For a moment his wry self, Zack said, "Suffice it to say, we had to.") As usual, they drove to a diner. Holly was agitated and trembly and afraid people were looking at her; Alan was crying. Alan had been drinking a lot of tequila. While he cried, he held his velvet hat on his head.

Some were starving for pancakes. Others couldn't eat. It was late—they gave up the Washington trip and decided to turn back. When they came out of the diner and into the huge parking lot, Alan suddenly wanted to drive—he grabbed Bibi's keys and jumped behind the wheel of her car. They yelled, "Alan! You can't drive!" But he started off, slowly.

To stop him, Zack stepped in front of the car. Tim and Bibi stood to the rear, so he couldn't back up.

But Alan locked the doors and started calling increasingly loud warnings out the almost shut window into the freezing night. They were all jumping around when he finally eased into second and started toward Zack. Before Zack could jump away, Alan speeded up. When the car touched him, Zack did a strange thing: he put his hands against the hood and tried to push it back.

Alan had the windows up now; he was calling something, his friends were running alongside yelling, he accelerated; Zack was backing up fast, pushing at the car, and through the windshield he could see the tears on Alan's face. Zack jumped on the bumper and flung himself forward onto the hood. ("Like Harrison Ford," Bibi said fondly, and I blinked at her. I thought she was talking about an American president whose face I had temporarily forgotten.)

Zack was face down across the car, and he grabbed the wipers and the edge of the hood right under the windshield and held on with his fingertips. Two of the guys were reaching for him to help him off, but the car was going too fast and Zack was going to lose his grip and fall under the wheels. Alan speeded up. Zack laid his face on the metal—it reminded him of lying with your face against sand and hearing footsteps. He thought, This is ridiculous. I'm gonna get killed. He would be this year's high school death—age seventeen, in front of a gleaming diner. He closed his eyes. The parking lot spun around him. He could hear Bibi's voice, feel the cold metal under his weirdly hot face. When, instead of turning out onto the highway, Alan rammed a wall sideways and the car stopped, Zack flew off almost slowly, he thought, and he could see behind his eyes the arc being described in the black air by his body—arms, legs, gelled hair—before, at last, he landed.

He passed out. Under his forearm was half a wine bottle. There was glass all around on the ground, like confetti, and Bibi knelt and brushed it away from him, making many little cuts in her hands, which showed up only later, after the others had pulled Alan out of the car and embraced him, and Zack had opened his eyes, and they were seated inside the diner again, ordering huge doughnuts and lots of cups of coffee, like long-distance truckers. They were all squeezed into one big booth, pressed against each other. They punched the buttons on the jukebox. They felt light and almost cheerful now. Zack laid his head back on the vinyl and tried to take Bibi's hand, and all the little cuts started to bleed. Then, Zack said, he and Bibi both began to cry.

It was morning. Outside, it was cold and sunny and still. I thought about their friend Alan, about his habit of holding the velvet hat on his head, as if against a stiff wind. We were still sitting at the table in our coats. "Look, I know this sounds crazy," Zack said. I was about to say it certainly does, how dangerous, how unwise, and also you passed out, you should be looked at by a doctor. Instead I said, "You seem so sad."

Zack said, "Well, we are sad. That's just it. We really are."

After that, things changed. Nora didn't go to Florida; five days before, she broke up with Mark and unpacked. Zack got into college in Vermont; we drove to the mall and bought long underwear and Arctic boots. Then something seemed to drift out of the house, like fog breaking up, almost as if the kids were already gone.

Spring came. I took to spying on them. On Saturdays I'd walk past Tempting Treats and try to catch a glimpse of Zack in his green apron behind the counter. Or a couple of times on the way home from work I drove to the grade school where Nora ran the theater program; I stood in the bushes outside the window and watched her apply makeup to the exalted faces of five first graders. She'd live at home one more year, a placid, celibate girl. In three months Zack would leave for college, never to return.

And then for the rest of the year nothing much happened—I expected it to, but it didn't—and we started living in a sort of timeless present. Things were as calm as they had been obscurely turbulent. At first this was unnerving, and we waited for more volatility. Finally, we settled down, but by then June had come and it all was essentially over. Zack graduated. The entire graduating class wore sunglasses with their caps and gowns; they threw their caps and bellowed; they patiently stood on the lawn, for a long time being grinned at by their triumphant, exhausted, overexperienced families, then went out to get shitfaced.

I remember standing there on the grass watching Zack and Nora and their friends strolling away. At that moment, as I might have expected but hadn't, a wave of feeling broke over me; it was an unfamiliar combination—real, deep sadness and heart-stopping relief. I would miss them so much I'd never get over it—I couldn't live without them! At the same time, for my purposes they weren't leaving fast enough. I couldn't wait another minute to start not caring so much.

I looked around. Willie was standing with some other people, laughing like a maniac. Steven, with whom I would amicably part, had gone to get the still-unblemished Porsche. For the moment, I was alone. I remember I was wearing a lot of jewelry and a beige silk dress. It was hot. But I shivered. I think I started thinking about a circus, imagining a life on the high wire—I shuddered, the way I bet you would if you had just crossed the wire for the first time, and now you were safe on the platform, folding your parasol, looking back, suddenly recognizing that you had recently been walking in air.

I was staying at the home of a friend, and in the night the clinking of the dog's chain woke me up, and as I was waking I realized that Zack, a character I'd been writing about for years, would at age sixteen get in a car with his friends and try to drive down to Washington to see the Vietnam Memorial. I got up and found some small index cards next to the kitchen phone and wrote, on ten or twelve of them, the story of Zack's long night out. The rest of "Poltergeists" built itself up around that recounting of the nighttime ride, which is now lodged in the middle.

J.S.

THE DAGUERREOTYPE

□

JULIA WHITTY

I have the death portrait of my great-grandmother's baby who died from the measles in 1871. The baby's name and sex are lost. My great-grandmother's name was Florence Belva Parnell and she was only nineteen years old when her firstborn child died. In the daguerreotype, the dead infant is propped upright in its mother's lap, draped in a white gown, probably its christening gown. My great-grandmother is wearing mourning taffeta, looking very young. She cradles the back of her baby's head in one hand and leans her own head into her other hand. She does not look at the camera but the baby does, straight at the camera, eyes partly open, the left lid a little heavier than the right. Its expression reminds me of my childhood doll who had too many sugar-water tea parties spilled on her so that when you laid her down to sleep and her eyes were supposed to close, one eye stuck open. Or when you sat her up to feed her, both eyes stuck closed. In the picture of my great-grandmother's dead baby, there is a smudge of dried blood under its nose that even now makes me want to take a handkerchief to it. It has five measle welts on its forehead that never got a chance to heal.

I first found this photograph while looking for my parents' copy of a sex manual which I'd found once before under my father's sweaters on the top shelf in his closet. I was ten years old and had dragged a chair up from the kitchen, pushed aside his shoes on the floor, and stretched up on my tiptoes on the top of the chair until my arches cramped. I was remembering the amazing drawings of penises and where they fit into women. Somehow, having seen these pictures once was not enough. I needed to confirm my own memories. Were such things possible? Were they likely? I worked through the closet by feel, sweeping my hand under my father's smooth merino cardigan, between two cotton crewnecks, on top of an oiled-wool Aran Isles sweater that was stiff with age. I found the old photograph under the V-neck with the leather elbow patches. The picture was inside a paper wrapping that said Britt's Daguerreotype Studio, San Francisco. I took the picture over to my parents' bed and studied it. I thought the dark-haired woman looked tired. I thought she was holding her child's head because it would not behave itself for the camera. I had no idea the infant was dead. But then again, I thought my father was hiding the sex manual from my mother.

Nine years later when I was in college and writing a term paper for an art history class, I asked my mother about the picture of the woman and the child.

"That was your father's grandmother," said my mother.

"What was her name?" I asked.

"She was also a Parnell," said my mother.

"What was her first name?"

"Florence, I believe."

"Florence? Just like me? Wow. Was I named for her?"

"I suppose your father might have been thinking of something like that. I just liked the name." She was painting a watercolor of the light as it dripped through a maidenhair fern in the window.

"Sunlight kills ferns," I said.

"Yes," said my mother. "But isn't it beautiful?" She continued to twitch her brush across the paper so that little pinpoints of tint bled into the wash of water and spread out far beyond the boundaries of her brush. Watercolor was the only paint that continued to grow after you put it to paper. I never could understand how my mother controlled it.

"And is this Dad's father?" I asked, pointing to the child in the photograph.

"No," said my mother. "That was a child who died."

"When did it die?"

"It's dead right there." She pointed with the long handle of her watercolor brush at the photograph.

"It's dead here?" I pulled the picture up close to my eyes.

"Yes," said my mother. "That's a death portrait." She was as matter-of-fact about the mysteries of death as about the mysteries of watercolor.

"Jesus," I said.

I switched the subject of my art history term paper from nineteenth-century portrait photography to nineteenth-century death photography. I learned that the Victorians took pictures of their dead more readily than of their living. In many cases, the death portrait was the only picture that ever existed of a person, particularly a child. Photographers took care to pose the corpses as if they were still living, sitting them up in chairs, eyes closed, hands crossed in their laps as if they were thinking pleasant thoughts while awaiting Sunday visitors. Sometimes they were posed reclining on settees, eyes open, hands crossed on their chests, heads tilted to the side, as if they were listening to poetry being read in the next room.

I sent my mother the finished report with the professor's "B+, nice work, interesting subject" on it, and my mother sent me back one of her characteristic handwritten notes:

Dear Florence,

Your typing is shaping up nicely. I noticed there weren't too many white-outs. Perhaps you could make a future for yourself in the field of secretarialism. Keep up the good work.

Love,
Mom

p.s. I've enclosed a snapshot of my newest watercolor of the light from a forest fire reflected on a calypso orchid.

When I was twenty-five years old, a secretary, and pregnant by the married man who employed me and whom I thought I loved, I found myself preparing for the ordeal of my first abortion. I took out the picture of Florence Belva Parnell with her dead baby. I sought information about her grief. I looked closely at the image of her hand as it cradled the infant's head. Hers was an unmistakably tender touch, the fingers curled around the little ear and pressed flat against the downy hair as if she'd been stroking it in the private moments while the photographer set up his shot. She was not appalled that this was the corpse of her baby. She was not in any way repulsed by its death. She was just sad. I thought she looked boneless from grief. I felt that way too.

As I grew older I became more interested in the story of this woman and pressed my father for information about her when I made trips to his cabin. He had chosen to leave my mother when I was thirty and live alone in the ugly scrub pines on the west slope of the Sierras. "I'm sick of her," he told me when I asked him why they'd gotten divorced after all these years. "If I want to live on cans of Dinty Moore stew and smoke in the house and wear dirty clothes, well by god, at my age I'm going to." I stopped trying to clean up around his place after that and spent my time just talking with him.

"Your grandfather told me a few stories about his mother, Florence," said my father one night as we sat in the old broken-down kitchen chairs that he'd scrounged from some flea market and set up behind his cabin. The only saving grace to his piece of property as far as I could tell was the stars. They lived in abundance out there, crowding the skies with light carried across trillions of miles of the universe. He had taught me the stars and constellations when I was a child, but here, on the land at the end of his life, the cosmos had grown larger and more brilliant than anything I had ever seen before. I realized then that I could never know all these stars. For the first time I understood that my father's sky glittered with worlds that had been extinct for eons, that existed only as traveling light.

"When Florence was sixteen years old, she went west with her parents on a wagon train from Iowa," my father told me. "They were headed out the Overland Trail for Oregon, but her parents died of cholera somewhere in Nebraska. Florence hooked up with a widower named Birthright Parnell who was on the same wagon train, only he took the south fork in Wyoming and went to California. She went with him. They got married in San Francisco and ran a saloon there and raised Birthright's son from his previous marriage along with his two nephews, which he'd taken on after his brother drowned during the crossing of the Platte River. Birthright, I guess, had a thing for orphans. When Florence was thirty-seven years old she gave birth to the only one of her twelve children who survived past the age of seven. That was my father, Lucky Parnell."

"And?" I asked as his voice trailed to a stop in the darkness.

But my father would only tell me that it was time to stop talking and start looking, because the Perseids were running. And he clamped his mouth shut and turned his head up to the big night overhead, forcing me to look up too. When my father was younger he had taken time-lapse photographs of the Perseid meteor showers that made it look as if silver stars dripped like stalactites from the roof of the sky. Somehow both my parents knew the secret to making small pictures grow larger.

I let my own head drop back, let my eyes drift off without focus.
I knew that to see shooting stars you had to set your eyes free.

"The Perseids were named because they appear to shoot like arrows from the constellation of Perseus, the archer," my father had
told me when I was a child as we watched the showers from the
dark hills on the far side of the Golden Gate Bridge.

"Who is Perseus?" I wanted to know.

"Perseus was the son of Zeus who slew Medusa and then carried
her head around with him, flashing it at his enemies and turning
them into stone. He rescued the beautiful Andromeda from Cetus
by using the power of the dead Medusa's head."

"How long did this head last?" I wanted to know.

"Forever," he said. "You see, Perseus is still in the sky. Every
night he plays out his fate, again and again. And every August he
shoots his quiver of arrows through the sky for us to see."

It took a few moments of relaxation in the cold air on my father's
mountain before I could see Perseus firing. I saw only single arrows
in the beginning. But within half an hour they were racing furiously
through the sky, bouncing off the edges of my sight, scoring a few
direct hits in the center. The Sierra night illuminated more of Perseus' arrows than I had ever seen before.

"It's a good year," said my father, resting his head on the back
of the old kitchen chair. "The Delta Aquarid meteors are running
right now too."

I listened to his words and let my eyes drift to a point of
such distant focus that they almost came full circle, to the point of
closest focus. I felt the stars swarming past my sight and into my
fiber.

"I wish we had a name for it," I said to my father.

"For what?" he said, his eyes still up to the sky.

"Florence's dead baby."

"No use," he said. "It's lost."

"Maybe we should make up a name," I said.

"No," he said. "It had a real name once and you can't change that."

But secretly I called it Independence.

When I was thirty-seven and pregnant for the third time, I decided to have the baby even though I was not married and could not hope to interest the father (another boss, also married) in parenthood. I knew that Florence had been my age when she gave birth to my grandfather Lucky. I knew I wanted this child. I told my mother the news while she painted in the front parlor of the old Victorian house that she had bought in Petaluma after my father died. Despite the divorce, he had left her his money and his property in the Sierras. "I want some history around me," she told me when I asked why she had bought an old house with all its aches and pains. "I want to feel part of some continuum."

"You never felt that way before," I said.

"No," she said.

But she was delighted about my pregnancy. She told me that motherhood was far better than wifehood and that I had chosen the right half of the equation to balance my budget on. Then she cleaned her brushes and wiped them dry.

A week later I received a little package from her in the mail. She had bought me a beautiful antique picture frame with leather edging and hand-worked wood carving:

Dear Florence,

    You can put the baby's picture in here when it's born. I am very happy about your news.

Love,
Mom

p.s. I won first place in the Art Fair for my painting of the light shining through Mrs. Rosen's window at night.

I intended to put my baby's picture in the old frame. But until its birth, I decided to put the picture of my great-grandmother and her dead child in it, and then I never took it out.

I knew before my baby was born that it would be a girl and I decided to name her Florence Independence Parnell. "For my great-grandmother," I told my mother. "Not for me."

"Well, I always thought it was a pretty name," she said.

But I called her Indy from the start.

After Indy was born I would hold her in my lap with one hand on her chest, feeling her heart beating fast and fluttery through the eggshells of her ribs. I would look down on her face and study the tiny blue veins under her skin, memorizing them, thinking: someday her skin will grow thicker, but I will always know the blueprint of her inner life. She would smile up at me with eyes so new that I couldn't tell if they were really focused on me, or on something further away.

When she was under a year old I took her to the pediatrician for her measles vaccination. When the doctor stuck her with the needle I started to cry too. "Wow," he said. "You're a pretty attached mother." But I was crying for the other Independence and the other Florence.

As Indy grew she learned the secrets of watercolor from her grandmother. We would visit Petaluma on Sundays and sit in the big sunny front parlor of my mother's house. My mother and Indy each had their easels and their brushes, and together they would paint the sunlight on the stems of cut ranunculuses in a vase of water, or the slats of light that fell on my mother's Oriental rug through the wooden blinds. I watched Indy twitch her brush across the wet paper, watched the color start small and grow outward, watched the light shimmer in her pictures like a moving thing.

"Well," said my mother, sizing up Indy's work. "Indy sure takes after me. She could be a great painter."

When Indy was eleven years old she asked me to fill in the gaps in her knowledge of the facts of life. She was reading *Little Women* that summer, feeling the deficit of both siblings and father and questioning me at length about her own history. I had already explained to her why I had never married her father and how he had died before she turned two. I told her that she came from a long line of single-child families: me, my father, his father. We looked through the old photo albums together, laughing at the snapshots of her infanthood: her love of peas (she would collect them off her plate and paste them on her head), her first day at the beach (crawling after seagulls to offer them cookies), her rides on the back of her polka-dotted rocking horse (which my father had built for me and I had passed down to her), Indy smiling with glee, gripping hard on the handles of the rocking horse's ears. "I always flew on that rocking horse," she told me. "We went to Persia and sometimes to Egypt. Did you fly on him too?"

"No," I said. "I think I enjoyed just rocking in place."

"If I had brothers and sisters," she asked, "do you think we could have flown to those places together?"

"I'm sure you would have," I said, hugging her, feeling her curiosity bursting through her bones, knowing that someday it would speed her on her way from me.

"I have a pretty good idea of how people do it," she said one day, regarding sex. "But I'm not sure about all the details."

I thought back to my father's manual and the line drawings of body parts. I thought of my bosses and lost boyfriends, of passion and mispassion. Then I told her the truth, about penises and where they fit into women, about eggs and sperm and embryos.

"Is it *fun*?" she asked, skeptical.

I offered my advice: "Sex is best for love or babies." She looked hopeful. I thought of the rocking horse and conceded, "Indy, sex may take you places I've never been."

When Indy was sixteen years old, in the aftermath of my mother's death, I showed her the daguerreotype of Florence Belva Parnell and her dead infant. We had packed up my mother's old house and put it on the market. We held an estate sale and auctioned off most of her belongings. We kept only her paintings, her photo albums, and her letters.

"This is your great-great-grandmother," I said, showing Indy the daguerreotype.

"Who's the baby?"

"That's a baby that died."

"When did it die?"

"This is its death portrait," I said. "In those days, people took pictures of the dead as remembrances."

"Really?" said Indy, taking the picture out of my hand for a closer look. "Why?"

"The pictures consoled them," I said.

"I can see that," said Indy, studying.

"Can you?"

She nodded. "Do you keep it because of that?" she asked.

I thought for a moment. "Yes," I said. "This picture has consoled me many times over the years."

When Indy was twenty-two years old she joined the Peace Corps. After four years away at college I had imagined that she might come back with me for a spell. I repainted her room, bought her a new comforter in midnight blue with flecks like stars in it, planned trips to the Chabot Observatory, to the redwoods, to Big Sur.

"I'm going to Ghana," she called me up to tell me.

"Ghana?" I said. "That's so far away."

"I know," said Indy. "Isn't it exciting?"

"What about medical school?" I asked.

"I'll go as soon as I get back."

"When will that be?"

"Not for two years," she said proudly.

During the two months before she left we talked on the phone often, Indy telling me about Ghana and the village near Duayaw Nkwanta in the hills above the Black Volta where she would live. She told me about her job in the local medical clinic, where schistosomiasis, sleeping sickness, and malaria were epidemic. "But I'm going to learn too," she said. "I'm going to study the herbal medicines of the region."

I thought of Africa, so far away that we would never even share the same sunlight. I thought of Florence Belva Parnell leaving her dead parents in long-forgotten graves on the Nebraska plains. I decided to give Indy one of my father's photographs of the Perseid meteor showers to take with her. I gave her the last painting my mother ever made of the light inside a honeycomb.

"What about you?" she asked. "I want to take something of yours with me."

"I'll think of something," I said.

I went through all my belongings: the antique gold wedding bands that I collected, the Depression glass, the old books, and postcards of places I'd never been. In the end I looked in the yellow pages for a professional photographer. San Francisco had hundreds. I saw a listing for Britt's Photography, and thought: it can't be possible. I called to make an appointment.

Two days later, I found a gray-haired man behind the camera in the old store front south of Market.

"I want a photograph to give to my daughter to take with her into the Peace Corps," I told him.

"Something special then," he said.

I nodded. "How long has Britt's been here?" I asked.

"Since 1869," he said.

"My great-grandmother had a photograph taken here in 1871," I said.

"Really?" He smiled in amazement. "My great-grandfather probably took it."

"Really?" I said.

"But it wouldn't have been here exactly," he said. "The old studio burned down after the 1906 quake."

"Oh," I said.

"What kind of a portrait would you like?" he asked, smiling.

"My daughter would probably like something glamorous," I said. "But I'm not sure that's possible."

"What would *you* like?"

I thought for a moment. "I would like a picture where it looks like I am watching the stars, or a meteor shower."

"That's a lovely idea," he said.

A week after the session he sent me the pages of contact prints and told me to circle the ones I wanted printed. There were pictures with my head tilted up, slightly to the right, down to the left, over the shoulder. I chose the one where my head rests in one hand and a bar of light, like in the old movies, illuminates my eyes. "Yes," I thought. "That is the look. That is the starlight."

I found two beautiful antique frames of velvet and gilt and put the prints of my pictures in each of them. I kept one for myself, wrapped the other one in the tissue paper that said Britt's Photography, and gave it to Indy to take with her.

This story emerged in a forty-eight-hour rush of writing, a few months after I had read an article by John Updike in American Heritage *magazine called "Facing Death." His description of the Victorian art of death portraiture led me to his original source, a fascinating and ultimately terrifying book,* Sleeping Beauty: Memorial Photography in America. *The pictures in this book were so painful that many people I know could not look at them. And yet to me they expressed the burden of love, passed down from an age more fluent in the language of death. I discovered that a photograph of my own great-grandmother was in fact a death portrait—she in mourning dress, holding a portrait of a dead child (I needed a magnifying glass to discern this). I decided to use "The Daguerreotype" as a kind of memorial for all the forgotten ancestors. Most of the names in it are from my own family tree. It was the first short story I ever wrote, and my success with it lay less in publication than in the realization that I could find the vein of history that runs through us and mine it for the emotional heart of fiction.*

J.W.

In the Gloaming

◻

ALICE ELLIOTT DARK

Her son wanted to talk again, suddenly. During the days, he still brooded, scowling at the swimming pool from the vantage point of his wheelchair, where he sat covered with blankets despite the summer heat. In the evenings, though, Laird became more like his old self—his *old* old self, really. He became sweeter, the way he'd been as a child, before he began to cloak himself with layers of irony and clever remarks. He spoke with an openness that astonished her. No one she knew talked that way—no man, at least. After he was asleep, Janet would run through the conversations in her mind, and realize what it was she wished she had said. She knew she was generally considered sincere, but that had more to do with her being a good listener than with how she expressed herself. She found it hard work to keep up with him, but it was the work she had pined for all her life.

A month earlier, after a particularly long and grueling visit with a friend who'd come up on the train from New York, Laird had declared a new policy: no visitors, no telephone calls. She didn't blame him. People who hadn't seen him for a while were often shocked to tears by his appearance, and, rather than having them cheer him up, he felt obliged to comfort them. She'd overheard bits of some of those conversations. The final one was no worse than the others, but he was fed up. He had said more than once that he wasn't cut out to be the brave one, the one who would inspire everybody to walk away from a visit with him feeling uplifted, shaking their heads in wonder. He had liked being the most handsome and missed it very much; he was not a good victim. When he had had enough he went into a self-imposed retreat, complete with a wall of silence and other ascetic practices that kept him busy for several weeks.

Then he softened. Not only did he want to talk again; he wanted to talk to *her.*

It began the night they ate outside on the terrace for the first time all summer. Afterward, Martin—Laird's father—got up to make a telephone call, but Janet stayed in her wicker chair, resting before clearing the table. It was one of those moments when she felt nostalgic for cigarettes. On nights like this, when the air was completely still, she used to blow her famous smoke rings for the children, dutifully obeying their commands to blow one through another or three in a row, or to make big, ropy circles that expanded as they floated up to the heavens. She did exactly what they wanted, for as long as they wanted, sometimes going through a quarter of a pack before they allowed her to stop. Incredibly, neither Anne nor Laird became smokers. Just the opposite; they nagged at her to quit, and were pleased when she finally did. She wished they had been just a little bit sorry; it was a part of their childhood coming to an end, after all.

Out of habit, she took note of the first lightning bug, the first star. The lawn darkened, and the flowers that had sulked in the heat all day suddenly released their perfumes. She laid her head back on the rim of the chair and closed her eyes. Soon she was following Laird's breathing, and found herself picking up the vital rhythms, breathing along. It was so peaceful, being near him like this. How many mothers spend so much time with their thirty-three-year-old sons? she thought. She had as much of him now as she had had when he was an infant; more, in a way, because she had the memory of the intervening years as well, to round out her thoughts about him. When they sat quietly together she felt as close to him as she ever had. It was still him in there, inside the failing shell. *She still enjoyed him.*

"The gloaming," he said suddenly.

She nodded dreamily, automatically, then sat up. She turned to him. "What?" Although she had heard.

"I remember when I was little you took me over to the picture window and told me that in Scotland this time of day was called the 'gloaming.' "

Her skin tingled. She cleared her throat quietly, taking care not to make too much of an event of his talking again. "You thought I said 'gloomy.' "

He gave a smile, then looked at her searchingly. "I always thought it hurt you somehow that the day was over, but you said it was a beautiful time because for a few moments the purple light made the whole world look like the Scottish Highlands on a summer night."

"Yes. As if all the earth were covered with heather."

"I'm sorry I never saw Scotland," he said.

"You're a Scottish lad nonetheless," she said. "At least on my side." She remembered offering to take him to Scotland once, but Laird hadn't been interested. By then, he was in college and already sure of his own destinations, which had diverged so thoroughly from hers. "I'm amazed you remember that conversation. You couldn't have been more than seven."

"I've been remembering a lot lately."

"Have you?"

"Mostly about when I was very small. I suppose it comes from having you take care of me again. Sometimes, when I wake up and see your face, I feel I can remember you looking in on me when I was in my crib. I remember your dresses."

"Oh, no!" She laughed lightly.

"You always had the loveliest expression," he said.

She was astonished, caught off guard. Then, she had a memory, too—of her leaning over Laird's crib and suddenly having a picture of looking up at her own mother. "I know what you mean," she said.

"You do, don't you?"

He looked at her in a close, intimate way that made her self-conscious. She caught herself swinging her leg nervously, like a pendulum, and stopped.

"Mom," he said. "There are still a few things I need to do. I have to write a will, for one thing."

Her heart went flat. In his presence she had always maintained that he would get well. She wasn't sure she could discuss the other possibility.

"Thank you," he said.

"For what?"

"For not saying that there's plenty of time for that, or some similar sentiment."

"The only reason I didn't say it was to avoid the cliché, not because I don't believe it."

"You believe there is plenty of time?"

She hesitated; he noticed, and leaned forward slightly. "I believe there is time," she said.

"Even if I were healthy, it would be a good idea."

"I suppose."

"I don't want to leave it until it's too late. You wouldn't want me to suddenly leave everything to the nurses, would you?"

She laughed, pleased to hear him joking again. "All right, all right, I'll call the lawyer."

"That would be great." There was a pause. "Is this still your favorite time of day, Mom?"

"Yes, I suppose it is," she said, "although I don't think in terms of favorites anymore."

"Never mind favorites, then. What else do you like?"

"What do you mean?" she asked.

"I mean exactly that."

"I don't know. I care about all the ordinary things. You know what I like."

"Name one thing."

"I feel silly."

"Please?"

"All right. I like my patch of lilies of the valley under the trees over there. Now can we change the subject?"

"Name one more thing."

"Why?"

"I want to get to know you."

"Oh, Laird, there's nothing to know."

"I don't believe that for a minute."

"But it's true. I'm average. The only extraordinary thing about me is my children."

"All right," he said. "Then let's talk about how you feel about me."

"Do you flirt with your nurses like this when I'm not around?"

"I don't dare. They've got me where they want me." He looked at her. "You're changing the subject."

She smoothed her skirt. "I know how you feel about church, but if you need to talk I'm sure the minister would be glad to come over. Or if you would rather have a doctor . . ."

He laughed.

"What?"

"That you still call psychiatrists 'doctors.' "

She shrugged.

"I don't need a professional, Ma." He laced his hands and pulled at them as he struggled for words.

"What can I do?" she asked.

He met her gaze. "You're where I come from. I need to know about you."

That night she lay awake, trying to think of how she could help, of what, aside from her time, she had to offer. She couldn't imagine.

She was anxious the next day when he was sullen again, but the next night, and on each succeeding night, the dusk worked its spell. She set dinner on the table outside, and afterward, when Martin had vanished into the maw of his study, she and Laird began to speak. The air around them seemed to crackle with the energy they were creating in their effort to know and be known. Were other people so close, she wondered. She never had been, not to anybody. Certainly she and Martin had never really connected, not soul to soul, and with her friends, no matter how loyal and reliable, she always had a sense of what she could do that would alienate them. Of course, her friends had the option of cutting her off, and Martin could always ask for a divorce, whereas Laird was a captive audience. Parents and children were all captive audiences to each other; in view of this, it was amazing how little comprehension there was of one another's stories. Everyone stopped paying attention so early on, thinking they had figured it all out. She recognized that she was as guilty of this as anyone. She was still surprised whenever she went over to her daughter's house and saw how neat she was; in her mind, Anne was still a sloppy teenager who threw sweaters into the corner of her closet and candy wrappers under her bed. It still surprised her that Laird wasn't interested in girls. He had been, hadn't he? She remembered lying awake listening for him to come home, hoping that he was smart enough to apply what he knew about the facts of life, to take precautions.

Now she had the chance to let go of these old notions. It wasn't that she liked everything about Laird—there was much that remained foreign to her—but she wanted to know about all of it. As she came to her senses every morning in the moment or two after she awoke, she found herself aching with love and gratitude, as if he were a small, perfect creature again and she could look forward to a day of watching him grow. Quickly, she became greedy for their evenings. She replaced her half-facetious, half-hopeful reading of the horoscope in the daily newspaper with a new habit of tracking the time the sun would set, and drew satisfaction from seeing it come earlier as the summer waned; it meant she didn't have to wait as long. She took to sleeping late, shortening the day even more. It was ridiculous, she knew. She was behaving like a girl with a crush, behaving absurdly. It was a feeling she had thought she'd never have again, and now here it was. She immersed herself in it, living her life for the twilight moment when his eyes would begin to glow, the signal that he was stirring into consciousness. Then her real day would begin.

"Dad ran off quickly," he said one night. She had been wondering when he would mention it.

"He had a phone call to make," she said automatically.

Laird looked directly into her eyes, his expression one of gentle reproach. He was letting her know he had caught her in the central lie of her life, which was that she understood Martin's obsession with his work. She averted her gaze. The truth was that she had never understood. Why couldn't he sit with her for half an hour after dinner, or, if not with her, why not with his dying son?

She turned sharply to look at Laird. The word *dying* had sounded so loudly in her mind that she wondered if she had spoken it, but he showed no reaction. She wished she hadn't even thought it. She tried to stick to good thoughts in his presence. When she couldn't, and he had a bad night afterward, she blamed herself, as her efficient memory dredged up all the books and magazine articles she had read emphasizing the effect of psychological factors on the course of the disease. She didn't entirely believe it, but she felt compelled to give the benefit of the doubt to every theory that might help. It couldn't do any harm to think positively. And if it gave him a few more months . . .

"I don't think Dad can stand to be around me."

"That's not true." It was true.

"Poor Dad. He's always been a hypochondriac—we have that in common. He must hate this."

"He just wants you to get well."

"If that's what he wants, I'm afraid I'm going to disappoint him again. At least this will be the last time I let him down."

He said this merrily, with the old, familiar light darting from his eyes. She allowed herself to be amused. He had always been fond of teasing, and held no subject sacred. As the de-facto authority figure in the house—Martin hadn't been home enough to be the real disciplinarian—she had often been forced to reprimand Laird, but, in truth, she shared his sense of humor. She responded to it now by leaning over to cuff him on the arm. It was an automatic response, prompted by a burst of high spirits that took no notice of the circumstances. It was a mistake. Even through the thickness of his terrycloth robe, her knuckles knocked on bone. There was nothing left of him.

"It's his loss," she said, the shock of Laird's thinness making her serious again. It was the furthest she would go in criticizing Martin. She had always felt it her duty to maintain a benign image of him for the children. He had become a character of her invention, with a whole range of postulated emotions whereby he missed them when he was away on a business trip and thought of them every few minutes when he had to work late. Some years earlier, when she was secretly seeing a doctor—a psychiatrist—she had finally admitted to herself that Martin was never going to be the lover she had dreamed of. He was an ambitious, competitive, self-absorbed man who probably should never have got married. It was such a relief to be able to face it that she had wanted to share the news with her children, only to discover that they were dependent on the myth. They could hate his work, but they could not bring themselves to believe he had any choice in the matter. She had dropped the subject.

"Thank you, Ma. It's his loss in your case, too."

A throbbing began behind her eyes, angering her. The last thing she wanted to do was cry. There would be plenty of time for that. "It's not all his fault," she said when she had regained some measure of control. "I'm not very good at talking about myself. I was brought up not to."

"So was I," he said.

"Yes, I suppose you were."

"Luckily, I didn't pay any attention." He grinned.

"I hope not," she said, and meant it. "Can I get you anything?"

"A new immune system?"

She rolled her eyes, trying to disguise the way his joke had touched on her prayers. "Very funny. I was thinking more along the lines of an iced tea or an extra blanket."

"I'm fine. I'm getting tired actually."

Her entire body went on the alert, and she searched his face anxiously for signs of deterioration. Her nerves darted and pricked whenever he wanted anything; her adrenalin rushed. The fight-or-flight response, she supposed. She had often wanted to flee, but had forced herself to stay, to fight with what few weapons she had. She responded to his needs, making sure there was a fresh, clean set of sheets ready when he was tired, food when he was hungry. It was what she could do.

"Shall I get the nurse?" She pushed her chair back from the table.

"Okay," Laird said weakly. He stretched out his hand to her, and the incipient moonlight illuminated his skin, so it shone like alabaster. His face had turned ashy. It was a sight that made her stomach drop. She ran for Maggie, and by the time they returned Laird's eyes were closed, his head lolling to one side. Automatically, Janet looked for a stirring in his chest. There it was: his shoulders expanded; he still breathed. Always, in the second before she saw movement, she became cold and clinical as she braced herself for the possibility of discovering that he was dead.

Maggie had her fingers on his wrist and was counting his pulse against the second hand on her watch, her lips moving. She laid his limp hand back on his lap. "Fast," she pronounced.

"I'm not surprised," Janet said, masking her fear with authority. "We had a long talk."

Maggie frowned. "Now I'll have to wake him up again for his meds."

"Yes, I suppose that's true. I forgot about that."

Janet wheeled him into his makeshift room downstairs and helped Maggie lift him into the rented hospital bed. Although he weighed almost nothing, it was really a job for two; his weight was dead weight. In front of Maggie, she was all brusque efficiency, except for the moment when her fingers strayed to touch Laird's pale cheek and she prayed she hadn't done any harm.

"Who's your favorite author?" he asked one night.

"Oh, there are so many," she said.

"Your real favorite."

She thought. "The truth is there are certain subjects I find attractive more than certain authors. I seem to read in cycles, to fulfill an emotional yearning."

"Such as?"

"Books about people who go off to live in Africa or Australia or the South Seas."

He laughed. "That's fairly self-explanatory. What else?"

"When I really hate life I enjoy books about real murders. 'True crime,' I think they're called now. They're very punishing."

"Is that what's so compelling about them? I could never figure it out. I just know that at certain times I loved the gore, even though I felt absolutely disgusted with myself for being interested in it."

"You need to think about when those times were. That will tell you a lot." She paused. "I don't like reading about sex."

"Big surprise!"

"No, no," she said. "It's not for the reason you think, or not only for that reason. You see me as a prude, I know, but remember, it's part of a mother's job to come across that way. Although perhaps I went a bit far . . ."

He shrugged amiably. "Water under the bridge. But go on about sex."

"I think it should be private. I always feel as though these writers are showing off when they describe a sex scene. They're not really trying to describe sex, but to demonstrate that they're not afraid to write about it. As if they're thumbing their noses at their mothers."

He made a moue.

Janet went on. "You don't think there's an element of that? I *do* question their motives, because I don't think sex can ever actually be portrayed—the sensations and the emotions are . . . beyond language. If you only describe the mechanics, the effect is either clinical or pornographic, and if you try to describe intimacy instead, you wind up with abstractions. The only sex you could describe fairly well is bad sex—and who wants to read about that, for God's sake, when everyone is having bad sex of their own?"

"Mother!" He was laughing helplessly, his arms hanging limply over the sides of his chair.

"I mean it. To me it's like reading about someone using the bathroom."

"Good grief!"

"Now who's the prude?"

"I never said I wasn't," he said. "Maybe we should change the subject."

She looked out across the land. The lights were on in other peo-

ple's houses, giving the evening the look of early fall. The leaves
were different, too, becoming droopy. The grass was dry, even with
all the watering and tending from the gardener. The summer was
nearly over.

"Maybe we shouldn't," she said. "I've been wondering. Was that
side of life satisfying for you?"

"Ma, tell me you're not asking me about my sex life."

She took her napkin and folded it carefully, lining up the edges
and running her fingers along the hems. She felt very calm, very
pulled together and all of a piece, as if she'd finally got the knack
of being a dignified woman. She threaded her fingers and laid her
hands in her lap. "I'm asking about your love life," she said. "Did
you love, and were you loved in return?"

"Yes."

"I'm glad."

"That was easy," he said.

"Oh, I've gotten very easy, in my old age."

"Does Dad know about this?" His eyes were twinkling wickedly.

"Don't be fresh," she said.

"You started it."

"Then I'm stopping it. Now."

He made a funny face, and then another, until she could no longer
keep from smiling. His routine carried her back to memories of his
childhood efforts to charm her: watercolors of her favorite vistas
(unrecognizable without the captions), bouquets of violets self-
consciously flung into her lap, chores performed without prompting.
He had always gone too far, then backtracked to regain even footing.
She had always allowed herself to be wooed.

Suddenly she realized: Laird had been the love of her life.

One night it rained hard. Janet decided to serve the meal in the
kitchen, since Martin was out. They ate in silence; she was freed

from the compulsion to keep up the steady stream of chatter that she used to affect when Laird hadn't talked at all; now she knew she could save her words for afterward. He ate nothing but comfort foods lately: mashed potatoes, vanilla ice cream, rice pudding. The days of his strict macrobiotic regime, and all the cooking classes she had taken in order to help him along with it, were past. His body was essentially a thing of the past, too; when he ate, he was feeding what was left of his mind. He seemed to want to recapture the cosseted feeling he'd had when he'd been sick as a child and she would serve him flat ginger ale, and toast soaked in cream, and play endless card games with him, using his blanket-covered legs as a table. In those days, too, there'd been a general sense of giving way to illness: then, he let himself go completely because he knew he would soon be better and active and have a million things expected of him again. Now he let himself go because he had fought long enough.

Finally, he pushed his bowl toward the middle of the table, signaling that he was finished. (His table manners had gone to pieces. Who cared?) She felt a light, jittery excitement, the same jazzy feeling she got when she was in a plane that was just picking up speed on the runway. She arranged her fork and knife on the rim of her plate and pulled her chair in closer. "I had an odd dream last night," she said.

His eyes remained dull.

She waited uncertainly, thinking that perhaps she had started to talk too soon. "Would you like something else to eat?"

He shook his head. There was no will in his expression; his refusal was purely physical, a gesture coming from the satiation in his stomach. An animal walking away from its bowl, she thought.

To pass the time, she carried the dishes to the sink, gave them a good hot rinse, and put them in the dishwasher. She carried the ice cream to the counter, pulled a spoon from the drawer and scraped off a mouthful of the thick, creamy residue that stuck to the inside of the lid. She ate it without thinking, so the sudden sweetness caught her by surprise. All the while she kept track of Laird, but every time she thought she noticed signs of his readiness to talk and hurried back to the table she found his face still blank.

She went to the window. The lawn had become a floodplain and was filled with broad pools; the branches of the evergreens sagged, and the sky was the same uniform grayish yellow it had been since morning. She saw him focus his gaze on the line where the treetops touched the heavens, and she understood. There was no lovely interlude on this rainy night, no heathered dusk. The gray landscape had taken the light out of him.

"I'm sorry," she said aloud, as if it were her fault.

He gave a tiny, helpless shrug.

She hovered for a few moments, hoping, but his face was slack, and she gave up. She felt utterly forsaken, too disappointed and agitated to sit with him and watch the rain. "It's all right," she said. "It's a good night to watch television."

She wheeled him to the den and left him with Maggie, then did not know what to do with herself. She had no contingency plan for this time. It was usually the one period of the day when she did not need the anesthesia of tennis games, bridge lessons, volunteer work, errands. She had not considered the present possibility. For some time, she hadn't given any thought to what Martin would call "the big picture." Her conversations with Laird had lulled her into inventing a parallel big picture of her own. She realized that a part of her had worked out a whole scenario: the summer evenings would blend into fall; then, gradually, the winter would arrive, heralding chats by the fire, Laird resting his feet on the pigskin ottoman in the den while she dutifully knitted her yearly Christmas sweaters for Anne's children.

She had allowed herself to imagine a future. That had been her mistake. This silent, endless evening was her punishment, a reminder of how things really were.

She did not know where to go in her own house, and ended up wandering through the rooms, propelled by a vague, hunted feeling. Several times, she turned around, expecting someone to be there, but, of course, no one ever was. She was quite alone. Eventually, she realized that she was imagining a person in order to give material properties to the source of her wounds. She was inventing a villain. There should be a villain, shouldn't there? There should be an enemy, a devil, an evil force that could be driven out. Her imagination had provided it with aspects of a corporeal presence so she could pretend, for a moment, that there was a real enemy hovering around her, someone she could have the police come and take away. But the enemy was part of Laird, and neither he nor she nor any of the doctors or experts or ministers could separate the two.

She went upstairs and took a shower. She barely paid attention to her own body anymore, and only noticed abstractly that the water was too hot, her skin turning pink. Afterward, she sat on the chaise longue in her bedroom and tried to read. She heard something; she leaned forward and cocked her head toward the sound. Was that Laird's voice? Suddenly she believed that he had begun to talk after all—she believed he was talking to Maggie. She dressed and went downstairs. He was alone in the den, alone with the television. He didn't hear or see her. She watched him take a drink from a cup, his hand shaking badly. It was a plastic cup with a straw poking through the lid, the kind used by small children while they are learning to drink. It was supposed to prevent accidents, but it couldn't stop his hands from trembling. He managed to spill the juice anyway.

Laird had always coveted the decadent pile of cashmere lap blankets she had collected over the years in the duty-free shops of the various British airports. Now he wore one around his shoulders, one over his knees. She remembered similar balmy nights when he would arrive home from soccer practice after dark, a towel slung around his neck.

"I suppose it has to be in the church," he said.

"I think it should," she said, "but it's up to you."

"I guess it's not the most timely moment to make a statement about my personal disbeliefs. But I'd like you to keep it from being too lugubrious. No lilies, for instance."

"God forbid."

"And have some decent music."

"Such as?"

"I had an idea, but now I can't remember."

He pressed his hands to his eyes. His fingers were so transparent that they looked as if he were holding them over a flashlight.

"Please buy a smashing dress, something mournful yet elegant."

"All right."

"And don't wait until the last minute."

She didn't reply.

Janet gave up on the idea of a rapprochement between Martin and Laird; she felt freer when she stopped hoping for it. Martin rarely came home for dinner anymore. Perhaps he was having an affair? It was a thought she'd never allowed herself to have before, but it didn't threaten her now. Good for him, she even decided, in her strongest, most magnanimous moments. Good for him if he's actually feeling bad and trying to do something to make himself feel better.

Anne was brave and chipper during her visits, yet when she walked back out to her car, she would wrap her arms around her ribs and shudder. "I don't know how you do it, Mom. Are you really all right?" she always asked, with genuine concern.

"Anne's become such a hopeless matron," Laird always said, with fond exasperation, when he and his mother were alone again later. Once, Janet began to tease him for finally coming to friendly terms with his sister, but she cut it short when she saw that he was blinking furiously.

They were exactly the children she had hoped to have: a companionable girl, a mischievous boy. It gave her great pleasure to see them together. She did not try to listen to their conversations but watched from a distance, usually from the kitchen as she prepared them a snack reminiscent of their childhood, like watermelon boats or lemonade. Then she would walk Anne to the car, their similar good shoes clacking across the gravel. They hugged, pressing each other's arms, and their brief embraces buoyed them up—forbearance and grace passing back and forth between them like a piece of shared clothing, designated for use by whoever needed it most. It was the kind of parting toward which she had aimed her whole life, a graceful, secure parting at the close of a peaceful afternoon. After Anne left, Janet always had a tranquil moment or two as she walked back to the house through the humid September air. Everything was so still. Occasionally there were the hums and clicks of a lawn mower or the shrieks of a band of children heading home from school. There were the insects and the birds. It was a straightforward, simple life she had chosen. She had tried never to ask for too much, and to be of use. Simplicity had been her hedge against bad luck. It had worked for so long. For a brief moment, as she stepped lightly up the single slate stair and through the door, her legs still harboring all their former vitality, she could pretend her luck was still holding.

Then she would glance out the window and there would be the heart-catching sight of Laird, who would never again drop by for a casual visit. Her chest would ache and flutter, a cave full of bats.

Perhaps she had asked for too much, after all.

"What did you want to be when you grew up?" Laird asked.

"I was expected to be a wife and mother. I accepted that. I wasn't a rebel."

"There must have been something else."

"No," she said. "Oh, I guess I had all the usual fantasies of the day, of being the next Amelia Earhart or Margaret Mead, but that was all they were—fantasies. I wasn't even close to being brave enough. Can you imagine me flying across the ocean on my own?" She laughed and looked over for his laughter, but he had fallen asleep.

A friend of Laird's had somehow got the mistaken information that Laird had died, so she and Martin received a condolence letter. There was a story about a time a few years back when the friend was with Laird on a bus in New York. They had been sitting behind two older women, waitresses who began to discuss their income taxes, trying to decide how much of their tip income to declare to sound realistic so they wouldn't attract an audit. Each woman offered up bits of folk wisdom on the subject, describing in detail her particular situation. During a lull in the conversation, Laird stood up.

"Excuse me, I couldn't help overhearing," he said, leaning over them. "May I have your names and addresses, please? I work for the I.R.S."

The entire bus fell silent as everyone watched to see what would happen next. Laird took a small notebook and pen from the inside pocket of his jacket. He faced his captive audience. "I'm part of a new I.R.S. outreach program," he told the group. "For the next ten minutes I'll be taking confessions. Does anyone have anything he or she wants to tell me?"

Smiles. Soon the whole bus was talking, comparing notes—when they'd first realized he was kidding, and how scared they had been before they caught on. It was difficult to believe these were the same New Yorkers who were supposed to be so gruff and isolated.

"Laird was the most vital, funniest person I ever met," his friend wrote.

Now, in his wheelchair, he faced off against slow-moving flies, waving them away.

"The gloaming," Laird said.

Janet looked up from her knitting, startled. It was midafternoon, and the living room was filled with bright October sun. "Soon," she said.

He furrowed his brow. A little flash of confusion passed through his eyes, and she realized that for him it was already dark.

He tried to straighten his shawl, his hands shaking. She jumped up to help; then, when he pointed to the fireplace, she quickly laid the logs as she wondered what was wrong. Was he dehydrated? She thought she recalled that a dimming of vision was a sign of dehydration. She tried to remember what else she had read or heard, but even as she grasped for information, facts, her instincts kept interrupting with a deeper, more dreadful thought that vibrated through her, rattling her and making her gasp as she often did when remembering her mistakes, things she wished she hadn't said or done, wished she had the chance to do over. She knew what was wrong, and yet she kept turning away from the truth, her mind spinning in every other possible direction as she worked on the fire, only vaguely noticing how wildly she made the sparks fly as she pumped the old bellows.

Her work was mechanical—she had made hundreds of fires—and soon there was nothing left to do. She put the screen up and pushed him close, then leaned over to pull his flannel pajamas down to meet his socks, protecting his bare shins. The sun streamed in around him, making him appear trapped between bars of light. She resumed her knitting, with mechanical hands.

"The gloaming," he said again. It did sound somewhat like "gloomy," because his speech was slurred.

"When all the world is purple," she said, hearing herself sound falsely bright. She wasn't sure whether he wanted her to talk. It was some time since he had talked—not long, really, in other people's lives, perhaps two weeks—but she had gone on with their conversations, gradually expanding into the silence until she was telling him stories and he was listening. Sometimes, when his eyes closed, she trailed off and began to drift. There would be a pause that she didn't always realize she was making, but if it went on too long he would call out "Mom?" with an edge of panic in his voice, as if he were waking from a nightmare. Then she would resume, trying to create a seamless bridge between what she had been thinking and where she had left off.

"It was really your grandfather who gave me my love for the gloaming," she said. "Do you remember him talking about it?" She looked up politely, expectantly, as if Laird might offer her a conversational reply. He seemed to like hearing the sound of her voice, so she went on, her needles clicking. Afterward, she could never remember for sure at what point she had stopped talking and had floated off into a jumble of her own thoughts, afraid to move, afraid to look up, afraid to know at which exact moment she became alone. All she knew was that at a certain point the fire was in danger of dying out entirely, and when she got up to stir the embers she glanced at him in spite of herself and saw that his fingers were making knitting motions over his chest, the way people did as they were dying. She knew that if she went to get the nurse, Laird would be gone by the time she returned, so she went and stood behind him, leaning over to press her face against his, sliding her hands down his busy arms, helping him along with his fretful stitches until he finished this last piece of work.

Later, after the most pressing calls had been made and Laird's body had been taken away, Janet went up to his old room and lay down on one of the twin beds. She had changed the room into a guest room when he went off to college, replacing his things with guest-room decor, thoughtful touches such as luggage racks at the foot of each bed, a writing desk stocked with paper and pens, heavy wooden hangers and shoe trees. She made an effort to remember the room as it had been when he was a little boy; she had chosen a train motif, then had to redecorate when Laird decided trains were silly. He had wanted it to look like a jungle, so she had hired an art student to paint a jungle mural on the walls. When he decided *that* was silly, he hadn't bothered her to do anything about it, but had simply marked time until he could move on.

Anne came over, offered to stay, but was relieved to be sent home to her children.

Presently, Martin came in. Janet was watching the trees turn to mere silhouettes against the darkening sky, fighting the urge to pick up a true-crime book, a debased urge. He lay down on the other bed.

"I'm sorry," he said.

"It's so wrong," she said angrily. She hadn't felt angry until that moment; she had saved it up for him. "A child shouldn't die before his parents. A young man shouldn't spend his early thirties wasting away talking to his mother. He should be out in the world. He shouldn't be thinking about me, or what I care about, or my opinions. He shouldn't have had to return my love to me—it was his to squander. Now I have it all back and I don't know what I'm supposed to do with it," she said.

She could hear Martin weeping in the darkness. He sobbed, and her anger veered away.

They were quiet for some time.

"Is there going to be a funeral?" Martin asked finally.

"Yes. We should start making the arrangements."

"I suppose he told you what he wanted."

"In general. He couldn't decide about the music."

She heard Martin roll onto his side, so that he was facing her across the narrow chasm between the beds. He was still in his office clothes. "I remember being very moved by the bagpipes at your father's funeral."

It was an awkward offering, to be sure, awkward and late, and seemed to come from someone on the periphery of her life who knew her only slightly. It didn't matter; it was perfectly right. Her heart rushed toward it.

"I think Laird would have liked that idea very much," she said.

It was the last moment of the gloaming, the last moment of the day her son died. In a breath, it would be night; the moon hovered behind the trees, already rising to claim the sky, and she told herself she might as well get on with it. She sat up and was running her toes across the bare floor, searching for her shoes, when Martin spoke again, in a tone she used to hear on those long-ago nights when he rarely got home until after the children were in bed and he relied on her to fill him in on what they'd done that day. It was the same curious, shy, deferential tone that had always made her feel as though all the frustrations and boredom and mistakes and rushes of feeling in her days as a mother did indeed add up to something of importance, and she decided that the next round of telephone calls could wait while she answered the question he asked her: "Please tell me —what else did my boy like?"

As a baby, my son hated going to bed at night. He fought and fought against that loss of consciousness, as if there were some danger posed to him in sleep. Or perhaps he believed he would miss something if he left us to putter around our apartment, unsupervised by his eager gaze? Before he learned to speak, our interpretations of his signals were a guess, and our responses were likewise uncertain: sometimes educated, often intuitive, and even more often an enactment of a piece of borrowed wisdom, in hopes that someone else's cure had broader applications. One night I even tried letting him "cry it out." The concept was anathema to me on every level—I equated it with the rat labs at college, all those appalling experiments in learned helplessness—but finally I became desperate and exhausted enough to try it. We both cried for over two hours, me in the living room, he in his crib, before I finally gave up on that remedy. All those babies who are said to squawk for a few minutes and then settle down . . . well, he wasn't one of them. He was my little boy, and we were charting our own map. More than anything, I wanted to understand.

At ten months, we took him out of his crib and gave him a futon. He was happier by far, but still needed company when settling down. I wrote most of this story while sitting next to him on the futon as he slept. I had a strong sense of all the women throughout history who'd sat with their children, in sleeplessness, sickness, anxiety, or pure communion. It was otherworldly, sitting there, watching over the sleeping child who had so recently not existed and who I could lose at any moment. Death was a presence in his tiny room as I forced myself through the litany of what ifs. I'd had a friend who'd died of AIDS not long before. I'd been wrapped up with him during his life and his illness, and with my own loss afterward, but suddenly I could think only of his mother. How much more can be asked of a mother than to help her child die? I imagined it, and wrote it down.

At four, my son still fights sleep. He still can't explain exactly why. That's all right. We have our relationship. I don't need to know everything.

A.E.D.

SWIMMING TO THE TOP

OF THE RAIN

□

J. CALIFORNIA COOPER

Mothers are something ain't they? They mostly the one person you can count on! All your life . . . if they live. Most mothers be your friend and love you no matter what you do! I bet mine was that way. You ain't never known nobody didn't have one, so they must be something!

Life is really something too, cause you can stand stark raving still and life will still happen to you. It's gonna spill over and touch you no matter where you are! Always full of lessons. Everywhere! All you got to do is look around you if you got sense enough to see! I hear people say they so bored with life. Ain't nothing but a fool that ain't got nothing to do in this here world. My Aunt Ellen, who I'm going to tell you about, always said, "Life is like tryin to swim to the top of the rain sometime!"

One of the things I always put in my prayers is "Lord, please don't let me be no big fool in this life!" Cause you got to be thinking, and think hard, to make it to any kinda peace and happiness. And it seem like things start happening from the moment you are born!

My mama died from my being born the minute I was born! Now if you don't think that changed my whole life, you need to pray not to be a fool! She left three of us. My two sisters, I call them Oldest and Middle, and me. She had done been working hard to support herself for years, I learned, and finally for her two children after my daddy left. He came back, one more time, to make one more baby. I can look back now and understand, she was grieved and lonely and tired from holding up against hard times all by herself and wished this time he was back to stay and help, so she let him back in her bed. Probly to be held one more time by someone sides a child. Then I was made and she told him. He got drunk, again, but didn't beat her. There's some whippings people give you tho, without laying a hand on you, hurts just as bad, even worse sometime. He left, again. He musta broke somethin inside her besides her spirit and her heart cause when I took my first breath, she took her last breath. I wished I could of fixed it whilst I was inside her, so she could live . . . and I could get to have my own mama.

She had already told my sisters what my name was to be. I was called Care. My first sister was "Angel" and the second "Better," four and five years old. But I call them Older and Middle.

We was alone, three babies.

Mama had two sisters we had never heard of. Somebody knew how to reach them cause one, Aunt Bell, who lived in a big city, came and got us and took us in. Had to, I guess. Cause wasn't nowhere else we could go at that time . . . three of us!? Musta been a shock for somebody wasn't expecting anything like that!

We think my Aunt Bell was a prostitute. Older say she was never in the little rooms she rented for us but once or twice a month. She would pay the rent, stock up the food, give us some little shiny toy or dress, lotsa warnings bout strangers, and leave us with a hug and kiss. If she had a husband we never met him. We were young and didn't understand a lot, but we loved that woman, least I did. Was somethin kin to me in her. She was so sad, even when she was smiling and laughing. I didn't see it, but I felt it. I'd cry for her when I thought of her and not know why I was crying! She took care us for about five years, then she was dumped on our front porch, stabbed to death! We opened the door for sunlight and found her and darkness. That darkness moved right on into the house, into our lives, again.

I don't know if they even tried to find out who did it. Just another whore gone, I guess. Never mind the kind of person she was, trying to do for us and all. We had never really been full too steady, but we had always had something!

We was alone, again.

I found out early in life you going to find a lotta mean people everyplace, but sometime a few good ones somewhere. Someone came in and prepared for the tiny, short funeral. The church donated the coffin and fed us. Somebody went through Aunt Bell's few sad things she had there and that's when we found out we had another aunt, Aunt Ellen. People should tell the children where to look and who to look for, just in case! Do we ever know what's goin to happen to us in this life? Or when?

Somehow they reached Aunt Ellen and she got there bout a week after the funeral. We was all separated and could tell people was getting tired of feeding and caring for us. Well, after all, they was poor people or they never would have known us anyway and they was already having a hard time before we needed them!

Aunt Ellen was a husky-looking, mannish-looking woman who wore pants, a straw hat, and a red flowered blouse. I will always remember that. I was crying when she came . . . scared. I stared at her . . . our new mama . . . wondering what was she going to be like. What would she do with us, to us, for us? Would she want us? I was only five years old and already had to worry bout my survival . . . our lives! I'm telling you, look at your mama, if she be living, and be thankful to God!

She picked me up and held me close to her breast, under her chin and she felt just like I knew my mama did. She took us all, sat us down and just like we was grown, talked to us. "I ain't got no home big enough for all us. Ain't got much money, done saved a little only. But I got a little piece of land I been plannin to build on someday and this must be the day! Now, I ain't got chick or child, but now I got you . . . all of you. Ain't gonna be no separation nomore, you got me. I loved my sister and I love you."

Three little hearts just musta exploded with love and peace. I know mine did! I remember holding on to her pants, case she disappeared, I could disappear with her!

She went on talking as she squeezed a cheek, smoothed a hair, brushed a dress, wiped a nose. "I ain't no cookie-bakin woman! But you learn to bake the cookies and I'll provide the stove and the dough!" My sister, Older, could already cook most everything, but we'd never had no stuff to cook cookies with. "Now!" she went on as she stroked me. "You want to go with me?" One nodded yes, one said "yes." I just peed I was so happy! I kept putting her as my mama! "We'll try to swim to the top of the rain together!" She smiled and I sensed that sadness again, but it went away quick and I forgot it.

When I hear people say "Homeland," I always know what they mean. There is *no place* like a home. She took us to that beautiful land on a bus, eating cold biscuits, bacon and pieces of chicken, even some cornbread. All fixed by our old neighbors. We stayed hither and yon while she mixed and poured the concrete and built that little cabin with four rooms. We lived in each room as it was finished. It was a beautiful little lopsided house . . . ours! Oh, other people came to help sometime, but we worked hardest on our own home! It took two more years to finally get a inside toilet and bath, but Aunt Ellen had to have one cause she blived in baths and teeth washing and things like that, tho I never saw her take one!

We lived there til we was grown. We tilled a little land, raised our own few pigs and chickens, and split one cow with another family for the milk. She raised us, or helped us raise ourselves.

Older sister quit the little schoolhouse when she was bout fifteen years old in the eighth or ninth grade and got married to a real light man. She just had to have that real light man! In a couple years she had two children, both girls. The light man left, or she left him and came home. Aunt Ellen said, "NO, no! I ain't holdin up no leaning poles! If you old enough to spread them knees and make babies, you old enough to take care yourself! You done stepped out into the rain, now you learn to swim!" Older cried a little cause I guess she was scared of the world, but Aunt Ellen took her round to find a job and a place to live. We baby-sat for her til she was steady. One day we looked up and she was on her own! And smiling! Not cause she was doing so good, but because she was taking care herself and her children and didn't have to answer to nobody! When her man came back, she musta remembered Mama, cause she didn't let him in to make no more babies!

Middle sister went on to the ninth grade, then went to nursing school. Just the kind teach you how to clean up round a patient. Aunt Ellen was proud. She was getting older, but not old yet, and said she would help anybody wanted to go to school long as they got a job and helped themselves too, and she did. That left only me home with her, but I didn't want to go nowhere away from her!

We didn't have no lot of money, helping Middle go to school and taking care of ourselves. I couldn't even think of getting clothes and all those kind of things! I had me one good dress and a good pair of patent-leather shoes I wore to church every Sunday. So after I got out the ninth grade I asked a lady who sewed for a livin to teach me in exchange for housework and she did. That's why I know there's some nice white people who will help you. After I learned, she would pay me a little to do little things like collars, seams, and things. Then I still watched her and learned more for free! I sewed for Aunt Ellen and me and Older's babies. We saved money that way. That's the same way I learned to play the piano . . . sewing for the piano teacher. I got to be pretty good. Got paid a little to play at weddings. Cause I won't charge for no funerals. Death already cost too much!

Middle graduated from that school, well, got out. Cause all they did was ask her was she all paid up and when she said yes, they handed her a paper said she was completed. She got married right soon after that to somebody working in a hospital and they moved to a city that had more hospitals to work in. Soon she had a baby girl. Another girl was good, but where was all our boy children? They necessary too!

One evening after a good dinner, me and Aunt Ellen sat out on the porch. I was swinging and she was rockin as she whittled some wood makin a stool for her leg what had started giving her trouble. She wanted something to prop it up on. Mosquitoes and firebugs was buzzing round us. She turned to me and said, "You know, I'm glad you all came along to my life. I did a lot of things I might never have got to, and now I'm glad they done! I got a family and a home too! I blive we gonna make that swim to the top of the rain! Things seem to be workin out alright! You all are fine girls and I'm proud of you. You gon be alright!"

Pleased, I laughed. "Aunty, you can't swim goin straight up! You can't swim the rain! You got to swim the river or the lake!"

She smiled. "Life is more like the rain. The river and the lake lay down for you. All you got to do is learn how to swim fore you go where they are and jump in. But life don't do that. You always gets the test fore you learn the swimming lesson, unexpected, like rain. You don't go to the rain, the rain comes to you. Anywhere, anytime. You got to prepare for it! . . . protect yourself! And if it keeps coming down on you, you got to learn to swim to the top through the dark clouds, where the sun is shining on that silver lining."

She wasn't laughing, so I didn't either. I just thought about what she said til I went to sleep. I still ain't never forgot it.

The next day when dinner was ready, Aunt Ellen hadn't come in from the fields and it got to be dark. Finally the mule came home dragging the plow. I went out to look for her, crying as I walked over the plowed rows, screaming her name out, cause I was scared I had lost my Aunt Mama. I had.

I found her under a tree, like she was sleeping. Had a biscuit with a little ham in it, still in her hand. But she wasn't sleeping, she was dead. I couldn't carry her in and wouldn't leave her alone so just stayed out there holding her all night long. A kind neighbor found us the next day, cause he noticed the mule draggin the plow and nobody home.

I sewed Aunt Ellen's shroud to be buried in. I played the piano at her funeral too. Her favorite song, "My Buddy." I would have done anything for her. I loved her, my Aunt Mama. She taught me so much. All I knew to make my life with.

I was alone again.

Older and I buried her. Middle didn't come, but sent ten dollars. I gave the preacher five dollars and stuck the other five dollars in Aunt Ellen's pocket, thinking, All your money passed out to us . . . Take this with you. Later, I planted turnips and mustard greens all round her homemade grave, cause she liked them best. Then . . . that part of my life was over.

I was alone again, oh Lord. Trying to see through the rain. You ever been alone? Ain't had nobody? Didn't know what to do? Where to turn? I didn't. I was alone even with my sisters living. This was my life and what was I to do with it?

The house and land belonged to all of us. I tried to stay in that cabin, intended to, but it was too lonely out there. Specially when all the men started passing there late at night, stopping, setting. Rain coming to me just like Aunt Ellen said. I didn't want to be rained on, so I gave it out to a couple without a home and moved on down there where my middle sister was, in the city. I got a job living-in and was making a little extra and saving by doing sewing. I was hunting out a future.

I went to church a lot. I stick close to God cause when you need a friend, you need one you can count on! Not the preacher . . . but God! I steered clear of them men who try to get a working woman and live off her itty-bitty money. I ain't got to tell you about them! They dress and sit while she work! No! No! My aunt taught me how not to be scared without a man til the right one comes, and that's why I'll have something for him when he gets here!

I met that nice man, a very hard-working man at a church social. Was me and a real light woman liking him and I thought sure he would take to her, but he took to me. I waited for a long time, til after we were married to ask him why, case he might think of something I didn't want him to think of. He told me, "I like her. I think she a fine woman, a good woman. But you can't like somebody just cause they light! Ain't no white man done me no favor by making no black woman a baby! What I care most bout skin is that it fits! Don't sag . . . or shrink when it gets wet!" He say, "I love your outsides and your insides, cause you a kind and lovin woman who needs a lotta love and don't mind lettin me know it! I need love too!" Then I knew I could love him with ease. And I did, through the years that passed.

My husband was a railroad-working man so we was pretty soon able to buy us a little home and I was able to stay in it and not go out to work. I made a little extra money with my sewing and teaching piano lessons. We was doing alright! We both wanted children but didn't seem to start up none, so I naturally came to take up more time with my nieces. That's when I came to know the meaning of the big importance of who raises you and who you raising!

I had urged Older to come to the city with her two girls, they were bout fourteen and fifteen years old round then. Middle didn't have no husband now, and her daughter was bout thirteen years old. I could see, tho they was all from one family, they had such different ways of doing things! With my husband gone two or three days a week, I had time to get to know them more.

Now, Older, she the one with the two daughters, she did everything for the oldest pretty, light one, leaving the other one out a
lot. The oldest one had more and better clothes and was a kinda
snotty girl. Demanding . . . always demanding! She was going to be
a doctor, she said, and true enough she studied hard. She volunteered
at the hospitals a lot. Getting ready, she said. She was picky bout
her clothes and since her mama didn't make too much money and
wouldn't let her work, she was always asking me to sew for her or
do her hair. Her best friend was a white girl, live up the street, from
a nice family.

I took to sewing, buying the material myself, for the youngest
brownskin one. She was a little hard of hearing and didn't speak as
prettily and clearly as her older sister, so they was always putting her
off or back, or leaving her home when they go out. Now, she was
not college-smart, but she was commonsense smart and a good decent girl, treated people right. That's what I like, so I helped her!
She was never asking for nothing but was grateful for the smallest
thing you did for her. That kind of person makes me remember my
aunts and I will work my butt off for people like that! I was closest
to her.

I spent time with Middle too. I love my family. Her daughter,
thirteen or fourteen years old, was a nice quiet girl. At least I thought
she was quiet. I found out later she was beaten under. She was scared
to be herself. Her mother, Middle, had turned down her natural
spirit! You know, some of them things people try to break in their
children are things they may need when they get out in that world
when Mama and Papa ain't there! The child was tryin to please her
mama and was losing herself! And she wasn't bad to begin with!
Now, it's good for a child to mind its mama, but then the mama
got to be careful what she tells that child to do! She's messing with
her child's life!

Middle was mad one day and told me she had whipped the child
for walkin home holding hands with a boy! I told Middle, "Ain't

nothing wrong with holding hands! Specially when you heading home where your mama is! Humans will be human! Some people wish their fourteen-year-old daughter was only holding hands!" I told her, "You was almost married when you was her age!" Middle told me I didn't have no kids so I didn't understand! I went home thinking children wasn't nothing but little people living in the same life we was, learning the same things we had to. You just got to understand bout life! I hear people say, "I ain't never been a mother before, how am I supposed to know what to do?" Well, let me tell you, that child ain't never been here before, been a child their age before either! How they always supposed to know what to do, less you teach em! How much do you know to teach em?

Several months later she whipped that girl, hard and long, for kissing a boy in the hallway. I told Middle, "She was in your hallway. What could she do out there and you in here?! If they was plannin anything special, they got the whole world out there to hide in!" Middle said, "I wish she was just out there holdin hands walkin home, stead of this stuff!" I looked at her trying to understand why she didn't understand when she was well off. "While you think you whipping something *out* of her, you may be whippin' something *in*! Talk to her more. Are you all friends? You know, everybody need a friend!"

She was so sad, my sister, I asked her, "Why don't you think about gettin married again? Get you some kissin stuff? Then maybe natural things won't look so dirty to you! You can be a mama and a wife, stead of a warden!" Middle just screwed up her face and say she know what she doing! Sadness all gone . . . madness too close. Things you feel sposed to make you think bout em! Think how you can help yourself. Hers didn't. She say, "The last thing I need is a man messing up my life again!" Well, it was her business, but it looked to me like she was gettin close to the last thing! I told my niece if she ever need a friend, come to me. I was her aunt and her friend, just like Aunt Ellen was to me! I left.

Life is something, chile! Sometime watching over other folks' life can make you more tired than just taking care your own!

Older's snotty oldest daughter had graduated with good grades from high school and was going out to find work to help send herself to college. Both she and her white girlfriend planned to go to college, but the white friend's family had planned ahead and had insurance for education. They both went out together to find work. They went to that hospital where Oldest's daughter had volunteered steady, spending all kinds of time and energy in most all the departments there. Her friend hadn't. But when they had their interviews, her friend got the job! Well, my niece was just done in or out, either one or both! But her white friend told her, "I'm a minority, aren't I? I'm a female! At least one of us got it! That's better than some man getting it!" Ms. Snotty just looked at her and I don't think they're friends anymore, least not so close. Anyway, my niece wrote a pack of letters and a month or so later, she went on East and got a job. I can tell you now, she didn't become no doctor, but she is a head nurse of a whole hospital. Her mama surenuff scrimped and saved and made herself and her other daughter go without to keep that girl in school. I was giving my other niece all she had to keep her from feeling too neglected. I loved that girl! I loved them both, but people with certain kinda needs just get me!

Middle had told her daughter, "No company til you are eighteen years old and through with school!" But she didn't give her the hugs and kisses and touches we all need. So the girl found her own. She was sixteen years old now, and she had gotten pregnant. She and the boy wanted to get married but Middle beat her and demanded on her to get an abortion. The girl wouldn't have one, so Middle was going to show her how her evil ways had cost her her mother, and how lost she would be without her! She put her child out of her rented house! Her own child! Seem like that was the time for Middle to act like the mother she was always demanding respect for! That was going to be her own grandchild! But . . . she put her out.

I didn't know it and that poor child didn't come to me . . . What had I missed doing or saying to show her I was her friend? Oh Lord, I prayed for her safety. You know on the other side of your door sits the whole world. The good people are mostly home taking care of their family and business. It's the liars, thieves, rapers, murderers, pimps, sadistics, dopers, crazy people who are out there . . . waiting . . . just for someone without no experience. Thems who that child was out there with, the minute her mama slammed that front door! And a belly full of baby, no man and no mama. It's some things you don't have to live to understand. I wanted my grandniece. I would have taken care of it for her. And Middle would love her grandchile. It's a mighty dumb fool won't let their own heart be happy! If she was worrying bout feeding it . . . she got fed! And didn't have no mama! Trying to show what a fool her daughter was, she showed what a fool she was! Your chile is your heart, your flesh, your blood! And sometimes, your way! Anyway, life goes on. I couldn't find her til way later.

Older's daughter had done graduated and was a surgical or surgeon nurse, and had her own place and car and everything! Older was planning to go visit her and did, leaving the youngest daughter to stay home and watch the house with my help. When Older got back she was hurt and mad. She didn't want to tell it, but we finally got it out of her. Her snotty daughter had made her wear a maid's uniform, the one she had for her regular jobs. She had to cook and answer the door and stay out the way when company came! Not tell nobody that was her daughter! Can you believe . . . even can you imagine that?! Her mother!? Well, it's true, she did and she still does it! Then, shame of all shames possible to snotty sister, her young sister got a job as a maid in a whorehouse! Snotty and Older hated that, but she made such good money, tips and all, and the girls giving her jewels and discarded furs and clothes and all. They wanted to use them, borrow her money but seem to hate her. Two ways. For having these things and for being low enough to work as a maid in a whorehouse! They made her sad. She was trying to swim to the top of the rain in her own way. I tried to love her enough, but there ain't nothin like your own mama's love!

Bout that time somebody told us about Middle's daughter. She was a prostitute trying to pay her own way, raising her daughter, living alone. She didn't have time to find a job before she started starving, so this was a way. She was trying to swim to the top of the rain, but was drowning. Middle took a gun down on that street and threatened to kill her! I talked to the young woman. She was still a good girl, just lost! But, loving her baby! That baby had everything! Was the fattest, cutest, sweetest, smiling baby I ever seen! Ohhh, how I wanted that baby! And I knew the pain, the great big pain I could see in her face she was going through. Who *wants* to sell their body? The *only* thing, no matter how long you live, that is truly yours, is your body. I don't care how much money you got!

Later, Middle told me, "Ohhhhh, I wish she was home just having one of them illegal babies! Oh, just to have her back home holding hands, or kissing in the hallway, even having that baby! I shoulda let her marry that boy when they wanted to! I'd rather kill her than see her be a prostitute!" She hurt and I could see it. It was the first time she had even blamed herself a little bit for her part in all this. I had a little hope for her.

The daughter brought the baby her mother had tried to make her get rid of and let her keep it sometime. Middle loved that grandchile so much, cause you see, she didn't have nothin else in her life. It was empty! I kept it whenever I could. That girl, her daughter, stayed sad . . . sad . . . sadder. She would look around her mama's house and make a deep sigh and go away looking hopeless. Her mama told her to come home, but she said it was too late.

I got involved round that time with Older's youngest daughter. She had fallen in love and was bout to marry a blind man. I thought that was good after I met him. He was so good-seeming, so kind to her, so sweet and gentle with her. My sister was going crazy cause he was blind! She didn't even think of his honesty and kindness and love for her daughter. She could only see he was blind. Oh Lord, deliver the innocent from some fools that be mothers, fathers, and sisters. She married him anyway, bless her heart, and my sister had a heart attack . . . a real one! Her daughter she didn't love so much and her blind husband took care of her, better than she took care herself when she could. Her nurse daughter said she couldn't! Didn't have time.

I was so busy being in my family's business I hadn't been in my own enough! My husband, have mercy, told me he was leavin me cause he had met someone he might could love and she was pregnant! I looked at him for bout a hour, it seemed, cause he was my life but I hadn't been actin like it! Been giving everybody else all my thoughts, time, and life. But I had done learned bout happiness and I understood if he wasn't happy here, he should be where he was happy! Ain't that what we all live for? How could I get mad at a man who had give me everything, including the chance to make him happy? I washed, cleaned, packed his clothes, and let him go, clean away. Then I went in the house, took the biggest bottle of liquor I could find, sat down, and drank for bout a week. Now, I ain't crazy and a hangover ain't the best feeling in the world. Life started again in me and bless my soul, even alone, I was still alive!

I went out in my . . . *my* yard and saw one lone red flower, dug it up and took it in the house. I told it, "You and me, we alone. We can survive! I'm going to plant you and make you grow. I'm going to plant me and make me grow. I'm going to swim to the top of this rain!" I planted it, it wilted, it lay down even. I let it alone cept for care. Let it grieve for its natural place. I loved it. I talked to it. I went and put it back outside, it's *my* yard too! It could be mine and still be free where it wanted to be! In a day or two, it took hold again . . . it's still livin! Me, I just kept carrying on with my swim.

I hadn't seen nobody, cause I didn't want to be bothered with their problems. I had my own! Then Middle came to me. My niece was in the hospital, dying from a overdose of dope in her veins! Ohh Lord!

When I got to the hospital, I stood in the door and listened to my sister talk to her daughter who could not hear her. "Don't die, my little girl, *don't* die! Stay with me. You all I got. What I'm gonna do . . . if you die? Stay with me, don't leave me alone. Hold hands with anybody you wants to! I won't say nothing! Kiss anybody you want to . . . I won't mind at all. Just don't leave me, my baby! Have many babies as you want! I'll love em all! Don't go. Child of mine, you can even be a prostitute. I don't care! Just live. I rather see you on dope than see you dead! Cause if you got life, you got a chance to change. Baby, I'm sorry. I'm *sorry*! Be anything you want . . . JUST LIVE . . . don't die! Come home! *Don't die!*" She screamed that out and I went in to help her grieve . . . cause the beautiful young woman was dead.

After the funeral, the good thing Middle had left was the baby she had tried to make her daughter get rid of. Her daughter had won that battle at the cost of her life, it seemed . . . so now, Middle was blessed to have someone to love and be with . . . in her empty life. I went on home to my empty life.

Things smoothed down. God is good. They always smooth down if you give life time.

One day, bout a year later, my doorbell rang and when I answered it, my husband was standing there with a baby in his arms who reached out for me the minute I opened the door. I reached back! I ain't no fool! He had got that young woman he thought he loved and she had got him, but after the baby was born, my husband wanted to rest and stay home when she wanted to play and go out. She left him with his baby. I tried to look sad for him, but my heart said, *"Good, Good, Good!"*

But he didn't look too sad. We talked and talked and talked and talked! I loved my husband and I knew he loved me, even better now. He wanted to come home and I wanted him home. And I wanted that baby. It was his and I musta not been able and she was. How lucky I felt that if I couldn't have one, he had give me one anyway. We didn't need to get married, we still was. Neither one of us had gone to the courts, thinkin the other one would. So I had a family.

Sometimes I hold my baby boy and look deep in his little bright, full-of-life eyes. I know something is coming in the coming years cause life ain't easy to live all the time. Even rich folks commit suicide. But I tell my boy, like my aunt told me, "Just come on, grow up, we gonna make it, little man, right through the storms! We gonna take our chances . . . and get on out there and take our turn . . . swimming to the top of the rain!"

LEAVING HOME

◻

SUE MILLER

"**G**o find Daddy," Anita said in the kitchen. "Where did Daddy go?"

Leah was in the closet in the living room, and Anita's voice sounded muted and thickened to her. The closet smelled of mildew and camphor, and was full of old boots and boxes of clothing. Leah knelt among them and listened to Anita cross from the kitchen to the foot of the stairs.

"The baby stinks, Greg." Anita's voice was closer, sharper. There was silence from upstairs.

"Did you hear me, Greg? The baby stinks and it's my birthday. I'm not going to change her." Anita walked back to the kitchen, past Sophie, who had followed her across the living room. Leah rose and stepped out of the closet to watch her grandchild. The little girl had just learned to walk and she held her amazed hands up in the air and waved them for balance with each exaggerated step, a miniature tightrope walker. There was a large wet stain down one leg of her overalls.

Greg lumbered down the stairs, and Sophie smiled up at him. Her bare feet curved inward at the toe. Greg squatted in front of her.

"Soph, you did it again," he said. Then he noticed his mother, standing in the closet doorway. "Isn't that something?" he asked her, as though Sophie had just performed some prodigious musical or artistic feat. His face was deadpan.

Leah laughed, pushing her curly hair off her face.

"Do you stink, Soph?" he asked the child. "Are you, in fact, a . . . *stinker*?"

Sophie smiled, watching him with delight.

"Are you"—he paused again, and in anticipation she made a small squealing noise—"a *stinker*?" She laughed and set her tiny hands on his face.

"Are you"—she had the game now, and was already laughing, but watched him rapturously until he had said it—"a *stinker*?" Her body gave itself up to laughter, and she suddenly lost her balance and sat down hard on the floor, still laughing.

"Look how smart she is, honey," Leah said. "She just picks up anything so fast."

"If she's so smart, how come she isn't toilet trained?" He scooped her up and held her balanced horizontally across his hip. A strand of drool dangled from her mouth and was suddenly gone, a drop on the floor. Sophie watched it, fascinated.

"What were you doing in the closet, Mom?" Greg asked.

"Trying to find the damn picnic basket."

"Didn't you used to keep it in the basement?"

"Yes, but we had a picnic just a week or so ago, and I thought I put it away up here."

He stood looking at his mother for a moment. She was still pretty, in a slightly plump, worn way. She was wearing jeans and an old T-shirt that had his high school emblem on it.

"Who is this 'we' that keeps cropping up?"

Leah blushed. "Just a man I've been seeing a little of."

"Just a man?"

She nodded.

"Wasn't there a movie called *Just a Man*?" He shifted Sophie on his hip.

"No," Leah said. "You're thinking of *Nothing but a Man*."

"No I'm not, Mom. I'm thinking of this movie *Just a Man*. It's different from *Nothing but a Man*."

"God, that was a good movie, that *Nothing but a Man*." Leah's hand strayed to her hair again. "And the sound track. I mean, it wasn't a musical, but do you remember that song 'Heat Wave'?"

"No, but you do." Sophie began to make complaining noises, and wriggled. "Okay, Soph, here we go," he said.

"I can't believe it," Leah said, as he turned to go up the stairs. "You don't remember 'Heat Wave.' "

He laughed. "That was your life, Mom."

Leah stood a moment at the bottom of the stairs and watched him carry Sophie up, jouncing her on each step. "Hup, hup," he said. Then she turned and crossed to the kitchen.

The kitchen was flooded with early-afternoon sunlight. Anita sat at the round wooden table by the windows, drinking coffee and reading the paper. The lunch dishes still littered the table. Anita had said she would do them. Leah had to will herself not to start cleaning up.

She sat down at what had been her place and sipped at the cold milky coffee left in her cup.

Anita lowered the paper. She was wearing her glasses, two clear, thick circles with steel-rimmed frames that perched weightlessly on her perfect nose. She was a law student. Most of the time Leah had trouble imagining her, delicate and frail as she seemed, in that competitive world. But now, wearing her glasses, she looked icy and determined. Leah didn't know if Greg had married Anita for her eggshell-frail beauty or for the steely competence that lay underneath it. Or both, of course. When he told her they were getting married, she asked him why. He seemed too young to Leah, hopelessly

young. "Because, Mom," he answered earnestly then, "she's someone I know I can live with the rest of my life." She was touched
by his conviction and ashamed of the impulse she had to mock him
for it. Now she looked at Anita. Why can't I ever tell what she's
thinking? Leah wondered. Why does she make me feel like the
younger of us two? She sighed.

"What's up?" Anita asked.

"Oh, just nothing's working today, and now I can't find the damn
picnic basket."

"What's it look like?"

Leah instantly felt annoyed. She didn't want Anita's help. She
didn't want Anita to find it for her.

"The way they look. A big square hampery kind of thing."

"Oh. I might have seen it, I think."

"Where?"

"The broom closet by the back door, maybe?"

Leah went to the broom closet and opened the door. The hamper
sat on the top shelf, beyond her easy reach. Joe, so much taller, so
much more domestic than she, must have put it away after their
picnic. She stood on her toes and, with the tips of her fingers, slid
the basket forward on the shelf until it leaned suddenly toward her
and she caught it. She had thought about asking him over tonight.
It was Anita's birthday, her twenty-fifth, and they were going to
have a party outside in the backyard. Greg had invited Pete Slattery,
his closest friend from high school, and his wife. She and Joe had
talked about whether he should come, but they had decided no.
Two of his children still lived at home, and when Leah and Joe were
together at his house they felt obliged to adopt a pose of almost
marital stability. They both liked the sense of freedom, of abandon,
they had at her house. Last Sunday after breakfast, they had made
love in the kitchen. Leah had sat in the bright summer light on the
counter amid the egg-stained dishes and chipped coffee mugs, the
sun warming her back and Joe warming her front; and she had cried

out, "Oh, oh, oh," as loudly as she wanted when she came. After all her years of negotiated privacy when Greg was young, of sneaking the occasional lover in and out of the house, as though she were the teenager, and Greg—heavily asleep in his room, which smelled of dirty socks and the sulfurous acne medication he wore to bed—were the parent, she was jealous of her long-awaited freedom, her claim to sexuality. They decided there was no rush for Joe to meet her family.

But a few hours before Anita and Greg were to arrive, he'd turned up at her back door with a present, a loaf of zucchini bread he'd made for the party. It was wrapped in aluminum foil, and it was still warm in Leah's hands as she stood with him on the back stoop.

"It smells good. Is it supposed to be your version of a silver bullet, Joe? Who was that masked man, and all that?"

She blocked the kitchen doorway. She was embarrassed for Joe to see how much neater the house was than usual. Even though he stood several steps below her, Joe's head was level with hers.

"It's supposed to make you remember me. You're going to eat a piece of that bread and want me in the middle of the family doings."

She held the present against her. The heat touched her breasts through her shirt. "If I had to pick something to remind you of me in my absence, it wouldn't be zucchini bread," she said, after a moment.

He shrugged and grinned at her. He was a skinny man, balding, with one eye that swiveled out as though to check on what was going on in the rest of the world. She had told him that she'd never have been attracted to him if it weren't for the wild freedom of that eye. She had felt a positive erotic charge trying to meet his difficult gaze when they'd been introduced, at a parent-teacher night in the high school, where his youngest child, a girl named Fiona, was Leah's student. "Well," he said, "actually we just had too goddamn many zucchini in the garden. That's the bald-faced truth of the situation."

"Oh, don't tell me the bald-faced truth," she said. "I never want to hear that." He kept grinning as he leaned forward to kiss her. His tongue came a little way into her mouth. Then he was gone, gone until this weekend of her being a mother again was over.

Now, as Leah brought the hamper over to the kitchen table, Anita got up lazily and started to carry the lunch dishes to the sink. What had bothered her most about the scene at the foot of the stairs, Leah suddenly thought, watching her tall daughter-in-law move across the kitchen, graceful as a giraffe, was that Anita had called Sophie "the baby." She ought to say her name.

Around three o'clock, with the house in a dazed silence because of the heat and Sophie's nap, Leah went out to the back steps to shell peas. The sun had swung around, off the stairs, but the heat rose, still and stifling and smelling of dirt from the earth in the backyard. Leah knew that the meal she had planned for this party was too elaborate, was taking too much of her time; but she knew, too, that she had organized it this way in part so that she could stay away from Anita and Greg and a vague feeling of anxiety they roused in her. She was glad to have this job to do, to be able to leave the house and come out here alone to sit.

Greg and Anita had had a small, quickly suppressed argument just before Sophie's nap, and Leah frowned, thinking of it, as her thumbnail slid along the seam of a bright green peapod. She and Anita had been working in the kitchen, and Sophie was standing on a stool by the sink, playing quietly with the soapy water Anita had run for her. She was wearing only her Pampers, and she carefully poured water from one plastic container to another in the sink. Her fat protruding belly glistened with what she had spilled on it.

Greg came into the room and began to play with her. Leah stopped what she was doing for a moment to watch them. He was wearing only cutoff shorts, and his brown body, with the big bones moving under the skin, gave her as much pleasure as Sophie's translucent roundness did. She remembered how homely Greg had been just before he entered his teens, a fat child who wasn't popular and who stammered in any new situation. Once he had used her razor to shave his eyebrows off. He hated the way he looked, he had said when she asked him why. "And this is better?" she countered in a tense, shrill voice. He had looked at her as though he'd like to kill her in some slow and painful way. "Y-y-y-y-yes," he said, his eyes not blinking under his smooth, naked forehead.

Greg made a waterfall, he blew bubbles with a straw he found in a kitchen drawer. Leah watched his muscular back, looked at Sophie's compact and delicate body on the stool next to him.

"Why can't you leave her alone for just a few minutes, Greg?" Anita said.

Leah looked away quickly; went back to peeling boiled potatoes for a salad.

"Why *should* I leave her alone?" Greg asked, standing straight. He shook the bubbly water from his fingers.

Anita's voice strained to be casual, reasonable. "Because you never do. She's perfectly content, playing by herself. And you always have to charm her with *your* game, your . . ." There was silence for a moment. "I just don't think it's good for her," Anita said finally.

Greg stood next to Sophie, looking at Anita. Leah looked at her too. She was staring over Sophie's head at Leah's son, with eyes that were free of love, free of any response to his beauty.

"Bupps, Daddy?" Sophie said. She had fished the soggy straw out of the water and held it up to Greg.

"Not now, honey," Greg said. He walked toward the door, his sense of injury apparent in the way he held his shoulders.

"Bupps!" Sophie shrieked after him. "Bupps," she wailed, and then bent over and cried, loudly and dramatically, with her head touching the counter, her face hidden against her small fat hands.

"Whoo," Anita said, moving toward her daughter and raising her eyebrows for Leah's benefit. "Nap time for this kidlet."

When Leah finished shelling the peas, she picked up the pot and the colander and went back into the kitchen. She glanced through the doorway into the living room. Greg lay on the floor, alone, reading an old issue of *Sports Illustrated*. Leah realized she hadn't seen Greg and Anita touch each other since they arrived.

Leah's house was like all the others around it, only with a slightly different "porch treatment" in front. It was part of a cheap suburban tract. She had bought it three years after she and Greg's father had been divorced, a year after she'd started teaching at the high school. The development was to have extended into the field and woods behind it, but by the time she and Greg had moved in, the first group of eight houses was already having trouble with its septic tanks. Until the town extended its sewer lines out as far as the development, which it didn't have any apparent intention of doing, no more houses could be built. Thus Leah had an unexpected park behind her. Deer sometimes wandered into her yard in the dusky mornings while she had her solitary breakfast; and on winter nights she occasionally went outside and listened to the snow fall with a hissing sound into the woods.

Anita's picnic was going to be at the bottom of the meadow, twenty or so feet before the woods started. They would be close enough to the house to hear Sophie if she cried, but far enough away so their noise wouldn't bother her.

While Greg got Sophie ready for bed and the steady pulse of the pump forcing water for Anita's shower thrummed through the house, Leah carried quilts and pillows, candles, and load after load of food and wine and beer down to the bottom of the lawn. She had changed into a dress and she had her shoes off and the grass felt cool and damp on her bare feet. Although it was still light outside, twilight had begun in the house, and she turned on the lamp in the kitchen as she assembled the final load from the clothes remaining in the hamper. Then she stayed outside, on her back on the faded and stained quilt, a glass of white wine within reach.

Greg called her and she answered halfheartedly, but she knew he couldn't hear her and she didn't get up. After a while the screen door smacked shut. She looked up and saw him walk across the grass to her. Over his cutoffs he wore a T-shirt that said "Computer programmers do it Digitally." He had worked for Digital since he'd graduated from Rutgers, since he'd married Anita.

"God, you did everything, Mom."

Leah propped herself up on an elbow. "I wanted to be able to just lie here without thinking about having to get up in a while to help."

"But you should have called me." He sat down on a pillow and reached into the cooler for a beer.

"Honey, you don't have to help with everything." And you shouldn't, she wanted to say. You shouldn't. She thought suddenly of all the years she had made him help her with the housework, even when she could have done it more efficiently herself; of all the times she'd lectured him on his responsibility to their tiny household. She had a vague, apologetic sense now that it had all been wrong, wrongheaded.

"What do you think," she asked, looking up at the first faint stars in the white sky, "was the thing that attracted you and Anita to each other in college?" She was embarrassed by the question as soon as she'd asked it, and rushed to qualify it. "I mean, looking back," she said.

He was saved from having to answer by the sound of a car in the driveway. "Ah. Guess who?" he said, and smiled. He got up and disappeared around the corner of the house, carrying his beer. She could hear voices raised in greeting, and in a minute they all appeared, Greg and Pete, and Pete's wife, Debby. Debby had been a student of Leah's years before. She was a sweet, stupid girl, with enormous breasts. She had had to marry Pete before she finished her junior year of high school. At the party Greg had thrown for them a few weeks after the wedding, Leah had found Debby crying in the bathroom; had cleaned up the vomit which had missed the toilet; and had tucked the miserable sixteen-year-old bride into her own bed for the night, while the noise of the party continued below.

They were cheerful now as they sat down and got beer and wine to drink. Pete told Leah how pretty she looked, and she made the mocking face she used at school when a student tried to flatter her. This teacherly manner had been her defense ever since Greg's friends began to turn into men suddenly, when she was alone and in her mid-thirties. It was like a joke they had all shared, especially she and Pete, the wildest of the friends, who had been sexually alert at an age when Greg still seemed to be sleepwalking through life.

When the screen door banged again, and Anita in a gauzy white dress stood poised a moment and then floated down through the fading summer light to them, Leah looked over at Pete and caught a look of sexual appraisal on his face.

"The birthday girl," Leah said quickly. Anita smiled at them all and sank down in the swirl of her skirts next to Greg.

"Hello, hello, hello," she said to each of them and leaned prettily, a frail reed, against Greg's shoulder. "What is there for me to drink, sweetheart?"

Greg poured some wine for her, let her lean. But he didn't look at her or respond to her. Even though Leah knew Anita was posturing slightly for the guests, she was moved by the younger woman's beauty, and irritated by Greg's stubborn unresponsiveness to it. She had the sudden conviction, as she reached over to light the picnic lanterns she had brought out earlier, that he would lose Anita and his marriage, and so, of course, Sophie. Her eyes momentarily filled with tears. She lighted the lamps and began to pass around the wicker picnic plates.

Leah drank too much during the meal. She poured herself glass after glass of white wine. The food she had spent all day preparing seemed tasteless to her. She ate a few small bites of the first course and didn't even cut herself a piece of Anita's birthday cake.

After they'd finished eating and were stretched out, drinking wine and beer, Pete lit a joint and passed it around. Leah remembered that she'd heard from someone else, some other high school friend of Greg's and Pete's, that he was dealing in a small way. She wrinkled her nose at the smell and leaned out of the circle. She had tried grass once or twice at Greg's insistence when he was in college, but it only made her sleepy and slightly nauseated. She thought it made Greg and his friends boring and she had told him so. He had shrugged and said, "It's just the same thing I feel about you and your friends when you've all been drinking."

Now their voices grew slowly more subdued and intimate. Debby was hunched over her glass of wine, talking at length to Greg, who nodded and nodded. Anita and Pete, more relaxed, giggled. Leah was sorry she hadn't invited Joe. She felt old and solitary, an observer. She wanted to clean up and go to bed.

She stood and walked slowly to the house, carrying her wine. At the kitchen door she looked back. The scene was beautiful in the yellow lamplight; and at this distance their soft voices seemed like a part of nature, like the sound of leaves in the wind, or the liquid murmur of a stream.

Leah went upstairs and looked a long time at herself in the bright light of the bathroom. Her eye makeup had smeared slightly. Her lipstick was gone. She pushed her hair back. Her face looked tired, weakened by age. She set down her wineglass and slowly washed her face, rinsing it over and over in the cool running water.

She went down the darkened hallway to Sophie's room. She stood just outside the doorway because Greg had told her that Sophie was a light sleeper. She listened to the child's regular breathing as she had listened to her son a thousand times when he was small. The air was full of the perfumed smell of Sophie's Pampers.

The screen door smacked shut downstairs. Sophie stirred; the plastic Pampers rustled gently. Voices whispered, there was soft laughter in the kitchen. Dishes clinked. Were they picking up? Leah should go down and help. Someone turned on the faucet and the pipes sang gently behind the cheap walls. She reached into the bedroom and slowly closed Sophie's door.

Leah went downstairs, and as she crossed the living room, she heard Anita's voice, thick with wine, grass, from the kitchen. "No, it's *not* that," she said. "It's just this endless mommy-daddy-baby shit. The endless threesomeness of it all. We always have to be so fucking responsible. It's as though I don't exist as a woman anymore."

And Pete's voice, slurred and soft. "I can't imagine that with you. If I were with you. I mean, I've always thought of you as one of the sexiest ladies I know."

Leah cleared her throat and then coughed, loudly enough, she hoped, to warn them she was about to intrude upon them. But when she stepped into the dimly lit kitchen in her bare feet, Pete was gently lifting Anita's hair from her face in what was unmistakably the beginning of an embrace.

"I'm here," Leah said stupidly. Pete's hands leapt back as if burned. Anita turned slowly, foggily, toward Leah and smiled. The orange light glowed behind her and Leah could see she wasn't wearing a bra under the gauzy dress. Let her be drunk enough not to remember, Leah thought.

"Are you starting to clean up?" she asked brightly. "I'll go outside and get some more." She turned quickly away from them.

Outside it was cooler. She stood a moment by the back door. The air itself lifted her spirits slightly; but as she approached Greg, she felt the return of her sense of helpless sorrow for him.

He and Debby sat on the quilt, talking like two earnest children. They didn't notice Leah for a moment at the edge of the lantern light, and Debby went on talking, telling Greg how much trouble she'd had getting her youngest child to give up a pacifier.

Then Debby looked up and saw her. "Leah," she said. "It's Leah."

There was a pause as they both looked at her. In the still evening air Leah could hear crickets, the clatter of dishes in the kitchen.

"Mom. Oh. You looked so weird to me." Greg stared at her with amazed, stoned intensity, and Leah bent down to start loading the hamper. "For a minute I thought," he said slowly, "I mean, I really thought, when I looked at you, that I was about ten years old again."

Later, after Pete and Debby had left, Leah sat on the edge of her bed upstairs and listened to Greg and Anita below in the living room. She heard the low metallic shriek that meant they were pulling out the foldaway bed, the lazy alternation of their voices. Then Anita's took over, a pressured monologue, with an occasional sharply articulated word—"never," or "fucking"—that floated up through the night air and the thin walls of the house. He didn't answer. Leah wanted him to. She sat in her room and listened to the sound of her son's marriage and wanted him to shout, to push, to hit. She thought of how he had sat, mute and resentful, when she had spoken just this way to him a hundred times, over the garbage not taken out, the bike not locked, the car dented, the curfew defied; thinking always that she was teaching him, teaching him the right way, the responsible way to get through life.

When she tiptoed past the living room on her way out, she heard them making love. The couch squeaked to their rhythm, he cried out in bewildered wild whispers, and there was a low mournful keening from Anita. They still had that, then. Did it make the rest easier? Harder? Leah remembered that she and Greg's father had made love, weeping, the night before he moved out of her life and Greg's forever.

For a moment, as she walked silently across the kitchen, she worried about leaving the house, about what seemed like an abandonment of Greg, of them all. But she had no power anymore—had never had the power, although at one time she thought she did—to stave off ruin, to guard her son against his share of pain. And for herself, right now, she wanted Joe. She wanted, just as Greg did, the illusion of wholeness, of repair, the broken parts fitting.

As she stepped outside and turned to shut the door, the porch light falling into the kitchen gleamed on the silver wrapping of the bread Joe had given her, the gift she'd forgotten to take to the party.

The genesis for "Leaving Home" is probably more complicated than the story itself. As briefly as possible, though: In 1980, just months after my mother had suddenly died, my father and I drove across the country in his old car, towing behind it a trailer with furniture and goods that had come from my mother's family, all the things of hers that he thought should now be his children's. We had one stop in Chicago and two in Colorado, where we unloaded the Victorian chairs, the china cupboards, the boxes of family dishes and silverware at my brothers' and sister's houses.

The arrangements I'd made for my son during these several weeks turned out not to be so great. I called him frequently, and frequently he wept into the phone. "When are you coming home?" over and over. Sometimes I wept after I hung up.

In Colorado, as we'd arranged, I left my father on his own to make the return trip, and I traveled west for another ten days or so with a lover. On one of the nights just before I started this leg of the trip, however, I stayed with my younger brother and his wife and their infant son—born, actually, the day my mother died. After we'd all gone to bed they argued, and I, lying in the guest room, could hear just their anger, no words. Though I didn't imagine that this argument meant much of anything (and indeed, in terms of the health or longevity of their marriage, it didn't), it fueled a line of thought and speculation—on love and loss and responsibility and pain—that absorbed and rearranged psychologically other aspects too of this somewhat peculiar trip. Within a year or so, I'd written "Leaving Home."

S.M.

ZOO BUS

□

EILEEN FITZGERALD

Elise opened the blinds and peered through the dusty slats, sifting the traffic for buses. Her feet ached; bones crowded against other bones, almost as if she'd grown extras during her eighty-one years. She leaned against the windowsill. On the street below, a young sweet gum tree held out a scant offering of pointy yellow leaves.

It was just like Gertrude to be late. Elise thought of poking her head out the window, shouting, "Gerrrtruuuude!!"; she imagined her sixty-year-old daughter hurrying down the street, trailing a jump rope. Elise almost laughed at the idea of Gertrude coming when she was called, or doing anything she was asked to do.

On the sofa, Alex, her downstairs neighbor, was chewing his ice cubes, although Elise had asked him not to. She shook a finger at him. "Don't eat that glass, Alex. It's part of a set." From now on, she would give him hot drinks, nothing he could nibble. Alex was twenty, the age her husband, Bill, had been on their wedding day. Elise tried to remember what it was like to be so young, to believe that one's teeth were immortal. She looked at Alex's long legs, sprawled halfway across her living room. Bill had not been such a casual man; he was a man who sat up straight. He had not been immortal either; less than two years after they married, he was killed in a train yard accident. Elise wondered sometimes how her life might have been, if it could have been easier.

In the distance Elise saw the hulking form of a bus. She watched its slow, smoky approach, frowning when she realized that it was the zoo bus. Now it would be another half hour, at least, before Gertrude got home. The zebra-striped zoo bus was one of the few old buses that remained in the fleet; the gaudy paint job advertised the African veldt section of the zoo. When Elise had still been riding the city buses—before she broke her collarbone in the bus accident—she made it a point of honor to wait for the next bus, no matter the delay. No self-respecting person rode the zoo bus. Now it groaned to a stop, and Elise watched to see who or what would disembark.

Alex gave his ice another crunch. Usually when he visited, Elise asked him to help with some small task and then rewarded him with a twenty-dollar bill. She decided to make him wait for his money today. She would let him wonder whether he should ask.

"Are you expecting someone?" asked Daniel, Alex's new roommate. His voice startled Elise; she looked to see if she'd mistaken the straight lines of his black hair. She'd always assumed Orientals were boat people, unable to speak English. But Daniel's voice was like a newscaster's, pure American. Elise wondered what he was— Chinese or Japanese? Korean? She knew that Orientals greatly respected their elders. She pictured herself as an Oriental grandmother in a soft, red chair. "Tie my shoe," she would say, and grandchildren would flock to her, anxious to help.

Below, the bus was already moving away, leaving behind a dirty cloud. A woman, grayish-brown hair twisted into a tight ballerina bun, stood on the grass patch that separated street and sidewalk, waiting to cross Brookside. Elise turned sharply from the window. "Of course she doesn't look up. Not Gertrude."

"Who's Gertrude?" asked Daniel.

"The daughter," said Alex.

"That's right. My dutiful daughter."

"Listen to this, Daniel—when Gertrude was a baby, she slept in a dresser drawer." Alex laughed. "When it cries you close the drawer."

"It certainly wasn't like that," Elise said stiffly. She turned to Daniel. "It wasn't unheard of," she explained, "to use a box or a basket for a cradle. It was the Depression. A baby doesn't remember."

"Is she coming up?" Daniel looked at Alex. "Should we go?"

Elise laughed. "We would grow cobwebs waiting for Gertrude." She thought of the last time Gertrude had been in this apartment, the day of the last collarbone appointment, the same day the settlement money for the bus accident had arrived. At the doctor's office, Elise showed the check to the nurse, cupping her hand over the numbers so Gertrude couldn't see. "I don't want her to slip arsenic into my soup," she whispered.

"Don't be silly," said the nurse. "Your daughter loves you."

After the doctor's appointment, Gertrude and Elise walked to the door, not speaking. Inside the apartment Gertrude made Elise demonstrate her range of motion. "Can you close the shower curtain?" she asked. "Can you function on your own?"

"Of course."

Gertrude stood like a stick figure, feet planted, hands on her hips. "Do you think it's cute? Talking about arsenic?"

"That was a joke," said Elise. "Levity."

"Do you honestly think that's why I'm here? For your money?"

Elise said nothing, and Gertrude left her alone then, with a vaguely aching shoulder and a single thought: The proof is in the pudding.

"Gertrude is a ne'er-do-well," Elise declared. She shook her head, dismissing the topic. But it bothered her, the way Gertrude marched across the street without lifting her hand to wave.

"We'll have lunch," she decided. "Would you boys like lunch?"

She knew Alex would go, but she wasn't so sure about Daniel. Maybe he only ate rice.

"I can't," said Alex. "Homework."

Elise turned then to Daniel. "You won't make an old lady eat alone, will you?"

"Certainly not. Lunch sounds great."

Alex lingered by the door until Elise ushered him out. "You study hard," she said, holding his elbow, giving him a tiny push. Her pocketbook hung on the hook by the door; the twenty dollars she'd earmarked for Alex rested inside. She would use the money to buy Daniel's lunch. "We'll go to André's," she said. "Gertrude will probably be there, but we'll just ignore her." There was only so much Elise could do; she couldn't force Gertrude to look up at the window and wave. But she could sit by her at the restaurant. She could sit so close that Gertrude would hear her breathing and know she was alive.

The door from the street opened into André's sweet shop, where display cases of cakes and chocolates lined the walls. Crocks of jam in wonderful flavors—*fraise, framboise, cassis, citron*—and loaves of shiny, braided bread crowded the shelves and countertops. Elise tilted her head back and inhaled, tasting the rich air with her nose, gripping Daniel's elbow for balance.

Behind the counter, two chocolate dippers were unloading trays of candies. Elise had spoken to the plumper man before; now she waved at him and smiled. "Did you fall in?" she asked, pointing to the chocolate smeared across his white apron.

"Franz dipped me," he said. "I'm selling for ten dollars a pound —going fast."

Elise didn't generally approve of fat people, but she forgave the chocolatier because he truly loved chocolate. "Save us a morsel of yourself," she laughed. "First, I must think of my young friend's good health. He's going to be a doctor." She leaned a bit more heavily on Daniel's arm.

The chocolatier patted his round stomach. "You skip the lunch," he advised. "It's chocolate that makes you strong."

Before the bus accident, Elise had not often gone to restaurants, preferring simple meals of tomato soup and toast. But in the past few years she'd grown fond of eating out. She liked saying "water" or "tea" or "check" and having the item delivered to her table by a smiling young person. At André's she'd become a familiar face; she'd made friends.

The sign in the front of the restaurant said PLEASE WAIT TO BE SEATED, but since the hostess was away, Elise led Daniel through the closely spaced tables.

"*Voilà!*" Elise whispered. Gertrude sat at the far end of the room, reading, fork hovering over a piece of yellow cake.

"Shall we ask her to join us?" asked Daniel.

Elise sat at a table with a view of Gertrude. "Let's wait to see what she does." Fork in hand, Gertrude turned a page. The cake looked untouched, and Elise wondered what kind it was—was it sponge cake? Whatever Gertrude was eating, Elise would pay for it. She would buy Gertrude's lunch, and Gertrude would be grateful.

Daniel stood beside the table. "Do you think she knows you're here?" he asked.

"She knows."

He looked at Gertrude, then back at Elise. "It seems funny, you sitting here and her over there."

Elise patted Daniel's hand. "Sit," she said. "We'll eat."

Once seated, Daniel's hands went to the container of white and pink packets, real and fake sugar. "Last year my mother and my sister had a terrible fight, and my sister ran away for two weeks. She took a bus to San Diego. I guess I know how it can be for a mother and a daughter, sort of ugly, even though you love each other." Daniel unfolded the menu in front of him, flapping the laminated pages.

"We'll get the special," said Elise. "It's always good."

A waitress maneuvered through the tables, loaded down with dishes. A bottle of ketchup poked out of her apron pocket. "We're ready," said Elise.

"In a minute." The waitress hurried to another table and began to dole out plates. When they had all been unloaded, the girl folded her arms and surveyed the scene. She pressed her forearms with her hands, kneading the muscles gently, like a delicate pastry dough.

Across the table, Daniel sat quietly, and Elise noticed that his hair was brown. "Where did you get that hair?" she asked. "I thought Chinese hair was black."

"It must be from being in the sun, playing tennis. Maybe it's from eating at McDonald's."

"Does your grandmother have small feet?"

Daniel smiled. "I never noticed."

Elise glanced over at Gertrude, at the piece of cake. It was just like Gertrude to order cake and then not eat it, to sit primly, back straight, legs crossed. She was wearing pale pink tights, a color that was charming for a girl but ludicrous for a sixty-year-old woman. If Elise complained, Gertrude would just say, "These are my work clothes."

"Hi, I'm Sandy."

Elise jerked her head, surprised to find the waitress inches away. The girl had one foot placed awkwardly in front of the other, almost as if she was pointing it.

"The special?" Daniel prompted.

"Not yet." Elise motioned discreetly toward Gertrude. "Do you see that lady with the pink legs? What kind of cake does she have?"

Sandy squinted toward Gertrude's table. She walked a few steps closer, then walked back. "Lemon."

"Thank you," said Elise. "We'll have the special."

Still the lemon cake sat undisturbed. Elise watched Gertrude's fork, thinking of the man she had seen on TV, who stared at a spoon until it curled into itself. She stared at Gertrude, willing the fork to sink into the cake. But she felt Gertrude pushing up, against her downward gaze.

Gertrude was the one who had resisted reconciliation, the one who held a grudge. Elise had tried. It had been late in December, after the bus money was snug in a savings account at Mark Twain Bank. Elise had not seen Gertrude for several months, but it was Christmas, the season of families and love. Early in December, Elise had prepared little gifts for her neighbors and helpers—dates stuffed with almonds, rolled in sugar—and several boxes remained, stacked on the kitchen table. She decided to make a delivery.

Elise bundled up, pulled on her galoshes, tucked the foil-wrapped gift under her arm, and stepped outside. Clean snow blanketed the sidewalks and piled inside the empty swimming pool at the Oasis Apartments next door. In the street, cars had churned the snow into mush. Along the curb, the white drifts were freckled black. Elise plunged through snow and slush, across Brookside to the Twin Oaks. During the holiday season, the building glowed blue with Christmas lights; in daylight the strings looked like vines, the unilluminated bulbs like bitter fruit. Inside, the corridors were brightly lit, festooned with strands of garland, and many of the doors had wreaths. Elise knocked on Gertrude's door.

"Well," said Gertrude. "Hello." She stood in the doorway in a light blue jogging suit and her stocking feet. Her hair hung down her back in one long braid.

"Merry Christmas, Gertrude," said Elise.

"You're brave to come out in all that snow."

"I like snow," said Elise.

The women stood facing each other without saying anything.

"I've always liked snow," said Elise.

"Would you like to come in?"

Nothing in Gertrude's apartment matched, but it all fit together, bright colors and bold patterns, scarves and fringed pillows. The rooms seemed out of place in a retirement community. Elise, timid among such exuberance, kept her fingers curled tightly around the dates.

A big book called *Yoga with Judy* lay on Gertrude's coffee table. "What in the world?" said Elise. "You're learning to hypnotize people?"

"You've heard of yoga," said Gertrude. "It's for meditating and relaxing. It has nothing to do with hypnosis." Gertrude had swung her braid over her shoulder. As a little girl, she had sucked on the ends of her hair. Now she was pulling on it, stroking it like a pet. "What are you holding there?" she asked.

Elise thrust the shiny box at Gertrude. "Dates."

"How nice! I haven't had one of these for about a hundred years." While Gertrude plucked at the foil wrap, Elise examined the other items on the coffee table. She flipped through a stack of large black-and-white photos that showed Gertrude with students. The students were doing basic ballet exercises, pliés and stretches at the barre. But there was something in their poses, something floppy and off-balance.

"One of the mothers gave me those," said Gertrude. "She called the newspaper, and the photographer sent the prints."

Elise studied a picture of four girls and one boy, each stretching one leg back in an ungainly arabesque. "Like jellyfish," said Elise. "No muscles."

"That's my special class. Didn't you see my picture last Sunday?" She handed Elise a newspaper folded open to the society page. The most prominent photo showed Brice and Allen Antioch at a holiday party, each gripping a sequined wife with one hand, a drink with the other. The picture warmed her, and she remembered them as boys, when she had been their nanny. Elise had seen this picture already—she'd been pleased to see her boys having fun—but she hadn't looked farther down the page. Other pictures showed black debutantes, giggly and glamorous in long dresses. Then, at the bottom of the page, under the headline, "Special Nutcracker," was a picture of Gertrude and the wobbly children.

Elise stared at the picture, mortified. They were mongoloid children. Gertrude was teaching mongoloids. Elise dropped the paper to the floor and wiped her fingers on her coat. It was horrible. She thought of Brice and Allen's reaction when they saw Gertrude's picture; she could imagine them laughing and laughing. She gathered up the foil that Gertrude had ripped from the box. She pressed the pieces into a tight ball and put it in her pocket. At home she would try to fashion a usable sheet out of the scraps. Gertrude could keep the dates—Elise had more boxes than she could use or give away already. But Elise would take back the foil; she would take back the box. "You'll have to get something for these," she blurted. "I need that box."

Gertrude brought a plate from the kitchen and began unpacking the dates one by one.

Elise watched, her face hot, her mind crowded with images of deformed dancers. She grabbed the box. "Don't be so fussy, Gertrude. They're not glass." She turned the box upside down, scattering sugar in a brief, gritty blizzard. Several dates bounced off the plate; they stuck on the table like squashed bugs.

Elise tucked the emptied box back under her arm. She took a date and held it in her fingers, pressing into the sticky softness. She wanted to slap Gertrude. She wanted to tell her not to walk around in her socks. "Thank you for helping the whole city to laugh at me," she said. "Thank you for that lovely Christmas gift."

In the bright corridor, she ate the date, hardly noticing its sweetness, although she felt the grains of sugar against her teeth. When she got outside, she cleaned her hands in the snow.

Walking home, Elise worked the foil wad with her fingers, pressing it tighter, harder, smaller. A cloying aftertaste hung in her mouth, a sickening taste of decay, of shame.

When Elise focused again on Gertrude's yellow cake, something seemed different. Gertrude had taken a bite. Elise took a deep breath; she stood and walked to Gertrude's table.

"How do you like the lemon cake, Gertrude?"

Gertrude looked up, her face calm. "Fine, Mother."

From so close, Elise could see the uneven surface of the frosting, where the knife had made dips and swirls. She wanted to shove her finger in. If I'm going to pay, she thought, I'm entitled.

"Was there something you wanted to say to me?" said Gertrude.

"Do you mind if I take a taste? I might buy a piece if I like it."

For a second it seemed that Gertrude hadn't heard, then she pushed the plate over. Elise picked a bit off the edge where the tines of the fork had made a jagged imprint. The crumb was so small it dissolved in her mouth; she could hardly get any taste from it, just a tiny tingle, a lemony pinprick.

The paperback book had fallen closed in Gertrude's hand. The title, *Zen and the Art of Motorcycle Maintenance*, didn't surprise Elise. Nothing about Gertrude surprised her, not even a book about motorcycle repair.

"In China," said Elise, "daughters respect their mothers. In China you would be a disgrace."

"Mmm," said Gertrude.

"You see," Elise said, pointing at Daniel. "Chinese."

"Yes."

"Answer me," Elise demanded.

Gertrude put down her fork. She folded her hands on the table, crossed her pale pink ankles. She said, "You haven't asked a question."

"I was nearly crushed by a bus," said Elise.

"Is that a question?"

"Don't make jokes. I could have died."

Gertrude nodded. "But you didn't."

Elise thought of smashing her fist into the cake, watching Gertrude's face crumple. "Tell me one thing, Gertrude—why should I buy this cake for you? Why should I?"

"There's no reason. I don't want you to."

"I have friends, Gertrude. Both young and old." Walking back to Daniel's table, Elise heard Gertrude's voice, quiet but clear:

"Then you must be very happy."

When the quiche came, Elise wasn't hungry. She ate bits of ham and left the custard.

"Why do you follow her around if it upsets you?" asked Daniel.

"I'm not following her. I'm living my life."

"Wouldn't it be easier to avoid her?"

"Gertrude is the one who is following me. She's the one who moved in at the Twin Oaks." Daniel nodded. He looked concerned. Elise liked him; he was so understanding and attentive. "You know, Daniel, we could make this a sort of ongoing appointment. I could treat you to lunch every Saturday. I could be your replacement grannie."

"I'd like to," said Daniel. "I would. Except that most Saturdays, I go cycling. But thanks. Thank you."

Elise knew he was lying by the way he stuttered. "How about another day?"

"I'd like to, but I have so much studying, huge amounts."

"You'll be old, too," she said, not caring if it made him feel bad. It was nothing but the truth. She gathered her belongings—pocketbook, scarf. "We'll split this one down the middle, shall we?"

Daniel cleared his throat. "To tell you the truth, I don't have any cash with me. Let me call Alex and have him bring me some money."

Elise let Daniel push his chair back, let him stand before she laughed. "I'm teasing," she said. "Didn't I tell you this was my treat?"

"I don't want to force you. I'll call Alex."

"I was joking," said Elise. "Joking."

At the cash register, Elise paid with a one-hundred-dollar bill. She liked big bills, enjoyed hearing the little gasps when she handed them to clerks. She got seven or eight of them out of the bank at once, to save herself time.

Elise chatted loudly with the cashier, as if Gertrude would bother to eavesdrop. Daniel stood at her side, quiet as a bodyguard. Behind the counter, the fat chocolatier was straightening the candy.

Standing at the cash register, waiting for her change, Elise was overwhelmed by exhaustion. Her body was no longer hair and toenails and veins; her body had become an accumulation of aches. She took Daniel's arm, felt him stiffen his muscles to support her weight.

"Miss?" called the chocolatier as Elise turned to go. "Excuse me, miss." He motioned her toward the counter, then handed her a small object wrapped in shiny red paper. "A chocolate walnut," he said. "Because you are sweet."

Elise spread the Sunday paper on the kitchen table and worked her way through. She read more carefully now, more warily, but Gertrude's notoriety had not been repeated. Brice and Allen Antioch, on the other hand, smiled at her from the society pages almost every week. When Elise turned seventy, Brice and Allen had surprised her with a retirement dinner—the biggest part of the surprise was the retirement itself; Elise had expected to work until she was no longer able to. She hadn't outlived her usefulness once the boys grew up.

She'd taken on other household responsibilities, like ironing and answering the phone.

At the retirement dinner, they ate on the Antiochs' finest china, on the tablecloth Elise had ironed that afternoon. The cook prepared lamb with mint sauce, baby carrots, new potatoes, lemon soufflé, and Gertrude—invited as part of the surprise—had embarrassed Elise terribly. Brice and Allen gave Elise a gold brooch and behaved marvelously; Gertrude wore slacks and refused to eat the meat. And she'd picked fights, blaming the boys for things that were not their fault, sticking her nose where it didn't belong.

"What do you think happens when a business moves out of downtown?" Gertrude had asked, elbows on the table.

Elise shot furious looks at Gertrude, who ignored her. The Antiochs didn't discuss business at dinner—Gertrude knew that. And they certainly didn't raise their voices. As Gertrude got louder, Brice's voice dropped to a murmur.

"The energy of the city is in Overland Park," Brice stated calmly. "That's a fact, Gertrude, I can't stop it. It made *sense* to move to Overland Park—I *live* in Overland Park."

"It's the little businesses that suffer," said Gertrude, "the ones that can't afford to move."

"This is business, Gertrude. We can't worry about how our decisions might affect every wig store and dance studio on the block."

"Of course not. And don't worry either about how every empty building makes downtown less safe."

Brice laughed. "So basically, if a ballerina gets mugged, it will be on my conscience."

Allen coughed softly. "Brice, Gertrude, I think a truce is in order. I propose a toast." He raised his wineglass. "To Elise, who loved us like a mother."

Elise lifted her glass daintily. "To the Antiochs. To my boys."

Elise had refused to speak to Gertrude until they were past the doorman, outside the Antiochs' apartment building. Then she spat words out angrily. "I have never been so ashamed. You know perfectly well how to behave, and you refuse to do so."

"I know how to behave," said Gertrude. "But I will not curtsy to the Antiochs' lemon soufflé. Those boys make me sick. You work there for forty years, and they give you a week's notice and a snooty dinner. No pension, nothing."

Elise spoke in a restrained, precise voice. "This was my dinner. The dinner in my honor, and you ruined it with your ugly talk and bad manners." She felt tears rising, but she pushed them down. She didn't need Gertrude; she had Brice and Allen. They weren't her sons, but they loved her. She could count on them.

After that Elise had made no effort to see Gertrude, and years went by. Gertrude sent money every week, but since the checks were for differing amounts, it was difficult for Elise to rely on them. Brice and Allen didn't send money, but Elise wore their pin on her coat and felt their love. After the bus accident, she had asked the desk nurse to call Brice or Allen as her next of kin. But they were both abroad, and Gertrude came instead.

Elise finished the paper and folded it. Sunday was a day so long and empty she could practically hear it flapping in the wind. The Antiochs had entertained on Sunday afternoons—leisurely parties with strawberries and champagne. Elise had been there sometimes, looking after the children. She decided that if anyone dropped in today, she would excuse herself into the bathroom and pinch her cheeks to make herself feel less drab.

On Monday Elise was restless. She considered taking a walk, but the weather was chilly, and she didn't really feel up to it. She used to walk around Loose Park quite frequently, but lately she was afraid of getting stranded. She didn't like the park as much as she usedy to anyway, not since the city installed a fountain in the middle of the duck pond. And she was uncomfortable with the number of black people who walked or jogged along the path. Loose Park seemed less and less like her park, and more and more like a park for anyone.

Elise walked from kitchen to living room to bedroom and back again, searching the floor for lint. She stepped into the hall, but she didn't expect anyone to be around on a weekday. She heard nothing at all, then, faintly, a typewriter downstairs, Alex or Daniel.

She could read or listen to the radio or turn on the television, but none of these sounded interesting. She thought of calling down to Alex and Daniel's apartment and asking who was typing. It didn't seem healthy to study so much. If they were doctors, they should know that too many books and typewriters could strain the eyes.

Elise didn't normally eat sweets, but she recalled a blueberry muffin mix tucked in the back of her cupboard. Brice and Allen had always clamored after cookies and cupcakes. She would bake and open the door wide and wait to see if any boys floated up from downstairs.

She took the box from the shelf, slit the cardboard with a knife. Inside was a sealed plastic bag of mix and a small can of wild blueberries. She poured the mix into a bowl, added water, oil, egg, then reached for the blueberries. But when she attached the can opener to the rim, she found that she couldn't squeeze with enough force to pierce the tin. She leaned her arm on the lever. But the opener slipped, nicking the skin on her wrist.

Taking the can and the opener, she went down the stairs. Once she had given Alex a can of green beans to open. Elise knocked softly on Alex and Daniel's door; she heard typing—the clatter of keys and the occasional ding of the carriage return. "Yoohoo," she called. "Alex? Daniel?" No one answered. She stood in the dim corridor, holding the can; the label showed tiny blueberries, the color of dusk. The bulb overhead had burned out, and Elise felt uneasy, even though she was in her own building. Alone in the darkness, she thought of the bus accident, felt the lurch, the turning and tumbling in her stomach; she waited for the crunch of bones. She remembered the concrete scratching against her neck and the strange cushion her bun had made, as if she were using a dinner roll for a pillow. She turned the can. Flat, paper berries spilled into her hand. She knocked harder. Nothing.

She rode downtown in a soiled cab, watched busy people rush by. Brush Creek trickled innocently, deceptively, within its cement banks, a dribble of dirty water; nearby buildings still showed marks from the flood. At 47th, the horse fountain galloped by, already shut off for the winter.

At the door of the brown brick building, Elise hesitated, clutching the blueberries. It would take Gertrude less than a minute to open the can. Not even Gertrude could refuse. She pulled open the heavy door. Inside, a narrow stairway led up to a glass door with black letters:

STAR GLAMOUR DANCE STUDIO

The stairs were speckled marble, pink and beige; at the center of each step, Elise could see an indentation where the marble had worn away. If she went up, she'd find a big, bare room, a wooden floor with dust along the edges. She'd seen enough dance studios to know that they were all the same—piano, mirrors, rosin, benches, students, mothers. She would not go up. She would not sit on a bench beside the mother of a mongoloid, watching Gertrude tilt heads and lift ribcages, watching Gertrude dance. She would wait for Gertrude to come down.

Framed recital photographs lined the walls—tap dancers in sequins and top hats, ballerinas of all ages. When Gertrude was just out of her teens, she'd been in the chorus of several shows in New York

City, but on the wall in the stairwell there were no pictures of Gertrude dancing.

At the top of the stairs, the door opened then closed. Elise moved closer to the wall, pretending to study the photos. Her body tensed, anticipating an onslaught of mongoloid children. They would engulf her, pummel her with ballet slippers. Elise glanced nervously upward, toward the door, where Gertrude stood waiting.

"We seem to be leading parallel lives," said Gertrude.

"I don't know about that," Elise said, confused and somewhat comforted by Gertrude's pink legs. She watched her daughter descend. At the bottom, Gertrude pushed the street door, and they stepped into the open air.

"What are you doing here, Mother?"

Elise held up the can of blueberries. "I can't open this." In her hand the can surprised her; it seemed so small and harmless. "I was making muffins." She pushed the can toward Gertrude.

"I don't understand. Do you want me to open it?"

Elise held the can and looked at the label, at its promise of plump sweetness and blue juice; she liked the way the tin held the berries in place. "No," she said. "Take it."

"I don't really want it."

"I want you to have it."

Gertrude kept her hands in the pockets of her overcoat. "This is my bus," she said.

Elise looked up to see a massive tire, an enormous bus. She took a step back, holding tight to the blueberries. The bus, camouflaged by soot, had snuck up on her. But she could see through the dirt to the black and white stripes below. Elise wondered if the pattern was authentic, if an actual zebra had posed while the artist traced and painted. Looking closely at the zoo bus, she noticed that the lines were blurred, the borders uncertain. The white stripes were dingy; the black stripes were gray. The door opened with a groan, and Gertrude stepped in. Elise glanced side to side to see if anyone was watching, then she lifted her foot to reach the step; clutching the railing on both sides, she hoisted herself up.

The driver wore a blue uniform with rolled-up sleeves. Elise expected to see him in khaki shorts and a safari hat. She expected to hear parrots and sultry tropical music. Gertrude tossed some change into the rattling metal money counter at the front of the bus. The door closed with a sigh, bureaucratic and indifferent.

"I'll pay for both of ours," said Elise.

"She already paid," said the driver.

Elise opened her billfold and pulled out her money—three one-hundred-dollar bills. She handed him one. "For mine."

"Can't change that. Exact change only." The driver's blue cap rested on the dashboard. He put it on, pulling at the slick, black bill.

Elise raised her voice. "Will a one-hundred-dollar bill collapse our city's economy?"

"Put that away," said the driver. "Before someone knocks you down and snatches it. The other lady already paid for you."

"She had no right to pay for me."

"I have a schedule. Sit down or get off."

Standing at the front of the bus, looking back, Elise felt as if she were about to enter a tin of sardines. Gertrude had taken a seat just past the middle of the bus, but Elise wasn't sure she wanted to sit there. She didn't want to sit beside a stranger either—someone who might turn out to be a criminal or a lunatic. The passengers sat with coats buttoned to their necks, shopping bags nestled at their feet, but years of riding the buses had taught her that there were no guarantees.

It would be best, Elise decided, to sit with Gertrude. She walked toward her daughter, grasping the metal headrests. She felt Gertrude's calm eyes but avoided looking into them—she didn't want to be hypnotized. Gertrude might be an expert by now.

Elise sat, the money folded in her fist. In the seat ahead, a baby in a yellow knit cap peeped over its mother's shoulder. The baby grimaced, then grinned, then began to cry. Elise jabbed the money toward Gertrude. "Take it then."

Gertrude's straight back barely touched the seat. Her hands, folded in her lap, were pale and freckled and wrinkled. "I don't want it."

"How much did you put in? Take what you put in and give me the change." Elise tried to drop the money into Gertrude's lap, but it fluttered to the floor.

Reaching to retrieve the bill, Gertrude whispered in Elise's ear. "Put your money away." Then, upright, in a more normal tone, she said, "You have to be careful. People kill other people for a bag of hamburgers."

"I don't want you to pay." Elise tried to push the money into Gertrude's hand again, but Gertrude wouldn't close her fingers around the bill.

"Really, Mother, it's my treat." She put her finger out for the baby to play with. "You're a sweet baby," she cooed. "Aren't you a sweet baby?"

Elise wanted to take Gertrude's finger out of the baby's grasp and put her own in. She wanted to touch the tiny fingernails, the little pompon on its cap.

"I had the toddler class this morning," said Gertrude, "eight little girls in tap shoes, very noisy. I'm getting too old for this."

"I could give you the whole hundred dollars," said Elise.

"I don't want your money."

Elise looked Gertrude straight in the face. "Don't you see? I can help you. I can put you in my will—I can give you money now. All you have to do is ask."

"I don't need it," Gertrude said firmly.

Silent, Elise sat and watched Gertrude shake her finger free of the baby's grasp. Elise wanted to grab Gertrude's finger and give it a twist. "You would want it well enough if no one was watching. You would help yourself—don't pretend you wouldn't."

"If you say so," said Gertrude. She reached up and pulled the wire that snaked around the bus above the windows. A sharp buzz sounded at the front of the bus.

"This isn't our stop."

"I'm getting out here." She gazed steadily at Elise, who looked away. "I'm sorry, but whatever it is you want from me—I don't have it."

"I don't want anything from you. I'm trying to give you something."

"Excuse me," said Gertrude.

Elise felt panicky; she held tightly to her purse. "I'm just trying to give you the bus fare. I'm trying to give you what I owe."

"When you get to the street before your house, pull the cord, and the driver will let you out. You remember." Gertrude edged past. She stood and walked away, tall and proud, like an African woman in a documentary, able to carry baskets in each hand, while balancing another on her head. Once she was off the bus, Gertrude stood on the sidewalk, facing the street. She was looking toward the bus, as if waiting for something else to happen.

Well, goodbye to you, thought Elise. Goodbye to Gertrude. Good riddance. She watched the baby in front of her. As the bus pulled away from the curb, the baby's head rolled from side to side, its neck flexible, unformed. Such a small baby—it was too early to know whether it would be sickly or ugly or mean. That tiny, lumpy package, that baby, could hold a lifetime of bitterness and hate.

The world through the window grew dim, day dissolving into darkness, and the zoo bus rolled along down Broadway. Elise wondered where the bus would take her if she rode to the end, if she'd end up at the zoo. If it were earlier in the day, she would do just that; she would go to the zoo—throw marshmallows at the elephants and ride a camel. She imagined walking through the zoo, pausing to look at a patch of pink, a flock of flamingos. There, at the edge of the lagoon, standing on one pink leg, was Gertrude.

Ridiculous. Gertrude was ridiculous. No one could love her.

Elise reached her hand out to the baby, but it didn't notice; its head was burrowed into the mother's shoulder. A circle of spit darkened the material of the mother's dress. Elise touched the baby's face with her finger and felt warm skin that was so soft it frightened her. The baby's eyelids opened halfway at her touch then closed heavily.

When Gertrude was a baby she slept in a drawer, but it was a drawer that Elise had removed from the dresser and placed on the floor. She would never have done what Alex suggested, closing the drawer with a baby inside. She would never do that. Elise had made the drawer into a cozy nest, and Gertrude had slept comfortably. Each night before bedtime Elise's husband, Bill, had filled a big mixing bowl with warm water and soapsuds. His hands were thick and oil-stained, and they colored the bathwater brown. But he loved to wash his baby, loved to dribble water from the washcloth onto her belly. Elise closed her eyes. She could see the dark-haired man, the dark-haired baby, the kitchen table, herself. She stood by the stove, watching Bill and the baby, waiting for the flatiron to heat; her long hair was tied back with a ribbon. When Elise opened her eyes, she was sitting in a bus that smelled of exhaust and sour milk. She tasted salt on her lips. She wanted to rush to the back of the bus and press herself against the window, push backwards through time and space as the bus rolled ahead. She wrapped her hands around the metal headrest of the seat in front of her and tried to stand, but the bus lurched beneath her feet, and she was standing and kneeling and clutching the seat.

Now? she thought. Would he love her now—a grown woman in pink tights? Would he love Gertrude now?

She called out to the driver, but her voice was swallowed up by the roar of the engine. A young man in a tan overcoat reached up and pulled the cord.

When the bus came to a stop, Elise stood and made her way to the front. All around her the passengers were goggle-eyed, like fish. She thought of the wobbly children in Gertrude's photographs, the awkward poses and soggy flesh. Her hands curled into fists. But if she saw the children in person, if she saw them dance . . . She thought of watching Gertrude's early dance lessons, many years ago. Gertrude had practiced past awkwardness and uncertainty, her movements becoming so fluid, so flexible that Elise had been tempted to press against her daughter's skin and feel for bones.

Standing at the edge of the bus steps, Elise caught her breath. The steps were steep as a precipice, and they led into darkness; she wavered at the top, afraid of falling. But by sitting down on the step, she made her way, pressing her fingers against the black rubber treads, scooting one stair at a time.

She was on Broadway, somewhere in midtown—she wasn't sure where. In front of her an auto dealership displayed hundreds of parked cars, prices painted on the windshields. An endless string of plastic flags—brightly colored triangles—marked the border of the lot.

She could find Gertrude still. She could go to her. Slowly, Elise began walking, moving toward where Gertrude had been, navigating by the plastic flags which flapped and fretted in the wind.

In Kansas City, where I grew up, there used to be a bus painted purple and black, zebra fashion. I guess it was an advertisement for the zoo, but I don't really know. One summer when my older sister was about fifteen, she had a job in a restaurant downtown, and she would take the bus to work every day. But she wouldn't ride the zoo bus; it was too embarrassing.

When I started "Zoo Bus," I had just gotten out of a bad roommate situation, and I used some of my pent-up roommate anger to fuel the story. I had always considered myself to be a mild-mannered person, so I was surprised to find that I had reached a point at which I was no longer willing to forgive this former roommate. I was thinking a lot about forgiveness and friendship and the limits of love, and it seemed to me that one of the strongest possible bonds would be that of mother and daughter, especially when the mother is elderly and somewhat dependent on the daughter. I wondered what it would take to sever a relationship that had survived for sixty years, through hundreds of fights and reconciliations.

"Zoo Bus" went through many rewrites, maybe twenty full-scale revisions. It kept ballooning up to forty pages, and I kept squashing it down again. I worked on the story for a year, trying to figure out who Elise was and trying to imagine what it was like to be eighty-one years old and mean.

E.F.